GHOST
STATION

ALSO BY **S.A. BARNES**

Dead Silence

GHOST STATION

S.A. BARNES

NIGHTFIRE

TOR PUBLISHING GROUP

NEW YORK

GHOST STATION

Copyright © 2024 by S.A. Barnes

A Nightfire Book
Published by Tom Doherty Associates / Tor Publishing Group
120 Broadway
New York, NY 10271

www.tornightfire.com

Nightfire™ is a trademark of Macmillan Publishing Group, LLC.

The Library of Congress Cataloging-in-Publication Data
is available upon request.

ISBN 978-1-250-88492-3 (hardcover)
ISBN 978-1-250-88493-0 (ebook)

Our books may be purchased in bulk for promotional, educational, or business use. Please contact your local bookseller or the Macmillan Corporate and Premium Sales Department at 1-800-221-7945, extension 5442, or by email at MacmillanSpecialMarkets@macmillan.com.

First Edition: 2024

Printed in the United States of America

0 9 8 7 6 5 4 3 2 1

For Allison Klemstein, Nathan Klemstein, Grace Barnes, Josh Barnes, and Benjamin Oldenburg. It is a joy to be a part of your lives. I am so proud of you!

Love,
Aunt Stacey

P.S. Some of you will have to wait to read this until you're older. A lot older. Also, when you do, please don't wake your parents up if you have nightmares. It makes Christmas super awkward.

1

The protesters outside are getting louder. Their chants are still faint, but somehow clearer than before. Or maybe that's just Ophelia's guilty conscience.

Their favorite seems to be "Montrose blows!" which does offer a certain pithiness, especially with the rhyming element. But there are plenty shouting "Fuck the Brays!" A perennial classic, though not usually directed at her personally.

But she certainly deserves it this time.

Ophelia flinches.

"Hold still, please," the young tech says politely. He readjusts his gloved hold on her wrist and then slides the needle into the still healing port on the back of her hand.

"Sorry." She tries to smile at him, pulling the crisp edges of the disposable gown tighter against herself with her free hand. She's naked beneath the gown on the mobile exam bed, and the cold air blowing down on her exposed neck is about to set her teeth chattering.

It's fine, though. She's about to be much, much colder.

"All right," the tech says a moment later, releasing her hand and peeling off his gloves with a snap. "Let's give that a few minutes to kick in. I'll be right back."

The digital name badge on his lab coat flashes "RAYON.

CALL ME RAY!" with a smiley face. But Ray doesn't meet her gaze as he pushes back on his rolling stool and then stands to exit the tiny prep room.

Shame floods through her, and she squeezes her eyes shut with a selfish prayer.

Please, please let this work. I need this to work.

In the silence of the prep room, broken only by those chants and the clatter of metal wheels somewhere down the hall, her QuickQ interface gives a friendly *bloop* sound.

Relieved at the prospect of a distraction, possibly in the form of her younger sister calling, Ophelia opens her eyes.

But it's her uncle's face that appears on the blue-framed interface in her right eye, as if summoned by the scent of her desperation.

Fuck. Ophelia's heart sinks. *Good old Uncle Dar, coming in for the kill.*

Her privacy settings allow her to see Darwin but not the reverse, a small blessing. His artfully silver-streaked hair rises above his preternaturally smooth forehead in a perfect peak. He is the image of the dashing, handsome CEO of a wealthy, multigenerational company, one who lands his air-veh to play an "impromptu" game of pickup with a group of Miami refugees from the encampment in Grant Park.

Until he opens his mouth.

"I know you can hear me, you little bitch," he says through his affable smile. "I've tried to be reasonable."

No, he tried to pull strings with her employer, which, surprisingly, hadn't worked. Probably only because her family's company and her employer are fierce competitors with a lot of hard feelings, not inclined to grant each other favors. Blackmail, espionage, rumors about hard-core kink preferences among senior executives. And that was just what she knew about.

"You need to think about the family for once. Come home to Connecticut and stay quiet. Let everything die down again. That Carruthers woman is digging again, and you're only making it worse." Darwin makes a scoffing noise. "What kind of a name is Jazcinda anyway?"

The name of a very respected journo-streamer, as it happens. Her channel tends toward the tabloid, but her own reports are solid. Very respectable. If you aren't worried about her turning your entire existence upside down and inside out.

The sensor monitoring Ophelia's heart rate gives a distressed bleat.

Darwin sucks air through his teeth, shaking his head in a tight jerk. "I knew you were trouble the first time I heard about you. We should have just left you there."

"Is everything all right, Dr. Bray?" Ray appears at the door again, glancing at her and then at the vitals monitor on the wall doubtfully. He is so young, maybe only a half a dozen years older than her seventeen-year-old sister. His hair does that swoop thing across his forehead that requires altering how the hair grows—no one's hair comes out naturally at a sharp right angle.

She gives him a smile full of reassurance that she does not feel. "Of course."

"Fucking pick up, Ophelia!" Darwin bellows in her ear, through her implant. "You're making things worse, drawing more attention we don't need."

Her pulse throbs in her neck, her hands tremble at her sides. But it's a vestigial fear, left over from childhood. That's all. She has vivid memories of Uncle Darwin leaning down to shout at her for some offense—real or imagined. She can still feel the warm spray of his saliva against her cheek, mixed with the bitter scent of his latest greens supplement.

But that was a long time ago. She's an adult and well outside of his reach now. Even with private security at his disposal, Darwin wouldn't send them here to get her. He's not that desperate. Or stupid. She's fairly sure.

Still, better to move this along.

"Is something wrong?" she asks Ray.

He shakes his head, stepping inside. "It's just I'm going to need to ask you to deactivate all communication implants," he continues, closing the door after himself. "It's to prevent the possibility of interference. You won't be able to use them out there anyway. Your messages and contacts will all transfer to the wrist-comm that has been assigned to you."

Ophelia straightens up quickly. "No problem." She concentrates on the six-digit code to deactivate her implant, while Darwin continues yelling in the background. She only left her QuickQ active in the hope that Dulcie—her younger sister, half sister, technically—would reach out. Ophelia is going to miss her eighteenth birthday next month. Wherein they were supposed to "ditch these mad dabbers and party like you're actually still young." But it seems Dulcie is still mad or, more likely, the family has gotten to her. The family gets to everyone.

The deactivation code numbers appear in her QuickQ interface right across Darwin's mouth, first hazy and then growing sharper. She double-blinks deliberately to confirm, and he vanishes. If only it were that easy in real life. Of course, he probably—definitely—thinks the same thing about her.

"Right, so you should start feeling some drowsiness," Ray says. "And then—"

Footsteps rush toward them behind the closed door, growing louder in their hurry. Ophelia grips the edges of the exam bed, fingers digging into the padding.

The steps stop outside the door, and Ophelia's breath catches in her throat as the door to the prep room swings open. But it's not the riot-masked, Pinnacle-branded mercenaries that she's half expecting.

Instead, it's another white-coated technician, accompanying a familiar figure, one with broad shoulders like an old-timey football player and a smooth, brown shaved head.

"Julius!" Ophelia sags in relief, grinning at him with a mix of bewilderment and delight. "What are you doing here? I told you last night I'd be fine."

"Like I was going to believe any of that nonsense." Julius waves his hand dismissively. But he looks rushed and ruffled, his vintage tie loose at the neck, and one crisp edge of his collar pointing upward above his bright yellow vest.

They'd said their good-byes at his apartment last night at her three-person—four, if you counted Marlix, Julius and Jonathan's daughter, sleeping upstairs—going-away party, less than six hours ago. It ended only after a little too much synthetic tequila (Julius and Jonathan) and far too much of the nasty grape-flavored prep drink (Ophelia).

She and Julius both came up through Montrose's Employee Psychological and Behavior Evaluation training program, several years apart. But they'd been friends as well as colleagues since the day she moved into the dingy office next to his.

As a bonus, he never once asked her about her family or even hinted that he knew who they were, though of course he did. Everyone did.

"I'm sorry, sir, but this is a private facility and—" Ray begins.

"First, it's 'Doctor,'" Julius says.

Ophelia works to not roll her eyes. He does like to trot that title out, usually when he's looking to impress. Or get away with something he shouldn't.

"Second, I'm her emergency contact *and* designated support person." He points at Ophelia. "I'm here to support."

Ophelia raises her eyebrows. That is . . . a shift from last night. Warmth like a tiny glowing spark flares in her chest. Even though he disagrees with her decision, Julius is here. That is the mark of a true friendship and—

Julius tightens his tie and smooths his collar and vest. "Can we have a moment, please?" he asks, in his this-is-not-a-real-question voice. "Alone."

The techs look at each other uncertainly.

The spark goes out, replaced by a coiling dread, like a length of chain piling up link by heavy link.

What's wrong? The words leap to her lips, but she clamps

down to keep them in. Old habit. Never talk in front of strangers. "It's all right," Ophelia says to Ray.

Ray looks back and forth between them. "Just a minute," he warns. "It's not a good idea to interrupt the preparation sequence."

Ray and the other technician, the one who brought Julius, leave the room, and Ray closes the door. But not all the way. It's sort of sweet, whether Ray is worried about her or the process he's responsible for. Working at a cold sleep facility, Ray has probably seen some shit.

"What is going on?" Ophelia asks Julius. "Is everything okay? Did Marlix—"

"I couldn't sleep last night after you left," Julius says, pacing back and forth in the tiny space, rubbing a hand over his smooth scalp.

"Synthetic tequila will do that," she says.

"No." He pauses long enough to hold her gaze fiercely, before resuming his movement. "You need to listen to me. I didn't want to say anything. Jonathan said to let it go because it's your choice. But I have to make sure you know." He blows out an exhausted breath, smelling faintly of fresh toothpaste and old alcohol.

She stares at him, unnerved. Julius is not the type to be easily rattled.

"You don't have to do this," he says in a rapid burst. Then he takes a breath, calming himself. "This . . . situation, it's going to blow over. The ethics committee cleared you. No one blames you."

Not true. She blames herself. She should have seen it coming. Every night, she plays the events over and over in her head. In retrospect, all the signs were there.

"The family's wrongful death lawsuit says differently," she reminds him, her voice more curt with the lump in her throat.

"That's bullshit and only because of who you are," he says.

Maybe, maybe not. Either way, the results are the same. A shiny wooden coffin at the front of St. Patrick's.

"It doesn't matter. You heard Paulsen," she says. Julius was in her office when Montrose's CEO himself, Richter Paulsen, projected in for a virtual meeting, all somber tones and barely disguised irritation. Ophelia suspected that if she were anybody else, he would have fired her on the spot, ethics committee be damned. And Paulsen still likely would, just later, when fewer people were watching. It was hard to blame him. No one likes picket lines and protests, media drones and bright-eyed, shiny-haired streamers, in front of their place of business. Of course, if she were anybody else, the public wouldn't have cared and the situation would be, sadly, a nonstory. Just another suicide from Eckhart-Reiser syndrome.

"They want headlines. Good ones. My name is going to get them, either way, so might as well be the right way." The world is starting to feel soft around the edges, her head swirling, thanks to whatever Ray gave her. But she's still very clear on one thing: she needs this job. Needs to help people, to make a difference. It's who she is. More than her last name, more than her DNA.

It's the only way she can—sometimes—sleep at night, without the guilt devouring her whole.

The relentless drive to do better, be better, remain above objection is exhausting at times. But the alternative is unthinkable. It was hard enough to get companies to take her seriously as a mental health professional eight years ago when Montrose hired her—likely more as a middle finger to her family's company than anything else. If Montrose fires her, it'll be next to impossible to find another opportunity. In the meantime, ERS is raging. She can't just let that happen. No, she needs to do whatever is necessary to keep that from happening.

Even if that means taking on a slightly out-of-scope assignment. Eighteen months with an R&E team on location.

Ophelia and her colleagues in Montrose's Psychological and Behavioral Evaluation unit have been pushing for earlier intervention for several years. Waiting until teams come back to Earth to treat them makes it so much harder to reverse the decline. *We wouldn't wait to set and heal a broken arm; why do we treat a broken brain differently?*

Ophelia had been especially proud of that line in their joint proposal—her contribution. Apparently this situation fell under the "be careful what you wish for" category. Or maybe the one about pride and a fall.

With her job on the line and an on-location psych resource being her recommendation—sort of—how could she say no?

Julius makes a disapproving noise in the back of his throat. "They're using you."

The temper she works to keep in check surfaces briefly. "You've said all of this, or some version of it, before," she points out. "Why are you here? Because frankly, I don't feel very supported by my 'support person' right now."

He doesn't answer right away. Then he moves to sit next to her on the exam bed, his gaze flicking to the door as if confirming it is still mostly closed. "Just . . . has it occurred to you that Montrose might be setting you up?" He can't quite look at her, keeping his eyes fixed on the floor.

She frowns at him. "What are you talking about?"

He leans closer, his voice an urgent whisper. "I mean, they blame the PBE unit for everything. Skyrocketing patient demand, lackluster results, insufficient treatment—"

"Not a staff meeting, Julius," Ophelia says. She's starting to feel a little dizzy.

He ignores her, continuing, "And now after . . . what happened, they're offering you this 'opportunity'? An opportunity that comes with no support structure, just you. An R&E team who, grieving or not, is going to resent the hell out of you for coming onto their turf. It's impossible to help people who don't want to be—"

"I haven't even met them—" she begins.

"You're one of the smartest people I know, Phe. Think about it." He takes her hand in his. She can almost feel it, through the curious numbness spreading through her body. "Montrose doesn't want the media heat for you, especially since you've been cleared. But if they send you away, they look cooperative and forward-thinking, and if you can't do it, the story won't be that they fired Ophelia Bray without cause. It'll be that Ophelia Bray failed."

His words, even as a hypothetical headline, land like an unexpected punch. Is he right? The concept sounds conspiratorial and overly complicated, but that doesn't mean he's got it wrong. In fact, it reads very much like a page out of Montrose's executive-level playbook. Nothing is ever their fault.

The gut-level uncertainty she's been feeling from the moment she signed on for this mission flares up again, acid burning through her stomach.

But . . . it doesn't matter. She has to do *something* to make up for her mistake, to save her career, and this is the best—the only—option on offer.

Ophelia draws in a breath and lets it out slowly, imagining her doubts dissolving into a white mist—like warm breath in cold air—then nothing at all. The pain in her stomach subsides slightly.

"I appreciate it, Julius." The words come out thick, slurred. "You looking out for me. But I'm going to be fine."

He squeezes her hand. "I'm just worried about you. Worried *for* you." He pauses, lowering his voice further. "We could just get out of here. Grab Jonathan and Marlix, take a vacation for a couple weeks, what do you say?"

Ophelia laughs. "With all of our free time? Right." She shakes her head. "You sound like my family," she says, teasing.

It's a small thing, a tiny twitch of tension, fingers tightening almost imperceptibly. She probably wouldn't even have noticed, if his hand hadn't been wrapped around hers.

Ophelia feels like she's falling, spiraling headfirst toward a hard stop. "Wait," she says. "Wait." Her thoughts are slow from the medications coursing through her veins, and her lips feel numb suddenly.

"Did you . . . Did my uncle . . ." She can barely say the words, can't even formulate the question, the idea both completely ludicrous and yet also perfectly, terrifyingly in character for her family.

But Julius doesn't need her to finish. "I *do* think this is a bad idea," he says defensively, lifting his chin up. "I didn't need someone else to tell me that. You're so desperate to make up for what happened that you're not thinking clearly."

That's not a denial.

Ophelia yanks her hand free, a yawning chasm opening up in her. Fury and betrayal churn within, each struggling for dominance. "What, were you just lurking in the parking lot, waiting for a signal?" Her voice cracks with the question.

He grimaces, which, in combination with his prompt arrival, is answer enough. "Listen, family is tough," he says quickly. "I know that. And I know you and your uncle haven't always gotten along," he says.

She can hear Darwin in that light, casual phrasing, making it sound like they argued over the implanted wishbone in the soy turkey one Thanksgiving. Her temper ignites, an open flame on a hair-fine fuse leading to years of stored-up fuel.

"What did he give you?" she asks, forming each word with care. "My uncle."

"He made some good points, Phe," Julius says. "I think he's really trying to help—"

"What did he give you?" she grits out between her teeth.

Julius draws in a breath, shame coloring his expression. Eventually he responds. "He said they might be able to pull some strings. With another artificial pregnancy license."

Oh. The sound is soft in her head, an instinctive reaction of surprise. Somehow, until that moment, until he confirmed the exchange, Ophelia had hoped it was all a genuine misunderstanding, a well-intentioned gaffe.

Julius reads the change in her expression. "You know how hard it is, and we've been trying to get that approval for a second—"

"Ray!" Ophelia calls.

"But, Phe, it doesn't matter. I only agreed to it because I care," Julius argues.

Ray appears immediately at the door.

"We're done here. Please escort Dr. Ogilvie out." Ophelia draws on every ounce of the Bray imperiousness to keep her tone from wobbling. The drugs, softening her defenses, aren't helping. "And change my emergency contact."

Hurt flashes across Julius's face, triggering a wave of molten rage in Ophelia. He betrays her, sacrificing a yearslong friendship, and he has the nerve to be hurt by her response?

To his credit, Ray simply nods. "This way, please." He holds his arm out in a gesture for Julius to leave. Ray does not, thank God, ask who should be her emergency contact, because at the moment she is out of family members and dangerously low on trustworthy friends.

Julius holds his hands up in surrender and turns to go. But he stops at the door. "Phe, I wouldn't have done it just for that. You know me, you know I love you, and I meant it. I think there's something wrong with this assignment," he says. "Please."

For a moment, her burning uncertainty returns. She wants to believe him, wants to believe he did this primarily for her benefit. Maybe the assignment is odd. Maybe the whole thing *is* a setup for her failure.

Or maybe her family is very, very convincing when they want to be.

She knows which one she believes more.

"Make sure you get what Darwin promised you," Ophelia says. "You earned it."

2

Three months later

White clouds of vapor drift in front of Ophelia's face—her breath turned visible—indicating that her eyes are open and she's at least somewhat alert. Above her, a smear of light filters down through the fogged-over circular window in the cold sleep tank lid. A faint ambient blue glow illuminates the side walls of her tank. She's awake. More so than before, whenever that was.

The last thing she remembers is . . . *Julius.*

White-hot pain slices through her at the memory of his anguished expression at the threshold to the prep room. But after a moment, it cools to a familiar and bitter disappointment.

It's just so damn predictable. She should have seen it coming. Allowing him—anyone—behind her purpose-built walls is a mistake. Her family will always find a way to use them. She *knows* that.

Besides, it doesn't matter, not now. There was more after that, after Julius. She focuses until it comes back to her.

Ray, holding her arm, which was bristling with sensors and tubes, not in comfort but in restraint, and telling her to lie back in the open cold sleep tank and take a deep breath.

It felt like squeezing inside a coffin, the sides of the tank pressing against her shoulders. Instinctively, her body rebelled against the rational part of her mind, refusing to relax, to lie fully back.

But she did as Ray said, pulling in a deep breath—her last one for months. A searing iciness spread upward and inward from her left arm, so cold it felt like being burned alive.

"No bugs, no bite," Ray said, giving the traditional R&E team sign-off.

And then . . . nothing. Not even the vaguely comforting sense of falling into unconsciousness.

Ophelia tries to blink, but her eyelids respond sluggishly. Once, and that's it. Then they stay closed, leaving her in the dark.

Somewhere inside the tank, a *drip, drip, drip*ping that taps at her brain, like an annoying fingertip drumming against her forehead.

A strained noise escapes her raw throat, startling her. Her mouth feels cold, her tongue like a slab of thawing meat. Foreign, thick, in the way.

Panic chews at the drug-induced calmness still drifting through her veins. Her hands, her legs, don't seem to exist at all, for all that she can feel them. And when she tries to open her eyes again, her eyelids flutter but remain closed. It is a terrifying feeling, to not be in control of your body when your mind is awake. Like being buried alive, encased within your own flesh and bone.

It's normal. This is all perfectly normal, she tells herself.

It's not as if she's unfamiliar with the waking process; patients talked about it all the time. But experiencing it directly is an entirely different world. And the only other time, she was so young that it—

She cuts off the thought before it can go too far. *Focus on the present.*

After a few more moments of forced, steady breathing, more feeling returns to her body and the panic recedes, giving her space to think. And when she tries to open her eyes again, her lids obey.

The sensors, tubes, and wires have been removed—the ones

she can see anyway—by the system in the early stages of bringing her back to consciousness. The strange pulling sensation on her lower legs is likely the artificial gravity. After months in a horizontal position, her tank is out of the cold sleep framework and tipped vertically for awakening. But her knees ache, as if she's been standing on an unforgiving surface without moving for months.

She tries to shift to alleviate the pain, the thick layer of biogel over her skin squelching around her, but the strap across her shoulders and chest is too tight for much movement. The lower strap, across her thighs, is looser, which is perhaps why it feels as though her knees are pressed against the tank lid. Her feet are tingling with the jabs of pins and needles as circulation works to normalize.

Any moment now, someone will be here to pop the lid, hand in a towel, and help her out. That's procedure. The only person who wakes alone is the mission commander, the most experienced traveler.

She holds still to listen, ears straining for the faintest sound of voices or footsteps. All she can hear, though, is that dripping. But the light through the window is steady. She's somewhere. She just needs to wait, stay calm.

Concentrate on something else, Phe. The team.

Reclamation and Exploration team number 356, one of the top-rated R&E teams, assigned to the *Resilience*, an Aeschylus class, short-duration exploration vessel, with capacity for ten. Modified StarPlus engines, but not the latest upgrades. Hence, the longer cold sleep times. The Somnalia VII cold sleep system, installed two years ago.

Ethan Severin, mission commander. Thirty-eight, divorced, no children. Raised in the Lunar Valley Colony support housing. Lost two siblings in the collapse of '76. Supports his mother and remaining sisters, who continue to live in the Lunar Valley Colony but in independent housing under the dome now. Recommended for Montrose's Distinguished Performance award, with over twelve years of unblemished service. Until this last mission.

Birch Osgoode, pilot. Twenty-eight, single, no children. Only child, born and raised on Alterra Station. So unobjectionable as to be virtually unnoticeable. His file contained only the basics of his work history and biographical data. Probably hired during one of the expansion rushes, when there wasn't time for or interest in a full background check.

Kate Wakefield, engineer. Thirty-two, in a domestic partnership with Vera Wakefield, two stepchildren. Daughter of two British refugees, fleeing the flooding that swamped most of the island in '83. One minor dust-up in a pub on her home station of Brighton that resulted in an arrest for assault, but the charges were dismissed. Otherwise a clean record. A twin. Her brother, Donovan Wakefield, is currently trying to make it as a farmer on one of the Trappist outposts.

Suresh Patel, inventory specialist. Twenty-seven, single, no children. Raised on Earth in New York. Three human resources complaints from previous team members in years prior for unspecified "inappropriate behavior"—a throwaway Montrose term that could mean anything from an obnoxious sense of humor to right-up-to-the-line sexual harassment—but nothing since he joined number 356.

Liana Chong, scientific coordinator. Twenty-three, single, no children. Aspiring astrobotanist. Working on an R&E team to save money for her PhD.

And finally, Ava Olberman, systems management. Technically, she's no longer part of the team, but her absence will loom over this mission to such an extent that she might as well be here. Ava was a widow, predeceased by her husband, Deacon, and survived by her adult daughter, Catrin.

In an ideal world, Ophelia would have preferred to talk with each of them individually first, to get a baseline before leaving

Earth, but with the unexpected end to their previous mission and the sudden change in her status, the logistics were impossible.

So she'll be meeting them all for the first time today. Assuming anyone ever comes to open her tank.

"Hello?" Ophelia calls, flinching as her voice immediately rebounds against the tank lid, seemingly twice as loud. "Someone out there?"

It's possible this is a prank. R&E teams are known for hazing new members. But it seems odd that they would bother with her, a temporary addition at best. Plus, this particular team is mourning the loss of one of their own. It's hard to imagine a prank fitting in with that dynamic.

Of course, it could also be a message: we don't want you here, and we're going to make sure you know that. But if that were the case, you'd think that someone would be nearby to ensure she received said message.

She holds her breath for a moment to listen better, but there's no muffled giggling or shuffling feet . . . just silence.

The first deep pang of dread reverberates within her, like the toll of an ominous bell. Did Nova screw this up? Mistakes, miscalculations do happen with cold sleep. Rarely, but still.

Or, is she in a warehouse somewhere, stored until her uncle decides what to do with her?

With that thought, her earlier panic returns, sharper than before. She thrashes against the straps holding her in place. "Get me out of here!" she shouts, ignoring the bounce-back of her voice. "Now!" A cold sweat that has nothing to do with her internal temperature or the defrost setting on her tank settles over her skin. A prickling numbness returns to her hands and feet.

Stuck in here forever. How long will it take to die? To feel thirst shriveling her insides? Or will she run out of air first?

Her breath shortens, pulls tightly in her lungs, and dizziness sends sparks of bright white through her vision.

It's only then, her mind racing through death scenarios, that the tiny rational portion of her brain manages to break through. The emergency release. Every tank has one. Ray had mentioned it in his overview that morning at Nova. Ophelia had even signed an e-packet that included a diagram of the release lever and where to find it—with a specific line on that page for her to initial her understanding. (Therefore, Nova could not be blamed if she suffocated in place. That was the idea, if not in so many words.)

Ophelia wriggles in the confined space of her tank until she can get her right hand up from where it rests by her thigh. It has to be here somewhere, on the underside of the tank lid.

Come on, come on.

Her fingertips fumble inside a depression, grazing over the lever and slipping off, the first time she tries to pull. The next time, though, she is successful in yanking the piece toward herself.

The response is immediate. The straps around her shoulders and legs retract into the side walls instantly, whipping across her skin in a manner that might have left friction burns were it not for the bio-gel, and the hinged tank lid immediately pops free with a rush of air, opening on the right side.

But she doesn't have time to celebrate or feel more than a bare second of relief. Free of restraints, her still-weak body obeys the stronger pull of gravity, tipping forward and sliding out of the tank before she can catch herself. She lands on the smooth floor in a heap, with a wet-sounding smack.

Dazed, she lies there for a second, cheek on the cold surface beneath her. Then she forces her wobbly arms to cooperate, propping herself up on her hands to get a better look around.

The automatic overhead lights are on, bright white illumination that hurts her eyes. A pile of plasti-sealed towels with the Nova logo rests on the metal bench screwed to the floor in front of her. Behind that, a series of ten lockers, six of which seem to have labels on them, not that she can read them through her squinting at the moment. A small circular opening on the far wall, no larger than her head, offers a bubbled view to the darkness of space beyond.

She's on the ship, then, the *Resilience*. This is the cold sleep room. She's exactly where she's supposed to be.

Relief is followed by an immediate spike in embarrassment, like that dream where you've arrived for an exam—*or the first day of a new job*—only to discover that you're completely naked and people are staring.

Only this is reality.

She shifts into a sitting position, her muscles and joints all protesting, crossing her arms over herself instinctively.

But unlike the nightmare, no one is here to witness her humiliation.

Two doorways on either side of the lockers, both of them standing open and empty, lead to what appears to be a corridor.

It's quiet, too. No voices. No footsteps, even from the corridor.

The only sounds are the deep thrum of the engines beneath her feet and the hushed susurration of the environmental system, pushing warmed and breathable air out into the room. It smells of burning dust, hot metal, and old meal-paks.

Where is everyone?

Shivering, she reaches up and grabs for one of the packaged towels on the bench in front of her. Out of breath and exhausted from even that small effort, she tears it open with fumbling fingers and wraps the white nubby fabric around herself.

With one hand on her towel and the other on the bench, she leverages herself into a shaky standing position after a few tries. But there's a prickling sensation, the feeling of being watched, dancing along the exposed skin at her back and arms.

She turns abruptly, nearly losing her balance in the process.

That's when she sees it. Rather, them.

Two tanks, alongside hers, tipped vertically for awakening. But hers is the only one with the door open. The other two are still sealed.

That sense of wrongness immediately returns, stronger than ever, and her accelerated pulse rattles through her, sending tremors like a mini quake.

I shouldn't be first awake. Not ever.

Carefully, she edges toward the other two waiting tanks. Dread uncurls within her, like a dark shadow stretching for room. She's not sure why at first; the tanks don't look damaged.

Then it clicks: they're dark. All the status lights and indicators on the front control panel—the panel that indicates the health and status of the occupant—are dead. Blank. Empty.

She moves closer to peer through the round window in the lid of the nearest tank, and her breath catches. The internal illumination system is down, too, but there's enough light from the locker room to see the shadowy profile of a nose, a chin, the top of an ear, and a sideburn shaved into a sharp point.

Someone is still inside.

"No, no, no," she breathes, lurching back instinctively. This can't be happening.

She forces herself forward again, lifting on her toes to peer into the second tank. This one, too, is dark inside, its occupant turned away from the window, like an actual sleeper trying to avoid the morning. Or someone who suffered a faulty awakening and whatever painful paroxysms that induced.

A glossy black braid runs neatly along the side of the head, above the delicate shell of an ear. Liana Chong, possibly, based on what Ophelia remembers of the crew photos.

Ophelia steps back, gripping her towel tighter. The Somnalia VII system operates on a viability standard, meaning it will wake the crew in the programmed order, unless there are . . . issues. In that case, it prioritizes the occupants most likely to survive.

If these are the first three tanks and only one of them—hers—was viable, that means the three tanks still in the framework are likely nonsalvageable. Along with their occupants. The system didn't even bother trying to wake them.

Mission failed before she even started. Even worse, Ophelia might very well be out here by herself.

The emptiness of the space outside, visible through that tiny aperture across the room, seems to press inward on her, as if it might crush the vessel and her inside of it.

Lost. Alone. On a ship she has no idea how to control or operate.

Panic is a blade in her chest, scraping at her lungs. She hurls herself toward one of the upright tanks, trembling hands fumbling across the control panel. There's a reboot option, in case of power failure. It'll run a shock through the tank system, acting as a restart for both the tank and the human within.

If, if she can remember how to do it. Her head is a swirling mass of anxiety and terror, thoughts sliding through her grasp before she can catch hold of any of them.

Then her gaze latches on to a small sticker above the control panel. Three numbered steps, written in red and excruciatingly tiny print, with an equally microscopic graphic of the control panel. The bold header on the sticker: EMERGENCY RESTART SEQUENCE.

"Please, please, please," she whispers, scrubbing the bio-gel from her eyes with the edge of the towel until she can see the words clearly.

1. Use only in the event of system failure. Death may result if restart function is applied inappropriately.
   (Nova Cold Sleep Solutions and Podrata Systems, manufacturer of Somnalia VII, are not responsible for misuse.)
2. Ensure tank is sealed.
3. Enter the following sequence:

The graphic of the control panel contains a series of confusing numbered arrows, indicating which buttons and touch pads to use in what order.

Ophelia follows carefully, pressing each one in the designated order. She holds her breath with the last one, watching, listening for any hint of the mechanism kicking in.

But the control panel remains dark, and there's no whine of activity. No sudden jolt of electricity, like a heart restarting itself.

Because she messed it up? Moved too slowly?

She draws in a deep breath and tries again, moving as fast as she can while still being accurate.

Still nothing.

Ophelia slaps the front of the tank, which does nothing but make her palm sting. "Fuck!"

On the off chance that it's simply a faulty tank, she switches to the other one. But her hope is draining away, like matter being sucked into a black hole. Inevitable. Quick. Violent.

She enters the restart sequence on this tank once, and then twice, with the same results as before.

The adrenaline spike that's kept her on her feet so far vanishes abruptly, and her knees give way, landing her in a messy heap on the floor again.

"Shit. Shit!" Blood roars through her ears, drowning out everything except her own panicked breathing. What is she supposed to do now? Does this ship even work without a living, breathing pilot to enter coordinates? She has no idea.

Ophelia senses a change in the air, a quick slip of breeze, before hands lock around her slippery arms and pull her upright.

Her throat locks on a scream—she can't scream, can never scream—and she twists to pull free, half falling, knee scraping against the bench as she turns to face her attacker.

A man in the orange and gray jumpsuit of R&E division glowers down at her. His dark hair is rumpled and too long, curling at the ends, and his beard is growing in, thick and stubbly. But she still recognizes him from his file.

The mission commander. Ethan Severin.

She shakes her head in disbelief. This doesn't make any sense.

"What is going on here?" he demands, staring at her. "Are you hurt?"

"I . . ." She jerks her chin toward the tanks. "Dead," she says hoarsely, staggering to her feet. How does he not know that already? "Something . . . someone . . . their tanks . . ."

He glances at the other tanks, and his expression shifts immediately. Not to grief or concern or even confusion. Just flat-out pissed. Mouth in a flat line, two hard dimples on either side, a mimicry of what he would look like when smiling.

She's not sure what she expects Severin to do in that moment. However, it's not to stride forward, around her, and rip open the door to the first tank.

"Wait!" she shouts. The only reason the bodies aren't rotting yet is because of the tank's seal, and the moment that changes . . .

Severin reaches inside and hauls out an arm, followed by a whole body in an orange and gray jumpsuit. Suresh Patel. Who immediately doubles over in laughter. Very not-dead.

Ophelia rears back. They were *alive* in there?

"Holy shit, you should have seen your face!" Suresh crows, his high cheekbones flushed with color. The central portion of his hair has been bleached and treated to a glittering white so it resembles frosted grass—or one of those wigs with sparkling powder on it. The latest trend.

Severin shoves Suresh back against the tank framework with a loud clank. "What the fuck is wrong with you?" Severin demands.

Suresh jerks his chin up defiantly. "It was just a joke."

"But the lights . . . your vitals," Ophelia begins, still trying to process what's happening.

The tank next to Suresh's opens, and Liana—her guess was correct—steps out with a sheepish expression. She gives a little wave hello. "It's a hack. A bit of paper in the latch to keep the tank from sealing. Just a dumb hazing thing." She grimaces.

Liana is right, Ophelia realizes belatedly; neither of their lids had given off the hiss of pressure releasing, as hers had.

A scrap of paper? That's all? Dizziness washes over Ophelia, sending her stumbling back toward the bench. She sits heavily, the heat of panic prickling her skin. But then anger boils up immediately in its wake. She could have killed them with the restart. The warning is right there on the tank lid.

Her fists clench in her towel, muscles straining to lash out at someone, anyone.

"This isn't bio-gel in her bunk, or spiders in her suit," Severin says, getting into Suresh's face. "You could have shorted out the whole system, killed yourselves, or her. Did it even occur to you what would happen if we had to try to make it home without cold sleep?"

Not all of them would survive. There are not enough emergency rations for the team to be awake the whole way home. Plus, the strain on the engine to keep environmental systems up and running the whole time . . .

Suresh pushes off against the framework, stepping into Severin's space, despite the fact that he has to crane his neck upward to meet the commander's gaze.

"This was your idea," Suresh says, flicking his hand at Ophelia. "You were the one who wanted her here. You were the one who said behave normally, treat her as a regular team member. So I did."

They look inches away from coming to blows, and that's exactly the kind of thing she's here to prevent.

Ophelia stuffs down her anger, pulls her ragged edges together by force, and draws in a breath. Transforming herself into the professional she needs to be. "Okay. I'm fine," she says, standing up from the bench. "Everyone's fine. Why don't we take a step back, and deescalate the—"

"Get back to work, both of you," Severin says, without looking at her. "Now."

"Yes, sir." Face flushed and eyes downcast, Liana hastily steps down from the tank platform and darts off to the corridor behind Ophelia.

Suresh holds his position for another moment or two, nose tilted sharply up, as if daring his commander to take a swing at him. Then he steps away, rolling his eyes. "Just a joke," he says again, not quite quietly enough, as he strolls toward the corridor, his hands stuffed in his pockets.

"Pod duty. First week," Severin says.

Suresh spins around, his mouth open in shock. "Are you serious?"

Ophelia grimaces. Pods, the packets of human waste routinely ejected from the toilet to a storage catchall outside the hab structure, were theoretically sealed, but they weren't always as leakproof as one would hope. And the pods that would be produced when the team ate solid food for the first time in months would not be pleasant. Generally the crew alternated days so no one was stuck with pod duty—or everyone was stuck with it equally, depending on how you looked at it.

"That's not necessary," she says quickly to Severin, her voice still rusty from disuse. Severin's punishment would only make it harder for her to gain the team's trust. "Ultimately, no harm done." Other than wanting to slap the bejesus out of Suresh Patel, perhaps.

That draws Severin's attention back to her, his dark eyes boring into her. A straight-up intimidation tactic, if ever she saw one. But luckily for her, she's been the recipient of stony looks and even stonier silence for so long now that both bounce off her with barely a dent.

She meets his gaze without a word.

"My team, my decision," he says to her, biting off each syllable. Then he turns back to Suresh, unrelenting. "First week."

Ophelia sees the argument building in Suresh's expression—the ugly twist to his mouth, the narrowing of his eyes. But then he catches her watching, and he shrugs with a forced grin. "Whatever."

Suresh wanders out of the room, following Liana's path, in a deliberately slower, faux casual manner. But his shoulders are stiff with tension.

"Get dressed, Dr. Bray," Severin says, once they're alone. "Meet me on the bridge." Then he, too, walks away.

3

Not exactly an inspiring start, Dr. Bray.

"Fuck," she mutters, scrubbing the towel over her skin, her assigned locker open in front of her. The blurry rectangle of shatterproof mirror inside the door catches her eye. Her dark red hair is darker still and hanging in clumps around her face, thanks to the bio-gel. The harsh overhead lights paint her skin an even paler shade of white, as if somehow all of her blood is not yet defrosted and circulating.

Patients try her temper and her composure all the time in the office. Sometimes because they want to inflict the hurt they're feeling on someone else. Sometimes because they just resent the hell of being sent to her in the first place.

Pretending to be dead, however, is a bit extreme.

She chucks the towel into the recycling bin built into the locker wall, banking it in.

And Severin? *My team, my decisions.*

Ophelia grits her teeth at the memory. He's not wrong, of course. But why agree to an on-site psych resource if he's not going to at least pretend to listen?

She reaches into the locker, where several plasti-sealed packages wait for her. After wrestling a T-shirt and compression shorts into place across her damp skin, she opens and shakes out the orange and gray jumpsuit until the arms and legs unfurl, sharp lines where they were folded.

Technically, the mission commander isn't her boss any more than she is his. She has the authority to pull anyone from duty, including him. But he is in charge of the success of the mission and everyone's safety. He can make her job difficult simply by not supporting her authority.

Or by supporting her a little too much, depending on how you look at it.

Punishing Suresh, while certainly within Severin's purview and thoroughly appropriate for that stunt, only makes things harder for her. She looks weak, ineffectual. Even worse, it firmly places her in the role of the outsider, the bad guy, a role that team members are already inclined to cast her in without any help.

Julius was right. It's a whisper at the back of her mind, her doubts and fears personified.

No. She shakes her head in emphasis as she steps into her jumpsuit. Julius might have been right about the team not wanting her here. That's hardly unexpected, even back on Earth. An employer-assigned therapist is rarely someone's first choice.

But this was still the best choice for her. And she's here now—that's the most important thing. She needs to focus on making a difference for them, on proving that she can.

If they'll trust her.

The zipper on her jumpsuit sticks halfway up, and she yanks at it in frustration.

Ophelia. Breathe. The thought that this is exactly what Julius would have said to her, were he here, were they still speaking, flits through her mind before she pushes it away.

She pauses for a moment, closes her eyes, centers herself. Focusing on the pattern of her breathing until it slows, regulates. The tension in her shoulders eases. *I can do this. They need me, even if they won't acknowledge it. Yet.*

If nothing else, that whole thing with the sleep tanks screams "cry for help." It can't be just a coincidence that Suresh and Liana would pretend to be dead on their first mission after Ava's actual death.

Ophelia is sure they would deny any connection between the two events, but that doesn't mean the connection doesn't exist, even on a simple subconscious level. Ava's absence is weighing on them. Which is only going to make things more difficult for them, on this assignment and every assignment going forward, unless they get the help they need.

Skyrocketing rates of depression, anxiety, sleep deprivation, domestic violence, workplace violence, and intoxicant abuse had been noted for decades among the space-based workforce, before Eckhart-Reiser syndrome and its triggering event forced the larger medical community to acknowledge that they weren't dealing with one-offs but a larger issue.

Humans aren't built for working and living in space. Circadian rhythms fall apart when people are in an artificial environment for too long. It's even worse for R&E teams stuck on a series of planets with day/night cycles that don't match Earth's. Then, add in the isolation, stress—in this case, grief and loss on top of work-based factors—poor diet, and lack of privacy, and you end up with a nice thick stew of contributing factors.

Talk therapy, medication, and regular exercise are all standard practice. But improved sleep—quality sleep, as determined by the three Ds: depth, duration, and disturbances—can also make an enormous difference.

The new iVR helmets Ophelia is charged with testing on this mission—a portable version of the same Montrose technology used back on Earth—will help reduce some of the physiological strain that comes from being off-world. Hopefully. But trial and error, particularly at the beginning, is inevitable.

Better to get started right away.

Ophelia opens her eyes, feeling calmer, more grounded. She knows her purpose, that she has the experience and the abilities to help. She *will* make a difference here. She is not a failure.

Pulling the baggy jumpsuit fabric tighter against her body, she returns to the zipper, and it rolls up smoothly this time. *There, see?*

She steps back from her locker, starts to shut the door, and then stops, her hand on the cool metal. A standard-issue wrist-comm rests on its side on the locker shelf above her head, a chunky screen on a thick black band. It's a poor substitute for her QuickQ implant, allowing only limited voice and text transmissions. But comms technology in the field is always a couple hundred generations behind. She—and everyone else in the crew—will have to rely on the ship to receive transmissions from home and then pass them on to these clunky old things.

The screen on hers is already flashing yellow, indicating waiting messages.

Her uncle. Julius, maybe, if he's come to his senses about how far over the fucking line he was. She should forgive him. Of all people, Ophelia knows how "persuasive" her family can be—persuasive like a knife to the throat of the person you love most. Besides, it's not as if she's going to trust him again, so there's no danger in it.

With a sigh, she reaches up and pulls the wrist-comm down, fastening the thick band around her wrist. She flicks through the notifications on the screen, deleting three messages from her uncle, most of which were received in the immediate aftermath of her turning off her QuickQ. One from an unknown number turns out to be a confused private practitioner trying to refer a former Montrose employee to her and somehow not understanding her on-assignment designation.

Ophelia forwards that one to Emery, her replacement, and then clicks on the next one.

A familiar number: Dulcie, her younger sister. The message is brief. "Ugh. Fine. I guess." A moment of quiet, then she sighs. "I miss you." Then the connection ends.

Ophelia's eyes sting. Dulcie is not just her favorite person in her family, but possibly her favorite person in the world. But she's doing this for Dulcie as much as herself. All this bad press about your older sister can't be easy for a seventeen-year-old.

Ophelia clears her throat and blinks rapidly to clear her

vision. Then she saves the message before moving on to the next. It's another unknown number with no text transcription.

That private doc not understanding, again, most likely.

A tinny voice emerges from the microspeaker. "Dr. Bray, this is Jazcinda Carruthers from the To Tell the Truth channel. I was hoping to speak with you."

Ophelia's heart stutters in her chest. Jazcinda has never reached out to her directly before. Ophelia's contact information isn't a secret; it can't be, in her profession. But the journo-streamers have mostly steered clear of her, thanks to the phalanx of Montrose lawyers shouting about privacy.

What has changed? Or, what does Jazcinda know that she's willing to risk it?

"But it seems I'm too late. Or a year and half too early." Jazcinda gives a self-deprecating laugh, one that's tinged with artificiality, in that it's designed to make people trust her. *Oops, I'm only human.* Ophelia has used a similar technique herself.

"If you'd like to reach out, this is my contact card." Information flashes on the screen. A momentary hesitation, then Jazcinda adds, "Hope to hear from you soon."

Ophelia immediately moves to swipe Delete, but something stays her hand at the last moment. Better to know the danger than to turn your back on it. That's been her philosophy for most of her life, and it's served her well so far.

At least she's several million kilometers away from having to deal with it right now.

While she's still contemplating Jazcinda's message and its meaning, the next message plays through. Another familiar number. But not Julius.

"Ophelia, it's your mother?" Her small, faint voice sounds even fainter this far away. Or perhaps that's just Ophelia's imagination.

Just turn it off, delete it. No good can come of this, you already know that. But it's difficult, nearly impossible, to stop longing for parental acceptance. It's embedded in the brain at such an early age.

"I'm worried about you," her mother says. In the background, glasses clink and someone laughs a little too loudly. She's at a party somewhere, a benefit, most likely, following her brother's—Ophelia's uncle's—directive to reach out. Too late, of course.

"I know why you feel you have to do this," she continues. "And I . . . I'm sorry."

Ophelia rolls her eyes. Her mother is always sorry, or so she says, but somehow the words never seem to amount to any action.

"But I think it's too risky." Her mother's tone shifts from soft regret to prim and pointed, a belated assertion of authority. "Don't go to that planet."

Ophelia sighs, waiting for the warning about Jazcinda, protecting the family, coming home to the compound in Connecticut. Her mother's mouth but her uncle's words—a skilled puppet show.

"I know it's been years since you've had an . . . incident," her mother begins, and Ophelia's eyes snap open. "But you must consider that this environment could trigger—"

Jesus. Her face hot, Ophelia slaps at the wrist-comm to silence her mother, resisting the urge to look around to see if anyone else might have heard. Unbelievable. They must be desperate to go digging that up.

Ophelia shakes her head and slams the locker door shut with a surge of gritty satisfaction tinged with familiar disappointment. She was right. Again.

Ophelia finds the bridge by following the signs, literally. Red directional arrow stickers marked BRIDGE in English, Mandarin, Russian, and Japanese are slapped on the gray metal walls, one on top of another, in crooked columns.

The red lettering on white background matches the Montrose logo, which is also plastered everywhere. It is, theoretically, an abstract representation of a mountain with a rose in front of it—a large triangle behind a smaller upside down one with a dotted line to represent the stem.

That said, every time Ophelia looks at the logo, all she sees is the little triangle peeing on the larger one. Probably a good thing the Rorschach test is no longer deemed a useful tool.

The closer she gets to the bridge, the quieter the hum of the engines becomes. The murmur of voices rises and falls in the distance. Tension arcs through her, urging her to hurry, but she keeps her steps deliberate, even. She will not rush, not on Severin's arbitrary command.

The corridor she's in eventually dead-ends into the threshold of the bridge, revealing a relatively compact room. Four padded swivel chairs—three of them currently occupied—sit interspersed among banks and wall panels of touch screens and displays. Slightly warmer air, heated by the equipment within, wafts over her at the threshold. Numbers and codes flash on various screens, accompanied by mild-sounding beeps and alerts, but nothing that screams "Danger!" Which is good, because she wouldn't have the faintest notion of how to respond, unless there's a big red EMERGENCY button somewhere.

The edges of the banks are worn from use, the floor is scraped and scratched—this is clearly a working ship—but it's a tidy space, free of distractions. That feels like Severin at work. It's not an imposing room, physically, but an intimidating one nonetheless, and Ophelia feels a pressure, like a force field, at the edge of it, reminding her that she doesn't belong here.

Across the bridge, on the far wall, Lyria 393-C hangs in the large viewport, an icy ball rotating slowly in the soothing black backdrop of space. Violent weather systems roil in the atmosphere, hiding most of the surface, including the jagged black remains of ancient nonhuman cities jutting out of the snow.

Lyria 393-C is one of a few dozen planets where humans have found signs of former intelligent life. It makes those planets extra valuable, but more for the oddity, the bragging rights, than anything else. These civilizations are so old, there's very little left of them. Despite what a certain popular conspiracy vid series would have everyone believe, humans—Earth and her various colonies—are still the only game in town.

On Ophelia's right, in the chair closest to her, a woman sits sideways, flicking the screen on her wrist-comm. Her legs hang over the armrest, feet jittering with a nervous energy. Her dark hair is pulled back on top, the shaved undercut dyed a bright blue. Kate Wakefield.

Dark obsidian stars pierce both of her earlobes and move up in a curved line through the cartilage. *Ah. She's a collector.*

Ophelia's had other patients who collect. One piercing for each planet visited/survived. It's sort of a new version of "the scars tell the story," and winner takes all. Kate might be in a pool of other competitors or not. Some do it just for themselves. On her right ear, though, there's a bright red patch, healing skin, where a piercing has been removed. Ophelia wonders if it's from the last mission, the one where Ava died.

Feeling Ophelia's gaze on her, Kate looks up from her wrist-comm. Her mouth drops open slightly, then she straightens up slowly, swinging her legs to the floor.

Kate recognizes her. Not surprising. Ophelia steels herself, bracing for the barrage of questions or the wave of hatred. Both her family and her career are known to trigger . . . powerful responses.

But then, after a second, Kate simply nods. "Doc."

"Hi . . . Kate, right?" Never assume. Even if you're right, you don't want to be the officious jerk caught memorizing personnel files. (Even if that is, in fact, what you've done.)

"That's me." Kate looks . . . relieved to see her, pleased even, which has the opposite effect one might expect.

"Dr. Ophelia Bray. You can call me Ophelia." Wariness

colors her response. No one is ever that happy to make Ophelia's acquaintance, just on its own. But maybe that says more about her than about Kate.

At the sound of their voices, the pilot turns in his seat at the front of the bridge. His closely cropped dark hair and smooth brown skin bring out the bright green of his eyes, which are narrowed in suspicion. His gaze skates over Ophelia from head to toe, but he says nothing.

Not an atypical response, but . . .

Ophelia catches herself in a frown. There's something familiar about him, something that didn't come through in his—admittedly sparse—file. The set of his shoulders, the clenched line of his jaw . . . She can't quite put her finger on it.

Birch Osgoode. Unusual first name. Is it possible he's from one of the mining stations in the Carver system?

Goliath? Her heart trips unexpectedly in her chest. No, not possible. Plus, she doesn't recognize his last name.

But it was tradition across all three stations—Goliath, Sampson, Jericho—to name children after things the miners missed back on Earth. Seasons, animals, landscape features, trees.

If he's from the Carver system, he's going to be pissed at Ophelia for reasons beyond the usual ones.

Ophelia stays still, letting him look his fill. But as soon as she opens her mouth to greet him, he turns away, facing the viewport again. Fair enough. For now.

Commander Severin, seated in the command chair at the center, still hasn't acknowledged her presence. She's drawing in a breath to clear her throat, when he finally glances back over his shoulder and nods at her.

Such a ridiculous power play. Irritation rises in her. *Back away from the trip wire, Phe.*

One of the hardest things in this field for her, for everyone, is navigating around personal emotional baggage without letting it affect the work. She struggles with people who like to wield their position like a weapon, forever caught between being desperate for their acceptance and pissed at herself for the craving.

But her ongoing and long-standing issues with authority and authority figures are not relevant here. She searches out the cool spot of calm in the center of her chest and focuses on that.

Severin rises from his chair. "Let me know when we're close, Birch."

"Affirmative, Commander," Birch says, his voice a deep rumble. An oddly formal response. Ophelia suspects that's due to her, either trying to not give her anything to write up in a report—even though that's not how she works—or signaling that he has no intention of being vulnerable in her presence. Like using someone's last name or title instead of their first to hold them at a distance.

Severin steps around his chair and walks toward Ophelia . . . then right past.

The cool spot of calm in her chest vanishes in a wave of molten aggravation. Gritting her teeth against an exasperated noise that she is too professional to release, she follows him into the corridor.

Severin stands, waiting, about three meters away, in a wide-legged stance, as if they were on a rolling vessel on the open ocean, arms folded across his chest. He doesn't need to be any more imposing. He's nearly half a meter taller than she is, and the same jumpsuit that bags awkwardly around her fits him perfectly. This is his territory, and she is the intruder; he couldn't make that any clearer than if he started peeing around the perimeter.

His dark eyebrows are disapproving slashes across his forehead. Or maybe that's his expression when he looks at her.

Ophelia lifts her chin. "Maybe we should start over," she begins, meeting his gaze, refusing to be cowed. She holds out her hand. "My name is—"

"To be clear, I don't approve of Suresh's 'prank,'" he says. "I sent them to retrieve you."

Ophelia lowers her hand, face going hot at the memory, at the impression she must have made. Naked, covered in bio-gel and babbling nonsense. "That is partially my fault," she says evenly, focusing on the center of his forehead. An old trick to create the impression of eye contact when the monkey brain is too overwhelmed with strong emotion for the real thing. "I should have anticipated that resistance to my arrival might result in—"

"But I don't want there to be any misunderstanding. I only agreed to this arrangement so that my team would be able to continue working instead of being forced into mandatory evaluation leave," he continues, as if she hasn't spoken. "You aren't needed or wanted here."

That shocks Ophelia into meeting his eyes for real. "I'm sorry?"

"We can't afford any . . . distractions. I'm down a team member, and I have three planets to document and survey."

"To be clear, you're saying my authorized presence and plan to treat your team is a distraction?" she asks, her grip on her temper slipping. *Fire in the hole, Phe.*

The corner of his mouth twitches in irritation, but he remains calm. "I don't have time for a rich girl playing at being useful, sitting in judgment on those of us who have to actually work for a living." The words aren't biting or hateful, more a simple statement of fact. But still.

Her jaw aches with the urge to unleash on him. Of all the reasons to object to her presence, at least this is a tried-and-true one. One she's been dealing with for the better part of two decades, with classmates, coworkers, the media, patients, the guy who sells her her ration of coffee from a cart on the corner. It's tired, yes, and tiring.

"Commander Severin, I have no interest in interfering. Or judging. I am here to help." She's not going to bother addressing the jab about her wealth—or rather, presumed wealth—and inefficacy. Trying to explain never ends well. "As an on-site psych resource, I can address mental health issues more easily and reduce their severity. Maybe even prevent full-blown ERS."

ERS, if it gets bad enough, if conditions are right, can result in a psychotic break, violence, and actual clinical insanity, known colloquially as a Bledsoe Break. As one of the corporations chasing the bleeding edge in human habitation and productivity in space and exoplanetary exploration, Montrose has a vested interest in keeping its workforce healthy.

Plus, ERS, like suicidal ideation, can be contagious. And with one team member dead under unusual circumstances, it would behoove Severin to take advantage of the help she's offering.

"In terms of mission efficiency," Ophelia says, "I think you'll find if we can work together, it'll only improve your stats."

Severin exhales loudly through his nose. "Don't do that."

"Do what?" she asks, frowning.

"The whole 'get them on your side' thing," he says.

"I *am* on your side," she says.

He snorts. "Don't bother. I've been through all of this before."

Ophelia draws in a breath and holds it for a second, trying to trick herself out of the fight portion of her fight-or-flight response. "With a treatment plan and the new technology Montrose sent, the iVR helmets for sleep deprivation, you may discover you're actually more—"

"Corporate just won't be satisfied until they dig into every nook and cranny of our brains, will they?" He smiles tightly.

"Yes, and what exactly happened to your lost team member?" she snaps, folding her arms across her chest to match his stance. If he wants to push, she can push too.

Ava Olberman, fifty-two, was last seen alive on Minos 972-C. She left the hab without telling anyone (a big no-no), and the geolocator in her suit was either turned off (a potentially fireable violation of mission safety guidelines) or broken.

Based on postmission debriefs conducted on their return to Earth, no one on her team, including Severin himself, seems to know why Olberman did it. She was a mission or three away from retirement, and looking forward to it. It made no sense for her to wander out into a hostile climate alone, and even less for her to stay out there past any survival point.

Ophelia can't make a definitive diagnosis without having examined Ava Olberman, but that sure as hell sounds like ERS to her.

Severin jerks back slightly, patches of color rising in his pale cheeks. She's hit a sensitive spot. He blames himself for Ava's death, if she has to guess.

She opens her mouth to apologize, but he recovers himself first, his mouth tight. "Are you sure you want to compare track records with me, Doctor?" he asks, his gaze boring through her.

Nausea slips through her stomach, marking its presence with a flood of saliva in her mouth. *He knows.*

Of course he knows. She gives herself an internal shake. Lots of people do, even those who spend most of their time away from Earth, apparently. That's why Paulsen was shitting himself about headlines. Because of who she is, because of what happened. Hard to find a juicier story than that.

She wants to hide, duck her head in shame. But she makes herself hold firm. "If you'd like." Her voice is a little too thin, too sharp, but he probably doesn't know that. "It's all the more reason to devote resources to understanding and preventing ERS."

He pinches the bridge of his nose in exhaustion. "Look, you can try to convince me you're here to do good, but we both know you're here for you. If we're good little heartbeats for you, then you get to feel better about yourself and your guilty conscience, and Montrose gets some good coverage out of it."

Ophelia flinches. Officially, R&E teams provide an on-site assessment of newly acquired planets, but their primary purpose is to establish a solid residency claim, per the International Space Exploration and Occupation Treaty requirements. Basically, they're just living, breathing bodies to be counted. A heartbeat.

And once upon a time, R&E missions carried the internal designation "HO." Heartbeats Only. A lot of displaced workers—former lawyers, teachers, writers, truck drivers, and doctors, whose jobs were eliminated in the previous thirty years with advancements in AI—had no choice but to retrain and take on work that would pay them well enough and provide benefits for their families.

Severin might be right about her being here for ulterior motives, possibly even selfish ones, but she's never thought of the R&E teams as just bodies, and she's sure as hell not here to escape her guilt—how can she, when it comes with her everywhere?

But it's clear that Severin will never believe that. He's already made up his mind.

"I'll need to meet with everyone individually for an evaluation and to establish an initial plan," she says finally. A group session would be the ultimate goal, but they'd have to work up to that. "There will also be some setup required for the iVR system."

He opens his mouth to object, dark eyes snapping.

"Everyone is, of course, welcome to opt out," she adds.

"But you'll report that," he points out.

"It will be acknowledged in the summary, yes."

He gives a humorless laugh. "Of course it will."

Ophelia waits.

Finally he shakes his head in disgust. "I won't make my team do anything they don't want to do," he says.

She clamps down on her rising offense. "I would never ask you to. But you can encourage them to take advantage of—"

"And you'll need to pull your weight as a team member while we're on-site," he continues.

"I'm happy to help with anything you need," she says, working to keep her voice even. "But my primary—"

"Just stay out of our way," he says, raising his voice to be heard, as he turns and heads back to the bridge. "If you can."

Ophelia watches him go, fighting the urge to scream. She's not sure who won—or lost—that confrontation, not that she should even be looking at a patient interaction in binary like that. But it's hard not to.

The only good news is that she doesn't have to worry about contracting ERS and wanting to commit violence against Ethan Severin. She already wants that.

4

The crew bunk room, when Ophelia finally finds it, is smaller than she pictured from the ship's schematic. It's tucked in an odd offshoot of a corridor between the engines below and the cold sleep room above. The sign is missing from the door, but there's no mistaking what the room is.

The space is vaguely hexagonal, with a built-in bunk in each wall and several drawers beneath for storage. Everything is that dingy, institutional white that only seems to make its appearance in small, high-traffic locations where some overly optimistic designer chose hope over practicality, believing the lighter color would make them seem brighter, bigger. Hospital waiting areas. School corridors. Space station security offices.

Her office back on Montrose's corporate campus isn't much bigger, and certainly is not in better condition, but it's cozy. She painted the walls a tranquil shade of blue and brought in cushiony chairs that offer comfort and invite confessions. It also has a door.

Here, the only privacy comes from an individual pull-down metal screen that closes off each bunk from the room at large, creating a nook that's only a little larger than the cold sleep tanks they just emerged from. The bunk room is only where they'll be sleeping when they aren't on the surface of one planet or another. A kind of home base of sorts. But conditions in a hab on the surface aren't likely to be much better.

No wonder patients return with such issues. The stress of working and living in such close proximity to one another is far too much even under normal conditions, let alone for the length of time R&E teams are away. It feels . . . tight already, too close.

How much smaller will it seem in the dark, with five other people in here, sleeping, snoring, murmuring?

The air seems to press against Ophelia's face, too warm, too thick. She shakes her head to dismiss the phantom sensation.

Tightening her grip on the slippery, sealed packages of company-issued clothing, she hoists her small bag of personal items higher on her shoulder as she searches for her name. Each bunk has the last name of each crew member on a small plastic tab, brown background with white lettering, mounted on the wall to the left of it.

Commander Severin's, closest to the door, has the metal screen firmly in place, revealing nothing of the interior. So, no clues there. Or that is the clue. The man clearly does not want anyone in his business. Which Ophelia can hardly blame him for, not without being a hypocrite, which she tries to avoid as much as possible, having grown up surrounded by the trait. That being said, he doesn't have to be such an ass about it.

Suresh's screen is half wedged open at an odd angle that suggests a broken or jammed mechanism, a tangle of covers visible inside the dim interior. A mirror on the back wall of his bunk space is surrounded by mobile press-on lights. Two overstuffed toiletry bags hang from a hook nearby. Unsurprising. That level of fussy handsomeness—not to mention his hairstyle—requires maintenance and dedication, especially out here.

Liana's bunk is wide open, her bed neatly made with a fuzzy purple throw and a variety of pillows in different shapes and sizes. A few digi-fotos of family wave and laugh silently from their positions on the wall. But most of her personal space is dominated by drawings on thin, rough hemp pages—stick figures holding hands in front of an ocean or a lake, and what might be the *Resilience* in the sky above, given the childish backward *R* on the outside of a spaceship-looking vehicle—in clashing shades of pink, purple, and blue. All of them are dedicated to Liana, in various misspellings of her name and title. Ont Lee-lee. Aunt Liannna.

She also has a set of those mini firefly drones that light up when activated and hover near the ceiling. They're dormant at the moment, clinging to the wall like the bugs they are meant to mimic.

Bugs. Ophelia shudders. They have so many legs to . . . skitter with.

Skin crawling with the sensation of imagined beetles, roaches, and millipedes, she turns away to the next bunk. Kate's is wallpapered in digi-fotos. Not a centimeter of blank space. They even line the outside perimeter of her bunk, nearly covering up the sign with her name. The constant motion in them—two or three seconds repeating—makes it hard to look at them or past them to the space within. Most of them seem to feature a beaming Kate on various adventures. Scaling a space elevator infrastructure. Cliff diving. Platform jumping on Mars at the threshold of the atmosphere. A man with similar features is grinning at her side in almost all of them—her twin brother, the colonist on Trappist? Probably.

Ophelia swivels toward Birch's bunk, to her immediate right, on the other side of the door. It's also tidily made but bare of any hint of personality.

Except . . .

The heavy blanket is corporate supply, thick faux wool blend with edges ragged from use. The cheap but durable blankets are thick and scratchy, meant to double as wall hangings to preserve the heat in your quarters in case of a station-wide outage.

His pillow is lumpy and uneven, a striking contrast to the tightly pulled blanket and sheets, but it's also familiar. Pillows were one of those things that took up too much space on supply and resupply missions. So the miners used a set of spare clothing in a pillowcase as a substitute, and then, by the time they could have pillows sent to them, their solution had become part of their cultural identity. If you use a real pillow on a mining station, or even in one of the communities made up of those from the stations, it's as good as declaring yourself soft or weak.

In fact, the reigning insult is "softheaded."

Birch is definitely from one of the Pinnacle mining stations. That perhaps explains why he seemed so familiar.

She ignores the tiny pinch of homesickness in her gut, along with the ever-present swell of anxiety whenever she thinks of the mining stations, and focuses instead on the last bunk.

It's the farthest from the door and from Severin, directly opposite him across the room. The privacy screen is closed, preventing her from seeing inside. But it has an empty, abandoned air to it.

It takes Ophelia a moment to realize why: the brown nameplate is missing.

She moves closer for a better look. Rough patches of white foam adhesive still cling to the wall where the identifier should be, where it has been removed but not scraped clean.

Olberman. This is . . . *was* Ava Olberman's bunk.

Ophelia had reviewed Ava's file before leaving, so it's easy to pull up a mental image of the woman—athletic build, silvery hair cut short, tired but kind eyes. In the digi-foto included with her file, Ava was posing with her daughter, Catrin. Catrin wore an ESS, an exoskeleton suit, surgically connected to her legs and upper body to help her stand and walk. Sometimes the spine simply could not be healed or even regrown. She had been paralyzed in and barely survived a horrific air-veh accident, the same accident that claimed the life of her father, Ava's late husband.

And now Ava is gone too.

For some reason, it hadn't occurred to Ophelia until this moment that this was where she would be sleeping. That she would not just be taking Olberman's seat on this mission but also occupying the woman's most intimate space—where she slept, where she dreamed, where she died.

No. Ophelia shakes her head. Not where Ava died. She ran out of air on Minos 972-C. With a malfunctioning geolocater and mostly likely a raging case of ERS that led her to act unpredictably. No need for added melodrama; the situation is tragic enough on its own.

She grips the handle on the privacy screen, cool metal against her fingertips, and pulls, half expecting to find it secured from the inside.

But the screen retracts easily and smoothly overhead, revealing the bunk inside. A harsh white light flickers on—now she can see why Liana and Suresh both have alternate sources of illumination—highlighting a simple bare mattress and a new pillow and crisp white sheets in the same plasti-seal as her jumpsuits. The faint smell of lemon-scented cleaner wafts outward.

Nothing ominous. And why should there be?

She's letting her nerves get to her, still jumpy from that stupid prank.

Ophelia opens the top storage drawer and dumps her company-issued clothing in. In the drawer underneath, the larger one, she tucks her whole bag. She's not sure what she wants to take with her to the surface yet, and there's no sense in unpacking just to repack.

Not that there's much in the bag to begin with. Pen and paper, to take old-school notes that cannot be uploaded or hacked into—that always seems to reassure her most paranoid patients. A cheap, disposable tablet that holds downloaded photos, music, and media, as her QuickQ implant won't work out here. Her birthday present from Dulcie last year—a necklace with a tiny delicate bird charm on a thin gold chain. Their mother almost swallowed her tongue when she saw it. Dulcie had assumed it was because of what she'd spent.

The rest is mostly clothes—thicker undershirts, warmer wraparound sweaters, and heavy socks. Space is cold.

After closing her bag inside, she straightens up and reaches for the sheets. But an unexpected flash of color stills her hand. There, just between the new pillow and the packages of bedding—pink.

Carefully, Ophelia pushes the sealed sheets aside, sending them slipping across the mattress, until she can see the source of the color more clearly.

It's a flower. Three of them, actually. Delicately folded bits of pink paper turned into origami lotuses. Dark veins of printed words run across the leaves and petals. A memorial of some kind?

Instantly, her mind flashes to the outer wall of her building on Montrose's campus. Two weeks ago, someone hacked it, so instead of running the latest corporate messaging, it showed emotional images of flowers waving gently in the breeze, balloons lifting into the sky, and messages that said things like "Gone Too Soon" and "Never Forget." Also, of course, "Montrose Blows!"

Instinctively, she shuts her eyes against the memory. But in turn, that only summons another, older one:

Dim corridors lined with carefully assembled bouquets of tiny greenery from the greenhouse, string or leftover scraps of fabric tied around their delicate stems. Weeping echoing from the mess hall. The slash of dark red paint across the door to their quarters, before her mother hurried her inside.

Her eyes snap open. No. Absolutely not opening that door to the past.

She reaches out to pick up one of the flowers by one of the tiny petals. Something about this—the color, the paper—looks so familiar.

Ophelia squints at the words, cut off in the leaf folds and overlapping each other on the petals until they turn to nonsense. Still, a few phrases immediately leap out.

. . . *no evidence of wrongdoing* . . .

. . . *(presumptive ERS), which* . . .

. . . *cleared for return to* . . .

It's the summary page of an ARD report. Assessment for
Return to Duty. A crew copy of one, anyway—those are always on pink paper, to differentiate from the original, and like
all official documents, still printed. In this case, so that the
employees in question can be handed the assessment in person,
in front of witnesses, and there can be no confusion about the
receipt.

A Pink, as they're colloquially known. Her patients frequently refer to "getting Pinked" or "waiting for a Pink."

After any kind of incident, especially one involving death
or severe injury, Montrose's Internal Human Behavior department is charged with investigating. They are an awkward balance of human resources and a privatized police force—both
hated and feared. IHB is responsible for writing the ARDs and
delivering the Pinks.

Working in the PBE unit, Ophelia has contributed to more
than her fair share of ARD reports, but it's rare for her to
have access to the unredacted final, even when working with
cases generated by an ARD incident. She's seen the pink cop-
ies before, usually in the hands of patients in her office, waving them around in protest of the results or holding them up
in triumph.

ARDs are highly confidential. Sharing an ARD report with
an unauthorized party, even a report in which the employee is
cleared of wrongdoing, is grounds for immediate termination.

And yet, here one is. Part of one, anyway. Cut into pieces and
transformed into flowers.

What a strange thing to memorialize Ava Olberman with,
the company's assessment that her death was her own fault.

Ophelia runs her thumb gently over one of the sharp, elegant
folds. A sign of guilt, perhaps?

That might make sense if a member of the team thinks they
should have found Ava faster . . . or caught the signs of ERS
earlier. Then again, guilt doesn't always work logically. It might
simply be someone with an overactive conscience, taking on

blame they don't deserve but can't seem to shake, nonetheless. People are strange like that.

She gently returns the first flower to its place and picks up the second to examine the words on it.

. . . left without notifying Commander Severin or her teammates . . .

All efforts to locate were unsuccessful, despite . . .

The body, likely in the collapsed tunnels on the southern side of the . . .

Ophelia's heartbeat speeds up, and it takes her a second to figure out why. This Pink holds no redactions. No perfect, solid black lines blotting out the words on this flower or the first. Unlike the version in her files, this summary page is seemingly whole.

Her fingers itch to unfold the paper, to see what she's missed, if there's anything important she doesn't already know. A more complete picture might help her better understand this team and how to help them.

But it's a violation—or the team will view it that way. And it is a little creepy, even with good intentions, to use someone's obviously private memorial as an investigative tool.

Plus, if she takes these flowers apart, she'll never be able to put them back together in the same way. And that will serve as an open declaration that she is the snoop/spy they likely think she is. Trust destroyed. No coming back from that.

"Hello?"

Ophelia jumps, startled, and spins around to face the door.

"Just me." Liana waves from the threshold and then steps inside. "I was looking for you. I wanted to say again how sorry I am for what happened earlier. We shouldn't have—"

She pauses as she approaches, her gaze falling on the flower in Ophelia's hand. "What are you doing?"

"It's . . . They were in the bunk," Ophelia offers, feeling both the lameness of that explanation for her nosiness and utter relief that she hadn't given in to the impulse to pick the flowers apart.

Liana steps forward and plucks the flower from Ophelia's palm. Her gaze slips to the bunk, where the remaining flowers are now clearly visible. "It must be for Ava," she says softly, her mouth turning down, carving lines on either side in her smooth skin.

So Liana hadn't been aware of the memorial until now.

"I'll take them. Get them out of your way." She moves past Ophelia and gathers the paper blossoms quickly but gingerly. Answers, information, disappearing right before Ophelia's eyes.

Watching her, Ophelia resists the urge to tell her to stop, to leave the flowers in place. "I'm sure it must feel strange. To have me here, in this space," she says instead.

Liana pauses. "You're just doing your job," she says quietly, her face still turned away.

"True. But that doesn't make the situation any less raw," Ophelia points out.

Liana steps back with the flowers in her loosely cupped hands, pink showing through the gaps in her long, elegant fingers. "I just miss her." Her dark eyes are bright, shiny with unshed tears.

Ophelia nods. "Completely understandable. You worked together, lived together. More like family than coworkers." If her other patients are the standard to go by, anyway. Not that family is any less complicated.

"Yes, exactly," Liana says softly, her thumb brushing over one of the paper petals. "I was so nervous when I first started, but Ava walked me through everything. Made sure I was okay." She laughs, shakes her head. "She was such a mom, you know?"

No, not really. But Ophelia can imagine it, based on her experience of other mothers.

"She missed her daughter. She only took this job to try to save for some experimental treatment for Catrin that her insurance wouldn't pay for. Something that would let Catrin walk again, I guess." Liana sighs. "She treated me like I was another daughter."

"She sounds like a good friend," Ophelia offers, leaving space for Liana to elaborate. In a session, well-timed silence is often just as important as or even more important than what she says.

Liana nods, her gaze remains fixed on the flowers. "She was, and I just wish we had—" She stops abruptly, straightening up, her shoulders stiffening.

"Wish you had what?" Ophelia prompts gently, when Liana doesn't continue.

"Doesn't matter." Liana shakes her head. "Accidents happen, unfortunately," she says. "It's sad. But that's just part of this life, isn't it?"

These sound like borrowed words, a speech Liana's heard dozens of times before. Perhaps after being told she was "too emotional."

Ophelia's mouth tightens. The outdated attitude that feelings are a weakness—or an inconvenience at best, instead of simply human and a necessity to address—lingers in this industry.

Liana's eyes are still slightly reddened, but the hint of tears has now completely vanished. She meets Ophelia's gaze steadily, unflinching, as if she's trying to impress the words upon her: *Nothing to see here.*

"Yes, it is sad," Ophelia says after a moment. "Which can be difficult to deal with sometimes. That's why I'm here. I can help, and I hope that you'll come talk with me."

Liana opens her mouth to say something further, but the ship shifts under their feet, as if a gentle wave has passed beneath them. The pitch of the engines, a constant background hum that Ophelia has already mostly tuned out, shifts to something lower, more resonant.

Liana's head jerks up, as if she's hearing a voice calling to her at a distance. Then a small smile breaks across her face. "We're in orbit. Almost there." She starts for the door, hands still holding the flowers. Ophelia is willing to bet they'll be hidden . . . or dumped in the first recycler Liana encounters, shredded and pulped to be remade into a cup or toilet paper. "He'll want to start landing prep soon."

"He," presumably, is Commander Severin. And not someone Ophelia wants to further agitate by being late or absent. Actually, that's exactly what she wants to do, but she will accede to her better judgment.

"I'll be there in a minute." Ophelia tips her head toward the bunk and the still sealed sheets, lying askew on the mattress now. "I want to take care of this first."

Distracted, Liana nods, hurrying out the door.

Ophelia tears into the packaging, releasing an overwhelming scent of *New*, and dumps the sheets out onto the bed, letting her mind wander as her body moves through the familiar motions.

It's hard, reading people. Especially when you've just met them. It takes time to get to know them, their body language, their conversational quirks and idiosyncrasies. Some people are more difficult to read, in general.

But in Ophelia's experience, extended forced eye contact like that generally only means one thing—lying.

It's a weird psychological quirk. People know that avoiding someone's gaze can indicate deception—which is true—but to compensate, they go overboard the other direction.

With the sheets in place, tight and smooth as she was taught so many years ago, Ophelia reaches for the pillow and begins to wedge it into the provided case.

Liana is lying about something related to Ava Olberman. Maybe it's simply that Liana is hurting from Ava's death more than she would like to acknowledge.

I just wish we had . . .

Known? Done more?

Maybe Liana feels responsible for only recognizing the symptoms of ERS in retrospect.

Or perhaps she has information about the events leading up to Ava's death, relevant and helpful details that might be found in the unredacted Pink.

There's no way to know.

With a sigh, Ophelia drops the pillow, twisted and awkward in its slightly too small case, into place at the head of the bed.

Or maybe Ophelia's just looking for something more to be wrong, trying to give herself another problem to solve so she can prove to Montrose she's good at her job. And worth the hassle.

"Everyone, prep for departure. Our window between storms is exceptionally tight." Severin's voice echoes through the bunk room via the overhead intercom.

Either way, one thing is clear: Liana is desperately trying to convince Ophelia that she's fine, everything is fine.

And Ophelia should know; she's been doing the same thing for most of her life.

5

Ophelia grips her safety restraints tighter, teeth rattling in her head so hard she's not sure she'll have any left by the time they land. Her chest aches with the pressure of increasing gravity, and her palms are sweaty inside her envirosuit gloves. Correction: all of her is sweaty.

The central part of the lander is a circular space with four bolted-down chairs, where she, Suresh, Kate, and Liana are all strapped in at a reclining angle. A short ladder leads to the command area above, where Birch and Commander Severin are seated. Another ladder on the opposite side of the space leads down another level, where they will exit through the airlock.

It's like plummeting to the ground in a child's version of an old-fashioned space shuttle, just thin metal between Ophelia and a horrible death. Bright flickering light, like flames, flashes outside the tiny circular window, her only view outside from this compartment.

"Seven minutes," Birch calls over the noise. The lander rattles ominously around them, sounding dangerously close to flying apart.

Ophelia squeezes her eyes shut. If only they could skip this part, stay in cold sleep until they're where they're supposed to be.

Not that being planetside is going to be so much better.

Planets are, for lack of a more precise term, dumb. The way they just sit there—all vulnerable, with no protection—in outer space. It took Ophelia years to get used to living on Earth, just being out under an open sky, where anything can fall on you, where the air might just suddenly vanish without so much as a warning alert. It's just a giant rock with no shield or propulsion. At least on a ship or space station, people stand a chance of getting out of the way of an asteroid or any other trouble that comes their way. Planets are always one significant collision away from being knocked out of orbit for good.

"All right, listen up, people. This is a standard residency package." Severin's voice, smooth and even despite the chaos around them, sounds in her ears through the in-helmet comm channel.

She forces her eyes open to find his image on the primary display inside her helmet, the others alongside him in smaller squares. Presumably her internal helmet camera was reflecting her image back to them in much the same way.

"Six weeks on and then we're out of here. Surface mapping, core samples, and—"

Next to Ophelia, Liana straightens in her seat and her hand shoots up as if she's been electrified.

"Yes, Liana, core sampling is yours if you want it," Severin says. Fondness mixed with amusement softens the harsh lines of his face, and Ophelia draws in an involuntary breath. It's a view into what he would be like in an unguarded moment, a moment when the weight of responsibility he carries is lifted. He's almost handsome. In a dark and broody sort of way.

She needs to get out more, clearly. Working too much—or an undetected oxygen shortage—has damaged her brain.

Liana pumps her fist in triumph, while Suresh shakes his head from across the lander. "Always volunteering for extra work," he tuts at her. "Have I taught you nothing?"

"Keep talking, pod boy," Kate murmurs.

He makes a sour face, while Liana snickers.

Their interplay makes an odd longing thump in Ophelia's chest. This level of camaraderie takes years—and a level of mutual vulnerability—to develop. Something she's only ever had with Julius. Except, obviously not.

The thought of all those Sunday mornings sends a staggering bolt of pain through her. Of arriving sleepy and being greeted by Julius with a cup of coffee in hand for her, of reaching across the table to cut Marlix's pancakes, of ganging up with Jonathan to tease Julius about his relentless need for a "civilized table," which always seemed to include fresh flowers, crisply pressed napkins that would have brought her grandmother's housekeeper to tears, and more silverware than any of them would ever use, considering one of them was a toddler.

Ophelia knew, of course, that it was all in reaction to Julius growing up eating scraps and street cart food, split among his siblings so that no one was ever hungry but no one was full either. In the same way, he knew that her reaction to her childhood was to rebel against the strictures of formality, which usually translated to wolfing down meal-paks at work or eating a cup of noodles on her ride home.

That's what it means to be known. And why it's a mistake. It only gives you an opening to hurt more. Because now she knows what it's like to have that closeness and to lose it.

At least she was smart enough—cynical enough, Julius would say—to keep the truly important parts of her past, the dangerous parts, to herself.

"We'll be launching the surface mapping drones as soon as the weather clears," Severin continues.

"We're going down without updated surface data?" Kate demands.

"Storms are too frequent and too powerful. We had to take our launch window when we could get it," Severin says. "But as far as mapping, we've got what came in the acquisition packet from Pinnacle."

Pinnacle? Ophelia works to keep her expression even. No wonder Severin was so cranky with her earlier.

"Which reminds me . . . Communication is going to be extremely limited once we're BOG," he says.

It takes her a moment to parse that one—"boots on the ground." Her patients, by the time they got to her, were accustomed to speaking to "civilians."

"So send your messages as soon as you can. We'll be cut off except for when the storms break temporarily," Severin says.

His tone is matter-of-fact, but that doesn't prevent a shiver from creeping along Ophelia's skin. Isolated on a dead planet and trapped with strangers by storms.

All the more opportunity to work without interruption, she tells herself firmly.

"Lyria 393-C is tidally locked, so we're landing in the terminator zone, target site 43B, near the remains of what was likely the largest city on the planet, also known as . . ." Severin's mouth twists as if he tastes something bitter. "Vatican City II."

Ophelia grimaces. Pinnacle is so terrible at naming things. Just . . . zero imagination. Even though they have an entire department dedicated to branding and naming.

"The most recent ghost station is Pinnacle's, so that's the one we're hoping to use," he continues.

His words send a jolt through her. "Wait. We're staying in a Pinnacle facility?" The question is out of her mouth before she can consider the wisdom of interrupting.

An extra beat of silence passes. "Is that a problem, Doctor?" Severin asks mildly. But there's a weight to his question that makes her feel like *she's* being judged.

"Of course not," she says quickly. What else is she supposed to say? There's no choice now. But she hasn't stayed in a Pinnacle facility since . . .

No, no. No!

"It's fine," she says, if a bit too loudly.

"Glad to hear it," Severin says dryly. "As I was saying, the plan is to use their station for our stay. It's a big one. Central hub and a dozen connected hab modules."

Severin's image in her helmet shrinks to the corner as a schematic pops up in the center, showing a layout of the station. It resembles an old-fashioned clock face, with the central hub in the middle and the connected hab modules as the "numbers" around the outer edge. But the modules aren't placed quite evenly all the way around, so it's a bit more like that melting clock painting. Still, it's the largest station she's ever seen or heard about.

Of course it is. It's Pinnacle.

What's odd, though, is that they've sold the planetary rights at all. Collecting planetary rights is a badge of pride for Pinnacle, particularly the ones with alien ruins. They're rare enough to be a big deal, even if, as far as Ophelia knows, Pinnacle has yet to gain any technological advances from what they've found. In most cases, there's no tech to be found. It seems those civilizations never even made it as far as humans did before dying out.

Kate splutters with a laugh of disbelief. "What were they doing, permanently moving in?"

"I have no idea." Severin's gaze flicks to her in the helmet display, and Ophelia senses trouble, a spark of mischief or perhaps challenge in those dark eyes, before he speaks again. "Perhaps Dr. *Bray* can illuminate us."

She opened the door by questioning the facility, and now he's making sure she pays for it. Asshole move.

"Dr. Bray?" Liana repeats softly, her voice rising at the end.

In another moment, another situation, the way her gaze and Suresh's whip around to focus on Ophelia might be funny. It's not as if she's hidden her last name—she's introduced herself multiple times for God's sake—but hearing it in this context, obviously, means something more.

The lander gives another hard jolt, and she clutches at her safety straps again, fresh sweat beading on her upper lip.

"Three minutes," Birch says loudly. Does he sound even more terse than before?

"Wait, wait. Bray, like the Pinnacle Brays?" Suresh asks, eyebrows raising to his vivid hairline. "Richest fuckers on Earth?"

Second richest. Pinnacle, the company her mother's family founded a century and a half ago, still hasn't conquered the second coming of the Carnegies—known as JPC Enterprises—despite their best efforts.

Ophelia won't argue the "fuckers" part, though.

Her great-great-grandfather was one of the earliest developers of the technology behind the QuickQ implant, specifically the wiring interfacing with the brain. It was meant to be a way to give patients suffering from degenerative diseases their voices back, helping them communicate and interact with the world even as their bodies failed them. What it ended up being, though, was sold for a shit ton of money.

So, instead of helping people who were losing the ability to communicate, now pretty much every brain in the solar system is wired and online every minute of every day. And the Brays still make money off all of them, not just the devices but also the user information gathered. Every search you run on your QuickQ, every keyword in your calls, is sold to someone who wants you to buy their crap.

Pinnacle has since moved on to exploring new avenues of revenue in space, from mining asteroids to new scientific discoveries. But the base of their wealth is still that one invention that commoditized humanity.

It's a family success story retold—and toasted to—every year at the holidays.

"Fuckers" is probably the best word for them, yeah.

"No, no way. That doesn't make sense. It's a common enough last name," Liana points out. "And the youngest one, she's too young to be . . ." She hesitates, glancing over at Ophelia. "Too young to be you," she finishes awkwardly.

"No, no," Suresh says with impatience, sitting forward. "The other one."

"The one that's a model?" Liana asks doubtfully.

No, that would be Portia. Ophelia's first cousin, Darwin's daughter. Portia is a model/influencer/actress, who still somehow never seems to have any occupation other than spending money. A bitchy thing to say, possibly, but when Ophelia was a scrawny eleven and Portia an overfed and overindulged ten, Portia had trapped her in the smaller wine cellar at Thanksgiving and stabbed her with a fork because she'd overheard her father saying Ophelia's blood was "contaminated" and Portia wanted to see it.

Ophelia can sit here and wait for them to run down all the various, possibly appropriate-aged women associated with her family tree, or she can end this torture.

She clears her throat, realizing belatedly that she sounds eerily like her grandmother in doing so. "He's referring to me," she says. "My mother is Regency Bray." The oldest daughter of the oldest daughter. It occurs to Ophelia for the thousandth time that this would be so much easier if she could have just changed her last name. But that remained a complicated and potentially risky endeavor, and for more reasons than just the family tradition of keeping the Bray name no matter what.

Suresh snaps his finger and points at her. "Yes, the one that showed up out of nowhere."

After all these years, Ophelia doesn't even flinch anymore. She's not sure whether that's a sign of improvement or cause for increased concern.

"I was born off-planet," she says, the words flowing out without hesitation. "My mother was on a charitable outreach mission to the terraforming colony on Celestia when she met my father." She braces herself for questions. People always have questions about Celestia.

Liana's mouth drops open. "The cult?"

Kate kicks at Liana in remonstration, though strapped in as they are, it's more a gesture than an effective deterrent.

"'Cult' is . . . a strong word," Ophelia says. "It's a privately owned endeavor. They wanted to make it on their own without a corporate sponsor." Which they hadn't quite succeeded at. Everyone can be bought—you just have to find the right price. If that's not the official Bray motto, it probably should be.

Suresh opens his mouth to say something, but Ophelia cuts him off. "My family history and connections are irrelevant here. I signed a nondisclosure and noncompete agreement, as we all did." Montrose—their employer—and Pinnacle are technically competitors, if only in the same way that a teacup Chihuahua and a Cane Corso are both technically canines. "I have no information on what Pinnacle is doing. I am not and have not ever been part of the family's plans." Her words are a little too sharp, but she can't seem to stop herself.

It's so strange. The outside world views her as part of them, one of the enigmatic, excessive Brays, while the Brays themselves cluster together with their backs turned against her, pretending that she doesn't exist. Or trying to, anyway.

"I am here to help," Ophelia says, trying to wrench the conversation back on track. "Most of my patients are R&E team members. Once we're settled, I'll meet with each of you to create a plan to address your needs. Some of it may be talk therapy or exercise—"

"Hear that, Birch? We're going to be running in circles around the inside of the hab," Suresh says with a sneer. "Getting our sweat on."

"A little busy here," Birch says tightly, as the shuttle gives another tremendous jolt.

"I also have the latest iteration of the immersive reality sleep bands from Montrose," Ophelia says. "They're portable now, and—"

A collective groan from Kate, Suresh, and Liana rises, startling her. Okay, no, the bands aren't the most comfortable, but their ability to simulate a soothing and familiar environment that is indistinguishable from the real thing is invaluable. Want to sleep in your childhood bedroom? No problem. Get your best rest in a hammock under the stars? That can be arranged.

Ophelia lifts her chin in defiance, though the gesture is likely lost behind her helmet. "It's important. An earlier and more active intervention makes a big difference. Especially when it comes to ERS."

"ERS," Suresh snorts. "Right."

Ophelia goes still. "I'm sorry?"

"ERS doesn't exist," he says. "Just a bunch of crybabies who can't handle the job."

She jams her tongue against the back of her rattling teeth to keep the spew of furious words inside. It's not the first time she's heard that, but it never fails to enrage. *Oh, do go on, Suresh. Please tell that to all the families who've lost loved ones to ERS. Like Ava Olberman's daughter. Please tell that to all the therapists and doctors struggling to keep ERS in check. Explain how it doesn't exist to all the children who have to watch their parents devolve into monsters who don't even—*

Ophelia forces herself to draw in a deep breath. This is just Suresh, being an instigator again. She makes a mental note—this is definitely something worth exploring in a session with him, what drives him to behave like such a jackass.

But no matter his motive, giving him what he wants, outrage and defensiveness, will only reinforce this unhealthy and morale-damaging tendency.

She pushes her anger down, deep down, with everything else that does not serve her or her purpose here.

"Sleep deprivation can be a major contributing factor for ERS, along with extensive cold sleep travel and isolation. And in your case, you have the additional issue of grief and loss," Ophelia says. Suddenly no one is looking at her, through her helmet display or across the lander. "So we're going to work on that. Together."

Silence holds for a moment.

"Is it true that your dad has private roads just for driving his air-veh?" Kate asks.

Ophelia blinks. But she should have expected this. "Hamilton Beck is my stepfather, not my—"

"And he only drives it once and then buys a new one?" Kate continues.

"What about your dogs?" Liana asks. "I heard that your dogs have a house to themselves, like, with a personal chef and—"

Fuck me. "I don't have any dogs," Ophelia says. "My aunt might be the one who—"

"—true that you own the ocean, like, the actual body of water?" Suresh joins in, showing genuine interest directed at her for the first time, rather than sheer disdain.

Irritation swells in her. Crashing and burning on the planet's surface below suddenly seems preferable. People have always been curious about her family, even the wealthy kids at the private school her grandmother insisted on, back when she first came to Earth. But most of those in the upper-crust and highly competitive strata preferred to pretend they knew it all and then whisper behind her back instead.

Where is Severin with his inconvenient need to defend, this time? Ophelia glances down to find his image still in the bottom corner of her helmet screen, his expression both amused and a little too smug. Of course, this is classic territorial behavior. *These are my people, not yours.* God, why did he have to be such a . . . man about it?

"Again, that is my family," she says, working to rein in her exasperation. "Not me. I live in a two flat in—"

"It's not the ocean, you twat," Kate says, scoffing at Suresh. "Just a part of it. In exchange for their technology to turn the saltwater into drinkable stuff."

Ophelia is fairly certain this isn't true, but knowing her family—or perhaps knowing them as little as she does—she can't rule it out.

Suresh flips Kate the finger, though the gesture is muted by the lander shaking and trembling around them such that his hand is barely aloft for a moment. "Is it true about the vault?" he asks. "That you have to provide a bone marrow sample for it to unlock?"

Her mouth falls open. "Bone marrow? Vault?" That's a new one. "What . . . There is no vault." And if there is, she certainly would not have access to it. Among other things, her controversial life choices—*Working for a living! For a competitor! Living on her own instead of at one of the family compounds!*—seem to herald an unpredictability that they view as a threat.

Her uncle—and her grandmother before him—seems to be of the philosophy that ignoring your problems is more dangerous than keeping a distant, disapproving eye on them and inviting them to Christmas dinner, for the photo op if nothing else.

"Again, I don't have much, if any, contact with—"

"Thirty seconds," Birch announces. A few more tooth-chipping seconds pass, and the lander's shaking slows, along with all the accompanying rattles, squeaks, and alarming popping sounds. Ophelia can't see much of anything from the window, across the circular space, but there seems to be less of that alarming "We're on fire!" light from the outside.

Thank you. She lets out a silent breath of relief at the reprieve, from both the shaking and the interrogation.

Until Birch continues with his question.

"Is it true that one of your patients killed himself by jumping out of your office window?"

6

Ophelia can't move, can't breathe for a second, air locked in her lungs.

It was inevitable. She knew that. Even with patient-doctor confidentiality, a suicide at the Psychological and Behavioral Evaluation offices, especially when emergency services are called, would make the news streams. Even without her name associated.

But her name was associated. Her voice was on the released QuickQ 911 tag.

"This is . . . Ophelia Bray. PBE for Montrose, Segura Tower. I have an attempted suicide. I need emergency services immediately."

"Tell me what happened," the operator says. Cool, dispassionate.

"He . . . he jumped. From the roof, I think. But he landed . . ." In the tag, Ophelia's voice sounds strange, broken, both because of emotion and because of the utter inadequacy and inaccuracy of that word. The planned and elegant movement it suggests. Her patient didn't land. He crashed. He smashed. He collided. *"He landed on the seventh floor, south side of the garden terrace."*

"Confirmed. We have your location. Emergency services en route. Is he conscious—"

She'd disconnected then to concentrate on moving as fast as she could from her office to the terrace below. Hours, years, eons passed in the time it took her to traverse those seventeen levels of stairs.

By the time she reached the garden terrace level and rushed through to rip open the door to the outside, she was dizzy and panting. A sharp breeze cut through her sweater to her damp skin.

Her patient lay on his stomach on the marble floor, perpendicular to her, head turned in her direction. His eyes were open, staring fixedly at her. But the side of his skull was now flattened, like an irregularly shaped melon. His scalp was both pointed and sunken in where it shouldn't be.

The sudden roar of nausea sent Ophelia's hand flying up to cover her mouth.

Then he'd blinked. He was still alive, somehow.

She'd raced to his side and held his hand, knees in the pool of blood around him, her pants soaking up the rapidly cooling liquid.

Rueben Monterra. A grandfather of two, kind eyes that held both sadness and intense drive to get better. One of Ophelia's favorite patients. One of her success stories. Her almost success stories.

He was a retired R&E pilot struggling a little with being at home full time with his beloved family for the first time in decades. Depression, anxiety, and mild cognitive damage from too many trips in the older version of the cold sleep system, known as NODD. Confirmed ERS.

But he had been doing so much better. Until he wasn't.

He died on the patio before EMS could arrive, died holding Ophelia's hand.

"It's not uncommon, you know," Julius had said, trying to comfort her. "They're confused, scared. Their brains have turned against them. God only knows what he was thinking or seeing. But they want someone to witness, to see them, to understand."

But Ophelia didn't understand. And quite selfishly, she wanted to know why her. Why had he chosen her? All she wanted to do was make a difference. A positive difference. But she'd failed. Failed him. Failed his family.

Shame scalds her neck and cheeks, and an internal fan kicks on, her suit's attempt to regulate her rising body temperature.

"It was the roof, actually," Ophelia says finally.

Liana gasps.

"Making Mommy and Daddy proud with more death and mayhem," Birch mutters.

Hamilton Beck is not my father! Ophelia wants to shout, as if that were at all the point.

"Enough," Severin says sharply. "Let's focus on why we're here." But his expression is troubled, brows furrowed like storm clouds on the horizon.

Birch changes their rotation then, pulling a stomach-swirling move. "We've got legs. Countdown to target," he says flatly.

Taut silence holds for several seconds, and Ophelia can feel them not looking at her.

"Prep for landing in three, two, one . . ." Birch intones, his voice trailing off just as a giant collision shakes the entire lander.

But there is no screaming, no panicked shouts for information, or even loud alerts. Just the faint soothing beep of what she assumes is the navicomputer announcing that they've reached their target destination.

Before she can unclench her cramped fingers from her safety restraints, Birch is scrambling down the ladder and past them into the cargo area, toward the airlock, without another word.

"Who pissed in his Toasty O's?" Suresh demands, shrugging free of his restraints.

"Toasty O's?" Liana asks, unclicking her own restraints.

"It's a saying," Kate explains as she stands and stretches.

Ophelia swallows, dry tongue sticking to the roof of her mouth. She has a water stem in her helmet somewhere, if she can remember how to trigger it. "He's from the mining stations in the Carver system." She means it as a question, but it comes out more like a statement. That's the only logical explanation for his . . . anger.

She unbuckles herself, hands trembling.

"The Carver system?" Suresh whistles.

"How did you know that?" Severin asks as he descends the ladder from the command area.

"The stations are Pinnacle's. Or they were." She stands, fighting the urge to fold her arms protectively across herself. It'll just make her look closed off and defensive. Besides, her suit is too bulky for the gesture to be effective. "My family shut down the stations twenty years ago, relocated the workers and their families to Avaris 796, in the next closest system." But going from station living to dirtside is hard enough even in good conditions, and these were not that. Avaris is pretty much a ball of rock with limited terraforming potential. Anyone living there is utterly dependent on outside shipments, and with the distance from the central colonies, receiving anything in a timely manner is a crapshoot at best. It's a difficult existence, but the only one that lets them remain near their former homes and keep their employment.

"Was this because of the whole Bloody Bledsoe—" Suresh begins eagerly.

"No!" Ophelia says, too quickly. "No. After that. They weren't making enough money anymore."

"That was shitty," Kate says after a moment.

"Yes. It was," Ophelia says vehemently. It's one argument, among many, that she's had with her uncle over the years. To no avail.

Oddly enough, her answer seems to satisfy them, like she's passed a test that she didn't even know she was taking.

Kate nods at her and then leads the way toward the cargo area, Suresh and Liana trailing behind.

"What's Bloody Bledsoe?" Liana asks, her voice loud and clear over the common channel in Ophelia's helmet.

"It's this guy who went nuts and killed a bunch of people on one of the Carver system mining stations," Suresh says.

Ophelia's hands tighten into fists. This is why she shouldn't talk about the Carver stations.

"Totally sick," Suresh continues. "Biggest mass murder in the last century. They didn't even know what was happening until his hauler docked and all this blood and body parts came pouring out of the—"

"It was a long time ago, when they first started seeing ERS cases," Kate interrupts. "Before they even knew what to call it. You don't have to worry about it."

"ERS," Suresh groans. "If I had a jackie for every time someone blames that bullshit, I'd—"

Their voices abruptly vanish in Ophelia's helmet.

She blinks, startled.

"I'll talk to Birch," Severin says, next to her. A glance at her helmet display reveals he's switched the two of them over to a private channel.

Ophelia turns to face him. "No. I should do it. He has a problem with me. That's not going to go away on command."

She steels herself to fight against his rebuttal, his insistence that Birch's problems are his problems.

Instead, Severin gives a brief nod inside his helmet, a flicker of what might be grudging approval in his eyes. "All right." He doesn't sound convinced, but he's not fighting her on it.

Well. If only she'd known that all she had to do to get them all on her side was to reveal the most soul-shredding fuck-up of her life . . .

Who is she kidding? She still wouldn't have done it.

"Come on," Severin says, tipping his head in the direction the others took. "We need to go. Clock's ticking on the next wave of storms."

According to Ophelia's mission brief, one side of Lyria 393-C is perpetually facing the sun, the other is in permanent darkness, but neither is warm enough for human habitation without interventive technology.

Their target destination is on the northernmost continent—which some joker had named Eden—in the terminator zone, the thin strip between light and dark that exists in perpetual twilight.

Despite knowing that, Ophelia instinctively braces for the sudden glare of light inside the crowded airlock as the door releases with a hiss.

Instead, gloomy gray illumination trickles in, along with a blast of wind and snow that knocks Ophelia back a step, into Severin.

He grasps her arms and steadies her. She pulls away before he can release her.

"Let's go," Severin says on the common channel. "We need to make sure the hab is secure before we unload cargo, and it looks like conditions are deteriorating fast."

Liana and Suresh struggle at the threshold, both trying to shove through the space at the same time as the other. Liana wins, by virtue of being shorter and more cutthroat; she elbows Suresh under his arm, which probably doesn't do more than surprise him, but that's enough.

She races ahead, leaning into the wind, helmet bobbling with her steps. "First," she says to him triumphantly, jumping off the end of the ramp into the snow. Ophelia can't hear the crunch, but her brain supplies it, thanks to all the years at her grandmother's Connecticut estate.

Birch follows them, studying a layout or map on his helmet screen, ignoring everyone. But the tension in his shoulders is readable even with the bulkiness of his suit. He's still pissed. But now is not the time to address it. Better to wait. And that's not avoidance of conflict, of discussion of her past, that's just . . . timing.

She almost believes that.

"You two idiots realize that dozens, if not hundreds, of people have been here before us?" Kate asks as she makes her way down to the frozen ground.

"Not in the last six years," Liana points out.

Six years? Ophelia frowns. That can't be right. Planetary rights have to be renewed every three years, at minimum. Even if Pinnacle had decided to sell the rights immediately after their last residency, that would be thirty-six months at most.

"Besides, you know it's not about that," Liana continues. "It's about being the first of *us*." As if that explains it.

Ophelia steps off the ramp after Kate. Her booted feet connect solidly with the ground, but it feels wrong . . . slightly off. Too light, too insecure. The gravity is just that much lighter here, perceptible, but not enough to alter their movements dramatically. No flying or leaping about, in other words. Which is just fine with her.

It occurs to Ophelia that, like Liana and Suresh, she should be more excited about, or at least interested in, her surroundings. She's literally setting foot on a planet where she's never been, where no human has been born, ever. A planet where aliens used to exist, intelligent life that was not from Earth.

Instead, she shivers in her suit, despite the heat pumping out to maintain her body temp. It's just so desolate here. So empty. And eerie.

The blue-gray light paints everything in shadow, turning everything into muddy, indistinguishable versions of itself. Drifts of snow and chunks of ice take on an ominous quality, as if they're hiding something instead of just existing. Her helmet light, automatically triggered by the dim conditions, casts a bright halo around her, but every time she moves, or the wind moves her, jagged shadows dance in the periphery. It's enough to make her wish for a sunrise, one that's never going to come, not here.

If nothing else, Lyria 393-C will be the perfect test case for the benefits of having on-site assessment and treatment for the depression, isolation stress, and anxiety that is sure to emerge during three weeks here. It looks to be an ideal location for letting dark thoughts get the best of you. For paranoia to set in.

In the distance, against a backdrop of snow-covered mountains, the ruins of the alien city loom on the horizon—beaten-down, indistinguishable humps of buildings; tall, jagged peaks of black crystalline structure poking up out of the snow and ice. The wind whips through them, creating a thin moaning sound that is picked up by the helmet's exterior mic, even from here.

From what Ophelia read about Lyria 393-C, the visible pieces of the city are the very uppermost part of the structures, and not much is left intact after so long in these conditions.

Kind of like if Chicago's skyline was suddenly buried in several hundred meters of snow, leaving only the air-veh landing platforms and communication towers visible.

Her stomach lurches suddenly with the realization of exactly how high up they are. As Liana races ahead, followed by Suresh and Birch, Ophelia grits her teeth to keep from calling out after them. How sure are they that the ice and snow here are solid all the way down? How sure can anyone be?

One false step and Liana might simply vanish, disappearing into a crevice no one even knew was there.

How many bodies are underneath them right now? The original residents of this city, this planet? Other teams who've lost members under the snow? Or buried them here after they died?

Like Ava Olberman on Minos.

Ophelia picks up her pace to follow Suresh and Liana. "So, based on the mission briefing I read, something catastrophic ended life here?" As soon as the question leaves her mouth, she realizes that contemplating mass extinction events is probably not the best way to shift her focus.

"Probably an asteroid," Suresh says with an unconcerned shrug. "Like ten thousand years ago."

"Nothing here now but us and a bunch of microbes," Liana says, breathless from her exertions, even in the lighter gravity.

Ophelia winces as Suresh shoves past Liana, nearly sending

her crashing into Birch, but Liana rights herself and then pushes back against Suresh, the loose snow at their feet rising up ghostlike in the wind.

But Severin would speak up if he thought there was any danger to his team members, she's sure.

A glance over her shoulder reveals Severin walking side by side with Kate, shortening his longer stride to stay even with her, listening and nodding as she speaks and gestures.

They're on a private comm channel, clearly.

His expression is intent, thoughtful, a furrow in his brow as he considers whatever she's saying.

None of the irritation or forced patience he's shown when Ophelia has spoken to him.

A flash of jealousy comes out of nowhere, taking her breath away.

What the hell, Phe?

The side of her boot catches on a clump of ice, and she has to face forward quickly to right herself before she falls.

Shut it down. Pack it up. Wanting—needing—to be needed, relied on by authority, is her weak spot. It's what both motivates and terrifies her, which, in psychotherapy world, makes her double the mess.

It doesn't matter whether Severin trusts her or not. Granted, she might be more helpful in this situation if he did, but he doesn't. Not yet, anyway. And that's fine.

"Two kilometers to our west," Birch says on the common channel, speaking for the first time since they left the lander. The map shifts and grows on his internal helmet display, casting his face in a shade of blue.

Ophelia keeps walking, head slightly down to avoid the worst of the wind. To her left, which is east according to her helmet compass display, mountains tower over them, even farther away than the old city.

Then, directly ahead of them, she catches sight of familiar bright colors—red, yellow, and blue. It's the Pinnacle logo, a giant *P* with the curve at the top shaped like a flag in the company colors, seemingly hanging in midair.

That can't be right.

Instinctively, she squints for a better look, though her helmet makes that both unnecessary and unhelpful. Finally, in a momentary break between the blasts of snow, she sees what she missed before.

The Pinnacle logo is indeed present, but it's plastered on the white airlock door of an exoplanet habitat. A big one, stretching out in both directions as far as she can see. All in white.

Her stomach tilts, giving rise to a wave of queasiness.

It's huge. Nothing like what she was expecting, even after seeing the schematic. She was concerned about not having enough space, about the lack of privacy contributing to other issues, but this is an entirely different psychological hot button. They could each take a hab module and likely not run into each other for days.

Looking up at the structure, she feels dwarfed by the size of it in a way she hasn't since she was a child. Somehow, the skyscrapers on Earth don't strike the same way. Perhaps because they are not and never will be the only thing standing between life and a horrific death. This station, this compound, for lack of a better term, is both a prison and salvation, all in the same place.

"Structure is generally intact. Generator is off," Kate announces on the common channel, after consulting a chunky handheld device with a tiny screen that she has produced from her suit pocket. "Syscon should be at the far end of the central hub."

Birch, first to the hab, does something at the control panel next to the airlock that causes the enormous door to pop open. Seriously, what was Pinnacle planning on bringing inside? The exterior airlock door is easily six meters across and nearly as tall.

Liana and Suresh tug it back, and then they lead the way in, followed by Birch, Kate, and Severin, who steps past Ophelia to enter.

Ophelia hesitates. The interior is inky blackness disrupted only by their helmet lights. But this airlock appears to be much larger than the one on the lander—big enough, in fact, for a rover that they don't have. On the far side of the lock, Birch's helmet light skims over what seems likely to be a charging station for that same missing rover. But even with the five of them inside, the corners of the space aren't touched by the light.

And this is just the airlock. What will it be like on the inside?

An enormous, enclosed environment with nowhere to run and thousands of places to hide.

Her heart shimmies in her chest.

It's been years since she's thought of . . . that time, that place, in this kind of detail. The nightmares stopped years ago, but clearly the effects are still present.

"Everything okay, Doc?" Kate asks, her thin eyebrows raised.

Ophelia refocuses in time to see all of them staring at her. "Yes, fine," she says, clearing her throat. Her grandmother's go-to move. "Just . . . thinking."

"Maybe think when we're, you know, safely inside?" Suresh smirks.

"Right." Ophelia steps inside to join them. But her knees are weaker and shakier than they should be, and it's not just the difference in gravity this time.

Then, before she can even get turned in the right direction to watch the gray light and snow outside vanish, the airlock door slams shut behind her with a heavy *thunk* that she feels in her bones.

7

"According to the specs, we're looking for a panel marked X326C," Kate announces, once the airlock door has closed. "In incredibly small print, most likely." She sounds exasperated.

"You ever think it's not the print but the elderly eyes trying to read it?" Suresh offers with a snicker.

"You ever think about what happens if I decide to leave you behind next time we're out?" Kate says sharply.

An odd beat of silence holds, a sudden tension thickening the unbreathable air.

"Sorry," Kate says after a moment, her voice strained. "I wasn't thinking. I—"

"Shut up," Birch snaps.

This has to be about Ava. Ophelia's interest sharpens.

But the moment is over as soon as it begins.

"Let's focus on finding the panel," Severin says, once again with that calm she can't quite decipher. Does he truly not feel anything for his lost team member? Or is he burying emotion so deeply that it can't leak out? Even with limited interactions with him so far, she suspects it's the latter.

Their blue-white helmet lights cast jumping and twitching shadows as they spread out, and boots *scritch-scratch* across the metal floor as everyone shuffles around inside the airlock, ice and snow in the treads gritting with every exploratory step. The noise is eerily familiar for some reason.

Ophelia freezes, all thoughts of Severin vanishing. A shiver runs down her spine, like someone unfamiliar tracing their fingers along the skin there. She knows that sound.

Not from frozen moisture on the floor but from a mix of dirt and rock that made it through the decon process.

When she looks down, as best as she can in her helmet, she's greeted with a glimpse of her childhood in gunmetal gray.

Pinnacle is famous for its brand individualization measures, including working with custom suppliers in bulk across multiple projects. Apparently, this squashed octagonal-patterned floor is one of those corporate identity tactics. The raised edges of the little oddly shaped indentations are meant to keep people from slipping, and they do, but without frequent and vigorous cleaning, the indentations are like tiny bowls that catch and hold everything.

Stray bits of rock. Clumps of dust.

Miniature lakes of blood.

Ophelia forces her gaze up, away from the floor.

"Over here," Liana calls from the far wall, near the empty rover charging bay. "I've got it."

Kate crosses the airlock to join Liana and pops the panel open. "No power," she says after a moment, with a frown in her voice. She consults her handheld. "Main genny's dead. I can't even get an automated response from my ping. They must have let it run down to nothing. I hope they haven't fried it."

"Better to find out now," Severin says, undisturbed. He is in his element now, it seems. "Manual." He gestures to the oversize crank near the interior airlock door.

Suresh groans, but he makes his way over to join Severin and Birch.

They get to work, and after several minutes of harsh breath sounds and muttered swearing over the comm channel, something mechanical rumbles in the distance, like a creature awakened after a centuries-long nap, and the interior door releases with a hiss.

A sliver of thick darkness waits in the gap between the edge of the door and the frame. Ophelia senses open space on the other side, even though she can't quite see it. It should be the central hub, according to the schematic on her helmet display. The common area used for meals, meetings, and emergency shelter.

"I've got to get to syscon to see what we're dealing with, if I need to replace parts or the whole thing," Kate says, putting the panel cover back in place. "Should be on the north side of the central hub."

Severin nods in acknowledgment, and Suresh steps up to pull the airlock door wider. His helmet light slices through the inky blackness, revealing nothing but an empty section of room, and then . . .

A metal-framed mess hall chair is facing the airlock door as if placed there deliberately, in a sentry position.

Only now it's tipped over, on its right side and slightly askew. Like the previous resident had been in such a hurry to get away that their feet had tangled with the chair's legs in their rush. On the floor behind it, meal-paks lie scattered, spilling out from a plastic storage bin in a near-perfect arc, as if dropped in surprise.

At first, the screams sounded like laughter, just loud bursts of punctuation in an otherwise rowdy conversation during the evening mealtime. But then people started running, their chairs tumbling over behind them as they shoved away from tables to flee. Her bare toes were pressed hard against the dirty ridged floor, ready to push off, to bolt, but she couldn't move.

Ophelia's breathing quickens at the memory, and she shakes her head, as if that will jar the images loose and send them fluttering away, back to the dark corner they came from.

"Creepy fuckers," Kate mutters.

"Oh, they're going to have to try much harder than that," Suresh says.

Ophelia frowns at him. Who is going to have to try what?

Suresh shoves forward through the airlock door, pushing

the chair out of the way. The meal-paks skitter away under his booted foot, making a slithering noise against the floor.

"Nothing else here," he pronounces after a moment. "But . . . this place is huge." He gives a whistle as he spins around the common hub, his light touching on neatly stacked tables and chairs on the opposite wall, near what appears to be a galley and food prep area on the far end. Then smaller airlocks on the right and left, draped in white plastic sheeting, presumably where the central hub connects to the smaller hab pods, the labs and living quarters, most likely.

Just from what she can see, the space would easily hold fifty or sixty people. That's, what, ten R&E teams? Way beyond standard mission accommodations. Why would Pinnacle have needed that much space? There was no way Lyria 393-C was intended for colonization. Maybe a more permanent science station? But then why would they sell the rights to Montrose? It doesn't make any sense.

Moreover, something about it, about this place, feels . . . wrong. Goose bumps creep along her spine and down her arms, despite her temp-controlled suit.

Or you're just being paranoid, reflecting decades-old, irrelevant trauma on current events. Which do you think is more likely?

"Kate, see what you can do in syscon," Severin says.

"On it," Kate says, slipping through the airlock entry, past Suresh and into the inky blackness.

"Birch, go with her," Severin continues.

Birch nods and follows Kate's path. The central hub grows slightly brighter from the force of their lights together as they head off for the far side of the hub. Syscon—the systems control room, where all the environment controls and generators and essentially anything required to keep them alive here can be accessed—appears to be somewhere behind the galley. Ophelia's schematic isn't that detailed.

"Liana and Suresh, take the east side, confirm structural

integrity on the outer units. I'll take the west side." Severin pauses, then glances over at Ophelia. "Doctor, you can just wait—"

"I'll come. I can help," she says firmly.

His expression says he very much doubts that. But he tips his head in acknowledgment. "All right."

Liana and Suresh lead the way in, followed by Severin.

Ophelia crosses the threshold into the central hub behind him, careful not to catch her boot against the raised ridge of metal where the airlock is joined to the central hub.

Once inside, her sense of the emptiness, the wrongness, only grows. But maybe it's just that sensation of overwhelming space around her, feeling tiny in an overly large environment. Exactly the opposite of what she expected here.

Ophelia trails after Severin, stepping where he steps, as if they're cutting a path through potential quicksand, but taking a good look around as she does. The squashed hexagons on the floor stretch out before her in an endless sweep of dull metal glinting in her helmet light. Scrapes and scratches indicate former activity. Tables being set up, chairs being pushed in. Carts and crates being dragged into position.

But Suresh was right; there's nothing else in here. The stillness, in place of what must have once been a hive of busyness, feels almost like a physical pressure.

Ahead of them, Liana and Suresh break off, heading toward the draped airlock on the right side.

She picks up her pace to catch up with Severin as he veers to the left. He lifts up the plastic sheeting, revealing an open airlock—the door completely pulled back—and dark corridor beyond.

The airlock on this side, and presumably the opposite side as well, are smaller than the one on the opposite end, but it's not as if Pinnacle would have needed to get the rover through one of them. These airlocks are probably only intended for use in the event of an emergency. The teams could seal themselves in the central hub and cut off the outer units if one or more of them were damaged or if they needed to conserve power.

That still doesn't explain why Pinnacle needed so much space.

Ophelia frowns, trying to think through any of the missions she's read or heard about, not that she's connected in any way to the inner circle there anymore, if she ever was.

Her grandmother would have had a fit about the unnecessary expense. She was, until the end of her life, obsessive about every detail when it came to Pinnacle, even those well below her pay grade. One time the media ran with a story about her ordering the removal of an entire park's worth of deciduous trees on Pinnacle's campus because the leaves were causing more work for the groundskeepers (which meant more money spent on something she didn't particularly care about). She replaced them all with bioengineered low-maintenance, low-scent, no-shed evergreens. Like a farm full of fake Christmas trees.

Uncle Darwin, on the other hand, never met a "business" expenditure he didn't like, and—

"Doctor?"

Ophelia looks up to find Severin staring at her, dark eyebrows raised.

She realizes, then, that she's stopped again. Right at the threshold from the central hub, leaving Severin waiting just inside the corridor beyond. Darkness and the unknown, lurking just behind him.

Ophelia's heart is pounding, and her subconscious is doing that tricky bob-and-weave maneuver again, bringing up old memories without her consent.

So many corners, so many shadows. Where are you hiding, Little Bird?

Goddammit. "I'm coming," she says a little too loudly.

Severin turns to the left first. He hunches slightly to avoid the ceiling. The connectors, white, semirounded tubes that attach to each other and to the individual units and central hub to create a passageway, rise over their heads, but Severin just barely clears it with the added centimeters from his helmet.

Coffee, or some other dark liquid, is sprayed all over the wall, a discarded cup in a frozen puddle of the same on the floor. A disposable fabric shoe, the kind designed to be worn inside the hab, nearly identical to the set Ophelia was given for this mission, lies flipped up on its side, as if someone ran out of it and didn't bother to come back for it.

"Looks like they left in a hurry."

"Or they didn't care," Severin says, kicking a pile of fabric out of the way on his side of the corridor. It's a shirt, dark stained and stiff with cold. Maybe someone used it to mop up the coffee. "We're placeholders, waiting for someone more important to arrive. Not sure that leaving the hab pristine is anyone's top priority."

Despite his level tone, that feels like a dig at her. "Listen, I feel like we got off on the wrong foot," she begins.

"There is no right foot, Dr. Bray. You're not needed here." He pulls open the first door on their right. It's unlocked, despite the impressive bolt across the outside of it.

Dim light filters in through three tiny round windows, so it's easy to see that this unit is a lab. Or it was. Most of the equipment—she recognizes a mass spectrometer, but that's about it—is still in place on the lab tables. But shards of polymer vials and tubes glitter all over the floor.

Severin steps inside, carefully avoiding the worst of the sharp pieces. "We look out for each other. That's all that's required." He makes a circuit around the outer wall of the unit, visually checking for leaks or weak spots. Then he checks again with a handheld, similar to the one Kate used earlier. Ophelia doesn't know exactly what the devices do, but she's not going to advertise her ignorance by asking.

He is protective of his team, his responsibility to them. That makes sense. He's accustomed to that role. From what she read in his file, he's the oldest of five children, raised by a single mom in the cheap seats of Luna Valley on the moon. That's the one where the whole colony was originally underground in an old lava tube.

"I understand that," Ophelia says. "And it's admirable, it really is. But there are things that I can help with that you may not—"

He straightens up from his position near the tiny porthole windows. "Doctor, we've agreed to your presence and your 'sessions.'"

He doesn't make the gesture, but she senses the exasperated air quotes, nonetheless.

"I'm not sure what else you want." He moves past her and back out into the corridor.

"What else I want?" she demands incredulously, following him. "ERS can be contagious. Like suicide ideation or even attempts at it. Not that you seem to care."

Apparently, Suresh isn't the only one here who can't resist under-the-breath observations better left unsaid.

"Uh, guys?" Liana speaks up in Ophelia's ear.

Kate is more direct. "Oi, Commander. You and the doctor are on the common channel. You're aware of that, yes?"

Shit.

But Severin doesn't seem disturbed. Not about that, anyway.

He spins around on her, closing the distance between them until he looms over her and she has to fight not to step back. "Don't you dare make assumptions about us. You don't know anything about us, about our lives. Do you even know what happens when you tag us with a PBE issue?"

Ophelia lifts her chin to meet his gaze. "Yes. You get treatment and the help you need to—"

He shakes his head, his skin a pale blue beneath the interior light of his suit. "Once you're tagged as questionable, no one wants you on their team. You're basically unemployable. Nobody wants to take the chance of another Bloody Bledsoe on their watch."

The nickname clangs through her, a harsh, discordant assemblage of syllables that makes her skin crawl.

"So forgive us for our lack of enthusiasm," he adds.

"At least you'd still be alive," Ophelia says, jaw tight.

His dark-eyed gaze searches her face and then he shakes his head with a sigh, some of the tension easing out of his frame. "This work is dangerous in any number of ways. We accept that when we sign on." He looks at her with what can only be described as gentle pity. "I realize someone with your resources may not see the difference, but for us, this job is everything. It's what keeps our families fed and our bills paid, better than anything else out there on offer."

The heat of humiliation races up her neck and into her face. He thinks she doesn't know what it means to need purpose? To need a regular paycheck? Or to worry about how many mealpaks are left before the next shipment of supplies, or what it feels like to dig under the cushions, hoping for lost water voucher coins? She may not know this team, but he doesn't know her, either. He can't. No one does.

She has to bite her tongue to keep from saying any of that, all of it.

"My family's money is not—" Ophelia begins, working for calm.

Severin holds up his hand. "You have a job to do, I understand that," he says. "Neither of us can do anything about that. But I don't want to spend the next twelve months fighting with you on different planets." He attempts a smile, his mouth thin and tight. "I'm happy to cooperate as much as is feasible.

You just . . . stick to your side of the road and let us do our jobs, okay?" He walks away, heading down the corridor to the next unit.

Fury leaves her with fists clenched, staring sightlessly after him. She's tempted to storm off, leaving Severin to his "side of the road." But that feels like giving in, and of all the character flaws she's been accused of having, near-pathological stubbornness is close to the top of the list, and the most accurate. Not to mention, she *needs* this to work.

She continues after him and steps inside the unit, and the back wall flashes her helmet light back at her, drawing her attention. Dozens of clear, sealed sample boxes are shelved in neat orderly lines, six across and six down, their contents a shadowy mystery.

Another lab unit, then. The metal lab table on her left confirms that suspicion.

But . . .

Ophelia squints. Two of the sample boxes, the end ones on the third and fourth rows, look strange. Cloudy. Almost as if condensation has coated the inside of the clear surface, but in a vaguely circular pattern.

"Almost done in here, Doctor," Severin says from his position over the window on the far right. "Weak spots near the floor seam are tricky sometimes. Syscon pops the locks on all the hab units if a leak is detected, to let personnel escape, so we need to make sure there's not a reason the doors are unsecured here."

Ignoring him, she moves closer to the back wall, trying to work out what she's seeing.

Halfway into the room, she realizes the sample boxes are broken. The polymer has shattered at an impact point, like a fist punching into the front of the box. Anger? Or someone trying to get something out? But why not just unseal them?

How biz—

The rest of the thought instantly evaporates when her foot collides with something soft on the floor.

She glances down and freezes.

White-gloved fingers rest against her ankle. Those fingers are attached to an envirosuited hand and arm, which lead to a torso and a blank-faced helmet, partially under the lab table but staring up at her.

A body. There's a body on the floor.

8

Ophelia's throat locks up, a scream trapped between her mouth and lungs, with nowhere to go as it grows and grows until it feels as if her flesh will split with it. Like the scream will explode from her throat, leaving a ragged hole behind.

Her peripheral vision whites out. For a moment, the body on the floor is Rueben, her patient, his shattered mouth moving in words that she can't understand, the metallic scent of fresh blood filling her nose as she kneels next to him. Warm blood on the cold terrace tiles, seeping into her pants as the distant wail of sirens fills the air.

Then—before she can stop it, before she can grab hold of her past and firmly wedge it back into the triple-locked vault where she keeps it—another memory surfaces.

Mari.

Marigold Trevor, just a few years older than she is, is curled up on her left side, half hidden under a mess hall table, though hiding had done nothing to save her. Her arm stretches out toward Ophelia, as if asking for help. But her face is shattered, concave where identifiable features used to be, one bright blue eye rolled up to look at her sightlessly from the sea of red and ruined flesh.

Mari watches over her sometimes when her mother has a shift at the mess hall and her father is out with his crew. Mari's braid always has a new ribbon woven through it, snaking in and out of the smooth blond segments, making her the coolest person that Ophelia knows.

But now, Mari's ribbon—a bright silvery spiderweb confection today—is stuck to a flap of scalp dangling from the top of her head, and Ophelia's bare feet are tacky, sticky with Mari's blood.

Run! *The urgency throbs through Ophelia like an infected tooth.*

"—Bray? Doctor, are you okay?"

She comes back to herself, arms rigid at her sides, her breath rasping in and out, fogging her faceplate in patches.

Severin is still across the room, device forgotten in his hand as he stares at her, the blue light inside his helmet highlighting his furrowed brow.

He steps closer. "You know it's empty, right? Just an empty suit."

Some part of her—a hard square of irrational terror in her gut—is convinced that if she looks, all she's going to see is Mari's empty, accusing eye staring back up at her. But after a moment, she forces herself to shift her gaze away from him toward that . . . thing.

Severin's right; the white envirosuit—with the Pinnacle logo on the chest—is mostly flat. It's just a fully assembled suit, lying on the floor in the shape of a person, one arm reaching toward anyone passing by.

"Right," she manages. "Empty. Yeah, I know." *Now.*

"What's going on?" Birch demands.

"On my way," Kate says.

"Negative, negative," Severin says, closing the distance between them, his boot nudging the arm of the suit. "It's just another stupid prank. Hazing for the next crew to find when they come in. A suit on the floor that looks like a person at a distance." He eyes her but says nothing more.

Ophelia waits another beat, but he doesn't out her as having fallen for it. Her immediate warm rush of gratitude instantly grates at the same time. She doesn't need his help. Nor does she need the way he's looking at her now, as if seeing her in a slightly different light.

"Damn, that's a good one," Suresh says in Ophelia's ear, sounding both awed and disappointed. "All we've got is a bunch of empty bunk rooms on this side."

"Nearly done here," Severin says. "We'll rejoin you in the central hub in a minute."

Then Severin turns to Ophelia, shifting them to the private channel again, his face in miniature on her helmet screen, and then larger right in front of her in real life. "Are you sure you're all right?"

His gaze pierces through her, as if he can see the memories so recently playing across her vision.

"Of course. I'm fine," she says, as crisply as she can manage. The lump of unrealized scream is fading from her throat, but the lingering rawness is a painful reminder. As is the rising crest of embarrassment. "It just took me by surprise."

Severin doesn't respond right away, just looks at her.

He doesn't believe her. Ophelia grits her teeth against the urge to explain, to babble justifications.

Instead she waits, her eyebrows raised in imperious question, as if daring him to ask—another classic Bray move . . . which she hates—until he finally nods.

"Back to work, everybody," Severin says finally, back on the common channel, in a tone that brooks no argument. "That next storm is coming in hard. T-minus twenty-three minutes. We want to be locked down before that happens."

"On it," Liana says.

"Roger," Kate says. "Environmentals are a go on your word."

Severin turns and walks out into the corridor without another word.

Ophelia lets out a slow breath, her attention drawn unwillingly back to the suit on the floor. Looking at it now, she can't even see how she thought there was a body inside. Yes, the positioning and the shape, but it's clearly not inhabited. Any normal person would have recognized that almost immediately.

It's this place. This fucking Pinnacle hab, unleashing shit in her head she absolutely does not need right now. Or ever. At this rate, she'll be lucky if Severin and the others don't report her to PBE.

But now that she's aware of the trigger—the unconscious connection her brain is making between past and present—she'll manage it. No problem. She will not allow the irrelevance of the past to fuck up her future.

Ophelia squares her shoulders and starts after Severin.

But, as she turns away from the suit, a flash of something bright catches her eye.

On the upper arm of the suit, a name patch is still in place, embroidered in shiny metallic thread that's frayed from wear in several places: M. DELACROIX.

She frowns, bending down to take a closer look. The white Pinnacle suit is dirty at the elbows, banged and bashed up from use on the chest plate, and the heavy-duty material gleams with the safety scaling, designed to help prevent tears.

This is not one of the emergency-only temp suits, designed to be used for a short period of time and then discarded, if something happens to a wearer's primary suit that can't be repaired.

This is a primary suit. M. Delacroix's, if the patch means anything. And there's no obvious damage that would render it unusable.

Why would someone leave their primary suit behind? Where is Delacroix now? Did he or she really go back to Earth with a temp suit? Or even on to another assignment?

That doesn't make any sense.

Then again, it didn't make any sense to her to pretend to have a tank malfunction, either, but clearly some R&E teams operate on a whole other level of common understanding.

"Dr. Bray?" Severin calls.

"Yeah, I'm coming," she says reluctantly, swallowing back her questions.

They're nearly done unloading, carting crates of food, equipment, supplies, and their own personal items from the lander to the hab, when the wind picks up suddenly, from a slight breeze to a sheer blast. The icy flakes turn to a blinding wall of white. Right at the start of their work, Severin had attached a bright orange guide rope to the leg of the lander on one end and to a hook on the outer edge of the airlock frame on the other. At the time, it seemed a strikingly antiquated and unnecessary gesture. Not anymore.

Their in-helmet visuals are lost with the storm, the connection to the *Resilience* temporarily gone. Only local comms between their suits are functioning, and even then, just within a short range.

That stripe of color at Ophelia's left shoulder is the only thing keeping her on track and reassuring her that she will make it back to the hab on this last trip. Eventually. The missing rover would have been really useful about now, but there's still no sign of it.

Leaning forward into the wind, she focuses on planting her booted feet in the gritty, crunchy surface and not dropping the slim metallic case in her hands. She insisted on carrying this one herself, even though it meant an extra back-and-forth journey. She didn't want to find it crushed between pallets of surveyor drones or "accidentally" lost in a drift somewhere along the way.

The case is not heavy; in fact, it might be easier if it were, less of a wind-catch. But the iVR bands inside are deliberately—and deceptively—lightweight for their power.

Her grip tightens on the case, both against the storm and

in determination. By the time she's done, team number 356 is going to be the most well-adjusted goddamned team in the—

The howl of wind around her rises to an unearthly shriek, an eerie, goose bump–inducing sound. From low to high, deep to shrill, like an animalistic moan of pain transforming into a scream. And it's coming from the city ruins to her left.

Beyond those dark crystalline towers jutting out of the snow at an angle, Ophelia can't see much. She gets only glimpses of the other shadowy structures when the storm takes a breath, holding back on the snow for a few seconds. But she knows what's there, according to the mission file anyway. The first team here called them, the beings who built the city so far below, the Lyrians.

They were, by Earth terms and definitions, mammals. Not all that dissimilar from humans, with a different bend in the evolutionary tree. From drone scans of the structures hidden in the ice, the consensus was they'd been communal, perhaps even matriarchal. Artist renderings depicted them as tall, slender, sloth-like creatures with long, elegant fingers, large, expressive eyes, and a thin layer of fur in a variety of colors. And sharp teeth, with fang-like incisors at the front of the mouth.

Those details, though, were just best guesses by astrobio archeologists, based on the one set of remains found— unintentionally mummified—on the next planet over, Lyria 393-D. A probe found one Lyrian dead, outside a rudimentary shelter, facing the direction of their home world, one arm outstretched as if trying to crawl home.

The Lyrians had been spacefaring, just not quite interstellar. They were advanced, building huge cities like the one beneath her feet and attempting to grow beyond their planet. But not fast enough.

They'd died horrifically. Likely starving or freezing or both. Millions of them, now crushed beneath the weight of snow, ice, and years.

More would probably be known about them and this planet except that once Bodhi 923-E was discovered, with more recent inhabitation and technology that might be adaptable to human use—meaning, weaponized—Lyria 393-C and others like it were knocked down to the bottom of corporate priority lists.

Planets like this one are now viewed as oddities, valuable only in the sense of their rarity and trophy status, interesting only in a vaguely scientific manner rather than anything that might be profitable.

This planet is a graveyard, forgotten and abandoned to the weeds and time. It should be sad. Or perhaps a warning that everything ends.

But standing here, rather than just reading about it, the eeriness is what rings through to Ophelia.

Her grandmother was on the board of a variety of foundations, including one advocating for the restoration of Pompeii after it was lost again to Vesuvius. Ophelia had seen the archival footage of the original site, after the twentieth-century excavation.

The plaster molds of the dead were made from the void where their flesh had rotted away in the ash, but their bones and teeth still showed through—ghosts that had physical form and shape. A burned loaf of bread still in the oven. Even a dog rolled up onto its back, exposing its belly in a grotesque mimicry of relaxation.

But more than that, it was that absence where there had once been life. Empty streets, abandoned baby cradles, kitchen tables with chairs still in place. Likely all of that and more—the Lyrian version, anyway—resides beneath her at this very moment.

The moaning grows louder, like vengeful voices rising in a chorus.

Ophelia doesn't even realize she's backed up, away from the ruins, away from the sound, until her shoulder smacks into something solid behind her.

She jolts and turns, stumbling over the ice, to find Severin behind her. "What—"

He reaches out to steady her. "It's just the wind," he says, his voice calm and even in her helmet. It drowns out the dreadful noise for a moment. "There's nothing else out here to interrupt it. To make noise."

As soon as he says it, she realizes he's right, of course. It's a flat plain of icy white nothingness, except for the jagged peaks of the former city.

"You need to stay on the line, Doctor." He nods his head at something behind her. She turns to look, awkward in her helmet, and realizes the orange rope is gone, lost in the violent flurries.

She couldn't have gone more than a step or three . . . but apparently that's enough. Her heart lurches upward in instinctive panic.

Stupid, Ophelia. Really stupid. Talk about an unforced error.

It feels like a small eternity but is probably only a few seconds before she sees a flash of familiar orange in a temporary break from the wind.

Without waiting for another prompt from Severin, she hurries toward it, like the lifeline that it is. She shifts the case to one hand and grasps the line with the other.

Severin moves back into place behind her on the line—the cord bobs and then straightens with the additional pressure. He insisted on coming back with her on this final run, while the others remained in the hab, setting up and settling in. Ophelia's (arrogant) assertion that she didn't need the help seems incredibly foolish right about now. To be fair, at the time, she'd been trying to prove that she was useful, not a burden, and she'd still been able to see their lander.

Now, without the rope, she'd have no idea even which direction to go.

At least he's not entirely empty-handed. He's carrying a

slim gray hard case, retrieved from the lander. It's marked with bright red warnings and has a coded lock. Standard mission firearm, the only weapon allowed. Though it's clear that they're not in any danger from claim jumpers at the moment, Montrose protocol indicates that the case should remain in the custody of the mission commander at all times. Only he—and his second, probably Kate—have the code to open it. And Severin strikes her as a very by-the-book type.

"Thank you," Ophelia says. She hears the edge of resentment in her voice but hopes he doesn't. It's not his fault. No matter how much she may dislike him, that doesn't change the fact that he's the one in his element here, not her. And it's his job to keep her alive, whether he likes it or not.

"It's all right, Doctor. The first on-planet assignment is always an adjustment. For everyone," he says mildly. "Especially here. The storms seem to roll up fast and hit hard."

She replays his words in her head, searching for the sneer, the superiority. But she can't detect even a hint of it. Severin either seems to have mellowed, now that they're finally on the surface, or he's ceased to view her as a threat.

Probably right about the time she froze up at the sight of an empty envirosuit.

She grimaces. She doesn't want an adversarial relationship with the mission commander; that would make accomplishing her objective here that much harder. Neither, however, does she want his . . . pity.

They both keep silent for the remainder of the journey to the hab. The only noise over the comms is their slightly labored breathing from the more strenuous effort required to return.

The lights are on when they enter the airlock this time. Whatever Kate is doing in syscon is working.

Ophelia follows Severin's lead, stamping her feet against the textured floor (*It's just a floor. Get a good look at it, and maybe then you can stop obsessing.*) to remove ice and snow while they wait for the airlock to run through its decon cycle.

A sideways glance at Severin, as much as is possible in her helmet, reveals that he is waiting patiently, staring straight ahead.

The impulse to fill the quiet with reminders about counseling sessions and what will be required, to piss him off and change the direction of his assumptions about her, thereby changing the imagined balance of power, is oppressive, almost a physical need.

Has it occurred to you that your issue is not with relationships but the mooch . . . much . . . mutual vulnerability that is occasionally required to connect with another human being?

Ophelia grimaces at the memory of Julius's words. He's lost friend status and all incumbent privileges, including telling her ugly truths about herself while they're both intoxicated. But she can't extract him from her memories so easily. And he wasn't necessarily wrong.

A very drunken session after her most recent breakup had resulted in that gem.

"You're more comfortable with patients than other people because you don't have to share anything of yourself with them." He'd patted her on the hand, eyes shining with unshed tears, as the bar around them continued to stomp and sing at the victory of a band she didn't know in a competition she wasn't familiar with. Maybe she was working too much—"too distant, too removed," as Baran, her ex, claimed.

"Sometimes I feel like I don't even know you that well," Julius had added.

At the time, she'd thrown her arm around Julius's shoulders, sloppily, reassuring him that he knew her best of all. Which was true. But it wasn't saying as much as it should have been.

Her real answer, if she could have told the truth, is the same now as it would have been then. Her problem is not with being vulnerable around others. If anything, it's the opposite. She's been—and continues to be—too vulnerable. All the time.

The inner airlock door finally releases with a mechanical clank and a slight hiss.

"Commander, when you've got a second . . ." Kate sounds especially formal over the comm channel. And for no other reason beyond that, Ophelia's stomach clenches up tight. That's trouble, whatever it is.

"I'm going to check with Kate." Severin nods at her, the gesture curt and perfunctory, but without the outward signs of hostility from before.

"Right," Ophelia says, even as the need to push back grows stronger, urging her to rebalance the invisible—no, nonexistent—power scales between them. *Drop it, Phe.*

Severin steps over the threshold of the airlock, into the central hub, heading toward syscon. Leaving her behind.

"Don't forget to see me later to set up your sleep settings for tonight." The words, clipped and sharp, slip out before she can stop them.

The immediate surge of relief is heady, familiar—that of bad news suddenly turned to simple miscommunication, of unexpectedly canceled family dinners, of vomiting after a series of poor alcohol choices. But then it vanishes, replaced immediately by the heated flush of shame. She knows better.

Severin pauses, his posture stiffening visibly, even through his envirosuit.

"Understood, Doctor," he says, without turning to face her. And the iciness outside has nothing on his tone in here.

9

Still kicking herself for antagonizing Severin, Ophelia shuffles into the central hub. Exhaustion burns in her muscles, adding sway to her posture. After standing still in the airlock, her body has stiffened up. Fever-like chills spill across her skin in waves.

The med-scanner is in a crate somewhere, but she doesn't need an official diagnosis. A cold sleep hangover, the teams call it. Too much exertion, too soon after cold sleep. With protein, iron tabs, and rest, she'll be fine.

Inside the central hub, most of the crates they hauled in earlier have been shifted to one side, organized, and stacked. It's brighter in here, too. The lights overhead beam down solid and steady.

Someone has set up a table and six chairs in the center of the space. It should make the hub feel livelier, fuller. Instead, the lone table amplifies the emptiness around it. It's easy to imagine dozens more tables and chairs in this space, the warm sound of conversation and laughter and humanity filling the air. The contrast to reality, then, is a bit bleak.

Suresh and Birch are on the side closest to her, facing each other with some kind of fabric game board between them. Shiny pieces, like flattened marbles in blue and yellow, lie in sporadic places across the board, glinting in the light. Though she's fairly sure that some of the tokens are replacement parts—unless a 316 hex bolt and nut combination is somehow a part of this game. Suresh is studying the board with the intensity of

someone disarming an explosive for the first time in the middle
of an earthquake, while Birch fidgets with a scrap of paper,
folding it and refolding it.

Liana is on the other side, head tilted back, her feet propped
on another chair and her eyes closed.

Their helmets lie cast aside on the table, their suits unfas-
tened and sagging around their waists.

"Doc." Suresh greets her, though his gaze remains fixed on
the game board. "Sit down before you fall down."

Without a word, Liana opens her eyes, straightens up, and
then waves Ophelia over to the chair next to her, across the
table from Suresh and Birch.

Ophelia makes her way over and drops into the chair. She sets
the iVR case by her feet, legs trembling, light-headedness swirling. Anemia. Something about the cold sleep process starves the
red blood cells. Completely recoverable but not pleasant, especially not at first, after the iron booster from the tank wears off.

Her breathing sounds too loud, too rapid in the silence of her
helmet.

"We're good," Liana says, enunciating carefully so Ophelia
can hear her through the external mic. She taps at the space
in front of her face where her helmet would be. "You can take
that off now. It'll be easier."

Ophelia reaches for the fasteners to unseal her helmet, and
then hesitates. She's not sure why. They're all sitting with their
suits sagging around their waists and their helmets off. It's not
like there's a gotcha in the waiting this time.

Confusion crinkles Liana's brow, then shame flashes across
her face before she smooths out her expression. She shrugs.
"Or not. It's up to you."

Guilt tugs at Ophelia. The tank stunt wasn't Liana's idea,
and it was just hazing, a phase they're hopefully past. Plus, if
she's going to do better than she has with Severin, now is the
time to start.

She pulls her helmet off, the cool air touching her skin and slipping into her sweat-dampened hair. It smells stale in here, vaguely metallic, and kind of bitter, like old sweat, scorched metal, and resentment.

Ophelia sneezes four times in a row, her nose burning.

"Sorry, Dr. Bray, the maid is off this week," Birch says with a sneer.

"Ignore him. The filters are still working to catch up. Lots of dust." Liana wrinkles her nose.

If it's like other sealed environments, not much of it, if any, is dust in the sense of planetary dirt, pollen, bacteria, and the like. It's more likely a combination of lint, hair, and, of course, the dead skin cells of the previous team, once the air settled after their departure.

That information is generally not well received by people who are used to fresh air and living in the open. To Ophelia, though, it smells like home.

The unexpected and unwelcome pang of nostalgia makes her eyes water.

But she's so tired, she can't work up the energy to berate herself for the reaction. Now that she's sitting, it feels like she might not ever have the strength to get up again.

"No, no, motherfucker," Suresh says in sudden revelation, shaking his finger at Birch. "What you did, that was not a legal move. Don't try that bullshit with me again."

"What?" Birch says, a protest of innocence. He lifts his hands, a tiny paper bird now perched on his finger.

"We're not playing by your weird-ass level seven rules or whatever," Suresh says with a scowl. He shoves a piece back toward Birch. "Go again."

Liana rummages in an open crate stashed under the table. "Here. This will help." She tears the plastic top off a protein booster and hands it to Ophelia.

Ophelia shimmies out of the top half of her suit as best as she can, to free her hands—the effort making her limbs feel even heavier—and then takes the booster.

When she squeezes the contents into her mouth, the first taste of faux peanut butter and banana activates her gag reflex—too sweet, and way too grainy, like someone ground up plastic bananas and mixed them with glue that had once shared shelf space with a moldy bag of peanuts.

But she puts her hand over her mouth and forces herself to swallow.

Suresh *tsk*s at her. "Woman up, Doc. The soy meatloaf one is way worse."

Liana pivots in her seat to face Ophelia, tucking her legs up under her in a calisthenic move that would be impossible for most in an envirosuit. "Can I ask you a question?"

Steeling for more questions about her family or her lost patient, Ophelia takes an extra second to force down another gritty swallow and then nods.

"How does the iVR system work?" Liana asks.

Ophelia blinks, surprised.

Liana tips her head toward the shiny case on the floor. "I've heard it's . . ." She pauses. "Creepy. Invasive."

Ahh, okay. "Like reading your mind?" Ophelia offers. It's not the first time she's heard this.

Suresh and Birch are ostensibly focusing on the game, but they're a little too quiet now, presumably listening in. Ophelia wonders how much of this fear is behind their resistance to her presence. No one likes to think that their mind, the last bastion of privacy, is going to be invaded, even if it is for their own good.

"It doesn't do that. It can't," Ophelia says firmly. "It's basically the same system you'd be prescribed back on Earth at one of our clinics, just upgraded for portability and faster results. All it does is draw on memories that you choose, and your QuickQ data, to re-create a sleeping environment. That's it. Good sleep is the basis for ERS recovery, and we're hoping to show that by instituting healthy sleep hygiene at the start of the mission, it can work as a preventative measure as well."

"Okay." Liana draws out the word, sounding less than convinced.

"It helps your circadian rhythms normalize, no matter what the light or"—Ophelia gestures toward the airlock doors and the perpetually gray twilight outside—"lack of light might be trying to tell your body."

Whether it's the temporary lift from the protein booster or Liana's interest in the iVR system, Ophelia is feeling more energetic. She leans over and grabs the case.

"Here, I'll set up a temp profile for you so you can check it out." Ophelia pulls the tablet from the case. The narrow headsets inside, six of them, gleam in the overhead light. "Think of it like a waiting room for sleep. You're going to visit and relax, and then you drift off to sleep, just like you normally would. Or even more easily than you normally would."

Studies have shown that sleeping in a familiar setting increases sleep quality, which reduces stress, which in the end improves crew communication and harmony. And all of that, combined with regular counseling sessions and medications, if needed, hacks away at their odds of ERS. Not that she's going to get into that now.

Ophelia walks Liana through a quick version of the standard recall questions for the purposes of establishing baseline settings. Ophelia's own setting is her cramped office at work on the Montrose campus—her safe space. Or it used to be, anyway.

Then, just as Ophelia would back at home, she demonstrates the flexibility of the band, which fits lightly on the temples, rising above the bridge of the nose. It's not meant to block vision so much as provide an easy connection to the QuickQ implant and remind the wearer that they're meant to focus on the images provided by the system, not their actual surroundings.

"Close your eyes," Ophelia encourages.

Liana does so with far less hesitation than Ophelia probably would in her shoes, and the system activates with a faint, cheerful chirp. Then Ophelia waits.

After a moment, Liana sits up sharply, surprise straightening her spine. "Oh."

Ophelia grins.

"It's the lanai at my tutu's house," she says, a little too loudly. The headset is using the same pathways that her QuickQ implant relies on for communication, so whatever she's seeing and hearing is overriding her current surroundings. Her hand reaches out, touching something that isn't there. "My cousins and I used to sleep over all the time. I can hear the ocean." Wonder transforms her face, smoothing out the baby lines of worry in her forehead. "The stars are coming out. I almost expect her to come out and tell us to settle down." She glances over her shoulder abruptly.

"It can't re-create people yet," Ophelia cautions her, raising her voice to match Liana's. Otherwise, Ophelia knows from experience, her voice will sound too much like a whisper of breeze or a voice murmuring in the distance. "It's too much processing power, and our brains are still too good at detecting AI impersonations when it comes to people we know."

"That would be weird anyway," Liana concedes. "She died when I was eighteen."

Slowly the tension drains out of Liana's frame, her shoulders relax, her hands unclench.

Elation surges through Ophelia. No matter how often she sees this, the first step in making someone whole, making someone better, is always such a high. This is what she's here to do. Why she's alive. It's not enough to make up for everything, no resolution for the greater karmic debt tagged on her account—nothing will be—but it's progress.

"Do you want to try it?" Ophelia asks Suresh, who is eyeing them from across the table.

Before he can answer, though, Birch jumps in. "Better real

nightmares than fake bullshit," he mutters. "Your move," he says to Suresh, waving his hand over the game board.

Ophelia turns her attention back to Liana.

But Liana tips her head to one side, blinking several times and waving her hand in front of her face, before focusing on Ophelia. "What happened? It went dark." She reaches up to pull the headset free.

Damn. "Wait. Let me grab the chargers." The headsets were supposed to have been in dormant mode, but it's possible that months in storage have drained them. Or maybe they're still a bit buggy.

She glances around for the bright green bag among the neatly stacked and piled crates and cases. "Where is—"

"Your stuff is in your office, Doctor," Birch says, making no attempt to hide his snideness, as Suresh grins at her.

And suddenly, without even asking, Ophelia knows exactly which module they've assigned as hers. The one with the fucking empty suit on the floor.

Suresh holds his hands up in surrender. "It's the farthest one out on that side, for privacy. Commander's orders."

Uh-huh.

"I'll be right back," she says to Liana. She gets up, careful not to entangle the arms of her suit in her chair.

"Hey, Bray," Suresh calls before she's gotten more than a few steps away from the table.

Ophelia looks back at him.

He holds his helmet up. "Remember, for when you come back. This is just my helmet. Not my head."

Birch snickers.

So even without Severin telling on her, they still knew. That she'd fallen for the suit prank, that once again she'd proven herself an outsider, unworthy.

"Suresh," Liana says sharply, her cheeks flushed with embarrassment on his behalf, or possibly Ophelia's.

Ophelia's temper flicks to life. *Who left?* That's what she wants to ask Suresh. With such anxious attachment issues, her immediate inclination would be Mom. But the desperate need for approval and use of humor even for negative reinforcement just screams "distant father."

The words are right there, on the tip of her tongue, and she can just imagine the stung expression on Suresh's face if she released them. How *good* defending herself would feel; how it would feel even better, making him shut the hell up.

But . . .

The vivid memory of sitting outside the headmistress's office settles over her. The uncomfortable wooden chair digging into her spine, the hastily sealed cuts on her fingers throbbing. It was her first year at Marchand-Brighton Academy. They were very intent on putting the "old school" back in "school."

"She has no control over her temper. She just exploded on that poor girl." The voice of Mx. Royce, the headmistress, drifts out through the closed door, worry and fear two taut threads.

The poor girl in question, who was most definitely not literally or figuratively poor, had been slashing the sleeve of Ophelia's uniform with tiny manicure scissors when Ophelia sat in front of her in class. Occasionally drawing blood in the process.

And Ophelia kept getting written up for dress code violation and being charged for new shirts.

She can still hear the *snip snip* of the scissors through the expensive fabric. The sting of the metal against her skin. The frustration of keeping her mouth shut, trying to be what her mother and grandmother wanted her to be. And knowing no one would believe her even if she told them what Anberlyn was doing.

She didn't remember turning and grabbing the scissors from Anberlyn, though the injuries to her hands spoke for themselves.

She definitely did not remember stabbing the sharp end of the nail scissors into Anberyln's shoulder—right, approximately, where she'd insisted on making her mark on Ophelia's clothing.

It was just . . . one minute Ophelia was gritting her teeth, working to ignore Anberlyn and memorize key dates related to the first colony uprising on Europa. Trying not to long for a home that no longer wanted her.

And the next, blackness. Literal dark dots flooding her vision. When it receded, Ophelia was standing over Anberlyn, hands bloody, while Anberlyn screamed on the floor.

In the confusion that followed, the scissors became Ophelia's—never mind the fact that she was not the one with the overgroomed and manicured nails—and the attack unprovoked.

"I told you, Regency." Ophelia's grandmother made no attempt to lower her voice to her mother, seated in the chair next to hers, delight and fury as prominent in her tone as the fear was in the headmistress's.

Anberlyn was fine, left with a pinpoint of a scar, which she had reshaped to look like a star for her first body-mod (of course) and a story. In the end, she did Ophelia a favor, ensuring that others would leave her alone. And the donation Ophelia's grandmother made went a long way toward soothing Marchand-Brighton's "concerns." Ophelia suspected her grandmother had selected that school for that very reason.

But Ophelia will never forget the look on her mother's face when she exited that office, the way she stared at Ophelia like she was a stranger and, more terrifyingly, too familiar at the same time . . .

"I'll keep that in mind, Suresh," Ophelia says calmly.

The look of disappointment on his face is almost as gratifying as letting loose on him would have been. Okay, not really, but it's not nothing, either.

Ophelia makes her way back to the module in question. The

suit that caused so much trouble is now jumbled up outside
the door, along with a scattering of detritus now swept up in a
pile—to be disposed of, most likely.

Her belongings, including her bag of personal items, are
neatly stacked inside. She immediately locates the bright green
bag and snags it, resisting the urge to check to see whether her
personals have been opened or searched. She has nothing to
hide in there, and if that helps them trust her, fine. Curiosity is
natural in this situation. So is, perhaps, deliberately provoking
a response, to an extent. It reasserts a feeling of control.

On her way back into the corridor, motion near the floor
catches her eye. Ophelia steps back automatically. *Rat.*

Rats were the second interstellar travelers, right alongside
humans. Where humans go, rats follow. Sometimes, even now,
they outnumber the official residents on farthest-flung space
stations and outposts. But there haven't been people here in
years.

This time, though, it's a dog. A digi-foto of one anyway,
resting on top of the pile of discarded belongings that have
been swept/gathered up outside the door.

In the foto, a dog with golden hair rushes across a wide expanse of grass toward a handsome man with a beard. The man
is crouching to greet him, only to be knocked over with canine
enthusiasm and his own laughter. Again and again, each time
resetting to this perfect moment in a life. Turning on the lights
inside the hab must have given the solar receptors enough juice
to start up once more.

The thin paper is cracked and torn in the corner, revealing
the wafer-thin circuits in the page.

Could this be Delacroix? He of the abandoned suit? Did he
leave behind this, too? Is he . . . dead?

There's no mention of that in the mission briefing.

Beneath the digi-foto in the pile, she catches the glint of
metal. Crouching down, she sets the chargers aside temporarily and picks through pieces of shattered polymer, discarded

meal-pak containers, dust bunnies, and wispy tangles of unidentifiable fluff that resembles the shredded insides of a pillow.

She finds the source of the gleam, pulls it out, and holds it up to the light. The "it" in question is a delicate silver band in an intricate filigree design. The edges are soft with wear, the metal scratched and worn. It's small, though, designed for someone with strikingly petite hands. Ophelia doubts it would even fit over her first knuckle.

It looks like a wedding ring.

Lost or left behind?

She frowns. R&E teams are often rewarded for austerity measures, at Montrose at least. The fewer items they take and/or come back with, the less fuel is consumed, and those savings can add up in a rebate for the team.

But this?

A photo and a ring are such small things, personal things. Things that wouldn't take up much space or add much weight. Things that wouldn't intentionally be left behind.

More likely they've just been forgotten. Right?

That uneasy feeling, the same one that came over her when they first closed themselves in against the storm, returns. Tiny hairs raise themselves along her skin like flags of alarm. In spite of herself, she glances over her shoulder.

Nothing but shadows between the gaps of the overhead lights.

Still . . .

She doesn't want to be back here by herself. Even the echoing canyon of the central hub feels more welcoming than this space.

After a moment of indecision, she tucks the ring inside the outer pocket of her suit. Perhaps she can figure out who it belongs to and return it to them, once this assignment is finished.

When she stands, the air displaced by her movement washes over the pile of debris, and several of the dust-menagerie make a run for it, revealing something she'd missed before.

It's small and white, smooth, with peaks and valleys and a curly upper edge. Familiar. She crouches down again and reaches for it, without thinking.

Then it clicks.

That familiar something is a fat white molar. A human tooth, right there on the ground.

10

Ophelia yanks her hand back immediately.

What the fuck?

Why is there a tooth on the floor? What happened? Who does it belong to? Why . . .

She stops and cocks her head to the side, giving the tooth a closer look. Something about it is wrong.

It's too white, too perfect. Too flat on the bottom, no roots.

With a grimace, she reaches out and flips it over, revealing a hollow underside filled with circuitry and two tiny dangling wires.

The air rushes out of her lungs in a relieved exhale, and Ophelia rolls her eyes at herself. Maybe she should try not assuming the worst, for once. It's just an implant. One of the old communication devices. Before QuickQ became the norm. Some older folks, in fact, refuse to make the switch, preferring devices that don't require surgery to remove or upgrade.

In her house, her grandmother had had a museum-like display of the companies/products Pinnacle had gobbled up or taken out of business. In an old-fashioned glass case, one that wasn't even fingerprint resistant or shatterproof, a white molar implant just like this one rested on a royal blue velvet stand.

Ophelia used to stare at it in fascination, wondering who it had belonged to, what stories it might have been part of, until her mother told her that it was probably just a product sample and to stop looking at it, as the household staff found her interest in it disturbing.

Still. Stuck out here on an R&E assignment was an odd time for someone to change or remove an implant.

Maybe she should mention it to Severin.

Only for him to point out that the implant is so old that it likely fell out? And that people forget things all the time? Or get divorced and deliberately abandon their wedding rings?

Ophelia purses her lips. *No, thank you.*

After a moment of hesitation, she picks up the implant and stashes it in her pocket with the ring. It feels like this is trying to tell her a story but she doesn't have all the pieces yet.

Or it's paranoia kicking in.

You need to be careful, Ophelia. Paranoia is the first symptom. How many times has she heard that over the years, from her grandmother, from her uncle, even from her mother, in response to, yes, occasionally an overreaction, but also every instance in which they didn't care for her response and wanted to end all conversation on a topic? It carries with it the unspoken question that's been hanging over her head her whole life: Exactly how much of her father is in her?

Annoyed with herself for going there, Ophelia collects the bag of chargers, stands, and then heads back down the corridor.

It doesn't matter—that has always been and continues to be her answer to that question. She doesn't hold some bizarre magical belief that DNA makes up the sum and total whole of a person, controlling their behavior. She makes her own decisions, about what to do and what not to do, based on her experiences and best judgment. Just like everyone else. She's not controlled by some outside force, driving her to . . . do what he did. She's not a passenger in her own body and brain.

Tightening her grip on the chargers, Ophelia turns toward the open door to the central hub to do her job.

But hushed voices on the other side of the draped plastic give her pause.

". . . burned out," Kate says, sounding agitated.

"We'll do what we can before we have to replace it," Severin responds.

They must have just come from syscon, returning from whatever problem Kate had referenced earlier. Their shadows, the two of them in gray scale and larger-than-life, flicker across the semiopaque screen of plastic in front of Ophelia.

"I'm telling you, it's bloody odd. No one does that. A departing team may piss on the floor and smear shit on the walls, but nobody fucks with the generator," she insists, leaning toward him. "They just left it. It could have started a fire and burned the whole place down."

"But it didn't," Severin says, with—from Ophelia's perspective—irritating calmness.

Kate tosses her head back with an exasperated noise. "Fine. Whatever. I'm just saying it means something. I don't have a good feeling about this one."

Ophelia starts to step forward, to offer her meager collection of oddities to Kate's argument. Maybe that would help. A double win—a contribution to the team and proving herself slightly better than useless, which seems to be their general opinion.

But then Kate continues. "You know Ava is going to be a problem," she whispers.

Ophelia stops. *Ava*. Kate has to mean Olberman. Who is dead. What does Ava have to do with anything?

Severin's shadow stiffens. "You let me worry about that. I've got it under control. She won't be an issue," Severin says.

She. The grimness in his voice raises the tiny hairs on Ophelia's exposed arms.

Is he talking about Ava . . . or her?

Involuntarily Ophelia takes a step back, moving away from the doorway. Out of sight, unless Kate or Severin were to lift the plastic and enter the corridor.

They don't, though. Kate mumbles her doubt about his

assertion and then they head toward the others at the table, with Suresh calling out a greeting and a reminder about the location of the meal-paks.

Ophelia waits a full thirty seconds after they leave to step out from the corridor into the hub.

Suddenly, paranoia doesn't seem like such an overreaction.

11

Creating a conducive therapeutic environment is a bit of a rough go when your only options are metal lab tables that look like something out of an autopsy suite, disposable plastic chairs, and a wall of cracked and battered sample boxes. The whole thing screams of sharp edges, impermanence, and shit going wrong—none of which Ophelia wants to bring to mind.

Ophelia tries covering the sample box wall with a discarded sheet she finds in the corridor, something left behind from the previous team, but oddly that only seems to amplify the morgue-like vibe of the rest of the room. She yanks it down.

Eventually she shoves one of the metal tables as far back as she can, against the sample box wall, and the other off to one side. That leaves the chairs, facing each other, isolated in the middle of the open space, like the center ring of an old-timey circus, but it is the best of a series of bad options. She hopes Liana will ignore the abandoned envirosuit now propped up outside Ophelia's office door, legs crossed at the ankles, like a patient waiting for an appointment. Talk about ambience.

Ophelia pauses to collect her mug of rehydrated coffee from the corner where she stashed it for safekeeping. It's her second already this morning, gone cold and gritty—grittier, if possible—while she rearranged.

She'd slept like the dead last night. They'd split themselves up between two neighboring bunk rooms. With all the space in the hab, there was no reason not to. Liana, Kate, and Ophelia in one; Severin, Birch, and Suresh in the other.

When Suresh noticed the division, he rolled his eyes. "How positively puritanical of us. Boys and girls to your opposite corners, like it's the last fucking century."

But everyone ignored him, too tired or too used to him to care.

Ophelia was the former rather than the latter. One minute, she was in her bunk, staring up at the gray-and-white-striped fabric covering Liana's inflatable mattress above her, while her mind chewed relentlessly on what she'd overheard. *She won't be a problem.*

And the next, she was waking up, her muscles stiff, and her iVR band still perched on her forehead in wait mode. She hadn't even had the chance to pull it into place. It was like a switch had flipped, her consciousness rolling up the sidewalks and pulling down the blinds without her consent or even awareness.

Her body was still recovering from the effects of cold sleep, evidently. She hadn't even dreamed, as far as she knew. When she woke, she felt a lingering sense of darkness, of loss and confusion, like she'd spent the night wandering down endless dim corridors, searching for something.

Not surprising, given the enormous hab complex she's in and yesterday's exploration of it—including the suit incident.

And the memories that being here has generated, which have broken free from the box she keeps locked tight and far away from her normal daily thoughts.

Ophelia grimaces and chugs the rest of her coffee, even the bitter dregs at the bottom. In short, despite the depth and length of her rest, she's just as exhausted now as she was yesterday when she stumbled out of the tank.

But she's determined to get her sessions off on the right foot.

Last night, after Ophelia returned to the central hub, chargers in hand, Liana had greeted her with enthusiasm for accessing the headset again. Kate and Severin were busy eating, talking off and on with Birch and Suresh. Everything was, in short, perfectly normal.

No strange pauses or avoidant behavior. No lingering or hostile stares at her except from Birch, which she was getting used to anyway.

In fact, all of them, even Birch, allowed her to set up their initial sleep profiles. And most of them—not Birch—had at least scheduled talk sessions for the days ahead.

For the individual sessions, Ophelia suggested alphabetical order—a structure that took away the stigma from someone volunteering to be first to meet with her. It also, not by coincidence, put Liana Chong first. Ophelia had seen enough to recognize that Liana, while a junior member of the team, held sway with the others. They were protective of her, despite being amused or annoyed by her enthusiasm, and her opinion would matter, even if it wouldn't completely convince them.

Plus, Liana was the one to ask about the iVR bands; she was clearly the most open-minded of the bunch. It only made sense to start with her and then let word spread, as it inevitably would.

All of this, of course, was dependent on the storm's duration and their other duties, as Severin did not hesitate to remind her.

But he'd offered nothing else remotely obstructive beyond that. Severin even wished her a good night's rest and reminded her to take her iron tabs before bed. And not in front of the others—as he might have, if he were wishing to use that as a conscious or unconscious move to establish authority—but in a private aside.

Why does that somehow make her more uncomfortable, like he understands her a little better than she would like him to?

Ophelia adjusts the chairs once more, moving hers to face straight toward the door and then stepping around to angle the patient one slightly toward the window. Maybe their seeming cooperation last night was all a front, but if so, she was going to take advantage of it for as long as she could, until she could convince them to *actually* trust her.

"Hello?" a soft voice calls from behind her.

Ophelia spins to see Liana poking her head through the half-open door, her expression uncertain. "Hi, good morning!" Ophelia says, a little too loudly, too cheerily, as she waves Liana in.

Take it down a notch, Phe, and maybe the caffeine with it.

But she can't help it. It's not just that Liana came, that her plan—okay, if it can be called something as formal as a plan—is working, and the accompanying elation. It's also the overwhelming relief of being back on familiar ground, doing what she does best. Even if it is on a creepy planet in a creepier-still hab.

Ophelia steps back, moving out of the way, making room for Liana to enter.

Liana hesitates, then heads toward the closest chair—the one Ophelia has designated in her mind as the patient chair—before stopping herself. "I don't . . . I don't know how to do this," she admits, turning to Ophelia, her hand resting on the plastic back. "I've never been in any kind of . . . session before. Except for our postmission debriefs. And the meetings after—" She cuts herself off.

Ava.

The urge to dig *right now* is a sharp pinch in her gut, but Ophelia ignores it. She closes the door and heads around to the other chair. "It's okay," she says easily, as she sits down. "This is just a conversation, not a test. There are no right or wrong answers."

Liana, rotating to follow Ophelia with her gaze, gives her a skeptical look, eyebrows raised.

Ophelia smiles. "Okay, yes, there are responses that might generate concern, but I'm pretty sure we're not there yet."

Liana's expression smooths out a little, and she takes her chair, sitting on the edge, as if she might leap up at any moment.

Ophelia leans back in her chair, giving off a deliberately relaxed but attentive vibe that she hopes will inspire the same in Liana. "How did you sleep last night? Did you find the iVR band helpful?"

Some of the tension eases from Liana's shoulders, and her face brightens. "Yeah, actually. It was great. It felt so real, just like when you showed me. I almost expected to wake up to the sound of the mynahs."

"That's exactly what we're aiming for," Ophelia says. "Any glitches or issues?" Her fingers twitch involuntarily for the sensation of her pen in hand, but taking notes always seems to make reluctant patients extra skittish, especially in the beginning.

Liana pauses. "Just a bit of a headache." Her hand flutters up to her forehead and then back down to her lap. Her fingers are squeezing together, interlocking, releasing, interlocking again.

"Totally normal," Ophelia says. "One of the possible side effects. It'll get better. But if you need a pain reliever, I'm sure whoever is in charge of the medikit would . . ." She trails off at Liana's wince.

Then it clicks. "Ava was in charge of the medikit," Ophelia says.

"Yeah," Liana says with a rueful smile. "Like I said, she liked taking care of—"

"What the hell, Birch?" Suresh's voice is tinny and echoing when it bursts to life in the room over their wrist-comms.

Ophelia and Liana both jump, startled.

"Did you take my good moisturizer again?" Suresh continues, his outrage only slightly muffled by a burst of distant static. "You know what this canned air does to my skin. I'm drier than a fucking sand lizard. Where are you?"

Liana rolls her eyes with fond exasperation. "He always does this," she says. "Accuses people of taking stuff and it's right there in his bag, probably hidden away for safekeeping."

The two of them, Suresh and Liana, seem the closest of the remaining team members, but more like siblings competing over Dad's attention than anything else. Ophelia makes a mental note.

"Maybe we could . . ." Ophelia holds out her arm, showing Liana that she's turning the volume down.

"Oh, right. Sure." Liana turns hers down as well.

Ophelia lets a beat of silence hang to allow the distraction to fade out and the silence to return.

"If it makes you feel any better," Ophelia says after a moment, "PBE therapists have required therapy sessions as well, when back on Earth. And I had no idea what I was doing the first time, either, despite desperately wanting to be in this chair." Ophelia taps the side of the seat beneath her. "You'd think it wouldn't have been that hard, since I know how the other side works, but if anything, that just made it more difficult."

That, and because lying in sessions, while expected, is frowned upon.

Liana gives a tight nod, but she's studying her hands, back in her lap.

"I can't read your mind. As silly as that sounds, a lot of people worry about that," Ophelia offers. "I'm not even trying. It's only what you feel comfortable sharing, and then, hopefully, as you get to know me, you'll want to share more so I can help more."

Liana fidgets with the cuff of her jumpsuit. "Right."

"How about if I start? You get along with your team, but I know that you miss Ava. That she was a good friend to you. That you're struggling with what happened to her." That last is a guess, but not a big one.

She nods, mutely.

"Is there something I can help you with? Something you're having a harder time with?" Ophelia tries to tread lightly. It's an impossible balance to find sometimes, wanting to help, needing information *to* help, but also trying desperately not to come off as the pushy asshole poking her nose where it doesn't belong.

"Not really." Liana stares out at the window. The dull brightness of the snow beyond reflects back on her face. She looks so small and vulnerable across the short distance between them. Ophelia feels a wave of empathy for her.

"I just . . . I hate that no one talks about her anymore," Liana says finally. "It's, like, Ava died and now we're all supposed to pretend that she never existed!" She folds her arms across her chest.

Ophelia nods. "For some people, it helps to talk about the person who died. For others, it reminds them too much of the loss. They need to contain their grief, only letting it out privately or when they feel they can manage it, which may not be often. It may look like they're pretending she never existed, but they're feeling it in their own way." Ophelia wonders which one drove the person leaving the paper flowers for Ava in her bunk, someone who wants to remember or someone desperately trying to forget.

"That's dumb," Liana protests. "We should be able to feel this together. We *lost* her together."

"I know, I get it, but people don't work like that." Or so she assumes. As someone who, like Liana, wanted to talk about things but was forced not to, Ophelia can only speculate on what her mother was feeling or not feeling. Years later, her own emotions are still conflicted, tangled-up knots of love and hate and confusion, which is why she keeps them tucked away. Her mother won that battle by default.

"I guess . . . I'm just wondering about how it works, then. Getting past it and, you know, forgiveness." Liana shifts uneasily in her chair. "How does that work if you can't even talk about it?"

Ophelia's attention snaps into hyperfocus, but she remains still, calm. No need to spook Liana. Figuring out what happened to Ava isn't what she's here for, except in whatever way understanding that might help her better understand *them*. "Forgiving someone or *being* forgiven?" Ophelia asks.

Liana doesn't answer; her gaze is fixed on a distant point. "If you did the right thing, the only thing you could do, then—"

BAM. BAM. BAM.

The loud pounding at the metal door explodes in the room, snapping the fragile thread of conversation and the nascent bond between them.

The door swings open before either of them can respond, and Kate sticks her head in, her hair rumpled and face pale except for bright patches of color on her cheeks. Liana jumps to her feet, looking ashamed, like an upper-level manager caught with naked persons cavorting on the background of his screen.

"Excuse me," Ophelia says sharply. "We're in the middle of a—"

Kate's gaze snaps to Liana, her mouth tightening with displeasure. "What are you doing? Didn't you hear me?" Kate demands, holding up her own arm and the attached wrist-comm.

Ophelia steps in before Liana can respond. "We turned down our wrist-comms so that we wouldn't be—" she begins.

Kate's eyes go wide. "Why the fuck would you do that?" She shakes her head, making a dismissive sound of disgust. "It doesn't matter. Come on." This last is directed to Liana.

"What's wrong?" Liana asks, following her out the door.

"We can't find Birch," Kate says grimly, the words drifting over her shoulder back toward Ophelia. "He's missing."

12

When Ophelia reaches the hub, just behind Kate and Liana, Severin and Suresh are standing together, near the long table, talking quietly. Suresh is explaining something, his hands shooting out wildly to either side in large gestures.

"What happened? What's going on?" Ophelia asks as she approaches.

"We're trying to work that out, Doctor," Severin says, without looking at her. He sounds calm, unconcerned, but the tension in his shoulders and arms, folded across his chest, is screaming, loudly. "Go on." He nods for Suresh to continue.

Suresh, after a sideways look toward Ophelia, shakes his head. "Not there. But I checked both bunk rooms, and all the permanent suits are accounted for." His usual teasing tone has flattened into something sharper around the edges.

Ophelia's heart plummets; they think he's outside. That he's left the hab.

Just like Ava.

"He wouldn't do that," Liana says, standing with Kate on Ophelia's left side. An odd beat of silence holds among the four of them. "He wouldn't," she insists.

Unless it's not a matter of choice, of Birch *choosing* to do anything. Or, rather, that rational thinking and logic would have anything to do with his choices. The drumbeat of fear that began with Kate's declaration of Birch as missing grows louder inside her.

"Did he say anything to anyone before—" Ophelia begins.

"No one has seen him since last night, and we can't reach him on comms," Severin says.

"What about the temp suits?" Kate asks.

Suresh hesitates, turning toward her. "That's a little more complicated."

"What the fuck?" Kate demands. "You're the inventory guy."

"Yeah, but I inventoried for a team of five during prep," he argues. "Temporaries are usually packed as a set of six."

"You don't know if Montrose left one out because we weren't at that point anticipating the doctor, or if one is missing," Severin says flatly.

"Correct," Suresh says.

Strange, but not impossible that an afflicted Birch would bypass his regular suit to dig out a temporary from the crates. Ophelia had an ERS patient once who was convinced that Montrose was intermittently screening his private QuickQ conversations (likely) and that it was triggered every time he used a word starting with the letter *M* (definitely not). So many sessions involving the awkward phrasing "your parent who is not your father."

Perhaps Birch's paranoia extended somehow to his regular suit and the tracking connected to it. It's hard to predict how someone, caught in loops of irrational thinking, would behave.

He cut them open; it's like he was looking for something . . .

Ophelia flinches but forces herself to remain focused, in the moment. Not the past.

"If he's out there, we should go look for him." Ophelia takes a half step toward the airlock.

"No," Severin says. "Conditions are improving, but I'm not risking the rest of my team. We won't have any way of knowing which way he went, if he's even out there."

"He wouldn't—" Liana begins again.

Kate cuts her off with a sharp look. "It could have been forty-five minutes ago or hours," Kate adds. "Any trace of his path would probably be wiped clean from the storm. We'd just be wandering around, gormless." She shrugs tightly. "Maybe fall into a crevasse."

"But we can't just stand around here and wait," Ophelia protests. And wait for what? The storm to clear so they can find his body?

In her mind, Rueben Monterra, smashed and broken on the garden terrace below her office, blinks up at her, his bloodied mouth moving. Ophelia shudders.

"Protocol says a thorough sweep of the hab," Severin says.

"You're joking," Ophelia says in disbelief. "You've looked for him in here already, haven't you?"

"A preliminary search isn't the same as—" Liana says.

"This isn't a cozy little Grant Park gated mansion, Doctor," Severin says. As always, his voice is mild while his words are cutting. "While the hab is meant to keep us alive, it's far from a perfect system."

"He could have fallen and struck his head in a far corner of some hab unit," Kate says. "Or come up with an embolism, run into a slow leak, and tucked himself away in a hypoxic delusion, or fucking choked on a meal-pak."

All true, theoretically. But clearly there's a reason why they're worried about the suits and whether Birch might have taken one.

Or maybe she is once again focusing too much on her worst fear—another patient with ERS that she was not able to help. She has to concede that is at least a possibility.

Ophelia nods curtly in acknowledgment.

"We need to go," Liana says. She's shifting her weight from foot to foot, like an impatient runner at the starting line. "Now. We need to find him."

Severin nods. "Liana, Suresh, search the C side again. Make sure you check every space large enough to fit a person, and even the ones you think might be too small. He could be disoriented. Hiding."

If someone fails to respond to comms, you treat it as if they're completely incapacitated and incapable of behaving rationally. Ophelia knows that. And yet she had never considered exactly how frustratingly difficult acting on that principle might be in a live environment. It's impossible to predict what Birch might have done, where he might be, when all the logical options have been eliminated.

"Kate will take the A side, and I'll handle syscon, the galley, and the central hub," Severin finishes. "Keep the common channel open, and call for help if you need it."

Based on her previous experiences, Ophelia half expects an argument about who is going where, doing what.

But Liana immediately hurries off, with Suresh at her heels.

Kate lingers, though, her gaze caught with Severin's in another of their silent exchanges.

After a moment, Severin's mouth tightens and he jerks his chin toward the table, off to the side.

Ophelia follows the motion to see a familiar case on the table; she missed it before. It's not the medikit, though, which would have made more sense. No, it's the thin gray case with the bright red markings and the code lock. The gun.

As she watches, Kate crosses the space in a few efficient steps and unlocks the case, removing the weapon.

"Whoa, whoa! What are you doing?" Ophelia steps forward, arms stretched out to block her path. "This isn't necessary. If he's ill or hurt, he's not a threat. Even if it's ERS, most patients are absolutely no danger to anyone other than themselves." With a few . . . notable exceptions.

"Plenty of ways to lose your grip out here that have nothing to do with ERS," Kate says grimly, stepping around her to head toward the A side.

What is that supposed to mean? Ophelia's arms sink slowly to her sides, then she turns on Severin. "You're seriously going to let her do that?"

He doesn't look happy, but he lifts a shoulder in a minute shrug. "It's self-defense only. Kate knows that."

Ophelia stares at him, then shakes her head, neck so tight

the muscles creak with the movement. "Fuck that. *Now* I'm judging you."

Then she takes off after Kate.

This unit is one of those that Ophelia checked with Severin yesterday, on the same side of the hab as her now-office but closer to the central hub. It looks virtually the same as it did then, except for the piles of swept-up debris.

Kate doesn't bother to look back at her, pushing farther in to check under the lab tables and associated desk.

When Kate's finished—a quick, efficient search, only made threatening by the weapon in her hand—she pivots and heads back toward the door, forcing Ophelia to step back out into the corridor to get out of her way.

This happens twice more before Kate stops at the threshold of the next unit.

She turns to face Ophelia. "If you're going to follow me, Doctor, you might as well make yourself useful and check the other hab units on this side."

Ophelia doesn't move.

Kate sighs. "Think of it this way: the sooner we find him, the better off he'll be. And if you find him before I do, you don't have to worry about this." She waggles the gun in a way that is disturbingly nonchalant.

Without waiting for an answer, Kate pivots and heads into the next unit.

As much as Ophelia hates to admit it, Kate has a point. It's not as if she'll be able to stop Kate from doing, well, anything. And if Birch is in trouble, they need to find him, fast. Tailing Kate is not exactly increasing their odds of finding him, which is the first—and primary—problem. The more time ticks away, the greater the chances that he'll be in real trouble when—and if—they find him.

Ophelia turns on her heels and heads to the next hab unit. The closed door is heavy but manageable.

This unit is another lab; it blurs with all the others on this side. Except it's clearly been closed off since their initial walk-through yesterday. Whoever was going through with the broom skipped this unit, and there's debris still piled up in the corners and scattered across the floor.

Ophelia shivers. Though the temperature in the hab is the same in each unit, a comfortable twenty degrees Celsius, it feels cooler in here. Darker, too. It doesn't help that the lights aren't on, part of Kate's order to conserve energy by making them inoperable in the unnecessary spaces.

Ophelia's cloth shoes grit across the shattered bits of glass and polymer. She hopes the pieces aren't too sharp, or that her soles are thicker than they look.

"Birch?" she calls into the small space, even though she's fairly sure she's the only one here. It's just an open-sided lab table, two desks, and a bunch of junk.

Ophelia bends down and checks beneath the first of the desks, one of the only conceivable hiding spots in the room. Nothing, of course.

But as she's pulling back from the desk closest to the door, she stops. On the underside of the plasti-fab desk, deep gouges mar the otherwise smooth material in parallel lines. Four of them.

Ophelia squints in the dim light, trying to understand what she's seeing. She kneels down and traces the lines, the rough edges of the grooves scraping her fingertips. What could have caused that?

Dark smudges are smeared along the desk's edge, wrapping around to the top.

Frowning, she straightens up carefully until she can see the top of the desk. There, beneath a thick coating of dust, is a matching mark, with more of the dark smears.

One on the top, but in direct alignment with the four underneath.

She holds her hand above the marks, without touching them. Thumb on the top, fingers underneath.

A perfect fit.

Someone clawed at this desk, hard enough to make actual marks.

Why?

Her brain immediately summons images, memories of bloody streaks on the floor, left behind by hands grabbing for purchase as people were hauled out of their hiding spaces.

No. Ophelia shakes her head. *Not here.*

But the back of her neck prickles with a chill of awareness, as if someone is just behind her, looming in the threshold, breathing just hard enough to ruffle the tiny hairs there.

Goose bumps spring up on her arms, and she whips around, hands up to defend herself from . . . something.

But no one is there.

She lets out a sharp laugh at herself. *Get a grip, Ophelia. What is wrong with you?* A question for the ages.

Whatever happened to that desk, whatever caused those marks, that (maybe) blood doesn't have anything to do with Birch. The smears were dry, the dust undisturbed until she touched it.

With a grimace, she starts for the door, and then she stops short, retreating to the other desk, the one under the window, to check it, just to be sure.

No marks on this desk. No dark smudges, either.

Motion outside the window catches her attention. Hard crystalline flakes, more ice than snow, click faintly against the window. Ophelia stares at them, watching them spin and move and collect against the rubber seal at the base of the window.

But then a swirl of darkness beyond pulls her gaze. The alien ruins loom, stark lines in the distance. This, however, is a person-size patch of darker gray, just above the frozen expanse of white, lurching awkwardly, first right and then left. As if fighting against the storm.

Horror curdles the coffee in her gut. *Oh fuck.*

Not person-size. That's a person. In the storm. It's one thing to talk about the possibility, entirely something else to witness it.

"Birch!" Ophelia pounds on the window. But he can't hear her. He's too far away already.

She rushes through the hab, out into the corridor, and races toward the central hub. Stumbling over the threshold, she rights herself and then bolts for the airlock at the opposite end.

It takes too long, so long. Even though it's only seconds, she can feel every one of them ticking down, like Birch's chances of being rescued before he's lost in the storm.

The airlock door is already open, and she throws herself inside. Only to find Severin, Suresh, Liana, and even Kate—with no gun in sight—standing there, on the far side, near the corner. They don't seem to be rushing into suits, though. They're gathered in a half-circle, staring down at something.

"Birch is . . ." she begins, panting. She waves her hand at the outer door, as if they'll understand that. "He's—"

Four heads turn toward her at once, like a choreographed action. Suresh watches her with his eyes wide. Kate and Severin exchange another of their patented silent conversations, which are so irritating. *Just say it out loud. We don't have time for this!* Then Liana steps toward her with a concerned frown.

"Ophelia?"

Ophelia opens her mouth to explain, but in the gap opened by Liana's movement, she can now see what they were all looking at.

Birch. On the floor, in the corner between the outer wall and the mobile sample containment unit they hauled in from the lander yesterday.

Not outside. In here.

He's sitting up, wrists resting on his knees, looking a little dazed and irritable but otherwise fine.

Suddenly, Ophelia feels like she's the one being battered by the storm, twisted up and spun around.

"—right there," she finishes weakly.

13

"Didn't you hear me say on the wrist-comm that we found him?" Liana asks, her forehead creased in confusion.

"No. I . . ." It dawns on Ophelia in that moment that she never turned the volume back up on her own device. "I guess I was . . . distracted." Pounding on the window and trying to get the attention of . . . who, exactly? Electric fear sizzles down the nerves in Ophelia's arms, making her fingers tingle painfully.

Liana and the others are all still staring at her.

I saw someone. Outside. In the storm. The words are perched on Ophelia's tongue, ready to leap off.

In the moment, it seemed so clear. She can still picture that pronounced left-right swaying of someone battling the storm to make forward progress.

But Birch is here. And so is everyone else.

Ophelia reviewed the pre-mission probe scans for herself—there's nothing alive on this planet except for them. Claim jumpers are always a (remote) possibility, but it seems unlikely that jumpers would wait for them to be settled in at the hab. Plus, the figure she saw, if she'd seen anything at all, was heading away from their facility, toward the city ruins.

So . . . a shadow, an optical illusion. The snow and wind creating odd patterns and the suggestion of movement. Plus, the team's obvious anxiety that Birch was outside probably planted the suggestion in her own sleep-deprived—and therefore highly suggestible—mind. You see what you expect to see and all that.

That *has* to be it.

Ophelia swallows hard. "It just occurred to me that the airlock was the one place we hadn't searched," she says.

That answer seems to satisfy them. Most of them, anyway. Birch is staring at her with open hostility, and even Kate is eyeing her, head cocked sideways with curiosity.

"Hell of a place to fall asleep, man," Suresh says to Birch, stepping forward and offering him a hand up.

"Yes. It is," Severin says, arms folded across his chest, stance wide again. "Explain it to me again."

Birch glowers as he pulls himself up with Suresh's help. "It's not that big of a deal. You know how it is the first night after cold sleep. I was awake, couldn't fall back asleep, so I thought I'd get up and check on the status of the storm."

Get up? Birch's words distract Ophelia from her own worries. He didn't get up last night. Not from what Ophelia saw on the iVR control tablet this morning. Wakefulness is one thing, but physical activity on that level would have registered with elevated heart rate and a change in breathing. No one was out of bed last night, based on the numbers. As far as those were concerned, Birch was asleep in his bunk—or, to be fair, wherever he initially dozed off—all night long.

"I sat down for a few minutes, and I must have fallen asleep," Birch finishes with a shrug.

"Inside the airlock?" Kate asks Birch mildly. Now that Ophelia is closer, she can see the outline of the gun tucked inside the oversize utility pocket on the side of her jumpsuit. "There are plenty of other windows to choose from."

Birch lifts his hands with an exasperated noise. "I don't know. I was feeling restless, okay?" His gaze slips past them, meeting Ophelia's for a fraction of a second before skittering away.

No matter how often it happens, it always strikes Ophelia as so strange how you can hear a lie sometimes. It's the fractional pause before the response. The thinness of the words, as if they're brittle ice, holding the shape of an answer but not strong enough to sustain thorough examination.

"It's no different than that time Liana passed out under her bunk," Birch points out.

Suresh snickers.

"Hey, that's not fair," Liana protests, her cheeks flushing pink. "You guys didn't tell me it was spiked."

"Liana, love. It wasn't spiked. It was called grog and just the smell of it incinerated my nose hairs," Kate says wryly.

"Why didn't we get an alert that the airlock was opened?" Severin directs this question to Kate.

Her mouth tightens. "I turned off the trip for the interior door. One less power draw. I didn't think I needed to worry about anyone wandering around in there for funsies." She glares at Birch.

"Okay, okay, got it." Birch rolls his eyes, scratching at his arm through his jumpsuit sleeve. The edge of the fabric near his wrist rides up, revealing a patch of angry red skin. Contact dermatitis, probably. "But you can't blame me for being a little stressed."

He sends a pointed look at Ophelia. It's a classic redirect, but it works.

The last of the tension of drains away from the group, their questions answered, their problem resolved. Almost as one, they step back and away from Birch, a precursor to breaking off and returning to whatever they were doing before.

But Ophelia steps closer. "I'm sure it's as you said, the remaining effects of cold sleep," she says, choosing not to call Birch out on his lie. Hard to do otherwise, when she doesn't have more information. "But I would still like to have a chat. Make sure everything is okay. Maybe we could run a couple tests through the med-scanner in the medikit."

She looks to Kate, who gives an uncomfortable nod after a beat. "Sure."

"No!" Birch says too sharply, at the same time. Then, with a frustrated exhale through his nose, he shakes his head. "No," he says again in a calmer voice. "I'm fine. Let's just get day one in the books."

Ophelia holds her hands up, palms out, in the classic "I mean no harm" gesture. "I'm just concerned, that's all," she says to Birch, but just as much to Severin. "We've found that disrupted sleep is not just a contributor but can also be a symptom of—"

"I don't have disrupted anything!" Birch snaps. "Just a headache that's as much from you as anything else. And that fucking thing." He points to the ground, where a discarded iVR band rests near his feet. Along with his wrist-comm.

Liana darts forward and picks up his wrist-comm, handing it to him by the thick black band. He nods his thanks, pausing in his scratching to loop the band—loosely this time—around his wrist.

Ophelia can't help but notice that Liana does not do the same for the iVR band. Part of her wants to scoop it off the ground herself before its delicate framework is damaged, but she resists the urge.

"What are we doing today?" Birch asks Severin. "Core samples? Updated surface scans with the drones?"

Silence holds for a long moment. Everyone, including Ophelia, waits for Severin to answer.

"We don't have a huge window between storms," Severin says finally. "Priority will be documenting the ruins, taking a few samples, and a couple other housekeeping items."

He's not going to do it. Disappointment swells in her, followed immediately by irritation flickering to life inside her chest, like flame caused by friction. Severin will not force—or hell, even encourage, apparently—Birch to get help. She should have expected nothing less. He warned her that he would not support her efforts.

She *could* push it. Demand that Birch submit to a session and a blood panel to check for low iron and T3 levels, both of which are known to exacerbate conditions leading to ERS, or be benched.

But that would only make Birch hate her more, if that's possible, and destroy any chance of him accepting her help when and if he really needs it, not to mention casting her firmly as the enemy with the others. Any progress she made toward trust with Liana this morning would be gone, if it isn't already.

Birch nods once at Severin, seemingly in gruff satisfaction.

"Suresh, you're on pod duty," Severin continues.

Suresh's mouth falls open in protest.

"But in this storm, no one goes anywhere alone. Birch, you're with him."

Suresh's protest turns into laughter.

Severin's glance briefly pauses on Ophelia, eyebrows raised, as if to ask, *Happy?*

That will keep Birch closer to the hab, which is probably safer, but nothing like an actual assessment.

Birch's mouth thins into a line. "Commander, I don't need to be babied because of—"

"Kate, Liana, you'll head into the city with me," Severin says, ignoring him. "The two of you will take samples from the towers; that's listed as our top priority on the mission brief. I'll handle the scan of the former excavation site, documenting what Pinnacle was up to. That's second on our list."

Leaving Ophelia to sit in the hab and twiddle her thumbs, apparently.

"If the storm gets worse, at all, if you even think that conditions might be deteriorating, head back immediately." The sternness in Severin's voice reminds Ophelia that this piece of common sense is not simply a nicety but a necessity among risk-seeking R&E teams, which most R&E personnel are, simply by the nature of the job. "If you get lost, stay where you are, we will find you. Be ready in twenty. We'll go out together."

Birch shoves past Ophelia on his way out, stomping across the airlock into the corridor. Suresh drifts after him. "Hey, it's not that big of a deal," he calls after Birch, but his gleeful tone is not going to help his case.

Birch is too far for Ophelia to hear his response, if he gives one at all.

Ophelia bends down to retrieve the iVR band, as Kate and Severin, discussing equipment needs, move to exit the airlock as well.

A quiet voice stops them in their tracks. "That plan leaves you going into the excavation site by yourself," Liana says. She's still standing where she was, rubbing her arms up and down with her hands, as if she's suddenly cold. "You don't know what the conditions are like there. You don't know if there's been a cave-in. Or if the support structure will hold. It's been six years."

"I'll be fine," Severin says, gently but firmly.

Liana shakes her head, mouth a stubborn line. "You said no one goes anywhere alone. It's an unnecessary risk. You could fall, get hurt, become trapped under a mountain of snow so thick you can't breathe and—" She cuts herself off, visibly steeling herself against the wave of emotion. But her eyes are shiny with unshed tears.

Ophelia lobs her own silent conversation starter at Severin. *See? Trauma. I told you.*

His jaw goes tight, the muscle jumping at the back corner of it. An acknowledgment of sorts.

"You could just wait," Liana continues. "Kate and I will finish at the towers and then one of us will—"

"We don't have the time for that, Liana," Severin says with patience, no evidence of the exasperation that Ophelia would have expected from him if he were dealing with anyone else, especially with the shortened timeline they're facing with the weather. Points to him for recognizing Liana's vulnerability. That also means Ophelia was right in her assessment of Liana's role on the team—she matters to them.

"I'm sorry," he continues. "But I promise, nothing is going to happen."

Ophelia raises her eyebrows. A bold statement, given the uncertainty of, well, everything in this place.

He leaves Kate and crosses back to the airlock to stand in front of Liana, forcing her to meet his gaze. "I'll stay in contact," he says calmly. "The team will know exactly where I am at all times."

He's good. Very good. Deep voice, soothing, reassuring, like a weighted blanket pressing tight over you.

Ophelia's resistance to him—a tension in her chest—softens. She finds herself wanting to believe him.

Until she catches herself, squaring her shoulders against the onslaught. He might mean it, but it's also a tactic, she's sure of it. He's just trying to keep all of his team members on task and focused. Fair enough.

"It won't be like before. And I don't want you to be distracted, worrying about me," Severin says to Liana. "This is the best solution, the only thing to be done. Unless you think the doctor wants to join me?" He cocks his head toward Ophelia.

Liana offers a cautious smile.

It's a joke, to smooth over the tension, reuniting him and Liana on the same side once more, the side of "this woman is an outsider and slightly ridiculous." Ophelia recognizes what he's doing, even if she doesn't like it.

But it's his exaggerated expression, a humorous version of a smirk, aimed at Ophelia, that does it—digs in, right beneath her skin. It's the tiniest up-flip in the right corner of his mouth, an expression that says how crazy an idea it is, that rich, useless Ophelia Bray might do some actual work.

Ophelia's seen similar looks before, from colleagues, classmates, even her various mentors. And she knows better than to be goaded by it. She absolutely has no business pretending to be a full-fledged R&E team member. Especially in a group that would, if not enjoy, be utterly entertained by her fumbling and stumbling around. Amused by her failure.

But Ophelia meets his gaze without flinching and lifts her chin, fury simmering just beneath the surface. "Ready when you are."

"Enjoying the walk, Doctor?" Severin asks, as the wind forces Ophelia to stagger sideways once more.

Stupid, stupid, stupid, Ophelia castigates herself. Studying the human mind and how it affects behavior has certainly given her better awareness of her own foibles. It has not, however, made her any less prone to falling into the pitfalls of her own personality.

Yes, of course, taking this trip to the city ruins might help garner her more trust, more respect. And passing up the opportunity to have one-on-one conversation with the man in an environment he is probably far more comfortable in would have been shortsighted.

But neither of those reasons are why she said yes. And they both know it.

"It's great," Ophelia says, trying not to pant so overtly over the private channel that Severin has opened between them. "Bright, sunny day. Fresh air. Exercise. What more could I ask for?"

The blank, snowy sheet of their surroundings is as dull and eerie in the vague blue-gray light as it's ever been. The only air is coming from the tank and recycler in her suit, and "fresh" would not be the word she'd use to describe it. *Thick plastic, with rich metal overtones* maybe. Or *fume-y*. Though obviously the air is clean enough to breathe or her suit would have been throwing an alarm.

The exercise part, at least, is true, though it feels a lot more like trying to chew through the thickened maple syrup filling in those weird cookies her sister liked to have shipped in from Independent Quebec. In other words, a lot of effort for very little reward. The walk to the outer edge of the city ruins might only have taken fifteen minutes in good conditions, but it's twice that today. And they are only halfway there.

Severin—six or seven meters ahead of her in physical form but right in front of her face on her screen—snorts, shaking his head. But Ophelia is secretly pleased to see the flush of exertion on his cheeks as well, even if his steps, even and smooth, don't show it.

Liana and Kate just broke off to head toward the towers, two spears jutting out of the snow. The towers look out of place, glossy and sharply angled at the ends, unlike the wind- and weatherworn edges of the rest of the ruins. Ophelia imagines that the Cloud Gate sculpture would look much the same to an outsider arriving to Old Chicago from another planet. Same with the tangled remains of the Calder sculpture, assuming any of it remained after the fire. Most of the former downtown has been permanently sealed off, cut off like a surgeon excising a margin of healthy skin around cancerous lesion.

"I don't appreciate you using my team to manipulate me," Severin says.

It's Ophelia's turn to snort. She did nothing of the sort. He's the one who opened his mouth. Now, granted, she might have guessed that Liana would latch on to the idea, refusing to let go of it, if Ophelia volunteered to accompany him. But that's his fault, too.

"And I don't appreciate you refusing to take advantage of the assistance I can offer for the betterment of your team," Ophelia says back. "So we're both full of nonappreciation, I guess, Commander. What would you like to do about that?"

Being categorized as baggage, useless, tainted, garbage—they're all tangled threads in her mind, leading to one giant hot button that she can't resist reacting to when it's pressed.

Granted, plenty of people want to give her too much value, fawning over her, but that's because of her last name, not in spite of it, and she's never been tempted to believe in it.

Ophelia suspects Ethan Severin has a similar sensitivity, only his is about his team and people thinking he's not doing enough.

He glares at her, and she can practically see him puffing up with the urge to defend himself. But he stops, his gaze darting to the side.

Ophelia freezes, her heart stumbles in her chest, and she automatically scans the horizon around them. But there's nothing except the city ruins growing larger in the distance as they approach.

Then it clicks. He's not looking *out* at anything.

The common channel remains open on the other side of her helmet screen, showing tiny images of Liana, Kate, Suresh, and Birch, though with the private channel open with Severin, she can't hear them, only read their transcribed words below their faces.

> **Suresh:**—completely disgusting! There's still shit in here from however many years ago. This is not what I signed on for.
> **Birch:** It'll go faster if you . . . try the shovel.
> **Suresh:** You try it!
> **Kate:** Keep scooping, pod boy.
> **Liana:** We're supposed to keep this channel clear!
> **Birch:** It'll go faster if you . . . try the shovel.
> **Suresh:** Bro, you said that already.

Ophelia frowns. Birch's gaze seems distant and unfocused.

Severin sighs on their open line, sounding tired, as he starts forward again.

She follows, struggling for a moment to pull her booted feet free from the icy layer of snow.

"You're genuinely concerned about him," Severin says, but it sounds more like a question.

Ophelia resists the urge to shoot back, "As opposed to falsely being concerned about him to amplify my own importance?" *Step away from the button, Ophelia.* Instead, she takes a calming breath and answers the question, ignoring the possible subtextual jab.

"I am," she says. And not just because the apparent response to someone's possible disorientation within the hab is to search for them with a weapon, though, frankly, she doesn't love that. It means the negative narrative about ERS and mental health in space in general is winning. "I don't know him as well as you do, obviously. But he seems a bit . . . disconnected. More so than before we left the ship."

"Do you think he was lying?" Severin asks, but she can't quite read his tone. There's something guarded in it. "About why he was in the airlock?"

She hesitates, and the only sound on their channel is their breathing, hers louder and far more ragged than his. "Yes," she says after a moment. "His iVR numbers don't match his story. But I think it would be a mistake to assume we know why. Trauma makes people do strange things."

She expects Severin to immediately protest the idea that his team is experiencing any aftereffects from Ava's untimely death. But he simply grunts an acknowledgment.

Ophelia sees an opening to continue. "I know you were concerned that he was trying to leave the hab, or that he was thinking about leaving," she says cautiously. *Like Ava.* "But we need to keep in mind that it might be something else entirely. I don't think he's progressed to the point that she . . . to that point. Maybe he was sleeping in there to guard the door, to prevent someone else on the team from leaving."

Severin's gaze jolts to back to hers abruptly.

"Just to help himself feel certain that it *wasn't* happening," she adds quickly. "Or it could be something as simple as needing to be close to an exit, to feel like he *could* leave, if necessary. Claustrophobia isn't unheard of as a reaction, even for an R&E team member." Particularly because Ava died, as far as Ophelia could tell, from running out of air. Leaving the hab to walk on a planet where the air is not breathable seems a contrary reaction, but it's instinctive in humans. Outside means more air. Period.

She stops, waiting to see if Severin will take the opening to ask another question or continue the conversation. But he doesn't.

Instead he gives her a curt nod and closes the private channel, switching them back automatically to the common one and Suresh's moaning about getting calluses.

Disappointment pings through her, but she pushes back against it. Building a therapeutic relationship takes time; she knows that. At least this is a start. That's enough for now. They have weeks to go yet.

14

"Watch your step," Severin says, as the ground dips unexpectedly beneath Ophelia's feet. "We're reaching the start of the excavation."

Finally, finally, they've reached the edge of the city ruins. The remains of the buildings are larger, more substantial than she expected; her sense of scale is off.

Ahead of her, broken rectangles cluster together in an uneven half circle, covered in a thinner layer of ice and snow. From the angle of their approach, Ophelia can see that at least three or four stories are visible above the ground on most of the buildings, with probably that many or more beneath the level of the snow.

The ruins loom over her, casting vague shadows on the snow like an unwelcome mat.

The so-called towers are to her right and slightly behind, and it's like she can feel them pulsing at her back, demanding attention, like a beacon. Probably because they're the only things around here that aren't white or gray or some shade of either.

On the other side of the towers, there's another clutch of ruined buildings, worn tops barely peeking through the drifts of snow. A similar set huddles in front of the distant mountains.

But clearly any work that Pinnacle did in excavation has been focused here—on this closest set of buildings, in particular the central trio that is grouped together, two shorter ones leaning toward a taller one in the center, like grieving family members relying on the strong one.

"They started out here, probably just to be able to get equipment in and the snow out," Severin says. Now that he points it out, Ophelia can detect the ongoing depression, almost like a pathway in front of them, leading to the targeted buildings.

"Field generators are still in place," he continues, gesturing toward small devices on tripods, stabbed into the ground at varying intervals along the path they are now following, like a perimeter. "That would have kept the snow away, until they ran out of power. Not enough light to keep the solar panels juiced without help."

She follows Severin down what's left of the carved path, and eventually they descend into a larger dug-out space near the buildings, where they are more sheltered from the wind and snow. The structures bobbing in the corner of her helmet-obstructed peripheral vision make her feel like either she's shrinking or they are unaccountably growing taller. As if she's that infamous Alice and she's lost her grip on what's real and what's not.

It sends shivers over her skin.

As they pass the first building in the trio, Ophelia can see now that it's not just leaning but has fallen over. Only the taller building in the center is keeping it upright. The quarried stone exterior is cracked and crumbling, but spikey shards of a glossy, orangish finish cling to it here and there. At ground level—or what passes for it at this point—the curved upper edge of a circular opening disappears into the snow below. The space is dark and alluring, promising mysteries to solve if one were to crawl inside. Until Ophelia is close enough to see that inside that particular opening is nothing but iced-over rubble, apparently from an internal collapse.

The central building, the one that appears to be intact and still standing straight up, is covered in a loose framework of scaffolding, behind which a dozen or so of those same rounded entrances beckon.

This is where Pinnacle set up shop. And where she and

Severin are headed, even though the plasti-fab boards and piping
that make up the scaffolding look shaky at best.

As Ophelia watches, a gust of wind tears past above them
and the uppermost level of the scaffolding sways away from
the building.

The thought of being on the fragile structure makes Ophelia's stomach lurch like she's falling. Her hands and fingers
tingle painfully, as if circulation has been cut off. "Severin,"
Ophelia begins.

"Yeah, I saw it," he responds. "We'll look for another way."

"Can't we just go in down here?" Ophelia gestures to the
nearest opening on her left side—dim, snow covered, but on
the lowest level of the scaffolding. They wouldn't even really
have to use it so much as crawl across the plasti-fab boards.

Severin shakes his head. "I don't know if there's a clear internal path between levels. It looks like they were using the
scaffolding for ingress and egress."

"Everything okay?" Liana asks, her smile uncertain on
Ophelia's helmet screen. As uncertain as the fucking scaffolding they're probably going to have to climb.

"We're fine. Just contemplating another way in." Severin
sounds easy, unconcerned, as he strides forward along the
building front, looking for something, but Ophelia wonders
how much of that is for Liana's benefit. She's beginning to suspect that Liana's concerns about a cave-in or other disastrous
outcome for this little adventure might not have been so out-
landish. This line item on the mission assignment requires a
thorough survey, with visual documentation of the entire excavation site. Montrose is desperate to figure out what Pinnacle
was up to when it was here.

"Just come back tomorrow with the drone," Kate says. Her
sharply angled bangs are hanging in her eyes, and she huffs a
breath upward to move them. "We don't need trouble on this
one. Liana and I are almost at the towers."

"Can't risk it getting tangled up in something we can't see,"

Severin responds, but he sounds distracted. Ophelia can't quite see him anymore; he's lost to the snowy background on the far side of the scaffolding, except for a few sharp motions that make him stand out. Whose idea was it to make envirosuits uniformly white, anyway?

"Here," Severin calls. He steps back into view and waves Ophelia forward.

She makes her way toward him, stepping in his footsteps, or trying to, despite his longer stride.

When she reaches him, he's standing at the base of the uncovered portion of the building, holding on to a ladder.

No. It is an assemblage of fraying dark green straps formed into a ladderlike structure, dangling from the upper-story window.

"You've got to be kidding me," she says, unable to stop herself.

"It's probably how they first gained access, working their way down," Severin says. "We're lucky they didn't remove it when they built the scaffold."

"Lucky," she repeats.

"It's perfectly safe," he says, a hint of exasperation entering his voice. "It's a portable ladder, probably pulled from their ship kit. Designed to withstand virtually any kind of environmental conditions. For a time, anyway."

He doesn't wait for her response but pulls on the ladder, and then even steps onto it with his full weight.

Snow falls from the rounded opening above, but nothing else. But the entire contraption scrapes from side to side just with his movement, let alone the wind.

"See? It's good." Severin steps back onto the ground but gives the ladder another tug for good measure. "Let's go. The snow is coming down faster now."

The harsh flecks of icy moisture do seem to be clicking against her helmet at a faster rate, that's true.

"Roger that. Same over here," Kate adds. "We're bagging and tagging samples now."

Ophelia is not afraid of heights, but being out of control? Being attached to wildly chaotic conditions with only the faintest grip on what's happening around her? She swallows hard, her palms damp with sweat inside her gloves. There's a limit to how far she'll go to get a patient to trust her.

Severin arches his eyebrows at Ophelia, looking at her directly through his helmet faceplate. His image does the same through the common channel, so it's a double dose of disapproval. "I assume that telling you it would be faster and more efficient for you to wait out here is pointless," he says.

Ophelia immediately feels a rush of returning fury. He thinks she can't handle it.

"I'll trade you," Suresh offers.

Everyone ignores him.

"You shouldn't go in alone," Liana pipes in.

"I'm here to help. Let's go," Ophelia says, all but daring Severin to take it back.

"After you," he says, holding the base of the ladder steady with one foot and a hand, waving her forward with the other hand. But she doesn't miss the self-satisfied smile flickering at the corners of his mouth.

Son of a bitch. She freezes, her foot caught in the first rung of the ladder.

He manipulated her. And well.

She's not sure which she's more unsettled by—that she didn't catch it or that he already seems to know how to effectively do so.

"We didn't have time to argue, Doctor," Severin says, when she glares at him. But beneath her irritation, grudging admiration pokes its grumpy head up.

That's all she has opportunity for, though, on that line of thought. Her entire focus is on gripping the rungs above her, one at a time, and pulling herself up onto the next without losing her balance. Severin's weight at the bottom helps, but not enough.

When she reaches the opening, she leans her upper body through it and half scrambles, half falls inside, kicking her legs free from the tangle of the second-to-last step.

There is a reason she has an office job. This is not her forte.

She lands on the floor hard enough to jar her teeth. The floor is gritty beneath her palms—not a sensation, obviously, with her suit gloves in the way, but a sound that comes through loud and clear on her external mic. She pushes herself up to her feet to look around, breathless.

Severin joins her in a matter of moments, neatly boosting himself inside.

"It's empty," she says, gesturing around herself. The space is essentially a block of rooms within a larger room, crumbled stone piles indicating where walls once stood. The ceiling is cracked and falling in in one corner. More rubble. The two metal stakes—she's not sure what else to call them—pounded into the stone floor to hold the ladder in place are pretty much it.

It's not as if she was expecting to walk in and find anything recognizable as furniture or tech—especially as the original residents weren't human, and how would she even know what she was looking at? But to find nothing but snow, rocks, and a thin layer of fine black grit over everything is disappointing.

He nods. "Upper levels were exposed longer, and I assume Pinnacle took everything, if there was anything left to find. We may have better luck on lower levels. They might not have gotten to all of those before they left."

Which means more time on the ladder. Fantastic.

Severin turns away from her, and the forward-facing light on the exterior of his helmet brightens. On her helmet screen, she sees his feed switch to indicate recording, with a red flashing circle above the view of the room. They'll all be able to hear him, but none of the common channel transmissions will interrupt.

"This is Commander Ethan Severin, documenting existing

excavation site identified as location of interest number 147B, formerly code-named the New Sistine Chapel in Pinnacle report briefing 113."

The New Sistine Chapel? Ophelia rolls her eyes. *Jesus, Uncle Darwin. Fire the naming department, please.*

The bright light turns toward her. "Dr. Ophelia Bray assisting, in a volunteer capacity," Severin adds.

Her own face, pale, small, and tinted blue in her helmet, appears in the feed. Her brow is furrowed in the image, and she looks unhappy.

Ophelia resists the childish urge to flip Severin and his external helmet cam a very unprofessional finger. Only because she's sure he'd insist on rerecording—and he'd be right to do so; she doesn't need to get fired over something so petty and stupid, what is she even thinking?—and she doesn't want to be here any longer than necessary.

Standing here in the center of this now open space, she shivers, feeling the tiny hairs at the back of her neck rise to attention.

Something about this place just feels . . . wrong. She's not even sure why at first.

She turns in a circle, trying to identify the feeling, tuning out Severin's narration for the recording.

Maybe it's just that all the *nothing* here is somehow eerier than finding unidentifiable detritus.

Like, there should be stuff here, signs of former life. Although she knows nothing about the decay rate of whatever materials might have been used for such things on this planet, or how long they would last in these conditions, it still feels as if something's missing.

No. That's not it. Not missing.

Hiding.

There's something—or someone—here. That's what it feels like. As if she and Severin have just missed someone sweeping through, removing all signs of themselves and anyone else. It's

not a scent left hanging in the air, obviously; even if that were
so, she wouldn't be able to smell it. It's not even a noise, echoing in the distance. Just a *sense* of not being alone.

She remembers the figure in the storm earlier, the one she
thought was Birch. The one she dismissed as an optical illusion, a trick of the mind. But what if it wasn't?

"Ready?" Severin asks, at her side suddenly, and Ophelia
jumps.

"Yes, right, okay," she says quickly, to cover. The recording
icon is no longer flashing on his feed. He must have paused it.
"Back to the ladder?" she asks, trying to sound like she's been
paying attention.

He looks at her oddly. "No, I thought we'd try the stairs."
He gestures toward a doorway on the far side of the room.

"The stairs? There are stairs?"

There are not stairs. However, there are two rows of pegs
extending from the wall in what appears to be a corridor of
sorts. The pegs are rounded and made of the same stone as
the building itself. Actually, the pegs look more like a natural
outgrowth of the stone—about a half meter in length and set
at regular intervals in a gently descending fashion. Of course,
Ophelia's not even sure if the building/wall is truly stone or if
that's just the closest human analogue. Because stone doesn't
really do that, right? Grow pegs without a seam or some other
sign of manufacturing.

Plasti-fab boards have been laid across the lower row of
pegs, lashed together and to the pegs themselves to stabilize
them. Somewhat.

They shift and creak with every step she takes, despite trying to follow Severin exactly. She finds herself reaching up
to grasp the pegs in the row just above her head for extra
help with her balance. They are smooth and worn, almost the

perfect size for grasping, just slightly too large for her hand and spaced at just the right intervals. That couldn't be a co-incidence.

Brachiation. The Lyrians might well have used their arms to transport themselves short distances instead of walking up-right. That's what one of the astro-bio archeologists had hy-pothesized in the mission briefing. The pegs would certainly support that idea.

The last plasti-fab board lies across the opening to the next level down, making it easy to hop off the pegs to the floor. Ophe-lia imagines that the Lyrians might have swung themselves over without needing the reassurance of something beneath their feet.

This level is virtually identical to the first one. Emptiness. Rubble. More of the dark grit, like ash but shinier.

It's the same on the next level down, and the one after that.

They find the bones on the first level beneath the snow line.

It's darker down here, not even the limited sunlight making it through the blocked openings. Though the Pinnacle team has shoveled out or melted most of the snow in the central room, there are still mounds of the stuff around the edges of the outer wall.

Along with other things.

Ophelia kneels in a corner for a closer look at a pile of what might be fabric remnants and a collapsed chain of rings made of some flexible material, each oval slightly larger than the next. When she gently lifts one edge of the closest ring, with one fingertip, to get an idea of how long the chain might be, of what the contraption might have been, she finds something familiar.

Dull yellowish-white stones, smooth and oddly shaped, ex-posed in a cracked and tattered leather wrapping.

It's the fingernails, though—black, flaking, and falling away at the opposite end—that give it away.

A hand, with even the tiniest of bones still in place. Undis-turbed by time, predators, or the weather. Just as if it had been left to deteriorate where it fell, skin and muscle rotting away to this mummy-like state.

Bones, bright white and splintered, poking up from a shattered mess of a hand, red blood and torn flesh. A last-ditch defense to protect the head, the face, but fingers and palm were nothing against the heavy swing of the wrench.

Ophelia stands up fast. "Fuck."

Severin must register the alarm in her voice, because he doesn't even bother to shut down the recording or berate her for injecting profanity into it, just cuts across the room.

"There's, uh, a hand over here." She points.

He crouches down and gingerly lifts the ring she indicates.

"Is that human? One of Pinnacle's, I mean?" Her boots grit on the floor as she turns in place, looking around for dried bloodstains, any sign of the chaos. People scrambling for their lives tend to make a mess.

"There's nothing in the Pinnacle mission report about it," Severin says with a frown.

"Like that means anything," she says before she can stop herself.

He looks up at her sharply, but she doesn't take it back. Seriously, does he expect her to believe that all mission reports are comprehensive collections of fact instead of shaded half-truths to protect the team and the company? She might have thought that once, but if so, this experience with this team and Ava have taught her otherwise.

He frowns. "It doesn't look quite right. The fingers are too long." He stretches his gloved hand out above it for comparison. "I don't think it's human."

The common channel crackles abruptly with static, startling them both.

". . . return . . . storm . . . samples. Copy?" Kate's voice is broken and fading with interference.

Ophelia realizes then that the images in the corner of her

helmet screen are frozen. The common channel is breaking up in the deteriorating weather conditions.

"Come on. We're running out of time." Severin stands. "It's just remains. Been here long before us and will be long after. Pinnacle probably just didn't see it."

"Except it's not just remains. Who leaves a hand behind? It's been cut off. Look, you can see it." She points to the blunt edge of the hand, where leathery skin and bone are both severed in a straightish line. Right where the wrist would be on a human. "And that cut does not look fresh, so it's not like Pinnacle was packaging up the rest of the body and just forgot it."

Severin glances at her for a moment too long, and Ophelia flushes, as if she's exposed herself. Dropped her envirosuit and her clothes to bare herself and her metaphoric scars.

"We don't know their rituals or practices," he says finally. "But this is documented in our findings now. We'll leave it for the archeologists, anthropologists, and whoever to work out. Not our job."

He's not wrong, and yet Ophelia can't shake her increasing unease.

Anything that happened here happened a long time ago. It can't hurt us. But that doesn't feel as reassuring as it should.

"Let's try to capture at least one more floor before we have to leave," Severin says, turning toward the central corridor that runs vertically through the building's core.

Reluctantly, Ophelia follows him down another set of "stairs."

But he stops abruptly as soon as he steps off the plasti-fab boards onto the next floor.

Ophelia sees why as soon as she does the same. The walls on the far side are crumbling inward, as if the building is being squeezed like a meal-pak. There is no getting to the next level or any lower in the building, at least not without special equipment.

Next to her, Severin edges forward. Pebbles crumble and clatter somewhere nearby.

"Careful," she begins. "I think—"

He stiffens abruptly, peering over the far edge into the debris.

Ophelia flinches, throws her hands out for balance, expecting the floor to give way on both of them. But nothing happens. And Severin is still just standing there, staring down at something.

After a moment, she cautiously moves toward him, one step and then another, until she reaches him.

When she looks down to see what he's seeing, it takes her brain a second to make sense of it, to convert the raw data of parts and pieces into . . . arms, legs, torsos, skulls.

Bodies. Piled on one another. Sightless eye sockets stare upward at them from above gaping mouths, teeth glinting in their helmet lights. The forms are longer, leaner in desiccation than they must have been in life, all stiffened and dried out. Hair or fur, Ophelia isn't sure which, or if it matters, strands in varying shades of orangish and white, stir in the air she and Severin have disturbed with their arrival above.

The remains match, more or less, the sketches from Pinnacle's astro-bio archeologists in the mission brief. The Lyrians are perhaps a little taller than predicted, more muscular, given the broadness of the shoulders. It's hard to tell with them in this condition.

Ophelia's gaze lands on a particularly confusing collection of limbs and faces, until her mind finally sorts it out. This is not an aberration, a two-headed being, but a child still clutched to its parent's chest. The tiny face stares up at her, as if looking for rescue far, far too late.

Maybe she should feel elation, excitement—this is one of the few instances of former intelligent life being found, even as remains. But she can't. Dread that she can't even articulate or fathom fills her, like weights pulling her beneath the surface.

"This should have been reported." Severin's voice is hoarse.

Reported? Pinnacle should have shouted about it, sending

out the news on every streamer channel it could find. But it had not.

The dread in her stomach increases.

"They must have been trapped, in an earthquake maybe?" Severin continues. "If it was an asteroid, then there might have been huge tectonic—"

"No." Ophelia shakes her head, grim comprehension suddenly filling her. Now, now she understands what her subconscious was trying to tell her a moment ago. "Look. They're stacked up on one another, not in a group." She can picture it easily, unfortunately. *Moving toward an exit that is no longer an exit, panicked cries.* "No one runs toward certain death unless there's something forcing them to it." Extraterrestrial or not, there are just some instincts that nearly all species are going to share, assuming evolution is in play—like the overwhelming drive to survive.

Once again she has the sensation that she's said too much. Severin turns his head to give her another, even more scrutinizing look. But she doesn't care. Not this time.

"I don't like this," she says flatly, expecting him to argue or dismiss her.

"Agreed," he says with a curt nod. "We're done here."

He turns, and they carefully, one at a time, edge their way back onto the plasti-fab boards and begin the climb back up.

Ophelia can feel that prickling sensation on the back of her neck again, that feeling of being watched or not being alone. Because of the bodies? No, that doesn't seem right. It's more ephemeral than that. Besides, the Lyrians are dead, gone. This feels more . . . present than that.

Or it's something else.

You need to be careful, Ophelia. Paranoia is the first symptom.

She shakes her head roughly to dismiss the thought—her family's bullshit, not hers. But with every step, she expects the boards to give out under their feet, a series of pegs crumbling, sending them plummeting back down. Or the walls around them to give a mighty groan and finally give in to gravity, burying them beneath tons of debris.

She and Severin make it out, though, to the level above, and then to the next one, without issue.

Severin, however, must feel a similar concern, because rather than leading her back up to the ladder, he heads to the outer wall window/door as soon as they reach a floor above the snow line and pushes through the accumulation of snow to exit.

It forces them to clamber over the unsteady scaffolding on the lowest level—another opportunity for catastrophe, for the entire structure to collapse on their heads. But they make it out unscathed.

When they're finally standing on the snow-packed ground, away from the building and the shaky scaffolding, in a blinding whirl of icy flecks and wind, Ophelia should feel better. Relieved.

Only she doesn't. Not entirely. The rock-hard pit of dread in her stomach remains.

They start slogging toward the hab, Severin at her side this time instead of ahead of her. She hopes he knows where he's going. She can't see anything, and there's no orange guide cord this time.

But he moves confidently, as if following a signal she can't see or hear.

The common channel buzzes intermittently in her ear, but she can't hear any transmissions and now the only face on her helmet screen is Severin's.

"I realize this may be against the rules or your personal ethos," he says a moment later, sounding uncomfortable, formal. "And I respect that, if so."

Ophelia waits.

"But the team didn't witness any of . . . what we found, because of the interference. And I'm not sure that they need to know about it. I'd prefer to keep this to ourselves. For now."

It doesn't require much imagination to conjure the varied reactions. Kate would probably be fine, and Birch would be . . . Birch. But it would worry Liana, who is obviously already struggling. And Ophelia could even see Suresh being unnerved by the development. Death isn't as funny when you're the one caught off guard by it.

"No need to inflict additional trauma," she says. "It's ancient history, literally."

He nods, his expression relieved, with a hint of grudging respect. "Thank you." At least they can agree on this.

But even that doesn't make the inexplicable dread in her stomach—and now also perched on her shoulders like one of those old-timey stone gargoyles that her grandmother added to more than one of her residences "for the look of it"—go away.

15

The hab is warm and inviting. At least by contrast to the storm now raging outside. It's still too big and uncomfortably empty for their small party.

But it is reassuringly human and familiar, which is a comfort after where they've just been.

As soon as she and Severin are released from decontamination in the airlock and shed their envirosuits, they're immediately pulled in different directions. After being scolded by Liana—and Kate, to Ophelia's surprise—for staying out too long in the storm, Severin heads toward the bunk room, and presumably his tablet, to transfer/save/upload or whatever needs to be done with the footage.

Then Kate recruits Ophelia to act as a witness as Suresh, fresh out of a shower with his hair sparkling like flecks of ice are clinging to it, takes official custody of the samples Kate and Liana brought back, adding them to the inventory.

As he lifts each vial and replaces it in the cold storage sample container, Ophelia gets a better look at what they brought back. Mainly jagged bits of rock, shiny like cinders. The largest is about the size of her thumb, but splinters of the same material, sharp and pointed, rattle soundlessly in the bottom of double-sealed polycarbonate tubes as well.

"Six vials," he says, carefully marking details on a tablet. "Each weighing between one-point-two-seven and five grams, according to the digital readout on the casing, put in place at the time of collection. Samples are irregular in shape. Black in color. Do you confirm?" He looks to Kate and then Ophelia and they both affirm the details.

"It was weird," Liana says, over Ophelia's shoulder.

Ophelia turns, raising her eyebrows in question.

"The towers. There's, like, nothing to them. They aren't buildings or anything. Just big hunks of that stuff."

"But they're smooth," Kate adds. "No signs of carving or jointures or anything. It's fucking weird."

"Thank you, ladies," Suresh says, snapping the lid back on the sample storage container and setting the lock on it.

While Liana helps him wheel/carry it back across the central hub to the C side module designated as inventory storage, Ophelia turns to Kate. "Have you seen Birch? I just wanted to check on him. See if his head was any better."

"He's here. Somewhere." She looks around the central hub with a frown. "Suresh was yelling at him about taking his toothpaste tablets about fifteen minutes ago." Kate rolls her eyes.

Ophelia nods. On her way past the galley she collects a protein pack, this one cinnamon soy, for a midday meal, and heads to her "office." She keeps an eye out for Birch, but without luck. Probably better that way. He needs to come to her on his own, or maybe with a nudge from Severin. Her seeking him out is only going to repel him further.

In the farthest hab on the A side, the noise of the others fades away, except for the occasional loud clang that travels up through the corridor, or possibly through the environmental system. Kate working on something in syscon, Ophelia guesses.

After forcing the cinnamon soy packet down, Ophelia drags a chair over to one of the lab tables and starts pulling the data from the iVR control tablet to set up a regular report, which she'll be able to use to create a full mission status at the end. Then she switches over to taking notes on her session with Liana, to help keep her memory fresh.

Exhaustion catches up with her quickly, her eyes heavy and

gritty as she tries to focus. Still adjusting to planetary conditions, post cold sleep. She props her head up on one fist.

What happened out there, what she and Severin found, it feels so far away, here in the hab. Like it's not real, just something she read in a novel or saw in a dream. Dead, mostly mummified nonhumans stacked up like cordwood is just not—

Bang.

Her eyes snap open abruptly against the heaviness of sleep, heart racing in her chest. The loud sound still echoes in her head, like a vibration hanging in the air. What was that? It sounded like the heavy crack of metal against metal.

Like a power wrench crashing into a space station wall just above someone's head.

She sits up, arm tingling from cut-off circulation, her back aching from her slumped-over position. How long has she been asleep?

Cocking her head to one side, Ophelia listens, straining her ears. But there's nothing now, just the sense of disruption. Hypnopompic hallucination, probably. Carson syndrome, formerly known as the horrifically named exploding head syndrome. Common with sleep deprivation and high-anxiety situations.

"Hey," a voice says behind her.

Ophelia jolts and spins in her chair, hand clasped to her chest in surprise.

"Liana," she says. "Did you hear that?"

Liana eyes her with confusion. "You mean me saying hi?"

"No, the bang before that," Ophelia says, already feeling foolish. "It just . . ." She shakes her head. "Never mind. What's up?"

"It's a team tradition to eat last meal together at the end of our first day," Liana says, then pauses. "Actually, we end up eating together most nights. Except for Kate. And sometimes Birch. They need their alone time." She pauses again. "Not *together* alone time," she adds quickly, her face flushing. "Anyway, I just thought you might want to join us."

"That's very nice of you," Ophelia begins. "But I don't know if that would be a good—"

"You're part of the team," Liana says, folding her arms across her chest stubbornly. "You should be there. Besides, it's fun and it'll help to get you know everyone better."

She's trying to help. The realization sends a flash of warmth through Ophelia.

Probably a thank-you, if Ophelia has to guess, for not letting Severin go alone today. It's a lovely gesture, though Ophelia is not quite sure the others will see it in the same light.

"All right," Ophelia says, standing up. Stiff muscles in her legs complain at the sudden change. Slogging through the snow and ice did a number on her today. She should be in better shape, though it's not as if she's planning on any more outdoor expeditions until they're heading for the lander to leave this place.

When she and Liana arrive in the central hub, most everyone else, excluding Birch, is already around the table. No one seems concerned about Birch's absence this time, though, so Ophelia assumes this is due to the aforementioned need for "alone time."

The relaxed chatter rises and falls gently, like water lapping at a shore, between Kate, Severin, and somewhat Suresh, who is also drumming an aimless pattern on the table. Meal-paks wait in front of them, along with a hot water dispenser.

Liana skips ahead, scooping a meal-pak from the open crate on the floor near the table, and settles into an empty plastic chair next to Suresh. She elbows him hard in the process, knocking him even further out of rhythm. Kate is on the other side of Suresh, the longer portion of her hair tied back, revealing a smudge of grease on her neck.

The three of them are on one side, Severin alone on the other, with two empty chairs to his left.

Great.

But to Ophelia's surprise, before she even has time to hesitate, he gives her a nod of acknowledgment and kicks out the chair next to him in welcome, all without breaking his conversation with Kate.

Ophelia feels, for one ridiculous moment, like she's back at Marchand-Brighton and being invited to sit with Anberlyn and her friends at the basketball game.

She grabs a meal-pak from the crate and takes the offered seat, hoping the heat in her cheeks isn't visible. She's supposed to be an adult. An objective, professional adult, for fuck's sake.

After dispensing a steaming blast of water into her meal-pak, Kate pushes the insulated container toward Severin, even as she drops her now heated pak on the table and blows on her fingers.

"Trust me, you want it hot," Kate says, seeing Ophelia's skeptical expression.

Suresh opens his mouth, a glint in his eye.

"Stop," Severin says as he fixes his own meal-pak. "Just don't."

"Fine." Suresh slumps back in his chair.

When it's her turn, Ophelia fills her meal-pak with the hot water, though with maybe not quite as much as Kate and Severin, and she leaves it to cool slightly on the table. She picked chicken tetrazzini, which appears to have the consistency of paste. She expects the flavor to be much the same.

"That's a mistake. Burns off more of your taste buds this way," Kate says in a muddled voice as she sucks in air to cool off her first mouthful. Once she manages to swallow—painfully, it looks like to Ophelia—she turns her attention to Severin. "If we've got time tomorrow, I want to head back to the lander for replacement parts."

As the two of them talk shop, Ophelia lets her focus drift,

words flowing around her in a comfortable haze. Until something Liana says catches her attention.

"—get to play with Marvin, Mabel, and Denise tomorrow," Liana says.

"Who?" Ophelia asks.

Suresh groans. "They're just autodrillers, Li. Not pets."

"You named the autodrillers?" Ophelia asks. Autodrillers are for ice core samples, she knows that much. Naming conventions around autodrillers, not so much.

"Of course," Liana says, surprised.

Severin breaks off his conversation with Kate to speak to Ophelia. "They had names to begin with," he tells her dryly.

Ophelia glances back to Liana for confirmation.

"M-426x doesn't suit Mabel's personality," Liana says with a shrug.

"You can tell the difference between their personalities?" Ophelia asks, amused. Anthropomorphism is such a human thing to do. People name their cars, their ships, their tablets, and apparently their autodrillers.

"Oh yeah." Liana nods emphatically. "Especially Denise." She makes a disgusted noise.

Ophelia can't resist looking over at Severin for his response. He rolls his eyes, fond amusement playing around his mouth, dimples appearing in stark relief.

It transforms him, utterly. Makes Ophelia's breath catch, her chest ache with the powerful tug of an emotion she can't identify at first.

Then it clicks. Longing. That's what it is.

Ophelia looks away quickly, her breath short and face warm.

Nope, no, we are not doing this. He's your patient, technically. He's also the mission commander.

"You should come with us tomorrow," Liana says to her, completely oblivious to Ophelia's inner consternation. "I can show you how they—" She stops abruptly, pressing the heel of her hand against her brow above her left eye.

"Are you okay?" Ophelia leans forward, concern pulling her out of her ruminations. "Is your head *still* hurting?"

"Just off and on today." Liana summons a smile that wavers at the edges. "Gone by tomorrow, I'm sure."

Ophelia frowns. "If it gets any worse—"

"It won't," Liana says firmly. She lowers her hand, as if determined to make a show of how fine she is. Then her gaze flicks upward.

"Hey, Birch," Liana calls, speaking past Ophelia. "We saved you a seat."

Ophelia twists in her chair to see Birch entering the central hub from the C side. He's striding with speed and purpose. Ophelia assumes it's hunger—or perhaps annoyance at the location of his seat, next to her—driving him, but he bypasses her side of the table entirely, cutting around the narrow end.

"Where are you—" Liana begins, as he moves past her chair to Suresh's.

"Hey, what's up, Bir—" Suresh starts to say, but he doesn't get a chance to finish.

Birch grabs the back of his chair and yanks him away from the table, then dumps Suresh onto the floor, like someone shaking trash loose from a can. Then Birch drops down next to him, draws his arm back, and begins beating the ever-loving shit out of Suresh.

A stunned silence holds for a second, the sudden violence as unexpected and unwelcome as a knock on the outer airlock door. Then Severin's chair screeches against the metal floor as he launches himself up and around the table.

Ophelia is frozen for a moment longer, the meaty smack of flesh striking flesh curdling her stomach.

"Jesus Christ! Birch, what are you doing?" Kate demands, yanking ineffectively at Birch's nonpunching arm.

Something about her voice, the fear and frustration in it, breaks Ophelia free from her temporary paralysis. She shoves back from the table and darts around to the other side to help.

Severin grasps the back of Birch's jumpsuit and hauls him off of Suresh, locking Birch's arm behind his back and bending him forward. She and Liana drag Suresh away, putting some distance between Birch and him in case Severin's hold fails.

Suresh's face is a bloody mask, with a gash beneath his eye, a split lip, and a rapidly swelling nose. "*What the fuck?*" he shouts, voice muffled, as he holds his hand to his mouth.

"What did you do?" Birch demands, twisting in Severin's grip.

"Relax," Severin says evenly. Only a tightened muscle at his jawline shows the strain of holding Birch in place. "Just relax."

"What are you talking about, man?" Suresh swipes at the blood trickling down his cheek, smearing it.

Ophelia stands and grabs for one of the recyclable cloths on the table that someone brought from the galley to serve as napkins.

"The samples. One of them is missing," Birch spits.

A deeper, thicker silence immediately floods the space.

Ophelia pauses, cloth in hand, unsure if she heard correctly. Samples from the towers? That's what this is about?

For the thousandth time since the start of this experience, she feels she's missing something important. Unspoken information that would make all of this make sense. It's like feeling the breeze of a near miss but never learning what danger you just dodged or what to look out for next time.

But Ophelia swallows back the questions rising in her throat. Asking now will only cement her status as an outsider, and experience says that even if they're angry with each other they'll close ranks more tightly against her.

"I don't know what you're talking about. I haven't touched them since we loaded them into the containment unit hours ago." Suresh sits up, all indignation, as Liana hovers nearby. "What are you doing, checking on them anyway? That's my job."

"There were six. Now there's only five," Birch says, ignoring Suresh's question.

"How did you even get in there?" Suresh demands. Ophelia

holds out the cloth, and he snatches it from her to hold it against the cut under his eye. "I changed the passcode for this mission."

Liana shifts uncomfortably. "It's probably still your birthday, just backward this time," she says softly.

Suresh glances up at her, both hurt and startled. "How did you—"

"Because it's what you always do," Birch snaps. "Because you're a vain, self-centered little—"

"Enough, enough!" Severin shouts, his voice booming through the central hub. He glances toward Ophelia, giving her an opening.

The opening, the one she's been waiting for, she realizes with a convoluted mix of surprise and appreciation.

She straightens her shoulders. "Everyone needs to take a breath so we can get this figured out," Ophelia says. "Shouting accusations—"

"But I didn't—" Suresh protests.

"—and denials isn't going to fix anything," Ophelia says, leveling a look at him until his mouth snaps closed. "We're going to take this one step at a time. Everyone will be heard."

"Or we could just see for ourselves," Kate says over the rattle of wheels as she emerges from the C side, half pushing, half carrying the mobile sample containment unit. Ophelia hadn't even realized she'd left the central hub.

Kate brings the unit to a point between Birch and Suresh. Her fingers fly over the prominent keypad on the front, and the lock on the sample containment unit releases with an audible click, giving truth to Liana's supposition about Suresh's passcode.

Suresh's mouth tightens, and he presses the cloth harder against his face, fingertips going white with the pressure.

A wave of frosty air billows over the edge of the containment unit, and Kate peers inside. "One, two, three, four, five . . ." She pauses, frowning.

"I told you," Birch hisses at Suresh, who holds his free hand up in a gesture of innocence.

"I didn't do it!" Suresh argues, then he turns to Ophelia. "I put six of them in there, didn't I? You saw me—"

"Wait, wait," Kate says. "Hold on." She reaches inside and delicately adjusts something. After a moment, she pulls her hand back out, a see-through vial with a sealed top in her fingers.

"It just slipped down in the holder," she says to Birch. "That's all, okay?" Her voice is gentler than Ophelia's ever heard it.

Kate replaces the vial and then edges the unit closer to him, presumably so he can see for himself.

After a moment, the tension slides from his body and Birch gives a defeated nod.

"I told you," Suresh says, but he's smart enough to keep his voice to a murmur.

Paranoia. Conflict. Violence.

Ophelia doesn't like how the pieces are fitting together. *What if it's ERS, oh, if it's ERS out* here, *and what if you can't stop it, what happens if it spreads, what happens if you—*

She shoves the panicked chatter in her head back into its box. This is exactly what she's here for.

"Can I let you go now?" Severin asks Birch, in that same unflappable tone.

Birch jerks his head in a sullen nod from his still bent-over position. "I'm fine."

"No," Severin says, as he releases him. "You're not. Both of you get checked out and patched up."

It takes Ophelia a moment to realize that he means for her to do it.

16

Birch shifts uneasily in the gray patient chair in Ophelia's office.

Suresh left a few moments ago, accompanied by Severin. She sealed Suresh's split lip and the gash under his eye with the portable medical unit from the medikit that Kate brought to her—though neither she nor Suresh was exactly at ease with it so close to his face. He didn't even protest when she made him wear the safety goggles, which was a relief. Ophelia has basic knowledge of how the PMU works—how everything in the medikit works—but absolutely no practical experience. She's not that kind of doctor. But she wasn't about to argue with Severin's order when it gave her what she wanted—a chance to talk one-on-one with members of the team.

Suresh was uncharacteristically silent the whole time, answering her questions with a word or two and only when required.

The normally taciturn Birch, though, is downright loquacious by comparison.

"I don't need this," Birch says, as Ophelia stands over him, holding the med-scanner wand near his forehead. He holds up his bloodied knuckles, the skin split from the impact with Suresh's face. "Just slap some gel-bands on my hands. I'm not sick."

Maybe not, but he doesn't look healthy either, now that she has a closer view of him. His green eyes are bloodshot, and his skin holds the grayish tinge of exhaustion.

"Just hold still. I'm being thorough. Commander's orders," Ophelia says.

He narrows his eyes at her. "That's convenient."

Ophelia ignores the comment. "You want to talk to me about what happened out there? With the samples?" she asks, keeping her focus on the med-scanner, mainly to give him the illusion that this is a casual, informal chat.

Birch gives a derisive snort. "With you? No thanks." He scrubs his palms against his jumpsuit, then his right hand drifts over to scratch his left arm, fingers worming beneath the sleeve of his jumpsuit to reach skin.

On the underside of his exposed wrist, Ophelia catches a glimpse of a memorial block—a solid black rectangle. Tradition on the mining stations is to ink assignments on your skin, an indication of the commitment. Like family. And when a significant death occurs, the assignment name is blocked out and covered by black ink, turning it into a memorial band for those who were lost.

"I guess I don't understand," Ophelia says. "Even if a sample were gone, it's not as if you can't get more." She tips her head toward the window and the city in the distance.

Birch stops scratching and looks up at her, past the med-scanner wand. His gaze searches her face, and disbelief slowly etches itself in his features. "You really have no idea," he says slowly.

Ophelia flinches, and the med-scanner wand chirps in protest. Quickly, she readjusts to keep the wand on task.

Birch shakes his head in disgust. "Jesus, how did you convince them to let you out here?"

Her face heats, and the desire to rattle off her every accomplishment, from graduating a year early from Marchand-Brighton to her journal publications on the effects of red dwarf light on the human circadian rhythm, is hard to suppress. Striving to prove herself is as ingrained in her as the repeated scoldings not to thank the help and the inner workings of the T118 station bot cleaner.

It's not about you, Phe.

"If I'm missing something, why don't you explain it to me," she says instead.

He barks out a laugh. "Are you kidding?"

Ophelia doesn't say anything, and he stops laughing.

"Listen, Doctor," he says with a sneer. "I realize that you're used to people cracking open, spilling their guts—"

His words trigger a graphic visual in her mind, and she represses a shudder.

"—to give you what you want, but that's not going to be me, okay?"

Ophelia moves the wand to hover over his right hand. "Hold it out, please. Palm down."

"Nothing's broken," he protests, but then, with an exaggerated sigh, he does as she asked. She suspects Severin's lingering presence somewhere in the corridor has something to do with it.

"I realize I'm not your favorite person," she says after a moment. "But I'm here to listen. To help."

He remains silent.

"Can you tell me about last night? Why you were really in the airlock?" she presses, as she waits for the wand to finish scanning for breaks and fractures.

Birch sets his jaw resolutely.

When the med-scanner signals that the bones in his hand are whole, she lowers the wand and steps back. He immediately begins scratching at his left arm again, almost as if he can't help it. But the med-scanner hadn't reported an infection or irritation. Stress, maybe. One of Ophelia's patients used to break out in hives every time she had to interact with anyone outside her team.

She returns the scanner to the medikit and settles across from him in her chair.

"Are we done here?" he demands.

"Not yet," she says. "I want to talk."

"Seems you've already been doing plenty of that," he mutters, his leg jiggling with nervous energy.

"Are you finding yourself worried or preoccupied with what the others are doing or thinking?" she asks.

Jaw tight, Birch stares at a point across the room, ignoring her.

All right, then. "Have you seen or heard things that couldn't possibly be real?" It's a risk, she's pushing too hard already, but she has to know. "Sometimes it may present itself as someone you know or it might simply be voices in your head that aren't your own."

A twitch rolls through Birch, like a full-body spasm. Then he stands slowly to loom over her, fists clenched at his sides. "Is this a game to you?" he demands, his voice low and gritty with anger.

Ophelia retreats slightly in her chair, caught between offense and an instinctive pulse of fear. "No, of course not. I'm just trying to ascertain whether you're a danger to yourself or—"

"Do you get off on this?" he persists, edging closer. She can't get up without colliding with him. "This sick, twisted mindfuck you've got going on?"

Ophelia gapes at him. "What are you—"

"Yeah, you do." A grim smile pulls at his face. "You put that shit in my head with that fucking band." He jabs his index finger at his temple, revealing vicious, red scratch marks down his wrist. "Now you want me to talk about it."

"What . . . I don't . . ."

Birch advances on her quickly, and she slides back in her chair until her spine is pressing tight against the plastic.

"What? . . . You don't *what*?" he repeats, in a higher-pitched, mocking tone as he towers over her. "I just happen to dream about that butcher for the first time in years, my brother's skull bashed in and his brains on the fucking floor, and you're here with your 'new system'?" Spittle flies from his mouth, landing a lukewarm splotch on her upper lip. "I see my brother calling to me from outside the hab, pleading with me for help, and that's a coincidence?"

Her ears are ringing, a high whine of panic and confusion, like a drill through her brain.

"I don't understand," Ophelia finally manages through dry lips, her tongue a dying husk in the bottom of her mouth.

Birch leans down, bracing himself on the arms of her chair, bracketing her in place and baring his teeth at her in a grin. They're pink. As Ophelia watches, a trickle of blood seeps out from his gums and into the seam between his front teeth.

What the fuck.

"You enjoy screwing with people's heads. Just like your old man. Well, not exactly, huh?" He raps his bloodied knuckles against his skull. "Mine's still intact."

Her throat closes off, sealed tighter than the imaginary Bray family vault everyone is so obsessed with. Her lungs rebel in her chest, struggling to take in air.

This is not . . . He cannot possibly . . . No one . . . I can't.

Her shock must show on her face.

"Yeah. Maybe we should be the ones asking the questions about you, Dr. Bray," he snaps. She tries not to flinch at the smell of hot metal and sweat emanating from him, the spray of saliva and blood against her skin. "Are you hearing voices? Seeing people who aren't there?" He mimics her again. "If anyone is a danger to the rest of us, it's you."

Birch leans closer still, and she turns her face away, her heart beating a frantic tattoo in her chest. "You think I don't recognize you?" He breathes against her skin. "I knew the moment Severin sent us your mission profile, *Lark Bledsoe.*"

Though spoken in a harsh whisper, the name seems to echo in the hab, in her head.

Birch pushes off her chair in disgust. "You look just like your father."

17

It's happened once before.

When Ophelia was sixteen, walking out of Marchand-Brighton Academy, bags in hand, for her first semester break, a man approached her on the sidewalk.

He was an up-and-coming journo-streamer, she found out later. At the time, she had assumed he was an older brother of one of the other students, or even an assistant on pickup duty. Early twenties, probably, dark coat, red-and-white-striped M-B scarf around his neck.

Lugging her bags, she walked past him without a second glance, her attention focused on finding the car her grandmother had said she would send, among the idling autocars at the curb.

"Lark," a man's voice called from behind her.

Her heart stopped for a moment, hearing that name again, and she stumbled, her toe catching a rough patch in the concrete. Down she went, duffel bag and backpack scattering to either side, along with her precious orchid, the one she'd resurrected from near death after a girl down the hall had thrown it out. Now the purple glazed pottery was in fragments, shattered around her, and the delicate white leaves of the orchid were smashed against the ground.

The man rushed over to her, hand extended to help her up. "It is you," he said, crouching next to her.

Still on the ground, she scooted away from him, heart crashing around in her chest like an animal frantic for escape, her hands and feet going numb.

"Field Bledsoe," he continued triumphantly, blue eyes lit with excitement. "Bloody Bledsoe. That's your dad. I've been looking for you for four years! Everyone thinks you're dead, but I knew it. I knew it!"

Her classmates milling about on the sidewalk, saying goodbye to each other, waiting for their parents, started to notice. Started to stare.

The man went on and on about transport receipts, security cam footage, wrong cargo hold weights, and illegal cold sleep facilities. Then he finally seemed to notice her lack of response.

He sucked air in through his teeth. "Sorry. I'm sorry. I've scared you. Hey, look, I don't mean any harm." He held his hands up in innocence. "My name is Alex Linley. I've been working on this story since that first rumor about the *Tarrytown* making an unscheduled stop at Goliath right after the news broke about Blood—" He stopped himself. "About the incident," he finished awkwardly.

Movement in the distance caught her attention. To her relief, Samson (not his real name), one of her family's private security personnel, stepped out of a car halfway down the line and charged toward them. The bright blue glow of the active QuickQ in his eye told Ophelia he was in contact with someone—her uncle, most likely.

The man glanced over his shoulder to see Samson barreling toward them, and he stood, face pale.

"It's all right, Miss Bray. I'll get your things. Why don't you get in the car?" Samson said, in a way that was somehow both comforting and menacing at the same time.

As she bolted for the car, she risked one look back. Alex was listening intently, frowning, as Samson pressed a piece of paper into his hands.

At the time—and for years later—she assumed Samson was giving him money. A link, perhaps, to an untraceable account. She might not have had all the details about how her Bray family operated, but she'd certainly seen them use money to make problems go away.

It wasn't until her early twenties, during graduate school, that it occurred to look him up. Alex Linley.

He was—still is—listed as missing.

Lark Bledsoe. Ophelia draws in her breath sharply. It feels like Lark is a whole other person, someone Ophelia used to know.

She doesn't really remember her, being her. When forced to consider it, she has memories of her childhood, normal memories. Hide-and-seek with other children, using service access ladders to avoid detection; snitching an extra flax cookie from the meal line; school lessons followed by a required shift in hydroponics or the crèche. But it's like those things happened to someone else, with Ophelia just watching from a distance.

Other memories, however, feel far too close.

Little Bird, where are you?

"I don't know what you're talking about," she says to Birch now, her voice barely a croak.

He straightens up. "Sure you don't. I don't know how you did it, but I'm betting that Bray money helped a lot, didn't it?" Birch folds his arms over his chest, one hand still scratching his arm, even through the fabric of his jumpsuit. "Nothing like what I had to do get out of the Avaris system after Pinnacle fucking dumped us off there. Blacklisted to keep their secret, no way out, no other jobs, no money."

The first half of her parents' story is like something out of an old fairy tale. The neglected daughter of a wealthy queen falls in love with the honorable but poor miner who is fighting for his struggling town.

Substitute CEO for queen and space station for town, and you've got the gist. Ophelia's mother was sent as a "Pinnacle representative" in a "good faith gesture" to quell rumblings of unionization with the Carver system mining stations—Goliath, Sampson, and Jericho.

The second half of their story was where the narrative twisted, jumping genres into one of those jump-scare, splatter-gore, nightmare fests starring a human monster named Bloody Bledsoe, good people who die for no reason, and the villain-adjacent who manage to escape with minimal harm.

Ophelia has dedicated her life since then trying to make up for it, trying to make up for them. Not just her father but her mother as well.

"Do you have any idea what it was like after the Brays swooped in to rescue their own and left the rest of us to burn our dead? Do you know how long that took? How many of them rotted in station storage while we waited for permission to take them to the ore processing facility? To destroy them like waste material?" His face distorts with rage. "I had to help my mother scoop my brother's remains into a bag."

Ophelia fights the mix of shame and anger that always rises in her when it comes to her family—either side, both sides. The Brays had despised the connection to her father even before he . . . did what he did.

Murdered almost thirty people, including men, women, and children, you mean?

But the Brays were just as bad, in an entirely different way. She doubts her uncle had Alex Linley killed. Too messy, too risky. More likely he was dumped on some desolate work camp colony with an implanted ID change, a fantastical story about the Brays, and no way to get home.

It feels like corrosion creeping up and down your skin. Like being made up of already damaged parts and struggling to make sure you're functioning as you're supposed to.

I have control of my actions. I make choices for myself. I am not my family.

It's the mantra Ophelia created for herself years ago, after she took her very first human psychology and behavior class at the academy.

Genetics are not destiny. Neither is environment. The two

together pack a powerful punch, but . . . *I have control of my actions. I make choices for myself. I am not my family.*

How much guilt is too much? How much is not enough? What can I do to make things better? Questions that continue to haunt her every single day.

But the one thing that will not make things better is for this to come out. She'll be fired, her license revoked, and possibly jailed for the lies her family told, the crimes they committed. There will be no more helping anyone. And the innocent in her family—there are a few, her sister, Dulcie, namely—will be destroyed.

She struggles to draw in a deep breath against the rising panic, and her vision pulses with black spots. But the medikit on the table to her right, almost in reach, catches her eye. Meds. Drugs that might make Birch forget . . . or fall asleep and never wake up again.

What is wrong with you? No. No!

Ophelia tears her gaze away from the medikit. "Birch, I need you to listen to me," she begins. "I—"

Birch's focus slides to a point behind her and, eyes widening, he takes a step back from her.

She flinches, imagining who he might see behind her. A full-blown hallucination of his brother? Or, oh God, her father? Birch said he'd dreamed about him.

The space between her shoulders prickles with awareness, as if the tiny hairs on her skin can detect a vision of the dead standing behind her, a sharp blade in hand.

Unable to stop herself, she spins around in her seat to look.

In the doorway, Severin raises his eyebrows at her. "Everything okay here?"

How much has he heard?

"Sure thing, MC," Birch says easily. "Just the doc and me having a discussion about getting more sleep."

Ophelia glances back at Birch, stunned by how normal he sounds now.

Then again, he must have some skill with deception. Montrose would never have knowingly hired anyone from Goliath for an R&E team, even if their pettiness tempted them to ignore a blacklisted status from Pinnacle. Not now that the medical community understands ERS a little better. It's too risky. Too many years of exposure to "less-than-ideal" conditions and "outdated" equipment and procedures. In other words, Ophelia's family company dumped their employees out there and then refused to upgrade to better, safer tech. As long as those teams were still pulling in ore from the asteroid, never mind that it meant up to six months a year in cold sleep as teams traded on and off.

No need to provide food or housing for dozens at a time. Just stuff everyone back into cold sleep when they are done with their thirty-day cycle. Wake them back up when they are needed again. What was innovative at the time is now deemed incredibly dangerous.

"Right, Dr. *Bray*?" Birch asks, drawing her attention back to the conversation. The emphasis on her last name is unmistakable, as is the veiled threat.

"Right," she says, her voice too thin.

Severin looks to Birch and then back to Ophelia, evaluating. "He's good to go, then?"

The second she tells Severin something is wrong, Birch is going to out her. She can feel it. But she can't ignore what's happening here, either.

"He should take it slow," she says finally, standing and facing Severin. *Do your job, Ophelia.* "And I'd like to get a blood sample to run through the med-scanner first."

"Not necessary," Birch says sharply.

"He's bleeding from his gums," she says to Severin. "Likely a sign of severe anemia, and it's possible his T3 levels are low, which can exacerbate certain conditions."

"I've been taking my iron tabs," Birch protests.

"All the more reason to just check it out," Severin says evenly, before she can respond.

"Fine," Birch snaps.

It takes less than a second to gather the needed drop of blood and set the med-scanner to work. She gives Birch gel-bands for his hands, her own hands trembling. "If that itching gets worse—" she starts.

"It won't. Can I go now?" he asks Severin, without even looking at Ophelia.

Severin steps out of the way and waves him forward through the door to the corridor.

"You'll let us know?" Severin asks her, as soon as Birch is gone.

You could be putting Severin's life at risk, along with everyone else's, by letting Birch go. Tsk, tsk. What happened to "Better safe than sorry"? How very Bray of you.

"Of course." Her voice comes out crumbly and thick, and she drops into her seat as he steps back into the corridor.

She closes her eyes. *Bloody fucking Bledsoe.* No matter what she does, she will never escape her father's legacy, her mother's response. She might have survived that horrible day, that horrible event, but apparently it will continue to linger like the ghost she should have been, no matter what—

"Everything okay, Doctor?"

Startled, she twists around in her chair to see Severin lingering in the doorway, frowning at her in concern.

It loosens something tight within her. "Do you ever feel like you're not enough?" she asks, the words escaping without her permission. Exhaustion has taken down her filter. "Like you'll never be able to do enough to make up for the past, for what you can't change, no matter how hard you try?"

His expression hardens. "I didn't come here for a counseling—"

He thinks she means Ava. "I'm not talking about you. I'm

talking about me," she snaps. "You know what? Forget it." She pushes to her feet.

Severin hesitates, fingers drumming a rhythm on the doorframe. "Yes," he says, after a moment. "But I think if you let the past haunt you, if you can't accept it, it's that much harder to make better choices in the future." He regards her warily, as if expecting her to slap back at him in some way.

But she nods. "That sounds good," she says, and she means it. But she's not sure she believes that's possible. Accepting the past, not being haunted by it. She's not sure he believes it, either.

"Good night, Doctor," he says, starting to turn away.

"Ophelia," she says impulsively. Julius is wrong—she does want to be known, just for more than her family, her history.

Severin pauses. Then he says, "Ethan."

Her cheeks warm, and for once it's not from embarrassment or frustration. "Good night, Ethan."

18

The walls are painted a soothing blue, with a hint of green for warmth. Every detail is carefully considered with patients in mind, down to the heavy knitted blanket tossed casually over the back of the couch for those still dealing with shock, and even the pointed tuck on the recyclable tissues in the gleaming metal cube on the side table. (Makes it easier to remove one when vision is blurred with tears.)

But at dusk, when patient hours are done for the day, that's when the space truly becomes Ophelia's.

Like right now. The sun is setting, turning the old skyline into black shadows against an orangey-red backdrop of sun. Old Downtown must have been something before the riots and the fire. The second one.

Ophelia sinks back into her desk chair, stretching her legs, contemplating the spread of her space. *Hers.* Her pen and notebook rest on the far edge, just waiting for her first patient the next morning. The image of her primary screen hovers in the air in front of her, projected from her QuickQ, flickering a dozen reminders to update files and progress reports.

The iVR is functioning just as it should, giving her a completely realistic version of her office back on Earth.

Ophelia settles in, relaxing. She's just starting to doze, that lovely, drowsy, relaxed in-between state, when she hears the automated office assistant's smooth voice.

"Dr. Bray. Rueben Monterra is here."

Her eyes snap open, and she bolts upright in her chair, hands clawing at the armrests, heart pounding. *What?*

"AIVA, I missed that. Can you repeat?" Even to her own ears, she sounds wary.

But AIVA remains silent, as she should. That functionality for the iVR is not enabled. No voices, no people, virtual or otherwise. Not to mention, that patient . . . Ophelia shakes her head.

She waits several seconds, but AIVA does not speak again. Odds were she never spoke at all. It must have been the start of a dream.

No, a nightmare. One that just happened to be set in the same location.

Because it couldn't be anything more than that. For one thing, Rueben, he always came in the morning. That's one of the reasons why everything was so—

The room goes dark abruptly, triggering the automatic lights overhead.

That . . . has never happened before.

Ophelia watches in horror as the windows across the room reveal a deep, black night with pinpricks of stars for bare seconds before transitioning to deep blue and then light gray, precursors to sunrise.

This is not right. No, no, not right. The scene in her office, it's always dusk. Always.

She pushes her chair away from the desk and stands. It feels sickeningly warm in here, as if waves of heat are radiating from the pale walls. What is happening?

A glitch? If so, this is one hell of a glitch.

She reaches up to pull the iVR band free from the receptors on either side of her temple. But her fingertips find only warm skin. No flex-metal. No trace of the headset at all.

Abandoning caution, Ophelia scrubs her hands over her face, a move that would normally send the device flying.

But there's still nothing there. No headset. Just the bridge of her nose, the quick brush of eyebrows, the heat of her panicked breath against her palms.

Ophelia snatches her hands away from her face, curling her fingers into her palms. It's just a dream. It has to be.

Except she's awake.

Okay, okay, just breathe. It's a lucid dream. Maybe triggered by the upgrade.

Never mind that this wasn't in the brochure and that maybe Montrose should leave the exposure therapy to actual therapists.

Ophelia takes a deep breath. She can manage this. All she needs to do is—

"Dr. Bray, Rueben Monterra is here," AIVA bellows. Her words boom in Ophelia's head, and she reaches up instinctively to block her ears, a primitive impulse that does no good when the sound is inside.

"*Dr. Bray,* Rueben Monterra *is leaving*," AIVA shrieks, just seconds later.

Ophelia freezes.

It's exactly . . . that morning. The morning that Rueben died. Not that AIVA was yelling then. She just kept repeating herself—"He's here. He's leaving. He's here."—in that flat monotone that expressed no confusion, no concern.

But clearly subtlety is not part of this new program.

Ophelia lunges for the door, moving on instinct, much faster than she did on the day when it really happened. If the headset is going to make her relive one of her worst days, she's going to do it better than she did the first time.

In the actual moment, she'd assumed a virtual assistant malfunction. What else could it be?

Now, though, Ophelia knows: her patient is pacing on the roof, one level above her office, triggering the virtual assistant's proximity sensor bubble—five meters in all directions, the grim-faced building engineer later explained—on and off and on again.

If Ophelia can stop Rueben, if she can just reach him before he commits to stepping off into thin air, she can change things. Even if it is just in a dream.

Her fingers curl around the too-warm door handle, and for a moment she's certain that the lever will not turn, that she will be forced to live through this moment of failing him again.

But the tongue retracts with an audible click—so real, the details—and she rips open the door.

The corridor outside her office in real life is decorated in light shades of gray and purple, with a carpet design that has made her wonder, more than once, if the designer was aware of its end location. There are tiny faces with a variety of expressions, hidden among the abstract flowers and geometric shapes.

She's already stepping out, her focus on reaching Rueben, before she realizes it's all wrong. The location. This is not the hallway outside her office. It's not even the right building.

A dim space station corridor stretches out before her, the lights at fifty percent to conserve power and the alert stripes on the wall flashing red, indicating the general alarm and containment to quarters for all but emergency responders. Not that it would do anyone any good.

Goliath. Home.

Unable to stop her forward momentum, Ophelia stumbles, and her foot—now suddenly bare—lands on the familiar squashed octagonal pattern on the floor. Her toes slip through the wetness of gathering condensation, dampening the grittiness they have already collected during her flight.

No. No, no, no. Her lungs shrivel up on themselves, retreating from their responsibilities. Nausea rides her hard, as if determined to crater her into herself. To turn her inside out.

The hydroponics deck looks exactly as she remembers it. Crowded and cluttered, with the extra jury-rigged humidifiers created from spare parts to pull any excess moisture from the air and rechannel it toward the small and frail food crops. But that also made it a good place to hide—in a game of hide-and-seek, where the stakes were simply losing a game. Not loss of life.

Ophelia clings to the door, which is still somehow impossibly her office door, refusing to look down at herself. The sticky blood and body fluids on her, from where she crawled under the table in the mess hall—they were all once people, people she knew and . . .

"Little Bird, where are you?" Her father's singsong chant sounds from somewhere in the distance behind her, and chills roll up her spine like a smooth, cold hand drifting over her vertebrae.

Ophelia gags, hard, and lets go of the door, hands flying up to cover her mouth.

And when she turns to reach for it, the door is gone. She's on Goliath, with no hint of it ever having been her office.

Enough is enough.

"I'm done now," she says through clenched teeth. "I'm waking up." She squeezes her eyes shut, hot tears leaking from beneath her lashes.

All she has to do is open her eyes. That's it. Just wake up and see the striped cloth of Liana's mattress above her.

Ophelia counts to ten slowly, ignoring the dripping of water near her and the thud of footsteps in the distance, but growing closer. *He's angry today. Hide. You need to hide!*

No. I need to wake up. This isn't real.

Ophelia draws in air until her lungs ache with it, and then releases it as she opens her eyes, certain that she'll find herself back in her bunk.

But instead of staring up, she's staring out across the corridor on the hydroponics deck, directly at the carved-out nook that she once used for shelter, pulling one of the raggedy humidity reclamation units in front of her for cover from her father. Who had murdered twenty-three people already, and then five more when he couldn't find her. If you counted him as a victim—and no one did—he reached twenty-nine. Just short of a perfect thirty.

Go! Now! Before it's too late.

"Little Bird, don't make it any harder than it is! I don't want to do this. You know I don't."

The vibration of his heavy tread reverberates through the metal floor beneath her. That should be impossible. But all of this is impossible. She's not eleven anymore. And he's dead. Long dead.

But the desire to run, to hide, is so strong her knees are trembling with it.

"You're infected," he calls. "You don't know, but you are. I have to save you. Please, let me save you!" A sob tears from his throat. "I love you. I—"

Coughing, a harsh-sounding jag, breaks in, interrupting him. The noise is somewhere nearby, closer even than her father somehow.

Ophelia frowns. That's not what—

The world around Ophelia rotates abruptly and she automatically throws out a hand to push off from any hard surface that she might smack into. Intermittent artificial gravity failures weren't all that unusual on Goliath back in the day, thanks to worn-out parts and austerity measures that made it difficult to get replacements.

As a child, she used to wish for gravity loss on the station like the children of Earth once wished for inclement weather to keep them out of school. Except, in her case, she and the others would spend the few minutes giggling and playing, shoving off each other and the walls, playing tag in the corridors, until the grav generators were fixed and they were tasked with helping to clean up.

But then her fingers brush over fabric, and her eyes snap open automatically.

Her surroundings spin into a blur that resolves itself into a gray-and-white-striped fabric overhead. She can, once more, feel the gentle press of the mattress against her shoulder blades.

Ophelia's back. Here and awake.

She sits upright with a gasp, like a diver breaking the surface from unknown depths. She reaches up to wrench the iVR band off her face, only to find it missing.

An immediate burst of panic makes a cold sweat break out all over her skin, until her waking mind finally kicks in.

Right. She's not wearing an iVR because she pulled them all last night.

No one objected when she retrieved the headsets to run a diagnostic. Just to be sure. It was new tech, after all.

Only Birch gave her side eye about it, but he said nothing.

Pulling her knees to her chest, she wraps her arms around herself, making her body as small as possible, just as she once did to escape her father. Her heart is still chugging hard enough that the beat of it taps against her upraised thigh like a fingertip keeping time.

You're fine. You're safe.

Dim light from the corridor spills through the window in the door, so Ophelia can see Kate across from her, gently snoring. In the bunk above, Liana murmurs in her sleep, but nothing indicates alarm or surprise. Probably one of them coughing had woken her enough to pull her out of the dream. She shudders to think how long it might have gone on without that interruption.

Just a nightmare, conjured up all on her own.

Not surprising. Given the stress. Given *Birch.*

She stares down past her knees, her knuckles turning white with her grip, the clutch of dread stronger yet this morning. She can't help feeling there's something more she could—should—be doing about Birch, but she hasn't been able to come up with a solution that doesn't seem inadequate. Or frightening.

Keeping an eye on him and trying to convince him that she's

not like her father, that she truly is here to help, is the best she's got.

With a sigh, Ophelia pushes back her blanket and stands. She doesn't know what time it is, but checking her wrist-comm is pointless. It's not like she's going back to sleep after that.

Maybe not ever again.

She reaches for her shoes at the foot of her bunk and stops.

Her right shoe is missing.

That's weird. Frowning, she checks under her bed, and then under Kate's. Nothing.

When Ophelia went to bed the night before, she lined up her fabric shoes at the foot of her bunk, just as she had the previous night.

Now, only the left one is there.

She tiptoes to the corridor and glances up and down. The same leftover junk from the previous team remains in piles. It's on Severin's list for cleanup, she knows.

But no sign of her shoe.

She creeps out into the corridor, closing the door to the bunk room gently behind her. The metal floor is cold and gritty against her bare feet, triggering memories of her dream. And that day.

He's angry. Hide. You need to hide! Now!

The panicked internal voice of the child she once was is loud in her head, until she forcibly pushes it down. She's not eleven anymore, and she does not need to think of her father.

Ophelia continues toward the central hub, with the thought that her shoe might have somehow ended up in her office. Not that she would have left it there, but perhaps someone is messing with her again. Suresh might have—

She stops short when she enters the central hub.

Her shoe is sitting alone in the shadowy space, a white dot on the open expanse of dark metal floor. Like a rowboat on the ocean, or an escape pod shooting deeper into space instead of toward home.

An uneasy feeling seeps through her as she edges forward to retrieve the shoe. The sensation of being watched raises goose bumps on her skin.

She doesn't believe in ghosts, not literal ones. Past trauma, sure. People reinflicting damage on themselves as they make fear-based choices to try to avoid more pain, inadvertently causing unhealthy cycles. But in terms of actual spirits reliving their past or torturing the living as vengeance, no. Never.

And yet . . .

The dimmed overhead lights flicker slightly—the generator struggling to keep up even with reduced demand.

Don't be ridiculous. No one died here.

Except for all of the Lyrians, buried beneath you, of course. And the ones just over there in the city. Their gaping mouths hanging open, pleading for help that's never going to come . . .

Shaking her head at herself, Ophelia heads deeper into the central hub.

Closer up, she realizes the fabric shoe is crushed in at the heel, like someone wedged their foot in quickly, not bothering to put it on correctly, and then accidentally walked out of it. Leaving it where it fell.

Pointing toward the airlock.

She bends down to pick it up, half expecting the fabric to feel icy cold or oddly warm. Instead, it just feels like her shoe.

Of course it does.

"What are you doing?" A voice behind her.

Ophelia jolts, nearly toppling over, and then stands, whipping around to face the speaker.

It's Kate, shivering in the compression shorts and T-shirt she sleeps in, arms wrapped around herself.

"I was just . . ." Sometimes the truth is the only option. "Getting my shoe," Ophelia answers finally, holding up the footwear as evidence.

Kate regards her with a confused frown. "Did you leave it out here earlier?"

"No. I don't know. I think maybe someone—" Ophelia stops herself before spouting theories that might sound like accusations she cannot prove. "How can I help you?" Clearly, Kate was out here—shivering in her nightclothes—for a purpose.

"I just . . . I woke up when you left the room, and I thought . . ." Kate trails off, one hand tugging at the embedded stars in her ear. She seems uncertain, for the first time in Ophelia's memory. "I wanted to talk to you, alone. About Birch."

That she was not expecting. "Oh?"

"You treated him last night after the fight. He went straight to his bunk after that, didn't talk to any of us." Kate hesitates. "Did he say anything to you?"

Ophelia works to keep her expression impassive, to hide the pulse of interest. "Anything, like what?"

Kate stares down at her feet, scrubbing her toe against the floor. "I'm just worried. He's never exactly been the cheeriest fellow, you know, but that was extremely out of character for him. He's never struck anyone before. I think . . . I think he's struggling more with what happened to Ava than he's letting on. And I wanted to know if he spoke to you about it." She looks up, then, a glint of hardness peeking through her somber mask.

What is this about?

"He didn't say anything to me," Ophelia says after a moment. More to see Kate's reaction than anything else.

Relief spreads across Kate's face for a split second before vanishing once again beneath the veil of concern. "Okay, I just—"

"But even if he had," Ophelia continues, "I wouldn't be able to discuss it with you. That's how confidentiality works."

A flicker of irritation creases Kate's brows, but she stamps it out immediately and nods. "I understand. Of course."

Ophelia gives her best professional smile and moves to walk past Kate, all the while thinking, *What the fuck am I missing?*

You really have no idea, do you? That's what Birch said to her last night, what's ringing through her head right now. And no, she really doesn't.

"I was thinking, maybe it would be better if you came with *us* today," Kate says.

Ophelia stops in surprise, turning to face her.

"If the weather holds, Suresh and I are heading back to the lander to get some parts for generator repair." Kate lifts her hand up, and the lights flicker on cue. "But the commander will probably have Birch launch the drones today for an updated scan. You could go, maybe just keep an eye on Birch?"

That is . . . exactly what Ophelia should do.

But why does Kate, a person who seems very concerned about what Birch might reveal in private conversation, want to give her another chance to speak with him alone?

"I don't think Etha—Commander Severin will go for that," Ophelia says, kicking herself. *One conversation, Phe? Really? One conversation and he's "Ethan" now.*

Kate waves a hand carelessly, not seeming to notice her correction. "Oh, don't worry about that. I'll talk to him. He trusts me." She eyes Ophelia clutching her shoe. "You should too," she adds after a moment, jerking her chin toward the shoe. "With . . . whatever."

There's a message Ophelia can't interpret beneath her words, only that it feels abrupt, a little hard, and in some way disingenuous.

Or perhaps this is simply her inherent distrust of people rising up to kneecap her, as it frequently does. One might even call it paranoia.

"Dibs on the lav," Kate says over her shoulder, as she heads back toward the C side.

"There are two—" Ophelia begins.

Kate points upward, still walking, and then Ophelia hears it: the faint off-key singing of a popular game show theme song, one that rhymes "prizes" and "sizes" with "thighses." Suresh, it has to be.

With a sigh, Ophelia heads toward the galley instead.

By the time she gets her turn in one of the lavs, everyone else is dressed and ready for the day, in their envirosuits, with helmets scattered around nearby.

When she emerges from the C side into the central hub, the antigrav sled is near the interior airlock door, which is standing open. The sled is full, stacked two or three high with crates and strapped-down equipment. Scattered crates are open all around it, exposing their soft gray padded insides and the shiny metal bits stored there.

"This would be much easier if we had the rover," Suresh says, lifting a closed crate to stack it on board with a grunt. "There's not enough room."

"Quit your whinging. It's fine," Kate says breathlessly, as she wedges a heavy-looking tool kit into place. The nearest crate tower wobbles, and Suresh and Severin rush to steady it.

"Oh, sure, it's fine," Suresh says through gritted teeth.

Once the crates are stable, Severin steps back, catching a glimpse of Ophelia. "Doctor," he says in greeting, turning his attention toward her. Liana looks up from a tablet where she's skimming something and waves.

True to her word, Kate must have spoken to him. Severin found Ophelia in the corridor as she was waiting for her turn in the sonic shower, told her she was welcome to join them today. He almost sounded like he meant it, too.

Perhaps she was wrong to be suspicious of Kate. Or maybe her suspicions of Kate had their origins in a baser emotion. *Jealousy is such an ugly emotion, darling. It'll prematurely age you like nothing else.*

A classic from her mother. Ophelia rolls her eyes and turns

her attention to something, someone, else. Birch is off to one side, scratching at his arm and staring off toward the airlock and the world beyond. At nothing. At everything.

"Listen up. We'll only have an hour or so outside," Severin says. "Kate and Suresh will be heading back to the lander to pull some supplies. Liana and I will be taking a few ice core samples. And Birch will be attempting to get a drone scan of the area, depending on conditions."

Birch, at the sound of his name, jerks to attention, blinking rapidly. He sees Ophelia watching him and immediately stops scratching, dropping his hands away from his arms with a scowl.

"Let's move, people," he says to his team. "Clock is ticking." Then he turns back to Ophelia. "Doctor, your suit?"

Shit. Right.

She turns and hurries as fast as she can back to the bunk room, grabs her suit and helmet. By the time she returns, the others are already in the airlock with the precariously loaded sled. Severin is the only one waiting for her on this side of the threshold, helmet tucked under his arm.

Ophelia can feel their collective impatience growing as she sits down to struggle into her suit. She manages to get it up her waist, and then, to her surprise, Severin—Ethan—approaches her.

He sets his own helmet on the table next to hers. "It's easier if you stand now," he says.

When she gets up, Ethan tugs the shoulder of the suit up and helps her get her arm inside, and then with rapid precision that speaks to his experience with this, he closes the fittings around the wrist and adjusts the elbow guard.

"Are you sure Birch should be cleared for duty today?" Ethan asks, not in a whisper but in a voice certainly too low to be heard by the others.

He's asking her opinion. Trusting her. All she's wanted from the beginning. An unexpected warmth curls through her, followed immediately by a sickening twist of conflict.

He keeps his focus on her suit, shifting to the other side to do the same thing to that arm.

"His blood work came back fine," she hedges. Which means next to nothing except that he doesn't have low iron or low thyroid levels making him worse.

When she got the med-scanner results back last night, his red blood cell levels were perfectly in range. No reason for his gums to be bleeding. White blood cells were up a little, but nothing that indicated an infection. Just some mild systemic inflammation, including what looked like a histamine reaction. The med-scanner suggested it was an unknown allergy.

"But you're still concerned." Ethan brings the zipper up from her waist, and for a flash, it feels too intimate, too close. Like being cared for. Heat rises in her cheeks.

"That's what Kate says," he adds.

Oh, well, if Kate *says it . . .*

Ophelia grits her teeth at herself, then nods. "I am. How long has he been part of your team?"

"Last six years."

"How well do you know him? Do you know anything about his past?" *My past.* "Have you noticed anything like this from him before?"

Ethan shakes his head. "He keeps to himself. Plays that game with Suresh. Likes word puzzles on his tablet. Makes little creatures and things from paper. Doesn't use a pillow. Won't drink coffee or any other 'stimulant,' he calls it." Ethan then gestures for her to lift her chin so he can close the fasteners at her collarbone. This close, she can see the faint freckles on his skin, where he must have been in the sun at some point or spent time under a sun lamp. Dark stubble is a shadow beneath the surface. The vulnerable underside of his jaw moves when he swallows.

"It could just be stress," she says reluctantly. "Like I said, loss affects everyone differently."

"But you don't believe that," Ethan says, stepping back. He holds out her helmet, and she takes it.

"I'd just like to keep a close eye on him for now," she says, trying not to feel like a despicable piece-of-shit liar. "Has he said anything to you? About Ava?" *About me?*

Ethan doesn't respond right away, picking up his own helmet from the table. "No," he says after a moment. "But he was up, wandering around the hab in the night."

"Are we going to do this or do you need to hold her hand some more?" Suresh's voice is small and tinny inside the helmet she's not yet wearing, but clearly audible. And impatient.

Ophelia glances over toward the airlock in time to see him lift his hands up in a *What are you doing?* motion.

Heat scores her cheeks. Suresh, she's certain, only meant to imply that she was incapable rather than anything inappropriate, and yet it feels like the suggestion is hanging out in the air now.

Ethan, back to blank-faced as ever, puts his helmet on, twisting with efficiency until it clicks closed. He gestures for Ophelia to do the same.

As soon as her helmet is in place, he pivots and heads back toward the airlock, without waiting.

"Make sure you stick close, Doctor," he says over the common channel.

Kate and Suresh lead the way outside, ducking their heads against the wind and tugging the sled behind them. Birch is at the back end of the sled, almost stepping on it in his eagerness to get out. He seems better now, more alert.

Liana is bent over her tablet, next to Ophelia, and Ethan brings up the rear.

"What do we think?" Kate asks, coming to a stop about ninety meters from the hab.

Ethan steps out of line and to the side, surveys the skies and the chipped-ice snowflakes spitting down on them. The wind swirls around him hungrily, but he remains stable, unmoved by it.

"Better than yesterday," he says. "But that could change fast. Just stick to the line. We can get the spiders started and then come your way to help."

"Spiders?" Ophelia can't help herself.

"Yeah, the autodrillers! Remember?" Liana tips her tablet toward Ophelia so she can see three individual schematics of what does, in fact, look like a four-legged spider, with a proboscis thicker than its legs projecting from the center "body."

"Meet Marvin, Mabel, and Denise." Liana beams at her. "I program them with coordinates based on the scans we got on the mission briefing, and they core out a sample. We'll do a couple of shallow samplings to gather data on the environment in the last few decades, snowfall, carbon dioxide levels, all kinds of stuff. They have diagnostic sensors that taste the ice and report back. But then we'll try for a deeper sample. Roughly one kilometer is thousands of years."

That piques Ophelia's interest. "So you might end up with samples that could tell you what happened here. Maybe even biological specimens—leaves, or whatever the equivalent might be."

"Exactly! If, for example, it involved volcanic activity, which is one of the theories, we'll be able to pick that up from the higher levels of sulfur and ash or whatever. If there was an asteroid strike on this continent, then we might see a big jump in ammonium ions."

As she's explaining, Kate and Suresh are off-loading three large crates from the sled and dropping them on the ground.

"Hey, careful!" Liana protests, hurrying forward.

"Liana, love, we go through this every time. They're in padded cases, they're fine," Kate says.

"Also, they're not alive," Suresh adds, sounding slightly out of breath. "Not pets, remember?"

Ophelia can't see Liana's expression, but her posture stiffens with hurt. Every team is, in some ways, like a family, with roles to play. When a family member is gone, there has to be some adjustment, or functionality can be impaired. Ophelia has no way of knowing whether Ava frequently intervened on Liana's behalf or if Suresh kept his mouth shut more often in Ava's presence, but her absence is notable at times.

Especially in that Ophelia finds herself stepping forward to defend instead of staying back, observing.

She catches herself and stops. *Not my job, not what I'm here to do.*

"You do know you're an asshole, right?" Liana shoots back at Suresh.

"Let's keep moving. Time is short," Ethan says. "You can work out your personal disagreements in your sessions with Dr. Bray. In the meantime, we have work to do. Birch, I don't know if the drones can handle this wind in a launch."

Birch, in the process of tugging a shiny silver case off the sled, doesn't respond.

Alarm flickers to life in Ophelia's veins, tiny spikes of unease.

"Birch—" Ethan tries again.

"I want to try," Birch says, hauling the case into his arms. It's apparently lighter than it looks. "It'll help if we've got updated survey data and visuals."

No matter what, it would be better if he can keep busy, his mind present and occupied with work, but it's not her call. Or at least not one she's willing to make right now.

Ethan seems to reach the same conclusion, though. "Fine," he says. "But don't wander too far."

With that, Kate and Suresh, still grumbling under his breath, venture off to the left, connect with the bright orange safety line, and vanish.

Liana makes herself busy dragging her spider crates into place, and Ethan helps.

"Here?" he asks.

Liana checks her tablet. "Still too close. The coordinates

will keep them from running into each other, but we don't
want to destabilize the ice pack."

Ophelia stays out of their way while keeping a close eye on
Birch, who is slogging, in the direction of the city. He stops
after a few minutes, kneeling to place the case on the ground.

She glances back at Ethan and finds him watching Birch as
well. He gives her a nod, acknowledging that he's aware, while
Liana rushes from one crate to another, opening the lids and
poking at whatever is inside.

Ophelia returns her attention to Birch . . . and the two
black crystalline towers, slender and knifelike, tilted at the exact same angle, like two giant blades stabbed into the ground
under the gray sky. No wonder the wind makes such strange
noises over there. Whistling, calling, screaming.

The blanket of snow at the base of the towers is dramatically humped and bunched, unlike the smooth waves, gentle
peaks, and rolling flatness all around her.

Then a mechanical whine loud enough to be heard over the
wind pulls her focus to Liana and her spiders.

The automated drills stand themselves up in their protective packing, shaking and stretching each limb and joint before
stepping out over the lip of the crate and skittering into the
snow.

Ophelia's revulsion is instinctive, automatic. She shudders.
There's no such thing as "good" insects or arachnids or other
pests in an enclosed environment. Weevils, the same ones that
once infested hardtack on long sea journeys, still manage to
work their way into Goliath's supplies from Earth, every once
in a while. Ophelia has no idea what weevils actually look
like, but as a child she always pictured tiny white spiders. They
ate nothing with flour during those months. Those were thin
months. People can travel to other planets and live in outer
space, but they always bring their troubles with them.

The spiders spread out and find their places, coming to an
immediate halt at some unseen signal, burying their feet in the

snow, and then locking them into place with a series of loud clonks.

Ophelia turns back to the city, back to Birch. He's standing now, but not moving, the case on the ground near his feet. She can't tell if it's open or not. But he appears to be staring at a fixed point in the distance, his hands clenched at his sides.

Fear zips through her, an electric shock to the nerves. Is he seeing someone out there? Is someone there?

She follows his gaze but can't detect anything beyond the now increasing snow. No shadows, no movements. At least, she doesn't think so. She can't decide if that makes her feel better or worse. If she were to see something too, would that mean she and Birch are both losing their grip on reality? It's a possibility that she has to keep in mind, unfortunately.

A half-forgotten memory surfaces abruptly. Ophelia's father, with his head propped in his bloody hands on their kitchen table, sobbing, while her mother stands in the corner, trembling, a dent in the wall just to the right of her head.

The dent isn't very big, but when the walls are thin sheets of plexiplastic over metal, it doesn't need to be.

Urgency for answers swells in her, drowning out everything else. Including, one might argue, the common sense to leave well enough alone.

A glance back shows Liana and Ethan occupied with the spiders. So Ophelia makes her way over to Birch, calling his name over the common channel when she's close enough. She doesn't want to startle him.

"I don't need you checking up on me," he says, without turning around. He kneels down to open the shiny case at his feet. A dozen or so palm-size drones are tucked neatly inside protective foam.

With a little bit of fumbling, she manages to send him a request to switch channels.

He doesn't move, and for a moment she thinks he's going to ignore her.

But then his hand shifts to his wrist, and a corresponding crackle sounds inside her helmet. "We're supposed to stay on the common channel, Doctor," he says. "Though, wait, are you still a doctor if all your qualifications were done under a false name?"

It's not a false name. Ophelia Bray is as real as anyone that money can buy. It's Lark Bledsoe who doesn't exist. Not anymore.

"I just need to ask you a question." Ophelia hesitates, but in for a penny, in for a pound . . . of flesh. "Did you really see your brother outside?"

Birch shoots to his feet, spinning around on her, his expression contorting with fury. "I am not—"

"I mean, did you see *him*?" she asks quickly. "Or did you just see . . . someone?"

Something like uncertainty flashes across Birch's blue-tinted face before it vanishes. "It was a dream," he said firmly. "From your invasive mind-fuck equipment. It doesn't matter." Another crackle, followed by a beep, indicates his departure from the private channel. He kneels in the snow and begins fussing with the drones in their case.

Ophelia bites her lip and starts back toward Liana and Ethan. Is it a coincidence or a symptom? She can't stop thinking about the shadowy figure she might or might not have seen through the window in her office yesterday morning.

Ahead of her, Ethan waves a hand, catching her attention. *Shit.* She forgot to switch back over to the primary channel.

"Everything okay over there?" he asks as soon as she's on. "Birch?"

"Yes," Ophelia says too quickly. "Just checking in."

"Yes," Birch says after a moment.

A beat of silence holds awkwardly, and she realizes she's waiting, air caught tight in her lungs, for Birch to give her away.

But he doesn't.

"Aww," Suresh says in a ridiculously sulky voice. "Where's my check-in, Doc? Playing favorites already."

The last thing Ophelia would want is Suresh doing her a favor, but at the moment his obnoxiousness provides the tension break needed.

"You're no one's favorite," Kate says with an audible sniff. "Now please focus on the task at hand if you want to keep breathing."

"Did everyone hear that?" Suresh demands. "She's threatening me, she's—"

"In the hab, you twat. If you want to keep breathing in the hab. Hand me the—"

A loud, metallic shriek interrupts Kate, making Ophelia jump. For a second she's confused, uncertain whether the noise came from inside her helmet or out.

"What was that?" Kate demands.

So, not something on their end, but loud enough that they could hear it.

"It's Denise. She's hung up on something," Liana says.

Movement catches Ophelia's eye: Liana approaching one of the spiders cautiously. Its whole body is shuddering as it tries to pull back from the ground, segmented legs flailing frantically in the snow, trying to gain leverage.

"This is a shallow dig, barely thirty centimeters down. There shouldn't be anything that close to the surface, not here." Liana sounds perplexed, tapping at her tablet before shaking her head. "She's not responding to commands. Her system is probably overloaded. Such a drama queen."

With a sigh, Liana sets her tablet carefully on the snow and edges closer, hands out like she's approaching a wild animal, as if she expects Denise to suddenly wheel around and attack.

More likely, it's in case the spider frees itself unexpectedly and momentum carries it back into her. Ophelia doesn't know how heavy they are, but it's almost as tall as Liana is, and the drill is certainly sharp enough to slice into her suit. Or worse.

Ophelia picks up her pace through the drifts. She might not be able to help, but she'd rather be close enough to try. The snow is coming down faster now, and the wind is moaning again, pushing against her and building to a howl.

"Liana," Ethan warns, stepping up to follow her.

"I've got it," Liana says, with a hint of ferocity. This is her domain, and she doesn't want anyone interfering.

At the spider's side, she stops, her hand moving with its undulations, until she's finally able to reach in and, quick as a wink, tap something on the underside of its core.

She jumps back as Denise stills, legs locking in place. "There, that's better," she murmurs, moving to its side again, patting it on its "head." "We'll get you all fixed up in no time, you ridiculous bitch." She looks over her shoulder to Ethan.

"Can you give me a hand?" she asks him. "I need to pull her back, clear the obstruction, and then reset."

Ethan moves to the other side of the spider, and they rock Denise back and forth gently until its legs come free, sending both of them stumbling backward.

Ophelia is almost there when Liana starts screaming.

19

"What is that? What the fuck is that?" Liana demands, her voice gone shrill.

She and Ethan are staring at something on the ground when Ophelia reaches them, panting.

Ophelia follows their gaze to Denise, now deactivated, on its side, legs slightly curled up toward its body. And then to the ice core, ejected from the drill's sample tube. The sample itself, about ten centimeters in diameter, is a frosty white at the top and then clear until the end, where the final chunk is a dark purplish-red with flecks of lighter shades within. An unmistakably bright red liquid, thawed temporarily by the heat of the drill, trickles down the edges to the bright white snow.

Uh-oh. Ophelia's stomach sinks.

"It's not possible, not possible," Liana mutters to herself.

"Someone tell me what's going on," Kate says grimly over the comm channel. "You have three seconds before I'm coming in hot."

"Negative," Ethan says. "We're fine here. Just an . . . unexpected development with the samples." He grimaces. Then he turns to Liana, moving in front of her, blocking her view. A moment later, Liana's mouth is moving rapidly, hands gesturing. Ethan must have switched them to a private channel.

Ophelia hesitates for a beat, then skirts around dead Denise and the drill hole to get a better look at the sample.

Ethan turns, keeping himself in front of Liana. "Doctor,"

he says, in that same warning tone he used with Liana. "Ophelia."

The sound of her first name from him makes her waver, almost turn back. A sudden yearning to be someone he should care about, to be a member of his team, under his fierce protection, is a hot coal in her chest.

Don't, Phe. Just don't. Even her internal voice sounds weary.

"We have protocols for quarantining—" Ethan begins.

"I'm not going to touch it. Believe me," she says. And if there's any airborne contagion that can penetrate through their suits, they're likely screwed anyway, which he knows.

He exhales in exasperation, loudly enough that it comes across the comm channel. But he doesn't move. If Liana weren't here, Ophelia suspects he would try to block her instead.

Ophelia kneels next to the discarded sample, which is rapidly refreezing to the icy surface beneath it. Yeah, that's definitely blood. And, uh, meat. Striations of skin, muscle, and grayish-pink tubing . . . intestines.

Her gag reflex kicks in and she presses her hand against the outside of her helmet, as if that will help.

Chips of bone along the bottom explain what stopped Denise. But that doesn't explain what this is doing here. She leans around for a better look at the other side of the mystery sample, but the top of it catches her eye. A scrap of bright blue fabric is stuck in the ice core, and beneath that, on the surface of the gray skin, mysterious dark lines that wind around in a familiar-seeming pattern that—

Fuck.

Ophelia jerks back. She blows out a breath as quietly as possible, trying to keep her stomach from lurching.

"Is it an animal?" Liana asks, leaning around Ethan. "There aren't supposed to be animals here!"

"Whatever it is, it was dead a long time before we got here," Ethan assures her. "Right, Dr. Bray?" The tension in his voice tells Ophelia he's not sure at all, and he's right not to be. Because none of this makes sense.

"Not an animal," Ophelia manages.

Unless animals on this planet were prone to wearing clothes and tattooing themselves with what she's fairly sure is an outline of Silly Bird, a popular sarcastic, cigar-smoking animated character from Earth.

"Did I clip . . . one of them? The Lyrians or whatever?" Liana's teeth are chattering. Shock. They need to get her inside. "Their remains should be much farther down."

"No, no. Nothing like that." Ophelia pushes to her feet, swaying in the increased wind. "I think we should go back in before the storm gets worse."

"What the hell is going on?" Kate demands in her ear.

"We can talk about it inside," Ophelia says firmly. "I think that's the best option."

She looks to Ethan, hoping he'll get what she's trying not to say aloud, or at least that there's something she can't say without switching to a private channel.

After a moment, he gives a decisive nod in acknowledgment. "Liana, pull Mabel and Marvin in. Kate and Suresh, do you have what you need?"

"We can make it work," Kate says. "But—"

"Good. Birch, we're heading back. Now," Ethan says, leaving no room for argument.

Birch. Ophelia completely forgot about him. She's expecting an alarming silence, but it's only a few seconds before he responds.

"Acknowledged."

Relief scores her insides, a cool balm against the preemptive panic.

"We'll regroup inside," Ethan says.

Liana steps back from Ethan to tend to Mabel and Marvin. Or so Ophelia assumes, until she makes a sharp right and pivots to come alongside Denise and the core sample, opposite Ophelia.

"Wait, Liana—" Ophelia starts.

From that angle, it must be clearer, or perhaps it's just an easier leap to make when you already know something is horribly wrong.

"Oh my God, it's a person," Liana whispers. "There's a person under here."

Denise managed to core right through the bottom half of an oversize Silly Bird, which, in combination with the intestines, suggests placement somewhere on an abdomen. A human abdomen.

Suresh has pulled together images from their collective feeds and stitched them together. His tablet runs through the grainy footage from Liana's helmet cam, and Ophelia's, as everyone huddles around the end of the table in the central hub to watch. Outside, the storm shrieks in outrage, as if furious at being denied the opportunity to have them join their poor compatriot outside.

With an irritable twitch, Liana shakes off the thermal blanket Ophelia tucked around her shoulders, even though she's still shivering. "This shouldn't be possible. The ground scans didn't show anything. I checked, multiple times!" She pounds her fist on the table.

"No one is doubting you, love," Kate says gently, before she turns away and heads for the galley.

"It's possible the scans weren't updated after . . ." Ethan pauses, seeming to search for the right word. "After," he finally finishes. He scrubs his hand over his face, the bristle of his stubble rasping against his palm, before moving up to press his fingertips between his eyebrows. His nail beds turn white with the pressure he's exerting.

"Do you have a headache?" Ophelia asks, alert.

Ethan lets go instantly, waving his hand in dismissal. "I'm fine."

"I'm going to go clean up," Birch says abruptly, straightening up and pulling away from the table.

Ethan's gaze meets Ophelia's for a fraction of a second in a silent question.

A bubble of inward elation—utterly inappropriate, and badly timed besides—rises in her. She shoves it down and lifts her shoulder in the slightest gesture she can manage, in what she hopes is a subtle communication of *It's okay with me if it's okay with you.*

After all, how much trouble can Birch get into if he's inside and everyone is here and awake, paying attention?

And though Birch hadn't phrased it as a question, Ethan nods. "Fine." He watches Birch leave, though, with a troubled expression.

"But I mean, who fucking buries someone this close to their front door?" Suresh demands, pulling their attention back to the tablet. He replays the footage. "They'd have to walk past him every single time they went out to do anything."

Liana makes a pained noise.

"Where's the fucking dignity in that?" Suresh shakes his head. "They had the whole planet to choose from."

"It's definitely not ISEC protocol," Ethan says. "There are regulations around handling remains."

"I hate to be the morbid one, but he—or she—wasn't buried," Kate says, returning from the galley with a steaming mug of coffee.

She puts the mug in front of Liana, who wraps her fingers around it, not even seeming to notice its sudden appearance with her focus on Suresh's tablet. Probably not the healthiest fixation at the moment. But pulling her away from it right now would likely only serve to increase her anxiety.

"What are you talking about?" Suresh asks. "Dude was literally underground. Or ice or whatever."

Kate opens her mouth, but before she can say anything, he holds up his hand to stop her.

"And before you jump all over me, how many female-identifying or nonbinary people do you know with Silly Bird tattoos? Particularly that one." He gestures toward the tablet.

The bottom half of Silly Bird does seem to be sporting exceptionally large testicles—probably anatomically impossible for birds or humans, proportionally speaking. Though, what does Ophelia know about bird reproductive systems? Absolutely nothing.

"No, it's not that," Kate says to Suresh in exasperation. "He's not deep enough."

"The ground is solid ice and snow." Suresh taps his finger against the table for emphasis. "They aren't going to be able to get much deeper without heavy equipment, which they wouldn't have had at the hab."

Kate rolls her eyes. "What's the average accumulation per year?" she asks Liana.

"Five centimeters, roughly," Liana says automatically. "Depending on conditions—"

"And we're assuming this is an R&E team member from Pinnacle," Kate adds.

Collectively, Ophelia feels their attention shift to her.

"Claim jumpers are always a possibility," she points out. She's not even sure why; it's not as if she has any loyalty to her family's capitalistic endeavors. But it's true—some smaller corporations or groups have attempted to claim planetary rights when there's been no activity and they think they can get away with it. But not usually with a company as litigious as Pinnacle. Or even Montrose.

Hard to hold a planet if you're blacklisted on all major transport companies and suppliers.

That said, Ophelia also has to be willing to consider that, selfishly, she just doesn't want to be associated with yet more awfulness from the people with whom she shares unalterable genetic ties.

"Dr. Bray," Ethan begins.

Ophelia sighs. "If that's part of a jumpsuit"—she gestures toward the images on the tablet and the captured scrap of fabric—"then, yes, the color looks right for Pinnacle. But there's no mention of any deaths in the reports that came with the rights package."

As soon as the words are out of her mouth, she wishes she could pull them back. As if they're all not well aware of how mission reports can be redacted, manipulated, or straight-up fabricated.

An awkward silence hangs for a few seconds, but then Kate clears her throat. "Well, let's just assume that was an . . . oversight."

Right.

"Pinnacle hasn't had a team here in, what, six years?" Kate asks.

Ophelia nods absently. If anything in the report can be relied on, which . . . who knows?

"Shit," Ethan says, letting his head hang down for a second, revealing the pale vulnerability of the back of his neck, the top knob or two of his spine.

The surprise of hearing the obscenity from him delays Ophelia's realization, but then it clicks. Basic math. "It just built up over the years," she says slowly. "The snow and ice."

Kate nods.

"So they didn't bury him," Suresh says, sinking back into his chair. "They just . . . left him."

This time the silence that lingers is heavy with grief and guilt.

"Who does that?" Liana asks softly. "Who does that?" Her voice grows louder, and she shoves back her chair to stand. "He was right there!" She flings her hand toward the airlock.

"They could have easily gotten him, brought him back with them. It's not as if they didn't know where he was or they couldn't get to him no matter how hard they tried." Her voice breaks, and tears slip down her cheeks.

What happened out there? Tell me, please!

But Ophelia swallows the urge to shout the words, because while she doesn't know the actual circumstances of Ava Olberman's death or why Ethan almost certainly falsified their mission report, she's fairly certain, for the first time, that Ava's teammates didn't have anything to do with her death.

Liana swipes at her face angrily and empathy pulls at Ophelia.

"I know this is hard." Ophelia leaves a pause, giving Liana space to respond, to engage.

After a moment, Liana gives a tiny nod.

"But the thing to keep in mind is that we don't control everything." Ophelia chooses her words carefully. "Other people make choices that we may or may not agree with, that we may not even know about. We don't have power over every variable, every outcome."

Ethan's dark-eyed focus holds on Ophelia like a physical touch, a firm hand pressing at the back of her neck. But he says nothing to stop her.

"You can't take that burden of responsibility on yourself," Ophelia continues. "It doesn't help anyone, even . . . the ones who are lost." She's walking a tightrope here, talking about Ava without talking about Ava. "We are just people. We do our best, but that's all we can do. You caused no harm here. In fact, you found him, so maybe in the end you're helping, acknowledging his death and loss."

Liana straightens up, taking a deep breath. The tension eases slightly, and Kate reaches out awkwardly and pats Liana on the shoulder.

"It's just . . . we can't even notify anyone," Liana says. "His family might not know what happened to him, if it wasn't in the reports. But we don't know his name."

Ethan clears his throat. "As soon as we can get a message through, Liana, I'll make sure mission control knows what we found. Someone will figure it out." He nods at her in reassurance.

Which may or may not do any good, given Montrose's history of petty competitiveness with Pinnacle, but that's neither here nor there at the moment.

If Montrose refuses to address it, Ophelia could always reach out to her—

She cuts off the thought before it reaches completion, ripples of shock shuddering through her. *No. Absolutely not. Not even to respect the dead. Not even to help Liana.*

Suresh holds his hand up. "Uh, Katey, your nose? It's . . . there's blood." He looks queasy.

Ophelia leans around Ethan immediately, in time to see Kate swipe her hand under her nose. It comes away bright red.

Ophelia's mind flashes to Birch's pink teeth earlier, and that lingering sensation of wrongness grows stronger.

"Excuse me." Ophelia pushes through the others to reach Kate. This, at least, she feels a little more confident with handling, as she used to have a patient who would get nosebleeds in times of high stress—or in recounting those times on her couch.

"Pinch closed," Ophelia says.

Kate nods, doing so. "I know," she says, her exasperation almost comically nasal, but then she leans her head back.

Ophelia reaches up and corrects her position. "Tip forward, not backward, unless you want it going down your throat."

Kate rolls her eyes, but she allows it.

"Does this happen often?" Ophelia asks.

"It's the dry air," Kate says with a muted huff. "That's all. The sooner we get the genny up to full capacity, the sooner I can bring secondary systems online, like adding some fucking humidity to make it more breathable in here."

Ophelia heads to the galley and grabs a handful of the general purpose cloths—though on this mission they seem to have a very specific purpose, soaking up more blood than spills.

"Any headache?" Ophelia asks, pressing a cloth into Kate's free hand. She releases her nose long enough to take the cloth with her pinching hand.

Kate starts to shake her head, then thinks better of it. "Just the normal one. It's because of cold sleep." Her voice is muffled.

"Still?" Ophelia asks.

Kate nods.

"How about your gums? Have you noticed any unusual bleeding?" Ophelia continues.

"Nooo," Kate says, drawing out the word in a manner that suggests Ophelia asked her whether she's experienced any unexpected finger growth. "I've been taking my iron tabs, like a good girl."

How about anything resembling hallucinations? How about that?

"Itchy skin?" Ethan interjects, arms folded across his chest. He's paying more attention than Ophelia thought.

Suresh exchanges a *What the fuck?* look with Liana.

"You know you can tell me," Ethan continues with an enviable calmness, though frustration tinges his words. "Any of you," he adds. "I expect you to tell me when something might be wrong, even if you're not sure."

Liana and Suresh are suddenly studying the table, and Kate shifts uncomfortably.

Kate's hand flies to her opposite wrist, before she forces herself to drop it. "It's just dry in here, I told you. That's all."

Ethan doesn't seem inclined to respond, just continues staring her down until she raises her chin defiantly. "I said no, didn't I?"

Liana raises her hand. "Uh, why are you asking these questions?" she asks Ophelia. Though quite reasonably that question should have been directed to her commander, the last one to ask a question. Something is definitely going on here.

Ophelia could defer her question to Ethan, but that feels somehow like a rejection of an overture, for reasons she doesn't understand.

"Just making sure I don't overlook anything," Ophelia says finally.

Suresh eyes her with suspicion. "No offense, Doc, but I thought you were more the type to worry about itchiness *inside* the old pate rather than the top of it."

"As I said, being thorough." Ophelia meets his gaze without flinching, and that seems to be enough for him to let it go. For now.

Fortunately, it doesn't take long for Kate's nose to stop bleeding, leaving her with sticky red smears on her hands and face.

"There. See?" She waves a hand in front of her gruesome but non-bleeding nose. "Fine."

Ethan studies her for a long moment, then seems to come to some conclusion. "Suresh, work with Kate as soon as she's ready. We want everything up to full operating capacity as soon as possible. We don't know how long this storm will last."

Kate turns away without acknowledging Ethan. Still in a huff about . . . Ophelia is not sure what exactly. But Suresh follows her quickly and they head toward syscon, behind the galley, heads together and whispering.

"Liana, if you're up to it, can you catalog the reports from Mabel and Marvin?" Ethan asks. "Write up the TLA summary and add it to the file."

TLA summary. In spite of everything, a laugh burbles up inside Ophelia. TLA. Top Level Assholes summary. In other words, break it down into small sentences, use short paragraphs, and include pictures, if possible, for the people making the decisions, who have no idea what they're talking about.

It's a term she's heard before from patients, but usually only the retired ones who have nothing to lose. So, either Ethan has decided she's worthy of that trust or he just doesn't care anymore.

"Sure. Of course," Liana agrees hastily, leaving even as the words are still exiting her mouth.

Ethan remains at the table, watching her go, then he turns to Ophelia, and the intensity in his expression makes her take a step back. "I've been doing this for twelve years, been on dozens of planets and asteroids," he says in a low voice. "First as a pilot and then a mission commander. I've never found a body like that. Never found a body, period. Any deaths have always been clearly recorded and the remains returned or properly disposed of. Leaving a body just out there, in plain view . . ." He takes a deep breath. "That does not happen. At the very least, it's a potential contamination source for the existing planetary biome. And that says nothing about the disrespect and degradation for the person that used to be." His tone harsh, he jerks his thumb over his shoulder in the general direction of Silly Bird's owner. "Combine that with what we found yesterday, and I have no idea what the fuck is going on here."

Ophelia opens her mouth. "It's not ERS," she blurts, before she can stop herself.

He frowns at her. "I never said that it was."

No, Ophelia is the one who is fixated with worry. Why? Because of a couple of admittedly strange incidents. Because she and Birch are both from Goliath. Or perhaps simply because it is her worst nightmare, what she's feared since she was eleven years old.

"I'm more concerned that something happened here, and that's why Pinnacle bailed without documenting anything." He jerks his head in the rough direction of the city ruins. Or possibly to indicate the dead Pinnacle crew member again. Both, maybe.

"It's possible," she admits. "But I don't think they would

have sold the planetary rights, then. That would have just brought more attention to . . . whatever."

He eyes her for a few seconds without saying anything, as if weighing his words and her potential response. "Have you known them to do something like—"

"No." Not that. But it wouldn't surprise her if they had. "I did find some odd things in here, though, the other day," she adds belatedly.

Ethan is not impressed by the wedding ring or the dog digi-foto, for all the reasons she imagined. But the removed molar implant and old bloody scratch marks on the desk are more intriguing to him.

"I don't like this. Any of it," he says, rubbing his forehead. "Not the dead guy outside, not the weird itching, nosebleeds, and headaches, or . . . the other stuff. When we got here, Kate found that the Pinnacle team had just left the generator running until it burned out. No one does that. They might trash the place, but not that. It might all be coincidence, but I don't like that so many of these things are piling up all at once." He takes a deep breath. "I'm going to ask Kate to run another diagnostic on our bio filters and the environmental systems. Just to be sure."

She nods. "Okay." Relieved—why does she feel relieved? He's talking about some kind of alien contagion so tiny or un-recognizable that it could bypass all their precautions.

It's not possible. As long as they've been following safety and decon protocols, which they have.

Ethan starts to move past her and then stops. "But, Ophelia, to be clear . . . this is not Eckhart-Reiser syndrome. Correct?"

Guilt twists in her, a thick, knotty braid of regret, uncer-tainty, and frustration. "Myriad physical symptoms can ac-company Eckhart-Reiser, including some of the ones we're seeing, but others too. Psychogenic itch, hair loss, agitation, lethargy, for example. The problem is those can all belong to other diagnoses as well." Ophelia folds her arms across her chest. *What is the game plan here, Phe? When are you going to say something?*

Not until I see more, not until I'm sure. There's too much at stake.

And not just for her, either. With two black marks in a row, this team will be locked out of any R&E work. Deemed too high risk. And not just with Montrose but any of the reputable corporations in this business. That matters, too. Ethan told her that himself.

Ethan's mouth flattens, but he doesn't press her on her nonanswer. He just nods at where her arms are folded. "You're scratching, Doctor."

She looks down and sucks in a breath. Her fingers, clawlike, are dug into her opposite sleeve at the elbow, nails reflexively sinking in and dragging back and forth. She drops her arms immediately. "I—"

But Ethan is walking away.

20

Ophelia waits until she's in the A side corridor and out of sight before she rolls up her left sleeve. Dry, bumpy red skin, scale-like, weaves in an uneven pattern along the back of her forearm to the inside of her wrist and up past the inner bend of her elbow.

What is that? Heat blazes from the afflicted skin; she can feel it radiating from the surface from centimeters away, like holding her hand in front of a fire.

Some kind of late-breaking infection from the port surgery? It is the same arm. But the port itself is surrounded by normal skin, not puffy or red at all. An allergic reaction, maybe. Birch . . . his results showed some kind of allergy, didn't they?

She touches her arm gingerly with a fingertip and watches in horror as the raised individual nodules . . . shift beneath her skin. They slip away from the pressure of her finger, collecting in a semicircle around it. The accompanying tickling sensation is followed almost immediately by a fiery itchiness.

Her skin crawls along her spine in response.

When she lifts her finger from her arm, a patch of clear skin is revealed beneath it. The bumps hold their pattern until, as she watches, one returns to the open space, then another, and another. Until it's no longer clear and no longer distinguishable from the rest of her afflicted skin.

She slaps a hand across her mouth, fighting the urge to vomit.

This is not hives or contact dermatitis or even psychogenic itching. Skin conditions don't move in response to stimuli.

Bugs. It's bugs! a panicked voice screeches in her head. *You're on a fucking alien planet, and there are alien bugs.*

Except there aren't any bugs. There can't be. The scans would have shown that. There's nothing alive here but the six of them.

Really, still counting on those super accurate scans, are we?

She ignores the voice in her head.

Besides, everything else is sealed tight. Their suits, the hab. There's no way in for anything.

That we know of. That's the key phrase she's missing. Because isn't the point of these missions to look for new things? Isn't that why Ethan is asking Kate to run another diagnostic, just in case?

Ophelia starts to call for Ethan, to tell him, but stops before any sounds escape. What is she going to say? He has the same information she does. Pulling him in before she has any answers is only going to make things worse.

She hustles for the med-scanner and medikit in her office. Birch may not have let her run an exhaustive check, but she can do one on herself. Just stay calm. There's a simple explanation. There has to be. Think it through.

Why did it have to be fucking bugs?

It still might not be. Several psychological conditions present themselves with body delusions. Ekbom's syndrome. Cotard's syndrome. Or, hell, even Morgellon's, though no one has had that diagnosis in the better part of a century, since it was wrapped under the umbrella of Ekbom's.

But if it's psychological somehow, then they're back to ERS, though it would be a variation of ERS that she's never seen.

And if that's the case, she needs to tell Ethan. Everything. Damn the consequences.

She's thinking so hard that at first she doesn't hear it over the air rushing through the ventilation system.

"... can't ..."

A pause.

". . . course, I want to . . . it's home. Home."

She stops. Whispers, somewhere ahead of her. Chills ripple across her skin, triggering another bout of itching along her arm, which she has to work to ignore.

Real voices?

Little Bird, don't make me find you . . .

Her father, the memory of him or a completely imagined circumstance, takes the cue to speak up. He sounds louder, but less solid than the other whispers somehow. His words are like water slipping through her closed fingers, there and gone.

Whereas this voice, while difficult to hear, lingers, clings to reality. A sibilant *S*. The huff of breath in front of the *H* in "home."

And it sounds like it's coming from her office, drifting out into the corridor from the open door.

Ophelia edges closer, scratching at her arm mainly so she can focus on what she's hearing instead of the burning desire to scrape her skin against the nearest sharp edge.

"Ash, please . . . don't . . ."

Ash. Who is Ash?

". . . can't ask me to do that. Not with her here."

Ophelia's only getting half a conversation, and she can't tell who's speaking. It's a man, she thinks. Suresh? Birch is showering, and Ethan didn't come this way. Did Suresh manage to get a direct connection to someone back on Earth? Ophelia didn't think that was possible this far out, even in clear conditions, let alone in the middle of another storm.

She closes the distance, moving as quietly as she can in her fabric shoes with their flat soles, and peers around the corner.

A tall figure is standing at the far wall of her office, staring out the window, angled toward the view of the former city. His breath clouds the duraglass in rapidly vanishing condensation.

His profile is immediately recognizable; it's Birch. His white towel is looped over his shoulders but it looks dry, still holding its creases from storage.

"Birch." Ophelia stops at the threshold. "What are you doing here?" She hadn't seen him cross back over through the central hub, from the C side to A, but to be fair, she and the others had been fairly distracted with the whole bored-out-chunk-of-a-human-on-video thing. "I thought you were going to clean up."

He doesn't respond. Continues staring out the window.

An uneasy feeling spreads its wings in Ophelia, preparing for flight. "Birch, are you—"

"Just looking," he says, speaking over her.

"Looking at what?" Anticipatory dread curls in her stomach.

Birch turns away from the window with what seems like physical effort. His eyes are unfocused and so very red. He's digging at his left arm again.

She opens her mouth to ask again.

"Looking for you. My head." He blinks rapidly, then raises his hand to his temple. "It's hurting. Can you give me something?" His words are coming faster now, like he's waking up.

"Oh. Yeah. Yes, of course." She turns to find the medikit. It's on the desk, where she left it last night.

Then she stops, the burning in her arm giving the sense of movement beneath the skin.

She faces him again. "Birch, can I check on your arm?"

He blinks at her, gaze distant, as if he's trying to interpret her words.

"Birch, can I—" she begins again.

"No, it's fine," he says. "Just my head."

"I really would like to make sure," she says. "If you can just roll up your sleeve, I promise, I'll be quick."

"I would really like a lot of things. Namely, not to be working with Bloody Bledsoe's kid." His voice rises in volume toward the end.

She flinches and automatically looks toward the door to see who might have overheard.

"But we don't always get what we want," Birch says, baring his teeth at her in a mockery of a smile.

Strangely, his gums don't appear to be bleeding anymore, but they . . . appear oddly dark. Little dark seeds appear to have sprouted in the gaps between his teeth. What the fuck?

"Doctor," he presses. "Unless you'd rather I express my pain in another way."

The threat, mild as it is, does its job, sending a wave of cold panic through her.

"All right." She heads toward the medikit. With her back turned, Ophelia feels somehow safer to ask the next question. "Who were you talking to, when I came in just now?"

He makes a noise, a grunt of surprise. "I wasn't talking to anyone."

She focuses on getting the painkiller loaded into the hypo. "Who is Ash?"

Birch's response is immediate, a sharp inhale, as if she's reached over and slapped him. "Do you think that's funny?" He crosses the unit in three strides to grab her arm and yank her around to face him. "What the fuck is wrong with you?" He gives Ophelia a shake, and it makes her teeth rattle in her head.

She's too stunned to react at first—like always—but the pinch of his too-tight grasp finally penetrates. "Let go. Now."

His face contorted in a sneer, he steps back, holding his hands up in a mockery of surrender. "You bring up Ash, and I'm the bad guy?"

"I didn't bring him up," she shoots back. "I heard you say the name. I don't even know who it is! You were talking and—"

"There's no one here," he says, throwing his hand out wide to indicate the space. "Who would I be talking to?"

"I saw . . ." Ophelia stops. Had she actually *seen* him speaking? She replays the scene in her mind: Birch at the window, staring out. Fog from his breath on the glass. But is his mouth moving?

No. The answer is no.

She heard his voice in the hall, but not once she was in the room. She never saw him talking.

Fear soars in her chest, and that sensation of falling while standing still returns. She was so sure that she'd heard it, actually heard it, versus inside her own head. How would she even have known what to imagine, if it was only in her mind?

It dawns on her then: Birch and Ash. Both nature names, in Goliath tradition.

Ophelia squeezes her eyes shut. Brothers would be a good guess, even though Birch's file lists him as an only child from Alterra Station. And based on his reaction, odds would suggest this is—or was—the brother who died at the hands of her father.

Which means that Ophelia, who once studied everything she could find about her father, if only to avoid becoming him, would definitely have known the name Ash.

Birch makes a disgusted noise, and she opens her eyes.

"Forget the meds. I think I'm better off without anything from you." He pushes past her without waiting for a response.

"But—" She starts to follow him but thinks better of it after a few steps. What, exactly, is she going to say? *Only one of us is right, and at the moment I'm not sure who?*

Hands shaking, she returns the painkillers to the medikit and reaches for the med-scanner. She's going to run every test she can think of on herself, on her arm, and figure out what's happening. If it's ERS—or rather, if she's ruled out everything else, as there is no definitive test for the syndrome—she'll tell Severin in the morning. Preferably before Birch starts talking.

Blood cools so quickly on the station's textured metal decking.

It turns tacky, sticky, losing that red vigor of life. Dark puddles of lost potential, pooling around collapsed skulls and unseeing eyes.

But it's a necessary evil to combat a larger one. And at this moment, it's also a useful one.

Perfect little high-arched footprints dance on the floor ahead, outlined in drying red. That second toe is longer than the first, sticking out above the rest, a daub of blood to differentiate. "Royalty," her mother said once, laughing. "It means we're descended from royalty."

This is her fault. She's one of them. *Those eyes, dark and cold, staring back at her through fake tears as she pretended to cower. And now Ophelia has no choice but to solve the problem she created.*

Ophelia tightens her grip on the blood-slicked handle of the pickax. "Little Bird, where are you? Come say hello." *Her voice, too deep somehow, rumbles out into the silence, sending a jolt through her.*

No response, no sound at all except the faint pings along the wall as the electronics of emergency alert continue to signal danger, alternate panels of flashing red and too-bright white.

She edges forward down the curving corridor on level seventeen. The weight of the pickax tugs painfully at her shoulder. Swinging hard and fast so many times has tightened the muscles across her back, but the adrenaline buoyant in her veins makes the sharp ache easier to ignore.

The mining ax is not meant to be a weapon, just an old-fashioned tool for the tight corners and small veins where their other equipment can't reach, but it certainly works to split flesh and smash skulls. Gobbets of torn skin cling to the far end of the ax, mixed in with splinters of white bone and grayish clumps of brain.

Signs of a job well done. Disease being cut free of the host.

She picks up the pace, stepping over the sporadic tangles of tubes and cords snaking across the corridor, white minerals crusting over the ribbing. It smells dank and fusty down here, as if there's rot just beneath the surface. HRUs, humidity reclamation units, cobbled together from spare parts, stick out from jagged holes in the walls, where they've been inserted to help pull every spare molecule of water from the air. Post-orbit modifications to carry and recycle more water to the grow labs. More people means more food needed.

Or so they say, but when have they ever told the truth about anything? Do they even eat? She doesn't know any-more. Sometimes it's hard to tell the difference between the ones who can still be saved and the ones who are lost.

Ahead of Ophelia, the footprints taper out to smudges be-fore disappearing. But that's all right; there's nowhere for her prey to go. Hydroponics is an essential service, so every door on this floor will be locked down during an emergency. Even the stairwell at the end of the level won't open without an ad-ministration access chip.

She steps around another HRU that's jutting into her path—this one not doing its job so well, judging by the glistening seepage beneath—and creeps around the final curve, hoping to surprise the child. Hoping the girl doesn't try to run. Ophelia wants this to be as simple and painless as possible.

Raising the pickax, she lunges out, away from the wall, to find . . . nothing. A patch of empty floor with dust and de-tritus gathering in the corners. The torn edge of a reflective wrapper from a meal bar winks and blinks back at her. The stairwell door is still shut tight, yellow light flashing "No Ad-mittance" on the panel to the right of it. The service panel to access the station's mechanicals is still bolted in place.

Ophelia smears a hand across her eyes, as if that will change what she's seeing. The girl came this way, she's certain.

Isn't she?

The pain in her head flares, the buzzing in her ears sending waves of dizziness over her that warp and bend her surround-ings, twisting them until she can't tell which way is up.

Ophelia is out of time. They're taking over. She can feel them changing her, altering her cells. Soon she'll be like the rest of them.

Her gaze falls to the decking, searching for any trace of footprints. But the floor around her is barren, except for the slow expansion of the water puddle beneath the nearest HRU. A puddle that's clearly new. Still emerging.

An idea flickers at the back of her muddled brain, rising above their influence.

She leans the ax against the corridor wall. Then, with an effort that feels like it takes every bit of strength she has left, she tears the HRU away from the wall. Water sprays into the air before cutting off to a dull trickle.

From the jagged hole in the wall, amid the tubes and wires, vivid green eyes—just like the ones that stare back at her from the mirror every morning—stare up at Ophelia. She is huddled to fit into the narrow space, her head down, knees pulled to her chest, and arms wrapped around her shins. Her dirty and bloodied toes stick out from beneath her blue school tunic and uneven leggings.

When Ophelia reclaims her ax, the girl offers no defense, no plea. She blinks once, a single tear streaking down one flushed cheek.

"I'm sorry, Little Bird." Ophelia raises her arm and—

Ophelia lurches upright in bed, gasping. It takes her a moment to reorient herself. She's in the bunk room, not hiding behind an HRU on Goliath or wielding a pickax over the child version of herself.

Her dream made her both her father and herself, both the murderer and his potential victim. *Jesus. That's messed up. Even for you, Phe.*

She drops back onto her mattress. Her left arm is throbbing, and her eyes are gritty with lack of sleep. The light in the outer bunk room window tells her nothing about what time it is, but Liana's mattress above her is still bent with her weight. So it must be early yet.

Ophelia spent hours yesterday, late into the night, searching for patterns, details she might have missed, looking everything up against every database she has access to out here, which is not many.

Now, she could probably diagnose and perform a routine appendectomy with the help of the Med-Bay medical unit on the *Resilience*, if they could get up there. But she found nothing that matches what's going on here.

ERS is, of course, the top contender, simply because of the frequency with which it occurs in this population (R&E teams) and the newness of the condition, which means they're still learning about it and variations may crop up.

So, Ethan then. She needs to tell him. All of it. Just in case. Maybe he'll understand.

He won't look at you the same, though. None of them will.

Ophelia takes a deep breath and then sits up. She makes herself look as she pulls her arm out from under the blanket. She's not sure what she's afraid she'll see—more of the bumps? Larger ones? Sprouting strange antennae?

She poked and prodded last night, even took a sample, which registered absolutely nothing on the med-scanner.

Which doesn't mean it's nothing, just that it's nothing their medical equipment has been programmed to recognize. Another point in favor of the alien something-or-other diagnosis.

Ophelia shudders, and it takes her a second to work up to looking down at the skin she's exposed, the few centimeters below her elbow.

Which is clear. Not a bump in sight. Just a few pale freckles and the thin white line of a scar from the sharpened edge of their table on Goliath.

Frowning, she tugs the blanket down farther. Still nothing.

Her arm aches like she's done a full day of biceps curls, but there's nothing visible. How is that possible?

Heart pounding, she shoves the blanket all the way down, revealing that her other arm is also completely normal looking, as are what she can see of her legs beneath her compression shorts.

That's good news. Whatever it was has resolved itself. The best possible outcome.

But it doesn't feel right; it's like she's missing something. How could something that awful just go away?

Maybe it was never there to begin with, a tiny whisper offers from the back of her mind. *You never saw bumps like that on anyone else. Maybe it's just one more hallucination that—*

No. *No.* She ran tests last night. She took a sample, for God's sake.

It was real. It was.

It's just . . . gone now.

But when she reaches out to touch the smooth skin of her knees, just to be sure, she sees what she missed before, in her search for skin disruptions: dried blood on her fingertips, creasing into her palm. Not a lot, but enough to be fucking alarming, since there should be none.

Tingles spread into her fingers and her feet, turning her extremities numb. Where did it come from? She doesn't see any obvious cuts or injuries, never mind having no memory of getting hurt. Her period is regulated by an implant, has been for years, and besides, the blood is not on her shorts or sheets, as far as she can tell.

But when she twists around looking, she finds it is on her pillowcase.

Ophelia freezes. Then she reaches up to touch her upper lip. It's sticky and stiff, and her fingers come away with more red.

A nosebleed. That's all. Relief makes her insides cave in. For a second she thought it was something utterly horrific, like the sudden evacuation of those bumps by force.

A nosebleed. *That* she can handle. As long as those fucking bumps are gone.

"I can handle it," she says in a whisper, more as a reassurance to herself than anything else.

"Ophelia?" Liana murmurs above her.

Ophelia goes still.

"Are you going to your office today?" Liana's voice is soft but not sleepy. Whatever this is, she's been awake, thinking about it for a while.

Ophelia tries to think, to move away from her own concerns and focus on Liana and what she's asking.

"I'm planning to, yes."

"I was thinking . . . I could come to your office again. Just to, you know, check in," Liana adds. "After yesterday."

Empathy pulses in Ophelia's chest. The discovery of a body in such a way would have been traumatic for anyone, let alone the person operating the autodrillers, who also happened to have suffered a loss recently. "Of course. Absolutely. Whenever you're ready." But speaking pulls at the stiffening mask of blood on her skin. She needs to get cleaned up before Liana or anyone else sees her.

Ophelia swings her feet to the floor. And Ethan . . . She hesitates. Well, it can't hurt to wait a little longer, until after she speaks with Liana. Based on the wind howling outside, they're all going to be trapped inside for at least a portion of the day. She'll find him then.

She wants this one last chance to help, to make a difference.

Ophelia gathers her jumpsuit and hygiene products from her bag under her bunk and keeps her head down as she leaves for the lav.

The lav is empty, fortunately. The wavy, shatterproof mirror on the wall in the narrow space provides a blurry shock. The blood from her nose is spattered and smeared all over the lower half of her face—thanks to her pillow, she would imagine.

It's unconscionable to use her water allotment this early in their first week, but sonic isn't going to cut it.

Once she's dried off and dressed, she passes through the central hub, stopping just long enough to make a coffee in the galley. She's exhausted, again. A loud clanging, followed by muffled swearing, comes from behind the galley. Kate—or Kate and Suresh—at work in syscon already.

Coffee in hand, Ophelia rounds the galley and cuts through the central hub to the A side airlock, her mind churning, reviewing what she knows of Liana from their previous, brief conversations and anticipating possible tracks their conversation could take. *This . . . this* she can address. The relief of having something manageable to anticipate, within her field of expertise, cannot be overestimated. It makes her feel like she can breathe freely for the first time in several days.

As before, Ophelia is greeted by the jaunty figure of the abandoned envirosuit, propped against the curved corridor wall outside her office. Even when she's expecting it, its appearance is still a bit of a jolt, given how person-like it looks.

The helmet and shoulders are more slumped today as the top-heavy suit is sliding toward the floor, but the legs are still crossed at the ankles, looking for all the world like a team member parked out in a patch of sun for a nap—minus the sun, of course.

With a sigh, Ophelia steps over the legs. She would be tempted to move it to the central hub, but she suspects that would simply result in it showing up in other places. The lav. Her bunk, with the covers pulled up.

She halts and then backtracks. DELACROIX. The name glints up at her in block text stitched on the shoulder patch.

What are the odds that this would belong to a crew member other than the one they discovered yesterday? The only person who doesn't need an envirosuit on this planet is, well, one in his condition. That also means he likely died inside the hab and then they . . . disposed of his body outside. Rather than an accident of some variety outside, which would then necessitate his retrieval and preparation for burial. Kind of makes sense, given how little preparation they did.

Her mouth tightens. She makes a mental note to tell Ethan. It might make his conversation with mission control go a little more smoothly if he has a name to share. Liana might find it reassuring as well, though, again, Ophelia suspects that Liana's reaction yesterday, even her decision to talk today, is more about her unresolved issues with Ava's death than about Silly Bird's owner, even if Liana doesn't realize it.

Ophelia's so focused on next steps that she doesn't realize something's wrong until after she pulls open the door and nearly steps on the shattered remains of her iVR system tablet.

She jumps back and stares at the remains of her office. The two chairs are overturned, the tables shoved out of place. The notepads she uses for patient notes are upended on the floor, pages creased and bent. The contents of the medikit are spread around the floor like someone spun in a circle with the case open until everything spilled.

Or like an addict tore up the room, desperately searching for something.

Shit. Ophelia should have locked the medikit up. Even if there aren't any known addiction issues on the team, she knows better than to leave meds of any kind out where someone can—

An unfamiliar sight snags her gaze along the back wall, below the shattered sample container units, and it takes her a second to understand what her eyes are telling her.

No, it's not another empty envirosuit or any other person-like substitute stretched out on the table that's been pushed into place against the wall. It's a person, Birch, resting on the table, as if that's the perfect place for a nap.

Or to crash.

"What the hell?" Fury boils over in Ophelia as she navigates her way through the mess, trying not to break or crush anything else. Getting back to the *Resilience* for replacements isn't going to happen for who knows how long. "Hey, wake up!" she demands.

As she gets closer, though, past the chairs and the other table, which were partially blocking her view, she sees that his left arm is dangling off the table, fingers brushing the floor. An awkward position for a nap, even a drug-induced one.

The blood spatter starts about a meter away, uneven and

chaotic, and then the droplets get larger and fatter, until they pool together, creating the drying red sea beneath his hand.

Blood, too much blood. Her grip tightens on her mug, but the tremors racking her whole body slop coffee over the edge anyway, burning her fingers. The pain registers in a dim, dissociative note, as if she's watching it happen to someone else, because she's transfixed by the scene before her.

The sleeve of Birch's jumpsuit is shredded to ribbons, and it too is hanging toward the floor. The skin on his forearm is sliced and raised in flaps, dangling like loosened bits of bark on his namesake tree, revealing the pink marbled muscle and tendons.

But worse than that?

The ragged chunks, like hacking cuts or bites, missing from both.

21

Ophelia stumbles backward, buzzing loud in her head. A chair leg catches at her ankle, and she goes down hard on her backside. It knocks the mug out of her hand, the air out of her lungs, and for a moment it feels as if she's going to be stuck here forever. Just frozen in this hellscape with blood and a body and—

Scooting backward on her hands, she frees herself from the thorny chair appendages, and then she turns over and scrabbles to her feet, bolting for the corridor.

She runs, not sure if she's running from or to, until she smacks straight into a solid body at the threshold to the central hub.

Ethan. He grabs her shoulders, pushing her back carefully, holding her steady. His mouth moves, but Ophelia can't hear him. The roaring sound is so loud in her ears, dark spots dancing in her vision.

Breathe, Ophelia. Breathe. She recognizes the shape of the words first, his lips forming the sounds in slow motion. Her first attempt at an inhale hurts with its shallowness. She tries again, and this time, air floods her lungs in cool, clean relief.

"What's wrong? Ophelia, what happened?" Ethan's urgency is conveyed in his firm grasp and the intensity of his gaze on her, but his voice is calm, level. That's why he's in charge.

Ophelia swallows hard and manages to croak out a single syllable. "Birch." Her hand flaps in the direction of the office before she can stop it.

Ethan nudges her back against the wall. "Stay here."

As soon as he releases her, she sinks to the floor, pulling

her knees up to her chest. She can't stop shaking. Trauma response. *Come on, Bray. You know this.*

Ethan sees it faster than she did, with a sharp intake of breath that she can hear even from around the curved corridor.

"Birch." The loud sounds of crunching glass and crashing furniture marks his progress across the room and then his search for something.

The PMU has a defibrillator function.

Fuck. She closes her eyes. She should have tried, she should have looked.

That much blood, already drying? It's too late.

Yes, but it would have been better to try.

Better for whom?

"Come on, Birch! Come on!" A distinct thump, one that can only belong to the defibrillator on a limp body, signals that Ethan's found and applied the device.

"What the hell is going on?" Kate appears at the doorway from the central hub a moment later, a streak of grease on her cheek. "I'm trying to fix the generator, which is hard enough without all the shouting and commo—" She pauses long enough to look at Ophelia, taking in her posture for the first time, it seems.

"Come on! Come on! Breathe!" Ethan's voice carries clearly down the corridor, now containing the first hint of furious panic.

Kate's eyes go wide. "No." She darts down the hall. A second later, her voice joins Ethan's, urging Birch to breathe, to come back to them.

But Ophelia already knows how this is going to end. Outside, the wind screeches in delight. Another permanent resident to keep all the others company.

"I don't understand. What . . . what happened?" Liana, seated next to Ophelia, asks again. Liana's breathing sounds ragged, on the edge of hyperventilating, but she's not crying. Not yet. She is focused on the few centimeters of amber in the bottom of her coffee cup.

When Ethan called the meeting in the central hub, Kate arrived with a bottle of highly questionable alcohol in hand. Not even a label on the bottle, just a sticker with "engine cleaner" scrawled in an uneven hand. Without a word, she slammed the bottle on the table and then gathered five mugs from the galley.

Ethan shakes his head. "I don't know. Bled to death is my best guess." He looks to Ophelia for confirmation.

"I think so." Her voice sounds rusty.

Liana takes a sip from her cup and coughs. "From what?"

He hesitates. "A wound to his arm."

Wound. That is an understatement, to say the least. It looked more like a dissection, with . . . gnawing. Ophelia presses the back of her hand against her mouth, against the fresh rebellion of her stomach.

It resembled what her father had done. Not what he's most infamous for—the rampage through Goliath with the power wrench and pickax, bashing in heads and faces of anyone who didn't scramble away fast enough. But the less talked-about deaths of his crew, before their transport even docked at the space station. Based on intraship security recordings from the mining transport, it seemed he was convinced that they were possessed by some unknown entity, something he called the Devourer. He broke into their cold sleep tanks and cut into them, trying to "save" them by digging into their chests, their arms and legs, searching for signs of it.

He thought Ophelia had been infected too. It's what he would have done to her, if he'd caught her.

She shudders. The memory is always chilling, but in this case, so is the coincidence. It rests uneasily on her, like a tower of rocks that have been stacked precariously.

"It might also have been the eye trauma," Kate says with a grimace.

Ophelia jerks to look at her. "Wait, what?"

Ethan and Kate both stare at her. "You missed the pair of scissors jammed into his skull through his right eye?" Kate demands.

"I didn't . . . I saw his arm," Ophelia begins. How had she missed that? His right eye was facing away from her, but still. Why the right instead of the left? Hard to guess the logic when he was clearly not acting on anything that would make sense to the rest of it. His QuickQ implant was in that eye. A symbolic severing of communication?

"It, uh, likely entered his brain," Ethan says, scrubbing his hands on his jumpsuit. He's not drinking. "Best guess."

"Oh my God," Liana whispers before shooting the rest of her drink. She puts the cup down, wheezing and sputtering.

Scissors he took from the medikit. The medikit that Ophelia had not secured.

In that moment, her memory flashes back to that small, warm security office on Goliath.

What did he say to you? What did you know? Why didn't you tell someone?

Suresh stands, toppling his chair. The clatter echoes through the empty space. "I want to see him," he says.

Kate shakes her head. "Not a good idea." She pours herself another drink. "I wish I hadn't."

"I don't care," Suresh snaps. "I don't believe it. Birch wouldn't do that to himself. He just wouldn't."

Before Ethan can respond, Suresh turns on Ophelia. "He said he was going to you for help with his headache. What did you do to him?"

Ophelia lurches back, stung. "He came to my office yesterday, not long after we came back inside. But I didn't do anything. He wouldn't even let me give him painkillers for his head."

"Why not?" Suresh demands.

She takes a deep breath. "He was . . . I thought he was talking to himself. I was concerned, and I tried to ask him about what I'd heard, but he refused. He claimed I'd . . . misheard. And he left without letting me help him."

Ethan frowns at her. "This is the first I'm hearing of it."

"What the fuck are you even here for?" Suresh asks, throwing his hands up. "Aren't you supposed to stop this?"

"Someone talking to themselves doesn't indicate suicidal ideation, or even mental illness," Ophelia shoots back. "And I wasn't sure. You can't restrain someone just because—"

"You weren't sure?" Suresh overenunciates the words, as if he can't believe what he's hearing. Then he turns on Ethan. "Seriously, why is she here?"

A roiling mix of humiliation and nausea churn in her. Because he's right, but also not.

"Enough," Ethan says. "This isn't productive."

"This is bullshit." Suresh turns and stalks off toward the A side.

This is it. Put or up or shut up.

"The damage to Birch's arm." Ophelia hesitates. "I've seen something like it before. Once." She chooses her words carefully. "With Bloody Bledsoe."

The silence in the intervening moment seems to make the name hang in the air, like toxic smoke.

"No, he smashed heads, remember? That's what Suresh said," Liana says, sounding small and younger than her years, someone relying on the details of a campfire legend to convince herself that the strange sounds in the woods are nothing to worry about.

"Not with his team. On the mining transport. He thought they were infected with . . . something. He cut them open, looking for it." Ophelia's voice is cool, distant, as if reciting from a textbook.

"Wait." Kate holds up an unsteady hand. "Are you saying

he was about to go Bloody Bledsoe on us?" she asks with a disbelieving laugh.

"No. I'm not." Her father certainly never inflicted any harm on himself, not until the end. "But I don't understand why—"

"You know what I don't get?" Kate sits forward, reaching for the bottle. "Why didn't he scream? He did that, to himself, and we never heard a thing. How is that possible? It had to hurt, what he was doing. What he did." She pours herself another healthy dose, then slides the bottle down to Liana, who fumbles to catch it, stopping it at the edge of the table. "And how did he stay conscious during that? I mean, he was either bleeding out when he stabbed scissors in his eye or he had scissors in his eye while performing surgery on his arm."

Liana's breath hitches and she pours herself more to drink, or tries to. The bottle wobbles in her hand, spilling around her cup, until Ophelia reaches out and steadies the neck of it. Liana nods in thanks.

"You're not suggesting that someone here is responsible," Ethan says to Kate. It's a question hidden inside a statement.

She gives a shrug. "If Birch was unconscious, that would keep him quiet, yeah?"

"Who? Who would do that?" Liana asks, eyes glassy with unshed tears.

Ophelia's mind immediately flashes to the shadowy figure that she—and possibly Birch—saw outside the hab. Maybe. But that's not possible. Even setting aside obvious issues with survivability on Lyria 393-C, there's no way anyone could sneak inside the hab without being heard or seen. She shakes her head to dismiss the thought, but it gives rise to another.

"I don't think we can make any assumptions about what Birch could or could not do," Ophelia says. "He was . . . not himself, and that means . . ." She stops, the words curling up and dying in her throat.

Blood on her face this morning. On her hands.

Instantly she pictures her reflection in the mirror earlier, blood smears from one side of her face to the other. Her stained hands beneath the shower water, turning the weak soapsuds pink.

Her head swirls in a vortex of dizziness. Suddenly she can feel the cool press of the scalpel in her hand, the warm spray against her cheek, and the thick metallic scent of fresh blood.

22

Ophelia can't move, numbness spreading throughout her body. All those years of her family's warnings and snide comments, her mother's fears—they proved to be accurate predictors. The tainted blood that her grandmother kept going on and on about was more than just her grandmother's snobbery and elitism. She wasn't just a classist bitch; she might actually have been right. Some people are more prone to psychotic breaks with ERS, and some of those, due to a combination of genetics and environment, are more prone to violence. That's proven. But Ophelia never considered that it might be an issue to truly worry about.

And now she needs to.

Last night she dreamed she was her father, hunting down a victim. And this morning she woke up with blood on her face and hands.

She could have killed Birch and not even realized it. Just disconnected from reality as easily as pushing a button to shut down Liana's beloved spiders.

Worse, in practical terms, is that Ophelia is the person with the best motive, the singular interest in keeping Birch quiet.

Acid, from the few sips of coffee she had before . . . before, scorches up the back of her throat. She presses her hand over her mouth. Her eyes water, blurring her vision.

"—calling it. As soon as the storm lifts, we're done," Ethan is saying. "We'll bring back the samples and data we've gathered so far, and that'll be it."

"Fuck," Kate says. "Are you sure? Ethan, if we go back now . . ."

He nods, responsibility weighing visibly on him, in the lines of weariness on his forehead. "I know."

Kate stays quiet for a moment, then her expression folds inward, morphing into blank resolve. "Okay."

"Let's get everything ready to shut down and close up, as much as possible," Ethan says. "I don't know when the weather is going to break, but I want to be ready to move as soon as we have the opportunity."

We're leaving. Ophelia sinks back into her chair. If she's the danger, they'll soon be safe from her.

Except she can't know that. To return, they'll have to put themselves in cold sleep, and based on what she remembers from protocol, Ethan and Ophelia will be the last to go.

Field Bledsoe, the crew leader, did the same thing. He sliced into his unconscious teammates. They never even had a chance to fight back.

Ophelia has seen the security videos from the transport dock. Her father emerging from the transport, covered in blood, head to toe, except for his eyelids when he blinked. Because of course his eyes were open when he was butchering his team, his friends.

"Roger that," Kate says to Ethan. Hands flat on the table, she pushes herself away from the table and then up from her seat. She sways slightly and then corrects herself, straightening her shoulders as she walks away.

"What about Birch? We're not leaving him behind. Not—" Liana lifts her chin. "Not like Ava."

Ethan flinches, a slight gesture, more near his eyes than anything. "Of course not." He looks to Ophelia. "But we'll have to make some temporary arrangements in the meantime. To make sure he is . . . taken care of." It takes Ophelia a second to realize he's looking at her, again, as a medical professional. Even though, again, she is not that kind of doctor. And another second to recognize the unspoken question about preservation.

"The cold," she manages after a moment.

Liana's jaw drops in disbelief. "You're going to put him outside?"

"Just for now," Ethan says. "We're not leaving him behind. I promise."

Something about this is ringing a faint bell, but Ophelia can't focus on it, not with alarms screaming in her head. Bloody Bledsoe! Bloody fucking Bledsoe.

Say something, Phe. Speak up. Tell him! If you had said something sooner, maybe Birch would still be alive.

Ophelia stands abruptly, her chair squealing against the floor. "I need to talk to you," she says to Ethan too loudly, the words exploding out of her mouth. "Now."

He looks startled, then wary. "All right."

Liana's gaze skates between them, but she doesn't say anything.

Ophelia steps away from the table, leading the way into the C side corridor, away from Liana, Kate in syscon, and Suresh somewhere on the A side.

Ethan follows at a slower pace. "I'll be right back," he tells Liana.

Ophelia paces a few steps back and forth in the corridor, waiting for him.

If she tells him, it's all over. Her patients, former and current, will know that she lied to them on the most basic level, that they were wrong to give her their trust. Same with her friends, her exes. She closes her eyes. *Julius.*

The consequences won't be limited just to her, either. Her family will be tried and convicted in the media, and while some of them deserve it, others don't—Dulcie has no idea who her older sister really is.

And that's if they don't put Ophelia and her mother in prison for their deception.

Deception. Ha. That's her grandmother's word, and she is conveniently too dead to take responsibility for the choices she made because she was too embarrassed to tell the truth. Lies, they're lies. Covered up by a ton of money, bribery, and blackmail.

Or, on the positive side, maybe Ophelia will end up locked in a secure facility, screaming about bugs, the Devourer, and being chased by her long-dead father. Not that she'll be aware of it. To her, that will be reality.

But no one else will die here. She takes a deep breath. That's the most important part.

"Ophelia?" Ethan prompts from behind her, making her jump.

She turns to face him, raking a hand through her hair, still damp from the shower this morning. How was that only such a short time ago?

"Look, I don't know how to even start—" She cuts herself off. "None of that matters. You need to restrain me until we can get out of here."

His eyebrows shoot skyward. "Excuse me?"

"Lock me up!" She throws her hands in the air. "Pick one of the unused modules. Toss a mattress and some meal-paks in one of the A side units, I don't care. Obviously not A-5, because . . ."

He cocks his head to one side, brow furrowed with confusion or concern or both. "Doctor, are you all right?" There's that command voice again. Smooth, calm, in charge.

She bites her bottom lip, feels it trembling beneath the pressure of her teeth. She releases it before she draws blood. "I think it's my fault. Birch, I mean."

Ethan's face undergoes a series of rapid emotions, landing on cold annoyance. "Doctor, if you're referring to your missed diagnosis, I don't have time to reassure—"

"Jesus Christ, Ethan, I'm trying to tell you I think I killed him!" Ophelia manages to bring her shout down by the end, but probably still not quite enough.

He steps back from her, repulsed. "What are you talking about? If this is some kind of joke, it's not—"

A hysterical laugh emerges from deep in her throat before she can stop it. "Why does everyone think I'm the one with the fucked-up sense of humor around here?"

He holds up his hand to stop her. "Just explain. Please."

She pauses to consider how to begin. "The other morning, I woke up and my shoe was gone. I found it in the central hub."

Irritation and disbelief war for dominance on his face. "Are you kidding me with this right now?"

"Just shut up and listen," she says. "I thought, at the time, it might have been another prank."

He grimaces.

"But now I think . . . I think I might have been sleepwalking. It's not uncommon for patients to experience more than one kind of parasomnia. Night terrors. Sleepwalking."

Ethan hesitates, then shrugs. "So you were sleepwalking. Sleep disturbances are not uncommon on R&E missions, as you've pointed out."

"Not usually this early on, but that doesn't matter." Ophelia folds her arms over herself. "And then, last night or this morning, I had this dream, but it was also part memory. I was there again." *Only, as my father.* Fuck, how had she not seen this earlier?

"Where, exactly?" Ethan asks, confused.

She swallows hard. "Goliath."

"The old space station in the Carver system?" he asks with a frown. "Why?"

"I'm . . . I was born there." It feels like letting go of a lit match she's been carrying for years, trying not to get burned, trying not to drop it.

A snort of disbelief escapes him, seemingly before he can stop it. He quickly regains control of his expression. "No, you weren't. You were born on that cult outpost."

"Commune colony," Ophelia corrects automatically. "That's what we told everyone, yes."

"Celestia whatever. Everyone knows that." He pauses. "Why are you saying this?"

Of course he's going to believe the media over her, the actual person involved. She wants to shout at him, *Do you think I don't know where I was born? Do you think I wouldn't want to forget this if I could?*

Okay, okay, breathe, slow down. She needs to build the case for him. "If I hadn't found that shoe, I would never have realized I was even out of bed. I would have just assumed I'd slept in my bunk without interruption. It might even have happened other times." Those dreams of wandering down corridors in the dark, had they not been dreams at all?

"You're telling me you think you killed Birch in your sleep." His tone is acid.

"It's not sleep, exactly. It's a memory. I'm reenacting a memory. Or a version of the memory, I don't know. It's confusing." She presses her fingers against her forehead and the headache throbbing within.

"Doctor, I agree with you that we have a problem here," he says, clearly struggling with his temper. "That's why we're heading home. But I don't think there's any reason to assume that Birch's death was—"

"I woke up with blood on my hands and face this morning. I thought . . . I thought it was just another bloody nose, like what Kate had. But it was a lot."

This time, Ethan's not quite as fast to respond. "It probably was a nosebleed."

"I wanted to check on his arm last night," Ophelia says. "My arm had this weird rash, breakout, I don't know. That's why I was scratching last night." She shudders at the memory of the movement beneath her skin. "Maybe it's part of this whole thing, maybe it's not. I wanted to check to see if Birch's was the same, but he wouldn't let me, threatened to tell everyone about me." She draws in a slow breath. "It's the same arm that was . . . dissected this morning."

"Breakout?" Ethan asks. "What kind of—"

"You're not listening to me," Ophelia says through clenched teeth. "I was born on Goliath."

"So you've said, which I still don't under—"

"I lived there until I was eleven, almost twelve." But that's not the real secret, is it? She feels like she's walking up to the cliff's edge, inching closer and closer, until pebbles are flying out from beneath her feet and the wind is pushing at her back. "My name was Lark Bledsoe. Field Bledsoe was my father."

Ethan rocks back as if she's taken a swing at him, clearly recognizing the name, but uncertainty still flickers around the edges of his expression.

Time to end that. End everything. Jump.

"Bloody Bledsoe is my father."

23

Before Ethan can protest, tell Ophelia that she's delusional—obviously not an impossibility, given their current situation—she continues. "I'd tell you to check with Birch. He recognized me. But obviously we're a little late for that." She flings her hand in a gesture toward her office and Birch's body within.

Ethan shakes his head, but he steps away from her, retreating toward the central hub. That hurts more than she expected.

"That doesn't make sense," Ethan says. "It's not possible. Bledsoe's family, they died in the attack. I was sixteen. I remember hearing that." His expression goes somewhere distant. "We had trouble getting food shipments in the Lunar Valley for a while because of the new transport regulations."

The lunar colony famine. More pain that could be traced directly back to her family.

"But I bet you didn't hear a lot about his family, did you?"

His silence is enough of a response.

"My mother fell in love with Field Bledsoe, and the Brays cut them off. They spread some story about her going on some special assignment somewhere because they were embarrassed. A Bray marrying an asteroid miner? Perish the thought. Brays are meant to work miners to death for greater profits, not procreate with them." Even the words taste sour in her mouth. "And after . . . after . . ." She swallows. "They paid. Everyone."

"No one can do that. Not even the Brays." But he sounds less certain now.

"I would agree with you, but the fact is, I'm living proof." Ophelia forces a shrug, more casual than anything she's feeling right now. "Goliath and the other stations were Pinnacle owned. Not to mention on the fuck-edge of nowhere. And when you have enough money, you can hide anything or pay people not to care." Sometimes she suspects it was more the latter than the former, which gives her even more doubt about humanity.

"But you work for Montrose. They would have done a background check and—"

Ophelia laughs, but it's a hopeless, empty sound. "They missed that Birch was from Goliath. I can guarantee you, my forged records are a lot better than his." And a lot more expensive. Plus, Montrose wanted her to work for them—all the better to rub it in her family's face. Even if they had spotted something odd, Ophelia doubts it would have mattered.

He scrubs his hands over his face and turns away from her.

She follows a step or two, then stops. "I don't know what's happening, what's causing the changes in behavior here, but I can't take the chance that I might hurt someone." Again. "Please, just listen to me. Put me in one of the—"

"Why are you here?" he asks. "You requested this assignment."

She stiffens. "I'm trying to help. I've devoted my life to helping prevent ERS. It was an opportunity to try new—"

"What I'm hearing is that you were so concerned with proving yourself and getting rid of your guilt that you put us, my team, in additional jeopardy just by being here. Is that about right?"

Shame washes over her. "I had no reason to believe that anything would—"

He spins to face her, so suddenly that Ophelia lurches backward. "How am I supposed to do my fucking job and keep people safe if no one tells me what's going on?" His face is flushed with fury.

There is still a part of her that wants to flinch away from a man, an authority figure, vibrating with anger. She hates that that part of her still exists after all these years. Part of her father's legacy, before he became Bloody Bledsoe.

She lifts her chin. "You're not hearing me. No one knew. I wasn't hiding it from you, specifically. Don't flatter yourself, Commander. You're not that important." She winces internally at the words and the coldness, even as she's still saying them. Hell of a time for her grandmother's influence to make an appearance. As much as she would have preferred that Miranda Bray had no hand or share in who she is, it seems that Miranda is impossible to escape.

Ethan glares at her, then his gaze skates away. "Never mind. Forget it," he mutters.

She's missed something, and she's not sure what.

"No," he says after a moment.

"No?" Ophelia repeats, confused.

"No, I'm not going to lock you away in a hab where you can wait for this to be over," he says icily. "Hiding is a privilege, Doctor, as it seems you already know well. The rest of us have to own up to our responsibilities."

She gapes at him as if he's slapped her. "I'm not hiding, I don't want to hurt—"

"Everything you told me is about what your father did. Not you."

"But Birch—" Ophelia begins.

"There's nothing to indicate that his death isn't exactly what it looks like. No footprints leading away from him. Please explain to me how someone would have done that to his arm without stepping in the blood. Particularly someone on some level unaware of their own actions."

That stops her. She hadn't thought about that. "Still, the genetic predisposition, combined with a violent upbringing—"

"Any of us might have that same predisposition. You're just the only one who knows for sure. And there's been plenty of violent upbringings on this team." He gives her a grim smile.

"So theoretically, we all have the same amount of risk, for all anyone knows."

Ophelia doesn't have an argument for that, damn it.

"I've lost another crew member under my care, and we're in a dire situation where we don't know the variables, other than the fact that we can't leave." As if in response, the wind rages against the hab, and Ophelia would swear she can feel her ears pop from a pressure change.

"I can't take the chance that locking you away is the better bet," Ethan continues. "I won't. I need all hands."

She opens her mouth to protest.

"And that's my call." He cuts her off. "I'll live with it. Well . . ." His mouth does that thing again where it quirks in a smile that is almost equally grimace. "As long as any of us will, I suppose." He pulls up his sleeve, tipping the inside of his forearm to her view.

Those little red raised nodules dot the surface of his skin.

"Shit," she breathes. She *knew* it was real.

Whatever this is, he's afflicted, infected, as well. "Nothing came up on the diagnostics I asked Kate to run," he says. "Not even anything unknown. The bio filter in the decon unit is supposed to hold anything it can't identify in stasis. But there's nothing."

She reaches out with a cautious finger and presses one of the raised areas.

As with her arm, the reaction is immediate. The nodules scoot away from the pressure.

Shuddering, Ethan yanks his arm away with a muffled curse. "What was that?" he demands. Even as he lowers his sleeve, he's running his short fingernails over the area, trying to scratch and not scratch at the same time.

"I don't know. Mine did the same thing. Vanished by this morning." Ophelia shows him her arm, now smooth and unremarkable as ever. But have they vanished, though? Or simply relocated to somewhere she can't see?

Dread swells in her.

They're in trouble. Really in trouble. And maybe not the kind of trouble she's been preparing for her whole life.

The memory of herself in that wavy mirror this morning, bloodied and uncertain, returns. She's been living under the weight of her father's actions for most of her life, fearing the possibility of becoming him, avoiding anything that reminds her of him. Maybe it's time to take a different approach.

"There's a sealable body bag in the medikit," she offers finally. "In the Kellerson pack."

His eyebrows lift slightly, but then he nods. "Good. Let's go."

It takes longer than it should, the whole process of just finding the scattered pieces of the medikit in Ophelia's trashed office. Ethan had insisted on wearing envirosuits to go back into her office with the antigrav sled.

"You realize even if this is some kind of biological contaminant, we're already infected," Ophelia pointed out as they suited up in the airlock. "Possibly even through the suits."

"We have no idea how it works, so we're going to follow level five quarantine protocol," he said. "By the book."

By the book. Ethan is very much a rules-exist-for-a-reason type of person. He must despise everything about her existence. Nothing by-the-book about it.

"I've got it," Ophelia says now, holding up the trifold fabric pack of old-school emergency instruments. It's much lighter than it should be, which makes sense, given where one of the scalpels and the scissors are. "It was under the desk." She pulls herself up with her other hand, using the edge of the desk. Even though their suits weigh the same inside and out of the hab, they are more cumbersome in an enclosed area.

Ethan joins her as she opens the pack. Most of the elastic

tool loops are empty, leaving her to wonder where the rest of the instruments are. Scattered on the floor, perhaps.

"Are you sure it's in there?" he asks.

The outer pocket of the pack looks much too thin to hold anything large enough for a body. And yet when she awkwardly sticks her gloved fingers in to search, something crinkles in response. With some clumsy maneuvering, she manages to tug the contents out—a thin rectangle of opaque plasti-seal the length of the open kit.

At Ethan's doubting look, she starts to unfold it.

It is horribly thin, but it should do the job. "I don't think it'll hold up under the weather out there for very long," Ophelia says. It's not really meant for this kind of a thing. More just a temporary solution until the deceased can be placed in cold sleep—cold storage at that point—back on the ship.

"I hope we won't need very long," he says.

With the bag expanded to its full length and width, it's harder to manipulate into place, flapping against Ophelia's suit every time she moves forward. The last thing she wants to do is snag the bag and tear a hole in it.

At Birch's feet, Ophelia hesitates. Theoretically, she and Ethan could drape it over Birch and then sort of wrestle it around the back of him, but sealing it would be tough.

"Here." Ethan shoves the other lab table parallel to Birch. "We lay out the bag here and then . . ." He gestures between Birch and the other table.

Ever practical. Though Ophelia wishes at this moment she could remind him once again that she does not have experience dealing with death and the dead, with a couple (big) exceptions. She can't even look at Birch, not without comparing and contrasting the living version with the empty flesh and bones that remain. His boots, not standard issue, are scuffed along the toes but otherwise highly cared for, and all she can think is that he won't have a chance to polish those scuffs out.

She closes her eyes for a second, steeling herself for what they're about to do. Then she steps to the other table.

With Ethan's help, she gets the bag situated and the opening pulled as wide as possible. The seal is a simple activation strip. Once the two sides of the opening are pressed together, she just has to remove the strip, which should activate the sealant, theoretically one strong enough to prevent leakage even on a microcellular level.

"You take his feet. I've got this end," Ethan says. If anything, he sounds colder, more professional than ever. His go-to defense when he's actually feeling more, she's pretty sure.

She moves to Birch's scuffed boots, traces the scratches with a fingertip. She didn't like Birch. Really didn't like that he threatened her. But no one deserves this.

Ethan steps to Birch's head. With a grunt of effort, he slips his arms beneath Birch's armpits and pulls.

Birch flops upright, like a zombie version of sitting up. His left eye is still open, staring at her, the iris already gone cloudy and gray. The right is closed, courtesy of the pair of bandage scissors pinioning the lid to the eye beneath. Bloody fluid rolls out from beneath the lid. And—

"Wait, wait!" Ophelia says.

"What?" Ethan asks, voice tight with strain, emotional and physical.

"Was that . . . Did I miss that too?" She leaves Birch's feet to point to the thick black fluid, like ink, slowly seeping from both nostrils. It screams *wrong* on a visceral level, raising prickles on her skin inside her suit.

But she has to ask, because if she didn't see the scissors, it's more than possible she missed this.

Ethan gently sets Birch's upper body back on the table and then shifts to the side to look. Ophelia knows the moment he clocks what she's talking about; the jolt of surprise runs through his whole body.

"What is that?" Ethan asks, retreating from the table. The calm in his voice is like reinforced steel, deliberate, unmovable.

"I don't know." Blood, drying blood, can have a blackish tinge to it, depending on conditions, but this is clearly not dry. And she's pretty sure it's not blood, either.

"No," he says finally. "That wasn't there this morning."

"It's coming out of his ears, too." More of the black sludge is slipping from Birch's left ear, presumably the right as well, curving into the topography of his outer ear.

Ophelia can feel it creeping, crawling into her own ear, and she instinctively reaches up to touch her ear, to reassure herself that it's just her imagination, but finds her helmet instead.

"All right," Ethan says. "Nothing's changed."

Ophelia wants to argue that, because unknown black stuff leaking out of major orifices qualifies as a big change in her book, but he's right. They still need to get Birch out of here, the faster the better.

Ethan returns to the table, at Birch's head once again, and a belated thought occurs to Ophelia.

"Hang on," she says, searching the ground. She finds an un-broken sample vial from the medikit, with the seal still intact, and then rummages until she finds a still-wrapped swab.

"I suspect we're going to have more than enough later," Ethan says.

Ophelia pauses, swab in her gloved hand. "Was that an actual sense of humor I'm detecting, Commander?" she asks. "Perhaps you're more ill than we realized."

"Carry on, Doctor."

Taking care not to get any on her suit, Ophelia swabs a gloppy sample from Birch's nose and quickly transfers it to the vial, scraping as much of it as she can from the swab before resealing the vial. In an ideal situation, they should probably take a separate sample of the black stuff rolling out of his ears, but they are far from ideal here.

She tucks the used swab inside a corner flap of the body bag, where it will be sealed in with Birch.

"There." Ophelia puts the sealed vial on her desk, which is still at odd angles with everything in the room after the chaos Birch evoked, and holds her hand over the vial for a moment, making sure it doesn't roll off. What they can do with it, she has no idea, but at least they have it.

"Can we do this now?" Ethan's prickly tone should get under her skin, but now that she knows he's using it to cover strong emotions, it's easier.

With grunting effort, they lift and then transfer Birch to the bag-covered table. More of the black sludge rolls out, as if their movements are pushing it out of him. Or like it's oozing out with a purpose and mind of its own. It drips from his ears, landing on the expanded bag with a splat she can hear even with her helmet on. Her skin crawls like it's trying to run away.

Moving as fast as she can, she hauls her side of the bag up and over Birch, and Ethan does the same on the opposite side. With some trial and error, they figure out that the side without the activation strip has to be tucked in, wrapped tightly around . . . the body. Emergency body bags do not come with instructions, and they should.

Once that's done, Ophelia tugs the activation strip free and presses the edge into place. It makes a hissing noise and the bag bubbles and melts where the strip touches it. A chemical reaction of some kind.

"Okay," she says, breathless.

Ethan ratchets up the antigrav sled until it's closer to level with the table, and they transfer Birch. It's not a good fit. The sled is meant for crates, cargo, equipment, boxed and stacked. Birch's frame is too long, too person-shaped. No matter what they try, his covered and booted feet dangle.

"He deserves better," Ethan says with harshness. "More dignity."

"He does," she agrees.

Ethan looks up at Ophelia in surprise.

"I don't have to have gotten along with him to recognize that this is a shitty end." Not to mention Birch had plenty of reason to hate her and more than enough terrible life experiences to earn him a better death, if things worked like that. They don't, unfortunately.

Together, Ophelia and Ethan pull the sled out into the corridor and then into the central hub.

Kate, Suresh, and Liana are suited up and waiting near the main airlock.

Ethan stops, forcing Ophelia to halt as well. "I told you to seal yourselves in on the other—"

"We're here for Birch," Suresh says, steadfastly avoiding looking at Ophelia. It seems his anger hasn't dissipated.

She can feel Ethan weighing his choices, whether the risk is large enough to push his authority on them or if it's better to let them join.

As always, the team dynamics here are complicated for reasons she doesn't understand. She's tempted to step back out of the way, to make room for Suresh to take her place at the sled next to Ethan. But she's beginning to suspect that her efforts to support the team, to help them see her as an advocate, have only raised suspicions about her motives instead of soothing them. Ethan thought she was trying to undermine his authority. She wasn't, she's not. But if you have a crew where leadership is in question from one side or another, it might seem like that. Ophelia came in trying to solve the wrong problem.

So she stays quiet and keeps her hand on the sled handle.

That seems to be the right move. After a moment, Ethan shakes his head. "Fine," he says with a sigh, and the thick lines of tension winding around everyone slacken a little. "Keep your distance, don't touch the bag. We don't know what this is yet."

Ophelia moves back to make room for Suresh, who takes her place with a sullen look.

The five of them make a somber procession into the main airlock and then out into the storm. The wind immediately tears at them, and the sled lifts and tilts under the gale.

For a second, it looks as though Birch is going to tumble off before they can even get clear of the hab.

Ophelia lunges forward to the side of the sled and then crouches down against the barreling force of the wind to press her hand flat on the bottom of the sled. Across the sled, Kate does the same.

In this slow, hobbling, uneven manner, they creep forward in the storm.

"Far enough," Ethan says. "We need to be able to find our way back." The snow clinks hard against Ophelia's faceplate, gathering at the seal just at the edge of her vision.

Suresh starts to reach down for the bag surrounding Birch.

"No," Ethan says sharply. Then he looks to Ophelia, and for a second she imagines she can see the battle being waged inside him, though in this weather it's likely her imagination, extrapolating.

Then he says, "Doctor?"

"Why?" Suresh demands. "He was my friend, not—"

"Because we know we've already been affected," Ethan says.

Suresh gives a derisive snort. "You don't even know what it is, let alone how—"

Enough. "Do you have a rash or any kind of raised bumps on your arm?" Ophelia asks.

"No," Suresh says after a moment, as if he wants to say yes just to prove a point. What point that would make, other than being a stubborn ass, she has no idea.

Which reminds Ophelia that they'll need to do a thorough check on everyone when they get back in. And then, after that, they should probably have all the exposed quarantine together until they can get clearance to take off. God, this would be so much easier if she knew what she was doing.

"Then stay back," Ethan says to Suresh. Ethan nods at Ophelia, and they move into the same positions as before, he at the head and Ophelia at the feet. But the storm makes it even harder, with the sled bobbing and wobbling and the wind tearing at Birch the moment they lift him. It's less a gentle transfer of Birch to the ground and more like a partially controlled fall, ending with an audible thud.

Suresh makes a pained noise. "Fuck," he mutters, kicking at the snow as he turns away.

Ophelia shifts to the opposite side, feeling very much like the funeral pallbearer that no one wanted to be there, and Ethan bends down to stab the pointed end of a makeshift flag into the snow. The bright orange fabric flaps in the wind, wrapping itself around the post.

Everyone stands in silence until Kate pushes forward to stand over Birch. At first Ophelia's not sure why, then she sees Kate's mouth moving. She's saying something to him, on a private channel with Birch, whose helmet and suit are of course back in the hab. It's a last chance to say what needs to be said.

When they retrieve Birch, they will be rushing to make the lander. Kate's right to do it now.

Ophelia's eyes sting at the final good-bye, one that so many can't have.

Liana steps up after her and does the same as Kate. Ophelia gives her as much privacy as she can by not watching, though from the corner of her eye she sees Liana's shoulders moving up and down in a gesture that speaks to crying.

Suresh moves into place, and just as Ophelia could read Liana's body language as sadness, his anger comes through even without his words.

"Permission to return?" Kate asks in a clipped tone, even as Ethan starts forward to take his turn.

He closes his eyes for a second, then opens them. "Granted," he says in that flat tone.

The three of them leave, hauling the sled behind them.

Ophelia's not invited, but even if she was, she would have remained. Ethan is a lonely figure in front of Birch's body. Empathy pulls at her. She wants to say something to help, but she doesn't know what.

"I can't keep anyone safe if they don't talk to me," he says. Almost exactly what he said before, only now he sounds more frustrated than angry.

Ophelia's first temptation is to react defensively, assuming his words to be directed at her—he is after all on a channel with her, rather than speaking to Birch as the others did—but then it occurs to Ophelia that it's not about her being Bloody Bledsoe's daughter. It's not even about Birch. Or not *just* about him. The damage is too old, too deep for that, both in Ethan and in the reactions of the others.

"Ava," she says, disparate pieces coming together.

He doesn't say anything at first. Then, after a moment, he says, "It was a routine assignment, just a drop and flop on Minos. HQ wanted a sample of some mineral that was registering on scans, but it was underground, through a system of old tunnels. Old." He tips his head toward the remains of the city in the distance, signaling that he meant millennia rather than decades or even centuries.

"But when we checked it out, the passageway was blocked, and the whole thing looked shaky as hell. I called it, sent us back to the hab. By the book," he says with a bitter laugh.

His sisters died in the Lunar Valley collapse; no wonder he was reluctant to push into those tunnels.

"So wait, if it wasn't ERS, you're telling me that Ava went back later on her own?" Ophelia is aghast. "Why?" There's no bonus involved in taking those kinds of risks. In fact, Ethan would have been well within his rights to write Ava up, and she would have been immediately removed from the active roster.

He tips his head back to look up at the storm. "We need to head back to the hab. Now."

"Ethan." Her legs are shaking from bracing herself in the wind, but she's not leaving, not until she hears the rest.

He shakes his head, and for a second she thinks he might just make good and walk away, forcing her to follow. But then he says, "I suppose that even if this isn't covered under doctor–patient confidentiality, I have my own form of certainty that this stays between us?"

Ophelia grits her teeth. "Correct." She waits for the threat, for the reminder of who she is.

But he just nods. "You know about the Challenge?"

She blinks, attempting to make the conversational leap. "What happened with Ava was about a dare?" Rumors of an underground competition among R&E teams to obtain the most valuable or rarest of items have been circulating for years. It's mostly urban legend, according to Montrose's Internal Affairs department. Something for teams to brag about over beers on leave and frighten the newbies.

"No, no. That is bullshit. Or maybe the Challenge was real once, I don't know. Now it's just a cover for the Nessers."

Every once in a while, in life, there's a moment where you sense that you're balancing on a precipice, a before-and-after, with a question in the offing that you're not sure you really want answered.

"Nessers?" Ophelia asks in a strangled voice.

"It's a bastardization of NSR. New Silk Road. A black market where samples or artifacts from claimed planets are sold to competitors. Or the highest bidder. It's not exactly a formalized process. Nessers are the ones who supply the product."

Ophelia gapes at him. "How—"

"Just clip an extra sample for your 'customer' and slip it through with your personals, or so I hear." He shrugs. "Other teams may sell on the market, but not my team, never my team."

That sounds like a point of pride for him, but Ophelia can barely focus on it because she's too busy reeling from the potential

ramifications. Personal items go through a general decontamination process and quarantine, but that's nothing like the
stringent protocols for anything extraterrestrial brought back
to their solar system from an assignment. "But the risks . . ."
She can't think straight. "That outbreak on New Rhodes, the
plague they couldn't get a handle on." Thousands dead on a
Montrose-claimed planet, an entire colony abandoned because
of the virulence of a disease they couldn't identify.

"Maybe the employers involved shouldn't buy on the market
then, if they don't want their people selling on it," he says flatly.
"Or, here's another possibility—they could treat their R&E
people less like disposable garbage. Unions, medical care, pay
increases for assignments with higher risk . . . all proposed, all
rejected."

"And that makes this okay?" Ophelia stomps toward him,
nearly falling over in the snow. "People died!" God, it makes
her dizzy thinking of all the lives lost.

"I'm not saying I like it," he snaps. "I'm saying I understand
it. If you leave a gap, desperate people will find a way to fill it.
Capitalism isn't only for the wealthy."

"At what cost?" Ophelia demands.

"The costs don't go just one way. And neither do the deaths,
as you well know," he says.

His sisters. Her father's victims. All of them, in one way or
another, could be listed as victims of greed. The Lunar Valley
should have been reinforced years before, with better infrastructure. Goliath and the others should have been retrofitted
with new equipment, new safety protocols.

But that's not what he means, not this time.

"Ava's daughter," Ophelia breathes. Experimental treatment
that isn't covered. That's what Liana said, back that first day.

"She needed the money. But I didn't know it was happening
until it was over. I would have stopped it," he says. "I would
have stopped her. I still don't know how she left the hab without it notifying us."

Disgust curls through Ophelia. "That hardly makes you the hero," she points out. "You know what's happening, and you haven't told anyone, when people are being hurt!"

He laughs, a dark, humorless sound. "How's the view from that glass house, Doctor?"

Ophelia takes a step back, stumbling a little, physically repulsed by the idea. "I . . . that's not the same. Not at all." *Isn't it, though, Lark Bledsoe?*

"If you say so," he says, in that same even tone that somehow manages to scream the opposite of his words.

Before she can even find an opening to argue, or decide how to argue it, he continues.

"Besides, reporting won't stop it. The companies, they're all too dependent on the market." He shakes his head. "They'll change the name, take it deeper underground. In the meantime, how many R&E teams would lose their jobs as part of the cover-up?"

In that moment, she can see it playing out. The press releases from Montrose, the grave statements of concern from Pinnacle, Generex, Mivida, Li Qi, and others, and the lower-level sacrificial lambs who would be fired or jailed to "make things right."

Ethan's right. It wouldn't matter. The power imbalance is tipped too far to one side, even with the existence of a black market. A swirl of despair—one that has always spun in Ophelia, sometimes a small dark cloud, other times a funnel cloud of hopelessness consuming everything in its path—lurches to life, gripping her chest and cutting off her breath.

"Anyway, none of that matters. The point is, Kate, Suresh, all of them, they don't entirely trust me anymore. I wouldn't let them go after Ava, once we figured out where she'd likely gone." Shame and frustration color his voice.

"That's your job," Ophelia manages. "To make the ugly choices and keep them safe."

"Yes, but doing my job then is making it impossible to do it now, if they won't tell me anything. Ava's death is my responsibility because she was my team member, but Birch's . . ." He takes a deep breath. "That's my fault."

"You can do the right thing and still end up being fucked," Ophelia says flatly. Not her finest moment, but at this exact second she can't seem to summon even a thin facade of optimism.

A glimmer of a smile emerges on Ethan's face. "That your professional opinion?"

"I think it's more along the line of a universal truth, but sure, if you want to go with that." She shrugs. "Not helpful but accurate."

"It might be more helpful than you realize," he says, after a moment. "Thank you."

Lightning flashes above them, followed by a booming crack of thunder.

"We're done. Now." Ethan turns toward the hab, authority back in place.

They haven't gone more than a few steps before she has to ask, "Are you . . . you're sure that all of them are involved? The corporations. The New Silk Road thing."

Ethan glances over at her with pity, and she hates herself for asking. But since she's going to hate herself anyway, might as well know. She's always struggled with her Bray side, but not nearly as much as with her Bledsoe half. "At least they never killed anyone" is not exactly high praise, but it's not nothing, either. Now she's not so sure she chose the right side of that moral conflict. If there even is a right side to it.

She's tried to build a new self out of the unobjectionable parts of her past. But now it feels like there are no unobjectionable parts, no ground on which to build her identity. Like she's creating an imitation of a semidecent human out of shit, blood, and corruption.

"Why else do you think the market still exists?" he asks. "None of them can rat out the others without being caught in the net themselves."

"Right." Ophelia nods, sickness welling in her.

When lightning slashes behind them, she can't help but turn and look back. The gray sky is violet now, the white lace of lightning spreading across it in jagged embroidered lines.

Back near where they left Birch, not far from where the flag twists and squirms in the torturous wind, a glint of metal in the snow catches the flash of lightning, a spark of brightness.

Liana's spider; it has to be. The one that found the Pinnacle R&E body. They must not be far from him, from Delacroix.

We're creating our own impromptu morgue out here.

That feels like an omen, or just fucking bad luck. Either way.

24

Raised voices in the hab greet Ethan and Ophelia as soon as the interior airlock door opens, after their (possibly pointless) decon session.

"—off your head!" Kate shouts. "Have you looked outside?"

"Better than just waiting around here because he's too much of a coward to try!" That's Suresh. "It's even worse now that *she's* here."

Based on the tone alone, Ophelia guesses she is the "she" he's referring to.

"For all we know, she's the one who caused all of this to begin. She's in his head, making things worse!"

Yep, definitely her.

Ethan, still suited, pushes forward into the central hub, and Ophelia follows at a distance.

"What's this?" he demands. All hints of his earlier emotion, his vulnerability, are gone.

Kate and Suresh face off across the table, Kate with her arms folded, Suresh pacing back and forth on the other side.

"Junior over here wants to take off in the storm," Kate says with a disparaging laugh.

Suresh stops. "First of all, fuck you," he says to Kate. "Second, what's the risk level here, really? We try to take off and make it back to the ship or we sit here and wait for perfect conditions that are never going to happen and—"

"Yeah, exactly how much piloting experience do you have?" Kate asks. "With Birch gone, Ethan is our only—"

"Dead. Birch is dead," Suresh says. "Because he took a fucking knife to his arm. And scissors in the eye!" He scrubs furiously at the inside of his elbow, using the fabric of his jumpsuit as an abrasive.

It was a scalpel, actually. But Ophelia's smart enough to keep her mouth shut this time. Besides, that doesn't matter now. She watches Suresh closely, though. He's scratching.

"We're not waiting for perfect conditions," Ethan says. "We're waiting for conditions that give us a better chance of reaching the *Resilience* than dying in a fiery crash or slowly suffocating to death, trapped in a damaged lander."

"You're going to wait us to death, just like you did Ava," Suresh snarls. "Because you're more worried about following the rules and what *she* thinks than saving us!"

Ophelia's temper flares, and this time, she can't tamp it down. "As I've told you from the beginning, my presence here has nothing to do with—"

"Your presence has everything to do with this!" Suresh cuts her off. "This kind of thing has never happened to us before. How do we know it wasn't your headsets that set this whole thing off in the first place? Maybe you did it intentionally, to mess with us in some kind of fucked-up headshrinker test."

Paranoia, check.

But it's the outdated and offensive-in-multiple-ways term that sets her over the edge. "Because, you asshole, whatever it is, I've got it too." Ophelia points to her left arm and jerks her chin toward his scratching.

Suresh looks down at himself and blanches, anger draining away to make room for fear. He quickly moves his hand away.

"And we're supposed to just trust you," Suresh scoffs.

"Really? Of the two of us, I think I have more right to say that, don't you?" Ophelia throws back at him.

He flushes.

"Enough," Ethan says sharply. "We're waiting until the storm lets up. Within reason," he adds. "Then we're going back. All of us." He looks to Ophelia. "Doctor, you have some thoughts on how to proceed?"

She hesitates. "We should probably try to avoid close contact with each other and . . ." Ophelia looks around. "Wait. Where's Liana?" She's missing from this tableau of dysfunction.

"She's resting. She said she didn't sleep well last night," Suresh says.

"Fine. Okay. We'll just need to keep our distance from each other, as best as we can. Those of us who are confirmed to be showing symptoms should wear our suits around those who aren't and—"

"It doesn't matter anyway," Kate says, sinking into a chair. "Even if we make it back to Earth, Montrose HQ is going to sic security drones on our ass. They're going to blow us out of orbit the second we tell them what's going on."

"That's a worst-case scenario," Ophelia objects, even as doubt niggles at her.

Kate laughs. "Really, Doctor? How many teams have you never heard from again?"

It doesn't work that way. Ophelia only sees teams after they're assigned to her, which by default means she only knows them after they've returned.

Ophelia opens her mouth to explain that, but Kate continues.

"Because I'm betting my number is higher than yours," Kate says. "They'll call it something else. Engine failure. Environmental systems overload. Fuck, even ERS, who knows. But the result is the same." She grins at Ophelia, blue eyes bloodshot and shimmery with unshed tears. *Boom*. She mouths the word, her hands miming an explosion.

No. They wouldn't do that. But Ophelia can't make herself say the words. Suddenly they sound far too naive.

"I need a drink." Kate shoves back her chair and heads for the galley.

"That's why we need to get out of here as soon as possible.

And just not say anything," Suresh argues. "Cold sleep will probably kill it all off."

"You're assuming this . . . whatever it is, is alive, that it's like anything we've ever seen before," Ethan points out.

Instantly her mind flips back to the plague on New Rhodes, the one that Montrose couldn't identify. Ethan implied that it was from R&E materials sold on the black market. If they—the team, including Ophelia—returned to Earth in a contagious state, that would be so much worse. Especially if they don't speak up.

Ophelia frowns. Something about all of this gives her the frustrating sense that she's seen this before, or heard about it . . . or something.

"—literally freezes us to death and brings us back. How could anything survive that?" Suresh says.

"Liana, love, what are you doing? I thought you were resting."

At the sound of Kate's voice, Ophelia looks up and toward the galley. Liana is drifting in from the C side, her steps slow, steady gaze focused on the distance.

"Liana?" Kate asks again, alarm sharpening her voice.

But Liana ignores Kate, moving past the galley.

"Liana?" Ophelia tries. But Liana gives no indication of having heard. There's a strange blankness to her, as if she's not really there, even though she's physically present. Ophelia's seen it before: sleepwalking—technically, somnambulism.

"Liana, where are you going?" Ethan asks as she crosses into the A side airlock.

Ophelia follows, with Ethan on her heels.

He reaches past Ophelia, as if to grab Liana. "Don't," Ophelia says quickly. It won't hurt Liana, not like the old superstition claims. But it can be stressful and aggravate anxiety, which they don't need right now, not with paranoia as a symptom. "Unless she's in distress, we need to just keep her from hurting herself."

On some level, Ophelia is anticipating Liana's destination

in the A side corridor. There just aren't that many places to go, and even beyond that, Ophelia is not a big believer in co-incidence. Still, when Liana stops and then executes a left turn with military-precision into her office, Ophelia's heart sinks.

Ophelia hurries to catch up. She doesn't want to lose sight of Liana, even for a second.

Her office is still a wreck. There's been no time to clean up, other than the quick attempt Ophelia made to gather up the remaining contents of the medikit so they wouldn't be further damaged or lost.

Liana stumbles over the shattered tablet on the floor but doesn't seem to notice. She doesn't even look down to see what it was, too intent on crossing the space.

She's going to the window, just like Birch last night. Ophelia's certain of it, even if she doesn't know why.

Ophelia picks her way to her desk and the remains of the medikit. Her hands shake as she preps the sedatives, trying not to feel like this set of motions is too familiar. Had she done this to Birch, too?

Across from Ophelia, at the window, Liana rises on her tip-toes. "Don't you see them?" she asks.

"What's she talking about?" Suresh hisses from the doorway.

Ophelia glances back and finds him and Kate hovering in the corridor. She hadn't realized they'd followed.

"Ava and Birch," Liana says, her speech slurred and awk-ward, as if she's speaking around a mouthful of pebbles. "They're out there." She points forward but uses her thumb to do so. It strikes Ophelia as odd, so much so that it takes her an extra second to recognize the gesture.

Then again, it's not nearly as odd as claiming to see your deceased team members outside.

Dread coils tight in Ophelia's stomach. She edges up to the window and looks in the direction Liana's indicating, half ex-pecting to see the unidentifiable shadowy figure she glimpsed once before. Or—worse—Birch, wrestling free from the sealed body bag, to rise and stagger around like the undead in those old folktales.

But there's nothing. Just a dizzying endless gray sky and snow blurring together, and in the distance, the dark, jutting crystalline remnants of the city.

Liana turns toward Ophelia. Liana's eyes are open, but they drift lazily in the sockets, unfocused. The whites are shot through with red veins, with tiny black spots on nearly all of them, like miniature ticks feasting at the source.

Ophelia sucks in a sharp breath.

Liana smiles, even as her irises float in opposite directions. "They want us to come."

"We are so fucked," Suresh says.

25

"I don't understand what you're waiting for," Suresh hisses. "Dose her!"

Much to Ophelia's irritation, he has summoned her to the corridor to have this conversation. Why does everything have to be a fight with this team?

Her head is throbbing. She and Ethan took off their helmets a while ago; there doesn't seem to be any point in trying to isolate themselves after all. But the muscles at the back of her neck are so tight that it's become difficult to turn to look at anyone. Which is fine, because she's not particularly in the mood to look at any of them. Other than Liana, her current source of preoccupation. Ethan remains inside what's left of Ophelia's office, just to the side of Liana, within reach and able to grab her if need be. But even that's not enough.

I need to be there, be ready.

"She's just standing there, looking out a window," Ophelia says to Suresh again, patience thinning to nothing. "She's not hurting anyone or showing signs of hurting herself."

Technically, Liana's standing there murmuring to herself. Words that Ophelia can't quite catch. Occasionally it sounds very much like gibberish. *Squash. Piccadilly. Remonstrative.* Listening sets off an awful clutch inside Ophelia's gut. She's not sure if Liana is in there anymore, or if she's buried so deep by whatever this is that it effectively doesn't matter. Honestly, Ophelia doesn't even know which is worse. She used to wonder about that with her father, if the part of him that was decent saw what he was doing, as if he was trapped behind glass and unable to free himself to take control. Her father had a temper; he could be violent with Ophelia and her mother, but never with strangers, never on that level.

Obviously. The mass murder level is generally one and done.

Still, it was hard to know what to do with the contradiction. The man who patiently played with Ophelia for hours, making up stories for her dolls and stuffed creatures, the man who taught her how to take apart and repair the station bot that cleaned the floor on their level, was the same man who terrified her mother on a regular basis, who taught Ophelia—unintentionally—to read the mood of a room with a single glance so she'd know whether she should freeze in place or run. The same man who lost his grip on reality and killed dozens of people.

Eventually, Ophelia had to stop trying to figure it out, which part was him and which was the disease. It was impossible to know—it was all of him and none of him at the same time. He hadn't been perfect before ERS; he wouldn't have been without it, either.

She loved him, she hated him, she feared him. It's all true.

"If I don't know what's causing this, I don't know what effect the sedative will have. It could make her worse," Ophelia says to Suresh. Liana seems to be functioning on some level between consciousness and sleep. She's partially aware, able to keep herself from falling over the debris, able to navigate to the window. And yet she's seeing what's not there, and how is she seeing *anything* with eyes that don't focus?

Ophelia shivers.

"Either way, I'm betting that it'll keep her from slicing at herself or any of us," Suresh says, his hands in fists at his sides. Trying not to scratch, if Ophelia had to guess. "What would be so bad about that?"

"Suresh, leave off. She's doing the best she can," Kate

says. Then she turns to Ophelia. "Doctor, what can we do to help?"

"Ophelia." Ethan jerks his head, indicating Liana.

Ophelia leaves the corridor immediately, gaze fixed on Liana, though Liana doesn't seem to be doing anything different.

"The back of her neck," Ethan says quietly, once Ophelia is close enough.

"The back of her . . ." Ophelia starts to repeat in confusion, and then it clicks.

She moves closer, and sure enough, familiar-looking raised nodules are spread across the vulnerable skin between the top of Liana's jumpsuit collar and the upsweep of her hair into a ragged ponytail.

Spreading? Or just presenting in a new manner?

Fuck. Fuck!

"Okay." With her gloved finger, Ophelia presses gently into one of the bumps. As before, it squirms away from the pressure, and the others scatter as well. This time, however, they seem to congregate together, joining with one another in clumps of two or three instead of simply fleeing the stimulus.

Huh. Ophelia raises her hand to try again.

Liana whirls around, startling Ophelia into stepping back.

"No," Liana says sharply. Her eyes still aren't working right, but that word was certainly clear enough.

Ophelia raises her hands in surrender and holds still, until Liana returns to her vigil at the window.

"If we can get a sample, maybe we can see what we're dealing with," Ophelia says to Ethan in an undertone. "Or maybe we can . . . remove whatever it is. It's near the surface." A little optimistic, given that the med-scanner hadn't recognized anything wrong in the blood samples she'd run before. And the similarity to her father's delusions makes her want to throw up. *You're infected, Little Bird.*

But they can't just sit here and wait for what happened to

Birch to happen to Liana, to all of them. In that way, Ophelia agrees with Suresh.

After a moment, Ethan nods reluctantly. "The PMU has a setting for foreign object removal," he says. "I've used it before."

Good. Then he can do this. The relief that she will not be the one operating—operating!—makes her knees feel weak.

Ophelia retrieves the sedative hypo from the desk, where she had left it within easy reach. Her fingers slip and slide inside her sweaty suit gloves.

She tightens her grip on the hypo as she moves next to Liana at the window, facing her instead of the view of outside.

Liana doesn't seem to register her presence, just keeps murmuring to herself.

Ophelia lifts her hand and it's over and done in a second, just a quick push against the side of Liana's neck, the hiss of the dispensed meds through the skin. She hasn't done anything like this since the training for her required rotation through Montrose's private locked wards.

Even then, administering sedatives was supposed to be a last option, to be used only if an orderly or nurse wouldn't make it in time.

Liana doesn't react to the injection at first. Certainly not the slow slumping forward or staggering that Ophelia expects.

Liana's hand flies up to her neck in a belated defense, and she turns toward Ophelia. Her expression holds no betrayal, even when she sees the hypo still in Ophelia's hand. The blankness of Liana's face is eerie, particularly in contrast to the frantic jitter of her eyes beneath their half-closed lids.

"It's okay, you're okay," Ophelia says quickly, attempting to reassure her, if she can still hear her.

The pain in Ophelia's head pulses suddenly, as if the blood is trying to push its way out of her eyeballs.

Jesus, am I having an aneurysm? Right now? She presses the heel of her hand against her left eye, unable to stop herself.

Liana lurches forward, not falling but running. Her elbow clips Ophelia's ribs as she passes, a sharp, shooting pain that distracts Ophelia from her head even as it sends her stumbling back toward Ethan. He catches Ophelia's elbow and steadies her before she can hit the floor.

Then he darts around her, fast but not fast enough.

"She's running!" he shouts to Kate and Suresh.

Kate makes a grab and catches hold of Liana's arm, but Liana manages to torque herself out of Kate's loose grasp and then bypasses Suresh's grab entirely.

"I thought you drugged her," Suresh shouts at Ophelia, as they take off after her.

"I did!" But the forced breathiness from Liana's blow to her ribs mutes the anger of her response. Ophelia staggers into the corridor to follow.

"She's going for the airlock," Kate calls over her shoulder.

"We can't let her get outside," Ophelia says, alarmed, still trying to catch up. The pain in her head is lessening slightly.

"You think?" Suresh asks, already crossing into the central hub after Ethan.

"Shut up," Kate says to him.

A moment later, though, as Ophelia reaches the entrance to the central hub, a loud thud echoes back toward her, followed by a series of grunts.

When she crosses into the hub, Ophelia finds that Ethan has Liana pinned to the floor about a meter or two from the airlock door, his body weight across her back, holding her down. But she's still struggling, bucking with her whole body and flailing her arms and legs.

"Ophelia," he says with gritted teeth. "Hurry."

She rushes to his side and drops to her knees to hit Liana again with the sedative. But it takes both Kate and Ophelia to hold her arm down long enough for Ophelia to administer it.

"She's freakishly strong," Kate pants.

The second dose does nothing except make Liana angrier. She manages to slither forward, and Ophelia catches a glimpse of her face, straining, red, but again curiously empty. No anger or fear or even pain. Thin streams of saliva slip from the corner of her mouth and down her chin.

"Doctor!" Ethan says.

"Okay, okay!" Ophelia leans forward once again with the hypo. This is all she has—three doses per vial. One of them should have easily taken down Liana. It should have taken down Ethan or Suresh, either of them much taller and heavier. Too much sedation might compromise Liana's breathing.

But this time, Liana finally goes still. Ethan, after a moment, levers himself up cautiously, prepared to drop down again if needed. When Liana doesn't move, he pushes up to his knees beside her.

"Turn her on her—"

Before Ophelia can finish, Ethan's already rolling Liana over to her side.

To Ophelia's shock and horror, Liana's eyes are open now, her gaze focusing on Ophelia. The confusion and fear Ophelia was looking for earlier run rampant. "What . . . why?" Liana manages, as tears well up and roll across her face, the bridge of her nose.

"Oh my God, Liana." She's back. Ophelia grabs for her hand to comfort her, but her fingers are cold and limp.

"Are you all right? What happened?" Kate demands, crouching next to Liana.

Liana makes a terrified whimpering sound. "I hear it. Don't you hear it?"

Everyone goes still. The only noises are Liana's panting and the wind moaning around the hab.

"It's the wind, love," Kate says gently. "Just the wind."

"No, no, no, nooo." Liana shakes her head, a tiny movement. "It's in me," she whispers, just before her body goes limp. Her head lands hard on the patterned metal floor with a reverberating thump.

It's in me. It's in me. Liana had one brief moment of awareness before she was gone again. Unconscious, this time, and unmoving.

Thinking as she paces the central hub, Ophelia tugs hard at the delicate chain around her neck, the tiny metal bird in flight, warm against her fingers. Her necklace from Dulcie, whom she might never see again.

The pain in Ophelia's head has receded to a dull roar. Her ribs ache, but she's otherwise fine. Except for the overwhelming feeling that they're making a mistake.

It's in me.

Maybe Liana noticed the bumps on her arm and never said anything. Maybe she felt them on the back of her neck earlier today.

But Ophelia can't shake the feeling that Liana was talking about a level beyond the merely tactile.

It's in me. It's in all of them now. Just to varying degrees.

"Doctor?" Ethan's voice brings Ophelia back to herself.

She turns to find him at the A side entrance. He looks exhausted, hair ruffled, a thin red line of a scratch on his left cheek. He and Suresh have moved Liana to Ophelia's office.

"We're ready. I would . . ." He pauses, seeming to search for the words. "I would appreciate your willingness to assist, if it becomes necessary."

If Liana wakes up. If she doesn't. Ophelia's not sure which he means. She doesn't think she wants to know. She's so far afield from where she expected to be. That—admittedly overly bright—vision of sessions in an office, with team members walking out feeling relieved, more rested, safer, none of that has even remotely come true.

Instead she's preparing to help with an impromptu surgery. Of all the kinds of surgery she's ever considered assisting with, which is to say none, impromptu would be the lowest on the list. She's never felt more helpless in her life, not even when she was hiding behind that HRU, praying her father wouldn't find her.

"I think we have to consider this might not be something we can just remove," Ophelia says.

Ethan raises his eyebrows. "This was your suggestion, Doctor."

"I know, but with what I saw—what *we* saw . . ." Ophelia corrects herself. "We're talking about multiple systems affected. Movement. Speech. Intent."

"Sleepwalking is—"

"Involves unconscious rote activity, usually. Maybe acting out a dream or nightmare. Not like this." Ophelia hesitates. "I'm saying Liana might be in there still, but she was not making the decisions. Not when she was running for the airlock door."

And that's what's going to happen to all of them. Slowly descending into madness, at best. Or quite possibly being perfectly aware but unable to move or speak while something else acts as them instead.

"You don't know that. You don't know what she was seeing or experiencing," he points out. "But even if that's the case, that's all the more reason we need to try to save her."

"She can't even give consent to what we're about to try," Ophelia argues.

Disbelief flashes across his face. "Are you seriously suggesting that we need to protect ourselves legally from trying to save her life?"

"I'm not worried about lawsuits, Ethan! I'm worried we're going to kill her. I'm not an expert at any of this. Neither are you." Ophelia already has so many deaths on her conscience, she doesn't know that she can stand one more. Not if Liana can't even consent; that seems wrong.

"Sadly, we are suffering a shortage of experts in any number of areas here," Ethan says wearily. "I still have a responsibility to my people. If it helps, I'm going to do this whether you're with me or not. Because if we don't figure this out, none of us are getting out of here alive." He scrubs his hands over his face. "Sometimes all we have is the ugly decision."

Ophelia bristles. "I'm not afraid of making—"

"It's not cowardice. It's selfishness. You're still hiding. And I don't have time for it. You don't want to be your father, Ophelia? Don't be him. You don't like being a Bray? Make your own choices."

His blasé attitude sets the remnants of Ophelia's patience alight. "You don't think I am? I've been fighting my whole life. To be better, to do better. You have no idea what it was like."

"You're telling me, the kid from the Lunar Valley slums, that I have no idea what it's like to fight?" He folds his arms across his chest, eyebrows arched. "To be despised and pitied at the same time?"

Ophelia's face heats. "Being poor isn't criminal."

"Neither is being rich," he says. "Or the child of someone who was criminal."

He's right, of course. Neither of those things is illegal, but for the effects of such, they might as well be.

"Who makes the rules, Ophelia? If you're trying to prove yourself, who decides when you're done? When you've crossed the finish line?"

She rocks back on her heels, breath stolen.

"If she dies"—he jerks his thumb back toward Liana—"but you weren't involved, does that make it better? Does that make it okay?"

"No, of course not!"

He shakes his head. "Then what are you doing?"

"I . . ."

He pivots and strides off toward the A side, without waiting for her answer, which she doesn't have anyway.

Her hands ball into fists. Ethan doesn't get it. He can't. It's not as if she's cornered the market on dysfunctional families, or even violent ones. But there is something to be said for being the blue-chip stock for both. It's a unique intersection of self-loathing and societal obsequiousness mixed equally with disgust. How is anyone supposed to claw themselves free of that? She's done everything she can to make a space for herself, separate from both aspects of her heritage, while still trying to make up for both.

It's impossible. Who she is always comes back to haunt her, one way or another, literally or figuratively.

But that question. *Who decides when you're done?* She feels it resonating through the middle of her, an emptiness vibrating from an unexpected blow, shaking and reordering things as it moves through. An earthquake of personal revelation, impossible to ignore.

He meant it, she's sure, as sarcasm. But in truth, it never occurred to her.

He's correct—no one is ever going to come up to her and say, "Enough. You're enough. It's okay that you're Field Bledsoe's daughter. That you're a Bray and you've been given great privilege despite not deserving it or being wanted by the Brays themselves."

That will never happen. For a variety of reasons, not the least of which is how few people know those details about her.

Ophelia blinks, processing that.

It's not that she's been anticipating this moment, exactly, more that she figured one day she would feel it, that she would reach some point in her life, some threshold or mountaintop where she would look around and realize that she'd accomplished what she set out to do. Attained a position that everyone would universally agree was above critique, beyond failure.

A snort of self-deprecating laughter escapes her, and Ophelia slaps a hand over her mouth, even as her eyes well with tears.

What the fuck, Phe. How did I miss this? Physician heal thyself. There is no finish line because she never set one. She just kept moving the tape with every accomplishment, with every attempt, because no one was there telling her she was done. Telling her she was enough.

But who would have done that anyway? Her mother? No. Her uncle, her grandmother? Please. And there's literally no one else in her life whose word she could accept, because no one else knows who she is.

Except, now, Ethan Severin.

Who makes the rules? Another of his questions that Ophelia doesn't have the answer to. But she knows what she wants the answer to be, what it should be.

Me.

26

The Portable Medical Unit is a bird-shaped device with the "wings" in a downward position to support the central body, which is a long, flat panel containing various instruments on the underside and a settings panel on the top. The wings can be extended or collapsed to fit the position needed.

It's designed for simple procedures while the team is on location, away from assignment. Healing sprains and minor fractures, treating frostbite, removing a bad tooth. Theoretically, it can mend clean breaks as well, but Ophelia isn't sure that she would trust her leg to it, especially in a running-for-your-life situation.

From what she knows, it's mostly for stitches. Hands and fingers. The occasional split lip, like Suresh's, or split skin beneath a black eye.

"Here. 'Foreign object removal.'" Suresh points to the settings, and Ethan bats his hand away.

"I've got it," he says. "Step back."

Liana is resting on the lab table on her stomach, her head turned to the side. Her eyelids are twitching with movement, but her breathing is slow and regular. For now. The PMU is positioned over the back of her neck, where, even from the doorway, Ophelia can see the bumps shifting and moving beneath her skin, roiling as though they can sense what's about to happen.

Ethan adjusts the wings, bringing the instruments closer to

Liana's vulnerable neck. So many nerves and veins, so many ways to cause permanent damage.

I hate this. "Maybe we should try it on one of us first, on the arm. On one of us who still has the . . . bumps."

"If it's a progression, we may not have time," Kate says flatly, swaying slightly in place. "Mine are gone, so are yours. If they're moving through the body, what happens if Liana's go deeper?"

Even though Ophelia had suspected at the time that Kate was lying about the bumps on her arm, her tacit admission of doing so still triggers a flare of irritation in Ophelia. She mentally stamps it out. Kate lying was not helpful, no. But there are bigger issues at hand.

Ethan rocks the device back and forth, ensuring its stability, and then, after a brief hesitation, he selects the menu option that Suresh indicated.

A faint blue light emerges from the instrument panel, a scan, moving left to right and then top to bottom.

Ophelia holds her breath, waiting. When it locks on, a matching blue X will appear on the desired area, asking Ethan to confirm.

Instead, it gives a distressed beep. "Target not identified," it announces, and the light vanishes.

"Something's wrong." Ethan frowns. "It won't lock on."

"Just override it. It did that last time, too, remember? It didn't want to pull the metal from my hand because it was too close to some nerve," Suresh says, waving his hand, palm up. A jagged white scar decorates his skin. "I'm fine. Just a little numb."

Jesus.

"It's probably because they're moving too much," Ophelia offers. "Safety restrictions on foreign body removal are more stringent."

The three of them, Ethan, Kate, and Suresh, turn to stare at her.

"What?" Ophelia shifts uncomfortably. "I took some training on it a few years ago. I wanted to know what my R&E patients were going through when they were away from home." Work is—was—her life.

Kate looks vaguely impressed—or that much closer to passing out. She's been hitting the "engine cleaner" hard. Suresh sucks his teeth in annoyance.

"Suggestions?" Ethan asks after a moment.

Well, I wouldn't fucking override the safeties. "Try to stabilize the target."

Ethan backs away from the PMU, holding his hand out in a gesture for Ophelia to take over.

"No," she says with a shudder. Cutting into someone, to help or not, is a bridge too far. A bridge too close to her father.

Ethan stares at her, mouth tight in frustration.

If you don't want to be your father, don't be him. As if it's that simple.

With a sigh, Ophelia finds a pair of long tweezers in the Kellerson pack. And that's how she ends up at the front of the PMU with Ethan back at the controls.

"Ready?" Ophelia asks.

He nods.

She tries to remember the exact instructions from the training. In that scenario, it was a patient who was moving too much and couldn't, for whatever reason, be sedated. Not exactly their situation here.

Her heart is beating so hard that the tweezers shake with her pulse as she zeroes in on the largest squirming mass beneath Liana's skin.

She's terrified that she's going to fuck up. That she's going to make a mistake that ends with Liana dead and Ophelia covered in her blood. But at the same time, Ophelia can't just hand this off to someone else. Suresh is a little too careless for her taste, and Kate is, she's fairly sure, too drunk.

Ophelia takes a deep breath and blows it out, then closes the tweezers around a bump, which looks like nothing so harmless now. It lurches left and then right, trying to escape her grip.

"Now," she tells Ethan.

The blue light reappears, scanning past her tweezers, correctly identifying them as surgical tools, and focuses on her prey.

That bright blue X appears exactly where it should. "Target locked," the PMU announces.

"We got it," Ethan says with obvious relief.

The PMU unleashes a cascade of instruments, including a laser scalpel and tweezers, miniature versions of the ones Ophelia's holding.

With a faint buzz, the laser scalpel zips a neat line across Liana's skin, right through the blue X, releasing the smell of burned flesh, and after a second, the first red beads of blood.

Ophelia swallows hard, looks away.

"Steady, Ophelia," Ethan says.

Her headache, never quite gone, grows in strength until she can feel pain in her jaw, shooting down her tense neck muscles as well. But she keeps as still as she can.

The PMU deploys tweezers with a *click-click-click*. *We're almost done. Please let us be almost done.*

"What the fuck is that? What is it?" Suresh demands.

"It looks . . . it looks like an exoskeleton." Ethan.

Ophelia's gaze snaps back to the PMU. Bugs.

Beneath the blood, she gets a glimpse of a black, shiny-edged . . . thing. It doesn't look like an insect to her; the lines are too straight. But the shiny surface does resemble a carapace of some sort. Then again, any bugs here are probably not like any they've ever seen before.

The PMU's tweezers have caught it, even as it attempts to squirm deeper.

"Where is it going?" Suresh leans closer, scratching at his arm. "God!" He glares down at his elbow.

The pain in Ophelia's head increases to lightning bolt strength and intensity. "I think we should hurry," she says. Nausea is building to the point of no return.

"Does anyone else feel ill?" Kate murmurs. When Ophelia glances up, she's pressing her hand to her head.

Could be the drinking. But . . . Ethan is pale and sweaty as well, a vein in his forehead pulsing.

The PMU pulls at the thing in Liana, and for a moment Ophelia sees it clearly, gone solid and still.

She gasps. It's not a bug, not at all. How is that possible? How is that *here*?

Then the invader seems to collapse under the pressure of the tweezers, spilling in little fuzzy lines back down to the incision.

Ophelia yanks her hands back. "Get it out, get it out!"

But even in the few seconds it takes the PMU to move a containment vial into place, it's too late. The thing has poured itself, like animated black sand, back into the incision and vanished.

Kate retreats to the corridor, her hand clapped over her mouth. A moment later, the sound of retching follows. The throbbing in Ophelia's head feels like movement now, like tiny knives slicing into her brain as they hack their way in deeper.

That's it. It's over.

"Close it," Ophelia says softly. "Before she loses any more blood."

"No, wait, we didn't get it out," Suresh protests, clawing at his arm without seeming to even realize it. He looks from her to Ethan and back again.

Ethan, however, is focused on Ophelia. "Birch's sample."

She nods, relief mixing with despair. He saw the same thing she did, recognized it.

As the PMU begins suturing at Ethan's command, Ophelia retrieves the sample from Birch on her desk.

The PMU has a magnification setting, probably for examining a patient's injury more closely. But it'll also work for their purposes.

Once the PMU has finished with Liana's stitches, Ethan changes the settings and slips the vial of black fluid underneath the central panel for a closer look.

"What is going on?" Suresh asks.

Ethan and Ophelia ignore him, leaning over the panel.

The curved glass of the sample vial distorts the view initially, but once the focus regulates itself, they have a clear look at the black fluid inside. The fluid from Birch's nose and ears. Except, under magnification, it's apparent that the liquid is actually clear. It's just filled, jam-packed even, with tiny black particles, all shiny and identical in shape. Angled at the top, sharp lines down the side.

At the moment, suspended in this fluid, they're cross-angled and scattered, some stacked into larger formations, others breaking down into barely visible particles.

All that same shiny black, that same familiar shape.

Ethan and Ophelia look up from the PMU to stare out at the crystalline towers jutting from the ground, flickering in and out of visibility in the storm.

An exact match.

27

Kate rubs her forehead. "I don't understand. You're saying we've got bits of a bloody building in us?" She still looks ashen. But she's upright and seated in a chair Ethan dragged over from the table in the central hub.

The three of them, Kate, Ethan, and Ophelia, are convened near the airlock door on the A side.

"That's the assumption we made. That everyone made. That those . . . structures were part of the city. But has anyone ever documented that?" Ophelia asks. "If someone confirmed it, that wasn't in any of the files I read." A fact that makes her feel like she's staring down at the ground from a dizzying height.

"Are we really trusting Pinnacle's reports?" Kate asks. "Either they missed something big or they're lying about it."

Heat burns up Ophelia's neck and into her cheeks. Kate's right. Ophelia has been operating under the assumption that, if anything, Pinnacle might have redacted or elided ugly facts that might have impeded a sale of the rights to Montrose. But this goes far beyond that.

The Bray greed strikes again. She doubts her uncle was directly involved, but he was certainly involved in the higher level decisions that had landed them in this mess.

His message, followed so closely by her mother's. *Don't go to that planet.*

At the time, Ophelia had interpreted it as her mother's fear of being exposed, as well as her perpetual fear of what the daughter of Bloody Bledsoe might do next.

But now . . .

Did her mother know about this planet? Did her uncle? Is that why they were pushing so hard to stop her? Were they trying to save her? Or, more likely, to save themselves, because she might find out what they'd done, lying to Montrose about the deal that landed them this planet.

Ophelia shakes her head. She can't handle this right now.

"They're not buildings. I don't know what they are. The stuff, it changes its appearance, stacking together and then breaking apart as needed. We saw that when we tried to take it out of Liana," Ethan points out. "It . . . they seem . . ."

Alive.

That's the word no one wants to use. They may not be organic, or organic in the way humans would define it. But they are *something.*

"It responds to stimuli," Ophelia says. "The pieces, they move when they want to get away."

"Yeah, so does an autocar. That doesn't mean anything." Kate props her elbows on her knees, resting her head in her hands, her shoulders hunched with pain.

"Are you all right?" Ophelia asks, bending down next to her.

Kate turns her head to give Ophelia a tight smile. "Head hurts. Nothing I can't handle. I've had worse hangovers."

Ophelia doubts that, but she understands. Kate's doing what she needs to do to keep herself calm. And if that's telling herself she's in control, then that's fine.

"So we landed on their planet, took chunks of them, and now they're pissed?" Suresh calls. He's in the A side corridor, where he can keep an eye on Liana, who's still unconscious. "Aliens. You're telling me we've got actual aliens inside of us?" His voice rises to a point that sounds more like a screech with the last words.

"We're not saying that," Ethan says quickly.

But we're not not *saying that, either.* Humans have visited thousands of planets and encountered weird animals, absolutely terrifying insects—as much as human classifications can apply to creatures not from Earth. But no one has ever found anything that indicates another intelligent species. Not one still active, anyway. The Great Filter theory, first posited a couple centuries ago as an answer to the Fermi Paradox, has been accepted as the reigning principle as to why.

As Ophelia understands it, basically all civilizations reach a point, some earlier than others, where they die out or extinguish themselves through violence, depletion of resources, or the inability to prevent natural disasters. Some never even make it to the animals-using-tools step.

But, for that matter, this could also just be tech, so far advanced that it simply looks alive. Probes sent from elsewhere to learn, to absorb.

"I don't think we can assume anything about motive or purpose," Ethan adds. "We don't know what we don't know."

"Who fucking cares? We just need it out of us," Suresh says, raising his voice. "So we can get out of here!"

Suresh has a point. They are not a scientific mission. What matters is doing whatever they can to get off this planet alive.

Ophelia meets Ethan's gaze. He gives a short nod.

"All right," Ethan says. "If we assume that—"

"How did it get in?" Kate asks suddenly, staring at something over Ophelia's head.

"What?" Suresh asks.

"I checked the bio filters," Kate says, nodding to Ethan. "Nothing. Not even in stasis. We're sealed in here, and if we brought it in with us—"

"What difference does it make?" Suresh shouts. "I thought we just agreed that—"

"Because even if we figure out how to get this shit out of us, that won't matter if we can't *keep* it out," Kate shouts back at him. "And if we can't do that, there's no fucking point to doing anything!" She winces and holds her head.

Ethan stays quiet for a long moment, then he asks, "Have

you checked the samples you took from the city? The towers?"
He meets Kate's gaze steadily.

Oh, shit.

"Pretty sure they're not actually towers, guys," Suresh yells.
"Fucking aliens."

Emotions flicker across Kate's pale face, one after another,
so quickly it's hard to catch them all. Fury, hurt, disbelief, then
a flash of fear before a cold hardness settles in. "Are you seriously suggesting that one of us . . ."

"It's happened before," Ethan says evenly.

Her eyes widen, and she darts a look at Ophelia. But whatever she sees on Ophelia's face isn't what she's expecting.

Kate straightens in her chair. "You told her?"

Ethan stays silent.

"Go ahead and screw us over, Commander," Kate snarls.
"We're never getting hired anywhere after this."

"Have you checked?" he repeats, unmoved.

"No! Not since Birch thought one was missing."

Ethan takes that in, then pivots and heads for the C side
corridor and the inventory room.

Kate stands. "No. I'll do it." She glares at Ethan. "I put the
sample unit in the airlock so we'd hear the alarm if anyone
went in."

She pushes past Ophelia and toward the airlock.

Ethan doesn't look at Ophelia—conflicted, no doubt—but
he follows Kate. Ophelia does the same.

The alert blares, just as before, the moment the inner airlock
door opens.

Once inside, Kate crosses to the sample containment unit,
bends down, and then uses Suresh's code to unlock the top of
the unit. The seal releases with a hiss.

She steps to one side and tips the top rack toward Ophelia
and Ethan. "See? All still present and accounted for. Double
sealed, and they don't seem to have moved or been messed
with." She dramatically lifts one vial, then another. "Weights

match what we originally noted. Nothing missing." She snaps the tray back into place and closes the lid.

"Satisfied?" she asks Ethan, but she doesn't wait for the answer before storming back into the central hub.

"Kate, it doesn't matter anymore," he says with a sigh, a step or two after her.

Ophelia trails behind them, thinking. So the exposure didn't come from those samples.

But then, it didn't have to, did it?

Random pieces she's been collecting all along without understanding how they fit together suddenly flow together, creating a cohesive line.

She stops abruptly.

The mess they found in the habs. The personal items left behind. The destruction in the labs, including the built-in sample containment unit in her office.

Only so much of that could be written off as a prank or a petty streak.

"It wasn't us," she says aloud, before she realizes it.

"What did you say?" Kate asks.

Ophelia clears her throat. "We didn't breach quarantine or steal samples."

"Yes, thank you. I know." Kate folds her arms over her chest. "Maybe you'll care to explain that to management so we aren't arrested, assuming we survive."

"What's happening?" Suresh calls. "I can't hear you."

"The team before us did," Ophelia says. "They were infected."

Ethan and Kate stare at her for a long moment in silence.

Then Kate makes a dismissive noise. "You can't possibly know—"

"Think about it," Ophelia says. "The towers—"

"Aliens!" Suresh interrupts.

"—are an obvious point of interest, especially here outside the largest ruins. Pinnacle would have required samples. And we have evidence that something went wrong here. This place was a wreck. Their fancy sample containment unit is smashed, but the lab equipment, the hab, the really expensive things, are fine. And they left personal items behind. Photos, a wedding ring, a molar comm implant! Who would do that?"

"You found a tooth?" Suresh shouts.

"That doesn't mean—" Ethan begins.

"And I don't think they put Silly Bird Tattoo Guy, Delacroix, out there and left him. They were intending to come back for him as soon as they were done, just like we are. They were following level five protocol." Ophelia looks to Ethan. "Just like us." The body bag would have disintegrated in the conditions, and maybe the flag blew away or they didn't use one, who knows. But she's right. She knows she's right, unfortunately.

"Guys," Suresh calls.

"In a minute," Kate shouts back at him, and then focuses on Ophelia. "You're saying that this happened to the Pinnacle team and, what, they fled and Pinnacle covered it all up? So they could sell the planetary rights?"

The all-too-familiar sensation of gritty humiliation and fury rises up in her. "Turn a loss into a net gain and hurt a competitor? I would say that it would not be out of character," Ophelia says tightly.

"And Montrose would be only too quick to bite," Ethan says.

"Making it their problem," Ophelia finishes. "Our problem."

"Hey, hello!" Suresh shouts. He's closer than before. "We have a problem."

When Ophelia swivels to look, he's backing out of the A side corridor, hands out in front of him. He stumbles over the threshold, his heel catching and sending him sprawling backward.

Liana steps over the threshold, perfectly, almost onto Suresh as he scrambles out of the way. Her eyes are open this time. But nothing about that offers the hope that she's getting better. Small portions of the sclera are still visible, but the veins and black spots have gotten larger.

"Oh my God," Kate whispers.

Liana pivots, heading for the airlock. "Out." The word is clear enough, and it's in Liana's voice, but without any of her warmth or life. It's flat, robotic sounding, as if something else is tugging on her vocal cords to make the word.

"She wants out, I say we let her," Suresh says, picking himself up off the floor.

"Suresh," Ethan says sharply.

"Not by herself!" He moves to join them, watching Liana disappear into the airlock through the inner door they left open. She can't open the outer door with the inner door still open, so she can't leave. "But, like, what if this is what they're pissed about? You know, we stole their shit, abducted their mothers or fathers or cousins or whatever that junk is." He flings a hand toward the airlock, and presumably toward the samples in the containment unit. "So let's give it back to them. Maybe then they'll leave us alone."

A dull thud echoes from the airlock. Then another, with the slap of flesh accompanying it.

Ophelia flinches. Liana's pounding her fists against the outer door.

"The storm—" Kate says.

"Is bad enough to keep us from taking off, I guess." Suresh sends a sidelong look at Ethan. "But we can see those fucking aliens from here. I say we go."

Ethan stays quiet. And Ophelia knows him well enough now to recognize that this means he's thinking, considering.

Oh Jesus. This is why R&E teams are not ever sent to planets without confirming that there will not be first contact with an extraterrestrial intelligence.

"This is a bad idea," Ophelia says. "We have no idea what they want. What they'll do. We don't even know if they're a 'they.' To your earlier point, this could be the equivalent of attempting to negotiate with the anticollision system on an autocar." She throws her hands up.

"Or it could be a hostage situation," Kate says quietly.

"Okay, fine. But who are the hostages, then? Us or them?" Ophelia demands. "How do you plan to communicate that you intend no harm?"

"I don't know." Kate raises her eyebrows. "Aren't you the people expert?"

"Are these people?" Ophelia shoots back.

"Do you have another suggestion, Doctor?" Ethan injects, before Kate can respond.

She grits her teeth hard enough that the enamel squeaks in protest. "No."

"Besides, don't you feel it?" Suresh asks, his voice softer. "It wants us to come back. To come home."

Ophelia, Kate, and Ethan turn to look at him. He's staring at the airlock as Liana continues her steady, even drumbeat of thumping. But more disturbingly, he's leaning in that direction as if being pulled by the shoulders by a not-quite-strong-enough magnet.

"Suresh," Ophelia says.

He doesn't respond.

"Suresh!" She snaps her fingers in his direction, a gesture she despises, both for its condescension and the vague connection to hypnosis and the chicanery sometimes still associated with psychotherapy.

But it jerks him out of his daze enough to flip her off.

"Can I check your arm?" Ophelia asks.

He scowls at her. But then he offers his arm, pulling the sleeve up.

She moves closer for a better look. His skin is red and abraded from his scratching, but the bumps have vanished. Only, they're not gone. She knows that now. They've just . . . progressed. The nosebleeds and headaches will come next. After that . . .

Thud. Thud. Thud.

"She's going to hurt herself," Kate says grimly.

"Now or later," Ethan agrees. Ophelia winces at the idea of Liana fumbling at her arm with a blade of some type.

Ethan tips his head toward the airlock. "Let's see what we can do to stop it."

Wrestling herself into her envirosuit is quickly becoming Ophelia's least favorite activity on an assignment that has been full of new lows. In the corner of the airlock, she struggles to pull her suit up over her shoulders. Opposite her, Kate and Suresh, already in their suits, are bickering while they attempt to shuffle Liana, who has gone quiet now that everyone is in here, into hers.

"Lift her foot. No, her other foot," Kate says. "Are you even paying attention, Suresh?"

Ethan approaches Ophelia, closing the fasteners on the front of his suit with one hand. Show-off.

"I know you're not happy about this," he says quietly.

"It's not about me being happy. I just don't know how to make this better. How to fix this." The fabric snaps out of her hand, too tight, or twisted somewhere that she can't see or reach. "Fuck," she mutters.

"If any of us knew how to fix this, we would do it. That's not your exclusive burden to bear, Doctor." Ethan reaches for the shoulder of her suit, meeting her gaze first, as if asking for permission.

He's too close, inside that half-meter perimeter designated for intimate acquaintances.

She nods jerkily, breathing faster. This is trouble.

"The trick with these things is you have to take it one limb at a time and roll up from there." His breath skates by her cheek as he talks her through it. The fabric at her shoulder loosens, his fingers working swiftly and efficiently, and yet she can feel every touch. He's her patient; this is not okay.

She closes her eyes quickly, tears burning behind the lids. This is her weakness. To be taken care of. She wants to be respected, needed, but at the same time she's so fucking soft for the slightest display of affection. She despises that about herself. Being aware of it doesn't help, either. It's like internal quicksand; struggling only makes it worse.

"It's hard to do everything at once," Ethan continues, his voice raspy. "To push constantly against what you can't control, what you can't change."

He's no longer talking about the suit.

Ophelia opens her eyes.

His exhaustion is plain on his face, but so, also, is the understanding. He knows—knows what it's like to hold yourself accountable for a disaster you didn't cause and yet can't seem to escape.

"Did you know that I was supposed to be at home the day the tunnel collapsed?" he asks.

The day his sisters died.

"I left them home alone to screw around with some friends at the power station."

His train of thought is not difficult to follow. "This isn't your fault," Ophelia says quickly. "Neither was Ava."

Ethan frowns, not acknowledging the truth in her words. "It's not yours, either."

She lifts her shoulder in a partial denial. "Feels like it."

He straightens her collar, pulling up the edges under her chin. "That's always the trouble, isn't it? When you take on one thing outside of your control, suddenly everything is your fault. Nothing is ever enough."

A tear spills over and rolls down to her chin. Ophelia swipes at the tear, turning her face away from him. "Sorry," she says with a half laugh.

"Nothing to be sorry about," he says. "Some of us are broken enough that we don't get to be fixed. And maybe we're better off that way. Not hiding from the damage like everyone else. Just accepting it and figuring out how to work around it. Just like we're doing. Like *you're* doing." His gaze meets hers and holds it. "It takes guts to face the worst of yourself, the worst of your fears."

His hands smooth over Ophelia's shoulders and down her arms, holding her for just a second. "But you need to stop blaming yourself for things you can't change and ask for help when you need it."

"You first," she murmurs.

He smells of coffee and the astringent dry soap from the sonic shower. But it's comforting, familiar, and she wants to rest her head, just for a moment, in the secure space between his neck and shoulder, to feel the edge of that stubble against her forehead.

The need must show in her expression. Ethan's throat works with an audible click and he looks away. But only for a second. Then his hand rises from her arm to touch her cheek, wiping away the track of that lone tear. His thumb brushes just beneath her mouth, and her breath catches.

"I . . ." Ophelia's voice is breathy and soft. She doesn't even know what she's saying or how she's going to finish.

A distant high-pitched shriek, like a woman or child in pain, pierces the quiet.

She lurches back from Ethan, her heart catapulting in a frantic attempt to escape her chest. Chills skitter across her skin and she wraps her arms around herself.

She looks toward the outer airlock door, as if she'll be able to see the source of the scream through it. Kate and Suresh are still arguing over Liana and her suit, now working her arms into the sleeves. They give no sign of having heard anything.

Fuck. Was that . . . Did I . . . She grips her arms more tightly, like that will keep her from shaking apart.

"I heard it, too," Ethan says, jerking her attention back to him. He nods, affirming his answer, as if she needs the reassurance, which she does. "It's okay," he says. "I heard it."

Her head bobs in wobbly acknowledgment.

Ethan takes a step back from her, resuming a more professional distance and tone. "It was the wind outside. It sounds a lot like . . . voices, I've noticed." He's not looking at her anymore, but at a point somewhere over her right shoulder.

Relief and disappointment course through her so strongly that she feels almost dizzy with the contradiction. It's for the best. But that knowledge does not drown out the selfish squall of deflected desire. Damn it.

Maybe she is crazy, wanting things she can't have at the same time that she knows better than to want them.

An exhausted laugh escapes her before she can stop it.

Ethan looks at her questioningly.

"Did you know my grandmother lost her mind at the end of her life?" she says.

He registers the change in tone and subject with confusion. "Miranda Bray?" he asks, with doubt.

"A little irony for you." Ophelia fumbles with the closures on her suit, making sure they're closed properly, trying not to notice Ethan following her motions with his gaze. "She despised my father for what she saw as his lack of mental toughness, a lack she was certain I had inherited from him. But then Alzheimer's got her in the end." Ophelia has mental illness and disease coming at her on both sides and crosswise in her family.

His brows draw together. "But that's—"

"Curable? Yep. But that would have meant stepping down from the board to get treatment." She gives him a hard smile. "Toward the end, I'm pretty sure she had half of the other members convinced that Andrew Busk had managed to resurrect himself from hell. She was so convinced he was a threat. In reality she was talking about events that happened decades ago. She could have saved herself, but she was too stubborn.

Too determined to get what she wanted, no matter the cost." She finishes the final closure with a snap.

His eyebrows arch, his mouth quirking in a thinly disguised smile.

"Yes, I know," she says dryly. "I've spent my whole life trying not to be her, trying not to be anyone in my family, only to realize exactly how much I have of them in me anyway."

It occurs to her then that if she'd recognized this sooner—and *accepted* it—she might have been able to be more open, more vulnerable with the people who mattered in her life. Her sister. Julius.

Julius ended up hurting her because she couldn't be honest with him, and her family used that leverage against her. If he'd known, truly understood her history with her uncle, he would never have done what he did.

Which means Ophelia's family has power over her only because Ophelia continues to give it to them. By keeping that all-important secret, a secret that's not even hers to bear.

"We ready?" Suresh calls, out of breath. He, Kate, and Liana are fully suited up, helmets waiting on the rack.

"In a minute," Ethan responds. Then he turns back to Ophelia. "At least now you can blame it all on alien possession."

"I have an idea," he says to Suresh, as he walks away from her.

It takes Ophelia a few seconds to realize that he was joking, that Ethan Severin made a joke. Gallows humor, but humor nonetheless.

Shocking what the prospect of death will do to change a person.

28

Suresh was right; the storm is weaker than before.

Still.

They stay within sight of one another, not that they have a choice. Ethan has linked them all together on another orange cord like the one that used to stretch from the hab to the lander. Turns out it's from Kate's mountain climbing equipment, in her personals. She had hoped to try for an ascent here.

"Cool, so we all get lost together," Suresh muttered, when they'd passed the cord from one to another, threading it through one of the fabric tool loops on the side of their suits.

"Better all of us together than one in every direction," Kate pointed out. "I can only rescue so many people in time."

Once, Ophelia would have bristled at the assumption that Kate would be doing the rescuing, or that any of them would require such efforts, but now she's just glad someone's thinking about it, putting a contingency plan in place.

Suresh is at the front, followed by Liana, with Kate keeping even with her, though Liana seems to be doing just fine. If anything, she is moving with more certainty and speed than the rest of them, as if she can hear a signal the rest of them can't.

Ophelia doesn't think Liana's seeing anything. At least not with her eyes. What is left of them.

Oh, God, please let this work.

Ophelia is behind Kate, who has the portable sample unit, with Ethan bringing up the tail. She's grateful to be in the middle. Fighting the wind and the snow and the slightly uphill climb isn't easy, even in the lighter gravity.

Ahead of them, the towers are sleek black blades sticking out of the ground, growing larger the closer they get.

Looking at them now, she's not sure how they—or anyone else—thought they belonged here. They're taller than anything else around, other than the mountains in the distance. The humped remains of the city beneath the snow are significantly lower, smaller.

The Lyrians were considered an intelligent species because they clearly used tools and they were, at least somewhat, spacefaring. But Pinnacle found no old satellites, no space docks, no colonies except that one lone Lyrian on the next planet over in the system. But how much of human technology would be detectable after ten thousand years? Maybe Pinnacle and Montrose assumed that the Lyrians were backward when the opposite was true. The Lyrians might have been more advanced, but because humans don't view advancement in the same way, they missed it.

The snow doesn't even seem to stick to the towers above the ground level; they're like arrows driven into the snowy surface. Ophelia wonders if they're somehow warmer than the surrounding air. Or if they're emitting some kind of field that keeps the moisture away.

Another possibility—these things arrived here after the snow started, after the Lyrians were gone.

That seems to stretch the imagination. Humans have found only a dozen or so other planets with signs of former alien civilizations, and this planet has two?

Three, actually, if you count us. Ophelia shakes her head. If Pinnacle and Montrose found something of value here, isn't it equally likely that some other species might have as well?

Humans have been operating like they have the universe to themselves just because they haven't found any other living civilizations. Doesn't mean they aren't out there.

Our arrogance might well come back to bite us in the ass when or if one of those other sentient species decides they're done with our bullshit. Ophelia winces, imagining the moment a corporation claims the exact wrong planet as "theirs."

Ahead of Ophelia, Liana is drawing even with Suresh in her eagerness to reach the towers. Is it *her* eagerness, though, or the stuff inside her, inside all of them?

Ophelia's not getting any closer to answers, but working through the possibilities keeps her from fixating on their fate. This extremely unlikely-to-work plan is their best bet, and it seems far more probable that they will all end up like Liana. Best-case scenario.

Ophelia bites her lip. If she doesn't have control, she doesn't know what she'll do. Even her grandmother, when she lost all sense of where she was, even of who she was, resorted to biting and punching anyone who came too close.

And you still don't know what happened to the rest of the Kellerson pack.

The rest of the surgical instruments, the different-sized scalpels, specifically, are still missing.

Ophelia takes a deep breath. Nothing she can do about that now. She needs to let it go. Just focus on the towers. Maybe this will all work, and the worrying will be for nothing.

The thought cheers her more than she expects it to. Oddly, it feels harder to hang on to her fears at this point, like trying to stop sand from slipping through the cracks between her fingers.

Almost like this is inevitable and they're finally reaching the end.

The end and we'll be together, it'll be so much better and—

"Hey, Doc," Kate says over the comms, startling her.

"Yes?" Ophelia tries not to sound too out of breath. What was she just thinking about? It's gone, vanished like a puff of steam in the air. She's lost not just her train of thought but also the entire station.

"I was thinking about it," Kate says, a little too casually. "If Pinnacle did what you think, if they covered up what happened here so they could sell the rights, then doesn't that mean they know how to treat this . . . whatever this is?"

Ophelia frowns. "What makes you think that?"

"Well, they had to know about it somehow. We only found one suit, one body. Maybe the rest of them made it back."

Ophelia hesitates. "It's possible, I suppose." Equally possible that there are more bodies tucked right next to Delacroix—and now Birch—that they just haven't found yet. "I don't think Pinnacle would have sold the rights, though, if they could figure out how to deal with it." Plus, knowing her family and how they operate, she thinks it's far more likely that Kate's earlier speculation about Montrose is probably true for Pinnacle as well. The team reported in, and now the remains of said team are floating in tiny exploded pieces in space somewhere.

"It doesn't matter, Katey," Suresh cuts in. "Even if they know, they're not going to share it with Montrose."

"Except we have the Pinnacle crown princess with us," Kate says.

Ophelia gives a choked laugh, something much closer to a strangled noise. "Crown princess?" That would imply that she's set to take over. Imagining the look on her uncle's face at that suggestion, the vein in his scalp that would pulse at the idea, is almost enough to make her genuinely laugh. "Like I told you before, my family and I aren't close."

"Not close enough to want to save your life?" Kate persists.

"No," Ophelia says flatly. "If anything, they would be relieved to be rid of me." She is the proverbial thorn in the side, the loose thread, the piano dangling overhead on a fraying rope.

"Oh."

Yeah. How does one follow up the blunt nonhyperbolic assessment that someone's family would prefer them dead?

They trudge onward in silence for several more minutes.

"Slow down, Liana," Suresh protests. There are dark shadows

ahead of Ophelia, but growing clearer as they approach the towers. The towers are huge, providing a dark background against which it's easier to see, especially when compared to the endless gray of sky and snow.

A high-pitched whine starts in Ophelia's ears. She turns down the volume on her comms, but it continues. She grimaces, automatically reaching for her ears to rub them, forgetting that her helmet is in the way.

Cells dying in the ear. It happens, more frequently with age. But unlike that experience, this doesn't fade after a few seconds.

A *ping* sounds, faint and barely audible. Someone summoning her on a private channel. "Do you feel it?" Ethan asks, after she accepts and turns up the volume.

For a moment, Ophelia's not sure what he means, too focused on the buzz in her ears, but when she takes stock, she realizes the perpetual tightness in her chest, the grinding dread, is gone.

"It feels better." His voice doesn't have that dreamy edge that she noticed from Liana, Suresh, and even Birch before he died. But it's softer than she's ever heard from him before.

"It does," Ophelia says, struggling against the urge to settle into the sensation, like sinking into a warm bath and surrendering to the heat. "But it's . . ." She pauses to try to find the right words to describe the feeling. Soothing, but with an edge of tension, a spring coiled beneath a smooth surface, a shark fin in the bathtub. "Too good to be true," she finishes.

"Like a predator luring in prey," he says after a moment.

"Yeah," she says, nodding. "That's it. Should we go back?"

"I don't think we can. Not without trying it. We just need to be careful."

Isn't that what we've been doing? she wants to ask, but that's not helpful. And she doesn't have any better suggestions.

When they reach the base of the towers, Ophelia has to immediately discard her previous assessment of the height and girth. Each of them is easily half a city block—or would be, if they were fully upright and rectangular instead of at an angle. It's as if skyscrapers had suddenly pitched themselves from above, into the ground. Staring up at them from this proximity, she can no longer see the top of them.

They are identical to one another, from what she can see. Smooth, black, mostly opaque, but with a sheen that gives them that crystal-like appearance. No obvious openings, cracks, edges. Each looks to be a singular, whole piece of . . . something.

She tears her gaze away from the towers—they are strangely enticing, for reasons she doesn't understand, like staring at the ground over the edge of a tall building and feeling that irrational fear that you might accidentally jump, but also a thrill at the same time.

"Stop, Suresh. That's close enough," Ethan says on the comm channel, drawing her attention back to the front of the line.

Suresh and Liana are moving quickly, too quickly, to the nearest tower. Neither of them responds to him.

"Stop!" Ethan charges past Ophelia, pushing the end of the rope into her hands as he passes.

Kate jolts as he rushes by her, seeming to shake herself awake. "Suresh! Stop!" She leaps forward, and Ophelia's forced to hurry along after her or lose her grip on the cord.

"What?" Suresh rocks to a reluctant halt at Ethan's hand on his shoulder. Only the tension on the orange cord between Suresh and Liana keeps Liana from proceeding without him. She's already straining forward, trying to close the final distance. Two, maybe three meters from the base of the tower.

"Didn't you hear us?" Kate demands.

The tower looms over them like one of those gods of old mythology, waiting to determine their fate. Except . . .

Home. Safety. Peace.

The impulse pulls at Ophelia, stronger now. That same promise of relief washes over her, enticing her to come closer.

Let go, Little Bird. Come join us. You'll feel so much better.

The lure is a lot easier to ignore when the voice in her head sounds like her father. A shiver ripples over her skin. This . . . whatever it is, in her head, it knows her. But it doesn't seem to comprehend that she might find his voice less than compelling.

"Hear what?" Suresh twists around, looking at them. He blinks slowly, looking drowsy. "What's wrong?" The words are slushy and slurred.

It's hard to read body language in suits and helmets, but the way Ethan stiffens, pulling himself upright, tells Ophelia that he's hearing it the same way.

"We need to keep our distance," Ethan says. "Come on. Back up." He takes the cord from Suresh's hands, pulling the slack into his grasp.

That seems to rouse Suresh from his daze. "No way! We came out here to fix this, and I am not—"

"Because it wants us closer," Ophelia blurts. "It wants us to give in and—"

The mental image appears in her head without bidding. Ophelia, pressed against the front of the tower, arms out in the parody of a hug, embraced by a bright white light. Fear, terror, worry, all just gone. Like they never existed.

In the visual, her shoulders droop with relaxation and the expression of utter peace glows in the white light. In that moment, she would be okay. She would be fixed. Whole in a way that she hasn't been since she was eleven.

Her eyes sting with the promise of it, and she has to blink to keep from letting the tears roll free.

"—be part of it," she finishes thickly. It's a thoroughly inadequate description. But she can't find the words to describe the sensation, the completeness the tower seems to be offering.

"That's good enough reason for me," Ethan says. He tugs

on the cord and pulls Suresh and Liana back, Kate and Ophelia along with them, closer to the old perimeter line.

The emotional effect lessens as they move away. Not a lot, but it's noticeable.

"The samples," Suresh says, jerking his head as if to clear it. "We need to give them back. That was the plan."

"I'll do it," Ethan says. He holds the cord out to Kate, gesturing with his free hand for the small sample case she transferred the vials to.

"No," Kate says sharply, pulling the case tighter against herself as if he might lunge at her and attempt to take it by force. "You're our only pilot. We can't get out of here without you."

"I'll do it," Suresh offers.

"Please," Kate scoffs. "You were already trying to throw yourself into the metaphorical fire." She takes a deep breath, and Ophelia knows what she's about to say.

"It should be me," Ophelia says. A surprising calmness fills her, just at the decision being made. It feels like she's been waiting for this moment her whole life.

Kate's brows arch in surprise, and Ethan's shaking his head. "No. Absolutely not," he says. "You did not sign up for this."

"I did, actually. I signed up for this assignment, whatever it entailed," she reminds him, using his words against him.

He flinches. "That's not—"

"Kate is your engineer. You might need her. If we don't all end up dead, you're going home. You don't need me to do that," Ophelia points out. "Let me do this."

Ethan steps closer to her, a mimicry of privacy only, because they're still on the open comm channel. His dark eyes scan her face, searching, the intensity reminding her of that moment in the airlock, when he stood so close, making her wonder exactly what he was feeling. "If this is about sacrificing yourself out of some sense of—"

"It's not," she says quickly. "It's just logical."

Mostly. I think. Wouldn't it be nice to save lives instead of taking them or worrying about taking them? The thought of never having to question her own motives ever again makes her feel like she's been cramped inside a tiny storage crate for decades and someone has just taken the lid off and offered to let her out to stretch her legs.

And the possibility of another taste of that peace, the bright white light . . . it's not *not* a motivation.

It'll kill you. The tiny portion of herself still dedicated to self-preservation raises its voice to be heard above the noise.

Maybe. Does she care? She's not sure that she does. Or maybe it's the alien sludge in her head influencing her, subtly nudging her toward the outcome it/they want. Does it matter?

She's tired of hiding, tired of running.

"She's right, Ethan," Kate says after a moment.

Ethan's mouth thins to an unhappy line. "Fine. But I'm going with you."

"No, that's not—" Ophelia starts to protest.

"I'll stay back, but I'm going," he says. "That's final." He turns to Kate. "You'll—

"Keep an eye on the brain-dead duo?" Kate asks. "Yeah. I got it."

He hands Kate his end of the cord, and Ophelia does the same with hers.

"That's really not necessary," Suresh says with a sniff, as Kate grips the lengths of cord tightly in her hand. "I'm not a fucking child."

"Sure," Kate says. "That's why you were running toward it like it was a fucking mirror with your name in blinking lights."

"That is incredibly offensive," Suresh says. "You know I don't ever rely on inconsistent lighting."

Kate kneels and opens the sample case, pulling one of the vials free. She holds it out to Ophelia. "Start with this, and we'll see what happens."

For a fraction of a second, Ophelia sees herself from a

distance, as if from a camera far above her. Not like the glowing, peace-filled version of a few moments ago but just her. Standing there, above Kate kneeling down and holding the vial out for her to take.

Am I really going to take it? Am I really going to walk up to this enormous alien edifice and offer it the chunks of itself that we took? It's such a bizarre idea that looking at it from an outside perspective triggers the momentary urge to laugh.

How the hell did she end up here?

Ophelia steps forward and takes the sample vial from Kate, taking care to grasp it firmly enough not to drop it in the snow.

She can't see any obvious place where the pieces came from, not from back here. So she just heads for dead center on the wide side closest to them.

Dead *center. Great, Phe.*

Ethan goes with her, maintaining his distance but swinging in a wide arc to stay in a straight line with her.

A private channel request pings. Ethan. She ignores it.

He won't try to pull her off course, either, because he knows there's no other option.

Once Ophelia reaches the center, or close enough, she stops. The tower looms over her, making her feel even smaller and more insignificant.

Tightening her grip on the vial, she breaks the seal, feeling the snap through her gloves rather than hearing it.

Then she edges forward.

29

The tiny slivers of sample tremble in the vial, clinking against the polycarbonate loudly enough that Ophelia's external mic picks up the sound.

She braces herself, preparing to be yanked off her feet or repelled backward.

But then she realizes it's just her hand shaking. The pieces aren't vibrating with the desire to fly forward toward their home. They're just sitting in there like the bits of inert material that they have been all along.

The towers themselves remain silent and still. No sudden hum or light show or mouth opening up to devour its scattered bits. Not even a faint rumbling of activity.

Ophelia feels the pull again, the temptation to let go and move closer. *Little Bird, you don't have to suffer anymore. Just come to me.*

She shudders.

But that's it, though.

Did they get this completely wrong? Maybe whatever is in them, whatever is causing this, isn't from the towers at all.

But she saw the shape; it's the same as the towers. All these little pieces adding up to these huge structures. Millions, billions? What was their purpose?

Her comm channel crackles. "Maybe try getting them closer," Kate says.

"Don't," Ethan responds immediately.

"I'm not suggesting she tackle it," Kate snaps. "Just maybe get some of the pieces within range for it to recognize them."

"How?" Ethan demands.

Kate makes an exasperated noise. "I don't know, try chucking them."

A gurgle of a laugh escapes Ophelia, the absurdity of the situation again striking her. It would be funnier if her heart weren't pounding like she was running for her life instead of just standing here with her trembling hand extended. The calm from before is definitely gone, overridden in the moment by her amygdala screeching at her to get out of there.

This isn't a bear or a saber-toothed tiger or even the sound of rushing footsteps behind her on a darkened street. But that primal part of her brain certainly recognizes it as a danger and wants nothing the fuck to do with it.

With a grimace, Ophelia pours a few of the slivers into her palm. She half expects them to come alive and try to burrow through her glove. But they don't. They're just pretty, shiny rocks.

"Do it," Kate insists.

Ophelia lobs them underhand at the black wall in front of her.

The wind skews them slightly over the few meters between, but they still connect, clicking when they hit the smooth surface.

Right before they fall to the ground and vanish into the new accumulation of snow at the base.

Damn it.

"Did you throw them hard enough?" Kate asks.

Ophelia turns her head to glare at her. "I don't know, I missed the training on pitching rocks at potential extraterrestrial entities."

"Just let me do it," Suresh says. "I can—"

"Ophelia." Ethan's voice holds an odd note. Preoccupied, uncertain.

The others must hear it too because they shut up, the comm channel going quiet.

Ophelia twists away from the tower, from the throb of its presence like the pull of leaving gravity for the first time, to find him.

He's still behind her, about three meters back, but staring at something off to her left, at the far edge of the tower, right where it curves out of sight.

"Do you see that?" he asks, without looking at Ophelia.

She can't see anything other than the long base of the tower. She's too close.

Careful to keep the remnants of the vial steady and upright, she moves toward him, turning to follow his gaze as she does.

"There's something over there," he says, pointing, as she approaches.

For a moment, she's certain she's going to see that shadowy figure from before, the one that she caught a glimpse of when they thought Birch was missing.

But no. Ethan's gesturing toward the squared, straight-line edge of something not made in nature. Covered in a thin layer of snow and ice, but clearly separate from the tower. Maybe waist high. As Ophelia shifts to get a better look at it, a light flashes on it for a brief second, then disappears. Is someone else out here after all?

She freezes. Nothing happens. But when she moves closer to Ethan, the light reappears. This time it holds steady as she keeps her gaze on it.

"It's just a reflection," she says, with relief. "From our helmet lights."

"No," he says. "It's a reflector."

Ophelia frowns. "What difference does that—"

He starts toward the light and the mystery object.

"Hey, what's going on? What are you doing?" Kate asks.

"Just stay there," he says, his tone brooking no argument.

Ophelia follows him, making sure that neither of them is

unconsciously being drawn too close to the tower as they go. This doesn't seem like a trick or a lure, but thus far, nothing about this assignment has been what it seems.

When he reaches the corner of the tower, he stops.

Ophelia joins him a moment later, halting at the sight before them, confused.

It's the missing rover, parked at the short end of the closest tower. The structure has shielded the rover from the worst of the weather, but it's still deeply crusted with snow and ice. Just not quite enough to make it an unrecognizable lump.

"I don't understand," she says. "Why would they leave this out here?"

"What is it?" Kate asks.

"The rover from hab," Ophelia answers when Ethan doesn't.

"Oh, shit," Kate says.

Ethan doesn't respond, just strides forward into the too-narrow gap between the rover and the tower.

"Ethan!" Ophelia scrambles after him.

He manages to stay clear of the tower, though she sees the sway in his steps, the magnetic pull of whatever this thing is that wants them to come closer, and she feels it in herself as well, as she trails after him.

Let go. Join us, Little Bird. Aren't you tired of being alone?

Ethan reaches the approximate location of the front passenger side door and scrapes at the snow and ice with his glove.

"Jesus, careful, please." Ophelia winces, imagining the tiny slices in the fabric and the slow slip of air from his suit, because from what she's heard, a lot of small tears are much harder to patch than one big hole.

But he soon unearths a door handle and pulls on it with both hands.

The door remains shut, but the sharp sound of ice cracking ricochets through the air like shots fired. It's frozen shut.

After carefully setting the open sample vial aside, upright in a clumpy patch of snow, Ophelia moves up to stand next to him. He shuffles over a step to make room, and then they both set their feet and grip the handle.

"On the count of three," he says.

"Right." She nods.

"One. Two. Three."

Her booted feet slip at first as she pulls, but then she manages to find some purchase.

The ice on the door creaks and pops, and then before she can adjust her stance, the door releases with a hideous shriek of cold metal hinges.

Her feet slide in the snow with the sudden change of leverage, ripping her hand off the handle and sending her legs shooting under the rover. They collide with something solid, stopping her forward progress, and she lands hard on the ground, her head banging around inside her helmet.

She tries to pull in a breath, but her lungs feel stuck together on both sides, the air completely knocked out of her. She can't move.

But she can see. With her head tipped hard to the left, she can make out a familiar shape under the rover with her.

Legs. In a silvery white envirosuit. Booted feet still locked in a half-crawling position, as if they're scaling a sheer wall.

A body. There's a body under here with her. That—not a tire or other piece of machinery—stopped her from sliding farther.

Blood rushes to her head, filling her ears with a roaring noise, and her lungs ache with the need to breathe.

"What's happening, Ophelia? Your vitals are all over the place," Kate says.

Dimly, Ophelia can hear the alarms signaling inside her suit. Involuntary goose bumps rise all over her body, a shiver running through her. She jerks her legs back and her knees slam into the underside of the rover. Fuck.

Bracing her hands in the snow, she scoots backward to free

herself, all the while expecting to hear a harsh skittering noise, followed by a cold, hard hand latching around her ankle.

"Doctor?" Kate presses.

Ophelia manages a tiny sip of air, and then another.

"I slipped," she croaks. "I fell." The beeps begin to slow. "I'm okay."

But whoever is under the rover is most definitely not.

The alarms in her suit stop, and Ophelia gathers herself up, outside the shadow of the rover. Knowing she'll regret it, she pushes up to her knees, and then, with a deep breath, she bends her head down to look beneath the rover.

A full person in an envirosuit is stretched out beneath, arms flung to either side. A pinnacle patch on the shoulder tells her it's a member of their team. The helmet is facing the other direction, though. Did they just climb under and freeze to death? When the rover was right here?

Ophelia straightens up. Her head is pounding, and she tastes blood, coppery and fresh in her mouth. She must have bitten her tongue when she hit the ground. She has to work hard against her gag reflex at the taste.

"Ethan." She stands, breathless, expecting to find him flung in the opposite direction.

But he's up already, or maybe he managed to hold on to the handle the entire time. He's leaning over the edge of the door to peer inside through the gap between the door and the frame.

Carefully, Ophelia staggers toward him. She'd slid toward the back end of the rover, farther than she'd thought. "I found. Underneath the rover. There's a body."

"Did you say a body?" Suresh demands.

Ethan doesn't move, just stays behind the rover door, staring in at something she can't see.

"Did you hear me? I said I—" Ophelia cuts herself off as soon as she reaches the rover's open door and looks inside.

At first, her brain can't make sense of it, like letters flipped upside down and backward, turning something as familiar as your own name into gibberish.

More envirosuits, like theirs, but with that familiar, brightly colored logo. Pinnacle. Arms pitched upward from the foot-well of the rover, ending in thick, lumpy black gloves over the hands. The faceplates on the helmets, the ones she can see, are blacked out. Legs in a chaotic tangle over the front seats.

There's two—no, three people jammed into the front. One is behind the wheel, collapsed forward and turned away from Ophelia, as if they're taking a nap before a long trip. The other two are wedged upside down and sideways on the passenger side, all higgledy-piggledy, as if they threw themselves into the rover without concern for fitting. Or as if someone else shoved them in in a hurry.

Ophelia takes a step back. "What . . ."

The body closest to her, the one with its arms flung into the footwell, wears a suit with a patch that says VIVIEN MARKELL, though the script is hard to read through the spatters of black on the outside of the suit.

Paint. They used black paint to cover their faceplates and their hands. Why would they—

A gust of wind whips around the corner of the tower, push-ing against Ophelia and setting off mini cyclones in the re-cently disturbed snow at their feet.

One of the cyclones spins past Ophelia and up to the rover, where it dissipates, scattering flakes inside the rover and over its occupants.

And that's when she sees it—snowflakes floating down inside Vivien's helmet. The faceplate on Vivien's helmet isn't blacked out. It's gone. Beyond shattered; simply no longer existent.

The face beneath is a thick mask of dried and frozen blood and fluids, the features obliterated. Her eyes, her nose, her mouth, they're just gone.

And her hands are the same.

From the tattered remains of her gloves at her wrist, tiny

black flecks shine back up at them under their helmet lights, but in the sparse gaps in the black, Ophelia catches the glimmer of white, of bone, where her fingers should be.

Oh, fuck, fuck, fuck.

"Pinnacle never even made it off the planet," Ethan says, his voice hoarse. "Three of them here, at least one back at the hab. Two more somewhere."

No, there's one under the rover. Ophelia subtracts from the total.

"They might have gotten the lander off the ground, but . . ." He shakes his head, his throat audibly clicking.

Shock. He's in shock. Which makes sense. Ophelia should be, would be, too, if she wasn't who she is.

She straightens up, forcing a deep breath through her still aching lungs. "Ethan. Hey. We need to go. Right now."

When he doesn't respond, she makes herself step closer to the rover door. Trying not to look at Vivien, not to think about the team member under the rover. *That's going to be our fate, our future.*

Ophelia tugs the door free of his hands and tries to close it. It stops well short, with another equally disturbing screech of the hinges. But there's enough room for Ethan to move past it now.

She grabs his arm and pulls him toward her.

"Take them back, you assholes! Wake up and take it back!" Suresh screams over the growing noise of the wind. Another front is moving in. "We just want to get out of here!"

A clattering sound Ophelia doesn't recognize echoes both inside and outside her helmet. "Suresh, stop! Stop!" Kate shouts. "Put them down."

The sample vials. He must be throwing them at the tower.

Ophelia heads for Kate, Suresh, and Liana, yanking Ethan after her.

"Ethan, I need help, I can't . . . Oh my God. Liana, stop! Come back!"

Ethan seems to wake up then. He twists his arm free from Ophelia's grasp and pushes past her to bolt for the front of the tower.

She rounds the corner just after him.

The hum she was expecting earlier kicks in now. Only it's not a hum, more of a high-pitched tone instead, like microphone feedback, increasing in intensity. Ophelia ducks, trying to cover her ears with her arms, though it does no good. She can feel the reverberation in her head, a bell that's been rung and won't stop. It feels like the bones of her skull are pulling apart, her brain turning to gray matter jelly.

She stumbles forward, away from the tower. She needs to get farther from the vibrations. The lure of peace and happiness is gone. Her father's voice is silent. This is its true face.

"Liana!" Kate shouts, her voice faded and distorted beneath the tone but cracking with desperation.

Ophelia twists around to look for Kate. For them. Where are they? Why aren't they running?

Ethan and Kate are hunched over, arms up in a useless attempt at defense, trying to stagger forward. Suresh is at the base of the tower, standing with his helmeted head tipped up as if listening to something Ophelia can't hear.

But Liana—oh God.

Arms flung wide in a parody of crucifixion, Liana is pressed up against the towers, like something is holding her there. Her feet dangle a couple meters above the ground, toes pointed downward. Her head leans forward against the tower in an impossibly straight and rigid position.

Exactly like Ophelia envisioned herself before. Only there's no white light, no sense of peace or becoming one.

And then the screaming starts.

30

Liana's body stiffens, and the thin shriek, like the whistle on the old-fashioned kettle Ophelia's grandmother insisted on for her tea, becomes a full-bodied scream.

The smooth and shiny surface of the tower . . . warps, shifting like a wave rolling across and up it simultaneously.

Liana's scream cuts off into a thick gurgling across the comm channel, followed by a sharp *crack*. A moment later, black bits flow like foaming smoke from her helmet in a stream Ophelia can see even at this distance here. Her faceplate. It just broke through her faceplate, like the Pinnacle team member in the rover.

We need to get her down!

Ophelia's not sure if someone said it over the comm channel or if she just thought it. It's impossible to focus on anything with the whine in her ears. It's like staring directly at the sun, only with sound instead of light.

Then Liana's hands lurch upward above her head, and her suit starts to move. Irregularly shaped lump and bumps press against the boundary of her envirosuit as they skim up her torso and down her arms toward the gloved ends of her suit. Whatever is in her is trying to get out, to get back into the tower.

Oh shit.

Ethan and Kate manage to reach the base of the tower and grab for Liana's feet, the only part of her in reach.

Gritting her teeth against the pain in her head, Ophelia slogs forward to join them. Only, just as she nears them, Suresh reaches out and presses his hand against the tower.

Motherfucker. He's going to be next.

Ophelia leaves Liana to Kate and Ethan and charges toward Suresh. She doesn't have a plan, she doesn't even know what she's going to do when she reaches him, which as it turns out, is to launch herself at him. Brute force, when all else fails.

Ophelia connects with him, her shoulder in his side, and her weight and momentum tear him away from the tower, casting them both to the ground. She lands on top of him, her abused lungs and back protesting the second jarring hit in a matter of minutes.

Ophelia straightens up as soon as she can, pushing herself back off him. "Suresh? Hey, Suresh!" She shakes his shoulders.

His gaze is fixed, unblinking, on the towers behind her. But then he shudders and his eyes cast wildly side to side until he finally sees Ophelia.

"What happened? I don't—"

"The aliens," she says grimly. Easier to use his terminology. "They pulled you in. We need to get you away from here." Before that magnet-like draw starts up again. She won't be able to stop him by herself if he decides to fight her.

"My hand! I can't feel it . . . I can't feel anything on this side," he says, panic in his voice.

He holds up his right hand, and his gloved hand flops forward, bending in the middle in a way that should not be possible.

It's probably better, then, that he can't feel anything.

"Can you stand?" Ophelia asks.

"I don't . . ." He shakes his head. "No. The whole right side of my body, it's . . ."

As she watches, he tries to move his fingers, and a combination of that blood and black sludge suddenly trickles through to his neck, pooling there, just visible through his faceplate. It must be rolling down his arm, back into his suit. Which means it is a not-insignificant amount of blood.

Ophelia looks away immediately, trying to ignore the swooping feeling in her head and gut at the sight of blood.

Okay, Okay. I need to think. "Keep your arm up." Above the heart. She hopes that's right. Or is that for a potentially venomous bite? Jesus. She never thought she would actually need to use this information.

She rocks back on her heels, thoughts spinning so fast she can't catch hold of any of them. *Tourniquet.* Suddenly the word and the idea pop into view. She fumbles through the pockets on her suit. Suit patches. Rations. All kinds of emergency stuff in there. And one of those things, she's pretty sure, is . . .

In one of the small pockets on the leg of her suit, her fingers latch on to a cord with a tiny plastic handle. "A tourniquet."

She loops the cord above Suresh's elbow and twists to tighten until he screams. *If they're not yelling, it's not tight enough.* The gruff instructor from her required training course, however, had failed to mention exactly how absolutely shitty it feels to deliberately inflict pain on someone, even if it is for their own good.

Ophelia blinks back tears. "Just try to stay calm. I've got you." She shifts around until she can get her hands under his armpits.

"Oh, yeah, much fucking better," Suresh says through clenched teeth.

It takes all of her strength to drag him backward. The snow helps a little, as does the marginally lighter gravity. But even with those aids, they only make it a half dozen meters before she has to stop, panting, side aching with the exertion.

When she checks the distance between their location and the towers, it looks as though she and Suresh have barely moved at all.

We're still too close. And—Ophelia checks her oxygen levels—*I'm sucking down air like there's a whole planet full of it.*

We're not going to make it. The realization is cold and

perfectly clear. She won't be able to get him far enough away before those things finish—it certainly seems like some form of eating, doesn't it?—and lure Suresh forward again, possibly everyone else as well.

Not to mention, Ophelia can't search for the hab behind her if she's dragging him. She might end up heading in completely the wrong direction in this storm. And they'll both die when their suits run out of juice. Assuming they even make it that far.

At the towers, Ethan and Kate are both now facing outward and pulling at Liana's legs, as if she were a cart to be tugged behind them. But the upper half of her body is glued to the tower. For now. Ophelia bets it won't stay that way. Not if the bodies they found in the rover are any indication. Someone tried to rescue them, but they didn't get very far.

Ophelia's not as quick about it as Kate, but she finds Liana's vitals on the display in her helmet faceplate. They're fading, but her heart is still beating.

Ugly choices. Ophelia spoke about them so cavalierly with Ethan before. Now, when she's actually faced with them, it feels like an entirely different situation.

"Doc, what are we doing?" Suresh asks in a gasp. "I'm not . . . the numbness is spreading."

I need help. And we all need to leave. "Ethan. Kate. Suresh is injured, and we need to get him back to the hab. I can't . . ." She takes a breath, forcing her voice to level out. "I can't do it by myself, and I think we only have a matter of time before *they,* whatever they are, try again with the rest of us. Please."

Hot tears roll down her face. She's condemning Liana to death. It's the only way forward for the rest of them. And Ophelia is the one pushing the issue, the one who will have to live with Liana's death, another death, on her conscience.

Kate hesitates. Ophelia sees her stop, and then Kate releases her grip on Liana.

The buzz in Ophelia's ears grows louder, as if the entities recognize that complete victory over Liana is imminent.

"Ethan, come on," Kate shouts. She pauses a moment, waiting for him, but he just leans forward harder.

She shakes her head and runs toward Ophelia. "Let's go." She takes a position at Suresh's right side, bending down to grip under his arm.

"Wait, we need Ethan," Ophelia says, startled.

"He's not coming," Kate snaps. "You're the one who said we needed to go."

"And you said he's our only pilot," Ophelia points out. Though that's not the reason. She just can't stomach the idea of leaving him here. Not when he could walk away.

"I'm pretty sure that's the least of our problems right now," Kate says. "Let's go!"

It's one thing to accept death when she doesn't have another choice, when death is the only option there is. But that's not the case here.

With a hole opening up in the pit of her stomach, Ophelia steps around Suresh and heads toward Ethan.

"Fuck," Kate snarls. "Doctor, get back here! If Severin is incapacitated, then I'm commander. I'm in charge!"

Ethan barely glances up when Ophelia reaches him. But he's still trying to free Liana. He's still in there, not lost to the tower, not yet. Which means this is him, making the choice. Trying to make up for past losses.

His eyes are bright with intensity, but Ophelia can see a familiar hopelessness in them as well. This is a man who is standing on the edge.

"Listen to me," she says, as calmly as she can, over Kate's cursing in the background. "I know you're blaming yourself for this right now. I understand that, better than anyone. You know that. But we need you. And if you don't walk away, we're all going to die." Her throat aches, but she keeps her voice as even as she can. "I'm not leaving you here to die just because you think you should, and Kate can't save Suresh on her own."

A convulsion runs through Liana's body, and the tower's pitch changes, going lower. Their time is running out.

"Doctor, don't make me come get you!" Kate bellows.

"You told me that I needed to stop taking blame for things I can't change and to ask for help," Ophelia says, backing up slowly. Step by step. "So, I did. I am. And I'm asking you to do the same thing."

Little Bird. Where are you? Her father's voice whispers through her mind.

"Ethan, please!" Ophelia begs.

A shout tears from deep within him. "Fuck!" He releases his hold on Liana and runs, grabbing Ophelia's arm as he passes and dragging her along with him.

The trip back to the hab with the three of them carrying Suresh through a building storm is over in a blink of an eye compared to the endless wait for the airlock to cycle through its pointless decontamination session. The system is set to prioritize decon over anything else, including repressurizing.

It seemed like a good idea at the time, three days ago.

"Can't you do anything?" Ethan asks, his breath fogging his faceplate. Oxygen is running low. Suit power is lower still. They might well freeze to death—or suffocate—before the inner door releases.

"Not from in here," Kate responds, her teeth chattering. "Is Suresh going to make it?" she asks Ophelia.

"I can hear you," he protests weakly from his position on the floor. Ethan has covered him with a cargo blanket, but she's not sure it's enough.

"Good," Kate says, all briskness and business. But she looks at Ophelia, still waiting for an answer.

Which Ophelia doesn't have. His right glove is alarmingly bloated, and he still can't feel anything on that side. "As soon as we're in, someone needs to get the PMU," she says. Though she already has her doubts about what it will be able to do in this situation.

"I'm on it," Ethan says.

Finally, finally, the airlock repressurizes, and with a final blast of air, as if they've been rolling around in dirt and need to be brushed off as well, there is the welcoming *beep* and a green light above the airlock's inner door.

Kate releases her helmet with an audible gasp of relief, dropping it to the floor, and then charges forward to shove open the door.

Ethan and Ophelia do the same. The air smells blessedly clean and medicinal, even though Ophelia knows it won't do a thing to help in this situation, just sting their eyes and noses.

Ophelia kneels down to take off Suresh's helmet as well. His skin has a gray tinge, shiny with visible sweat. Blood and black spatters dot his chin and neck. Beneath the collar of his suit she can see where both have soaked into his jumpsuit beneath.

"Why?" she asks. "Why did you touch it?"

"I . . . I heard my mother," he says quietly. "She was calling to me. Telling me that my aunties were waiting, that our meal was ready. It felt so real." A tear breaks loose and rolls down his temple. "It was like I was there. My mother was pulling on my hand, tugging me closer, and then . . . then you were there and I was on the ground."

"She's alive?" Ophelia asks, on impulse.

He frowns. "What? My mother? Yes. As far as I know. Why would you—"

Ophelia shakes her head. "Never mind."

Ethan gives her an odd look as she straightens up. "What are you thinking?"

"I don't know." Still trying to figure out the unfigureoutable. She hesitates. "Your mother, Suresh . . . you love her?"

Ethan stares at her.

"What are you talking about? She's my mother. Of course I love her!"

Ophelia holds her hands up in surrender. "Okay, okay." Love and hate are both strong emotions—usually complicated ones as well.

A loud clattering comes from inside, followed by the unmistakable screech of metal on metal.

"I moved the table in the central hub closer," Kate says, breathless on her return.

That's a good idea. Better not to waste time hauling Suresh back to Ophelia's office. Plus there's a limit to how long a tourniquet can be in place before the limb is lost. She remembers that, but not exactly how long that is. Her training only covered this old-fashioned crap as a last-ditch measure. More as an oddity, like using two pieces of wood to create friction to start a fire instead of just using a fucking plasma lighter.

"Ready?" Ethan asks, crouching behind Suresh to lift his upper torso.

Ophelia nods.

"Ready," Kate says.

With a grunt of effort, Ethan lifts Suresh, and Kate and Ophelia pull Suresh's legs up from the ground. He is quiet. Not so much as a whimper.

The three of them—four, technically—make their way awkwardly over the threshold and into the central hub, where the table is, as promised, much closer.

Ethan steps carefully to the side of the table and swings Suresh sideways over the table, letting him down gently when Suresh's backside connects with the table. Ophelia and Kate follow suit, placing his legs down in alignment.

"Don't roll off," Kate warns Suresh, as Ethan disappears down the A side corridor to grab the PMU.

"So much fuss over little old me," Suresh murmurs, his eyelids fluttering down.

"And try to stay awake," Ophelia adds abruptly.

Kate's eyes go wide. "Why the fuck would he want to do that?" she demands. "He's in pain—"

"Because I think it matters. It seems to get worse, the symptoms, when we're not conscious." And Suresh is not in pain, which Ophelia thinks is very much the issue. Some part of him seems to be already lost to that thing. If he goes to sleep, they might lose him entirely.

Kate rolls her eyes, but she pokes Suresh in his shoulder. "You hear that? Mean doctor says you need to stay awake."

"Crazy bitch," Suresh says, with a hint of his former spark. "Trying to save me from the nice alien torturers."

Ethan returns seconds later with the PMU.

"Leave the tourniquet in place. I think," Ophelia says to Kate, who has stepped to the other side of the table, her hands hovering above the looped cord. "We need to take off his glove."

With a grimace, Kate steps back and out of the way, holding her hands up. "Machines, not people, Doc."

Son of a bitch. Fine.

Ophelia moves around the table and fumbles with the latching system at Suresh's wrist. It's backward to what she's used to, putting them on and taking them off of herself.

Ethan steps in, nudging her out of the way and taking over. He twists at the wrist, and the glove clicks in release. Then he lowers it carefully over the cuff edge of the suit.

The sound, oh God . . . Ophelia's not sure any of them will survive this, but if she does, the wet splotching sounds of his flesh and that mix of blood and black sludge hitting the metal floor will stick with her forever.

Suresh's hand is a shredded mess. Skin and ligaments dangle from bone. And the black stuff is everywhere. It's as if the tiny pieces exploded his hand from the inside. And maybe they did, trying to get to the tower. Only his suit—and the fact that he wasn't quite as infected as Liana—saved him. The pieces were not able to get out and rejoin the whole. Liana's faceplate cracked. But his glove held. That's it.

Ophelia tightens her lips and presses her tongue against the roof of her mouth, resisting the rise of bile.

Ethan draws in a sharp breath.

"Oh, shit, am I going to lose a finger?" Suresh asks.

The color drained from her face, Kate pats his shoulder. "Nope. All five alive. Going to be baby smooth and good as new." She glares at them.

"Med-scanner," Ophelia says after a moment. "I need it. I'll be right back."

She turns away for the A side corridor, her breath trembling. She manages to hold it together until she's out of sight, tucked around the bend in the corridor. Then her trembling knees give.

Ethan follows her. She doesn't look up, but she knows it's him by the familiar rhythm and firmness of his steps.

"We can't stitch it," Ophelia says to the tops of her knees. "There's nothing to stitch, and the PMU is useless unless you're willing to risk amputation. Assuming there's even a setting for that. He needs more care than we can do here. Probably even more than we can give him on the *Resilience*." The ship, orbiting on autopilot, kilometers above them, seems as unreachable as home right now. "And I don't even know . . . I'm not even sure he'll survive cold sleep. The system uses our circulation to move the coolants, and he's lost so much blood, and with that sludge, those *things*, in there, I . . ." Ophelia shakes her head.

"The shock to his body might be too much," Ethan says, sinking down to crouch next to her.

"Yeah." Ophelia clasps her hands together to keep them from shaking, resting them on her knees. After all they've done, after all that's been sacrificed—Liana, Birch—they're just going to end up stuck in here, watching each other die or progressively lose their minds.

"No," Ethan says.

"No?" She raises her eyebrows.

"We just need to get the bleeding stopped as best we can. Stabilize him. And then we are getting the fuck out of here. Now."

She looks up at him, startled. "But you said the lander can't handle—"

"It can't." He amends a moment later, "We shouldn't. But we're past the point of 'should' right now." He pauses. "You were right."

Ophelia raises her eyebrows.

"Ugly choices." He tips his head at her in acknowledgment. "If I'm going to be responsible for deaths, I'd rather it be in trying to save ourselves. Period."

The hollowness in his expression, though, tells Ophelia what she already suspected. This is going to damage him further. To risk all of their lives by taking off in a storm, knowing it may well end badly. To put Suresh in a tank, knowing he may not survive.

But does anyone get through life without taking damage from a risk in one form or another? Her entire career—hell, her life—suggests that's an impossibility.

Ophelia sits up straighter. "Okay," she says slowly.

Ethan takes her hand and pulls her up to her feet.

"In the medikit, there should be casting gel," he says. "I've used it to set a broken arm or two in the past. It makes a watertight seal. You think we could use that to stop the bleeding long enough to get Suresh back up to the *Resilience*?"

Dizziness washes over her. Probably from standing up too quickly. Lack of food. Lack of sleep—her eyes are burning with it. Stress. A tickle in the back of her throat. The urge to laugh, even though there's absolutely nothing funny about any of this. "Maybe," she begins. "It's off-label use, for sure, but I can't think of—"

Little Bird. I found you.

She stiffens, freezing in place. Just past Ethan's shoulder, her father appears. Not see-through, vague, or even in shadow.

His gray jumpsuit is dusty with the remains of work, despite the best decon efforts. Just like it used to be when he returned from a monthlong stint on the P3X147 mine. His fists are clenched at his sides, knuckles bruised and darkened from colliding with rough edges on machinery and punching random walls in a fit of temper. His silvery curls are cut short on the sides. Exhaustion is creased into his face. Anger simmers in the heavy brows, ready for the lightning-quick shift from smooth to convulsive fury.

Ophelia hasn't seen him, not like this, in decades. In the media coverage, they used his employee photo, a blank-faced stare into the camera. Or, worse, the muddled sec cam footage of him exiting the transport, a bloodied and small figure barely distinguishable from his surroundings.

But this is her father as she knew him most of the time.

Pissed. On the edge of an explosion.

Her shoulders hunch automatically. *Stay still. Quiet. Hide, if you can. Wait it out until it's safe.*

The impulse to follow those tried-and-true measures is so strong it's hard for Ophelia to even look at him, as if making eye contact might set him off. It used to, if her mother wasn't there to intervene, to try to defuse him. She did, occasionally.

Why did you make me search for you? Didn't you hear me calling you? You answer when I call you, Lark! His voice booms in her head.

Hearing it, the implacable build of fury within, makes her heart flip-flop with terror, even as an adult.

It dawns on her that this is likely what her mother felt as well.

Small, frightened, alone. And trapped.

Ophelia has always known that her mother must have been scared, even if she refused to talk about it. That being afraid kept her on Goliath and with him. That the rift with her family didn't help, because she felt she had nowhere to go, no resources to help her escape.

As a small child, Ophelia saw it as two adults who seemed equal in her eyes. One who hurt her and one who allowed it. But that assessment, like everything else in life, was far too simple for a complicated situation.

Her eyes water, and she blinks to make them stop. *This is not real. This can't be real.* No matter what the panicked rhythm of her heart is saying, her father's long dead. No longer able to hurt her. But fuck if it doesn't feel as though he could reach out and grab her at any second. Shake her until her teeth rattle in her head, leaving fingerprint bruises on her skinny-as-a-stick upper arm, just like he used to.

Ophelia shuts her eyes for a moment, trying to shake off the vision. Hallucination. Whatever. Clearly those things have finished . . . processing Liana and are starting back up again. "Let's try the gel," Ophelia says to Ethan, her voice croaky with distress.

And—thank God—her father is gone when she opens her eyes.

But Ethan is watching her with an odd expression. Then he steps back suddenly, putting distance between them.

"What, what is it?" Ophelia asks. Or that's what she says in her head.

Because only then does she hear herself, the disconnect between the words she's thinking and the ones coming out of her mouth.

"First, first siren coffee?"

31

"Order school eat!" Ophelia bleats. Her voice is not her voice, too soft, too dreamy. And not saying what she wants.

She claps a hand over her mouth. *No, no, no. What is happening?*

"It's okay, it's okay," Ethan says gently. Then he turns and calls over his shoulder. "Kate!"

Terror pierces Ophelia, cold blades tearing inside. She's not as lost to it as Liana or even Birch seemed to be. But possibly only because she's still awake. For now.

Kate appears in the corridor. "What is taking so long? The med-scanner should be—" She stops abruptly as soon as she sees them. "What are you doing? What's wrong?"

"We're losing her," Ethan says quietly.

"No, I'm still here. I don't know what's wrong," Ophelia insists. But more nonsense spews forth from her mouth. Her lips, teeth, and tongue feel like strangers, no longer obeying her commands.

Kate stares at her, mouth open slightly.

Ethan moves to grab Ophelia's arm, but acting on impulse, she darts sideways, farther down the A side corridor, out of reach. Her limbs, for now, are doing as she asks. But that's no guarantee for an hour from now, or even five minutes.

Her breath catches hard in her throat, a whimper escaping before she can stop it. *I can't. I can't do this. Be present and feel my mind deteriorating around me.* This is her nightmare coming true. Losing control of herself and still being dimly aware of what's happening.

"Ophelia, I'm not going to hurt you," Ethan says, his voice low, hands out in front of him as if he's approaching a feral animal. "I just want to make sure you're not going to hurt yourself, right?"

Part of her wants to roll her eyes at him. She understands him perfectly well. But he has no way of knowing that because she can't tell him that.

She can't breathe. Her lungs are tight, like they've turned to solid stone. Incapable and impervious to air.

What am I going to do? She shifts her weight from foot to foot as Ethan approaches slowly, cautiously. She knows what *not* to do, as unhelpful as that might be at the moment. Sleep will only make it worse. Birch, at least, had some awareness, but Liana . . .

Wait. She stops moving. She'd avoided giving Suresh a sedative because she didn't want to lose him to the towers, to whatever this is. She hadn't considered what would happen if she attempted the opposite. If their sleeping minds give this thing some kind of an advantage over them, then what would happen if she made herself, well, more awake?

Ophelia turns on her heels and heads for her office, where the medikit was the last time she saw it.

Fortunately, it's still on her desk.

Ethan and Kate follow her at a safe distance.

"What is she doing?" Kate asks, as Ophelia rummages in the kit.

"I don't know. Be ready to grab her if she's got the scalpels," Ethan says grimly. "Ophelia, just come with us and—"

"Grass. Chair sky benediction. Chair sky benediction!" She shows them, with trembling fingers, the ampule.

"A stimulant, I think," Ethan says to Kate. "I don't think that's a good idea," he says to Ophelia. "It's supposed to be for extended—"

She presses the hypo against her neck. A cool sensation rushes beneath the skin and then sweat instantly bursts out all over her skin, along with chills. Her teeth chatter.

"It's in the frontal lobe, the language center," she tells them, tremors racking her body. Her heart is pounding like she's running sprints. Uphill. "But I can still understand everything. Ethan, I'm still me."

Gibberish again.

Ethan cocks his head to the side, looking at Ophelia intently. Then he turns to Kate. "Can you give me a second?"

She folds her arms across her chest. "Not a great idea, Commander."

"It's fine," he says. When she doesn't move, he straightens. "Kate. Now, please."

Commander voice. It's effective.

She scowls at Ophelia. "I'll be right outside." Then she pivots and stalks toward the door, making a show of stopping just over the threshold.

Ethan edges closer to her, hands still up, but he seems more certain now. "I need you to come with me. Someplace safe. If you can understand me, you know why I have to do this. I can't risk you hurting yourself or us. And . . ." He hesitates. "With your history, with what you've told me, I need to be cautious." The compassion in his gaze, meshed with implacable kindness, makes Ophelia simultaneously want to cry and to dig a hole in the ground and vanish forever.

Bloody Bledsoe strikes again. But she understands. She would insist on nothing less.

She's never felt more tainted, more damaged, in her life, though.

Ophelia takes a chance and tries nodding.

Relief spreads across Ethan's face.

"I knew you could understand me. We're going to prep the lander, get Suresh in place, and then I'm going to come back for you. We're all getting out of here. Okay?"

"If it'll even let us leave," she says bitterly. "It might just yank that stuff right out of us the second we break atmosphere. We'll end up nothing but puddles of black goo inside a crashed lander." Which might, for that matter, be exactly what happened to any remnants of the Pinnacle team, assuming there were any.

Ethan's eyes widen. And it takes her a second to realize what she's said. Actually said.

Excitement courses through her veins like electricity. "That made sense! You understood me!" Ophelia doesn't wait for him to respond. She has no idea how long this limited window will last. "Listen, you can't sleep. Don't even let yourself get drowsy. Our conscious minds seem to be able to hold it off somewhat. But probably not forever. Use whatever we have of this to stay awake, at least until you've made it to cold sleep." She holds up the remaining doses of the stimulant.

"It's fine," he says, waving away her words. "You're fine. You can—"

Ophelia takes a step back from him, much as it kills her to do so.

Ethan frowns. "What? What's wrong?"

"You were right. I'm too big of a risk. Right now, I have control. But there's a good chance this is temporary," she says. "It's in my head. I can feel them . . . waiting."

Several emotions flicker across his face before he lands on one. The Commander is back.

"We need everyone, Doctor. You can't just—"

"Not this time," Ophelia says.

He opens his mouth to argue.

But Ophelia has one last card to play, her worst fear and her largest vulnerability simultaneously. "Don't let me hurt anyone. Please."

Ethan and Kate determine that the bunk room Ophelia shared with Kate and Liana is the best place to serve as Ophelia's temporary holding cell. The farthest from the towers and the easiest to clean out.

Ethan walks her over through the central hub. Suresh watches silently from his table/gurney. Someone must have filled him in.

"It's going to be fine. We'll be right back for you," Ethan says, as Kate finishes shoving all of their personals, including Ophelia's, into the corridor. Eerily, it reminds Ophelia of how they found the hab when they first arrived. All those personal items discarded, left behind.

Ophelia nods, almost afraid to speak now, to find out that the ability is gone again.

Kate steps back, giving her plenty of space to enter the module. The only things left are the beds themselves. Even the sheets and blankets are in a heap in the corridor.

Kate is sweating, and her eyes are glazed. She's struggling against the influence of the towers, just like everyone else. But she meets Ophelia's gaze, openly hostile, as she swings the door shut, and suddenly Ophelia doubts very much that anyone will be coming back for her, if Kate has her way.

She doesn't blame Kate. Learning that you've been working side by side with the daughter of the most famous mass murderer in the last thirty years, and that said daughter is now experiencing hallucinations of her father, is probably more than a little frightening, not to mention infuriating. And it's safer for all of them if Ophelia is not on the ship. Trust is essential. It only takes a few seconds to disrupt a cold sleep tank and turn the prank that Suresh staged into reality. And someone always has to be the last one in. Kate doesn't trust Ophelia, and now Ophelia's not sure she would trust Kate.

Ophelia doesn't know whether Kate will succeed in convincing Ethan. If she does, Ophelia hopes she won't be aware of being left behind. Starving to death or bashing her head against the door to try to get out sounds like an awful way to die.

Outside the bunk room, the door lock clunks into place, and Kate's face vanishes from the porthole window.

Ophelia makes herself back up, away from the door. Hovering won't make it open any faster, if it opens again at all.

Though it was never a large space, the bunk room feels cavernous with just her. No snoring Kate or Liana asking her questions.

Out of habit, Ophelia drops back onto her lower bunk. Her hands are sweaty, her heart still racing.

Figure, what, a few minutes to gel-cast Suresh's hand, make sure it's holding. But then they have to work out how to get the glove over his hand. And his suit hasn't been charged. Ours haven't been charging long enough.

But even when that's out of the way, they need to get Suresh to the lander and strapped in. Then, only then, would they come back for her.

So at least an hour. Maybe more like two.

And every second that ticks by is one less second that she has control of herself. Her father, he will be back. She can feel it. As if he's standing just at the corner of her vision, where she can't see him but senses that he's there.

He used to do that sometimes. Sneak up on Ophelia and her mother. On a good day, it was to surprise them with an earlier arrival, to present them with unexpected gifts from the latest shipment of supplies, orders he placed in secret.

On a bad day, Ophelia and her mother were being too loud, using too many of the rations, enjoying themselves too much without him. And it was his job to make sure they stayed in line; as union president and a crew leader, he had a reputation to maintain.

Some of that, she now knows, was the ERS-fueled paranoia that people were plotting against him. Some of it was not.

Ophelia has always blamed herself for not speaking up, for not getting help for her mom and for herself. In that tiny security office, the station officers hammered at her. Did she know something was wrong? Why didn't she say anything? Was she aware of how many people had died?

It dawns on her now, though, that even if she could have gotten over her fear of her father's retribution, who would she have gone to? Who would have believed her or thought it was anything more than overly stern parenting?

A kid who says that their father is acting strangely, lashing out, and talking about a mysterious cabal of "them," when the parent is a respected member of the community and seemingly still holding it together at work and outside the home—who is going to act on that?

Nobody. So even if, at eleven years old, she'd had the foresight to recognize that something was wrong and gathered the courage to speak up . . . it probably wouldn't have done any good.

It wouldn't have done any good.

It wasn't her fault.

The realization—and the fact that it took this situation for her to finally reach it—makes her want to laugh.

Ophelia holds her hand over her mouth to keep it in.

There's no small amount of irony here. The thing her father feared, the paranoid delusion of the people around him being possessed, is actually what's happening here. And that is what it took for her to truly accept that she wasn't at fault.

Outside, she hears the muffled sounds of voices and movement. The whine of the antigrav sled being adjusted. They must have figured out the suit issue.

There are extras, it occurs to her. Birch's. The temporaries.

Kate and Ethan are getting ready to take Suresh to the lander.

And leave you behind, Lark, her father whispers. *But you don't have to be alone.*

That pressure-like sensation in Ophelia's head, the anticipation she had told Ethan about, feels like a wave hanging over her, just waiting for peak height before crashing down and drowning her.

When Ophelia visited the locked facilities, the patients who'd experienced complete psychotic breaks, lost from this world to one that ERS created for them, were more sad than frightening. They could be treated, at least.

But the ones who just vanished within themselves, who broke and couldn't connect with any world anymore, the so-called coma ward . . . visiting that floor always took more from her. The vacant gazes. The impatience of even the most well-meaning aides. Bodies that needed to be turned and rotated. Chins that needed to be dried of silvery strings of saliva. Food that needed to be spooned in until they forgot or no longer cared to swallow.

This isn't the same. But it feels close enough that the horror is more than reminiscent. There but for the grace of God, except maybe God isn't feeling very graceful at the moment.

Ophelia turns her wrist over, examining the veins just beneath the surface. Blue, faintly raised. Pumping blood and foreign contaminants into every millimeter of her body, past even the blood–brain barrier. Her own workings turned against her.

She wonders if that's what made Birch dig into his own skin. The desire to be free of it on his own terms.

Ophelia shakes her head, which is feeling thicker by the moment. They're coming back. Ethan said he would come back.

But you know that he's not. You know that you're not worth it. You've never been worth the trouble. You know that, Little Bird. You talked him out of walking away from Liana, some-one he cared about. Why the hell would he bother with you?

Her father appears once more, his booted feet at the edge of her vision. Like they did when he was searching for her to "cure" her. Peering through a crack on the side of the HRU, she watched him pace up and down the corridor, white sparks dancing in her vision because she was too scared to breathe.

Now Ophelia scrambles back on the bed to stand up, half hunched, the mattress knocked askew beneath her feet. She keeps her eyes down, away from him. Not real, he's not real.

"Little Bird," he croons. "I'm the only one who cares, Lark. Come to me. I can save you."

This version of her father, the one who sounds gentle, kind, and sad for her—as opposed to the wild-eyed, bloodied option—is harder to resist. It's a direct arrow to the part of her she's worked hard to deny—she loved her father, even though he killed people. Even though he hurt and scared Ophelia and her mom. Ophelia still wanted to love him. And she didn't know how to untangle those feelings, so she just pretended they didn't exist.

And that's been fine. Mostly.

Until now.

He holds out his hand. So familiar to Ophelia—blunt, squared nails, calluses on the palm. The same hands that held a tablet to read to her, the scarred knuckles that she used to poke at, asking where each mark came from. The same hands that lifted her off her feet, dangling her by the shoulder joints, demanding to know if she'd taken the candy that Mx. Solomon offered at school because *we don't fucking take charity.*

Tears burn her eyes, and her nose starts to run. Wouldn't it be better to go with him, just accept what's coming to her?

"I can't get out," Ophelia says, her voice choked.

"Sure you can," her father says easily. "Go to the door. Call for them. I'll help you. I'll help your friends, too," he adds. "None of you have to be alone anymore."

A fleeting sensation of that white warmth, the comforting glow Ophelia felt at the towers, returns briefly, and longing hits her like a punch to the lungs.

"I'm so tired," she whispers to him. Tired of hating him, tired of loving him, of trying not to do either in her drive not to be him. Or be a Bray. It feels like no soft place to land, and there's only so long she can glide.

"I know, sweetie. Come on," he says. It's almost a coo, but she can hear the impatience growing beneath it. You only get one chance with him in a good mood; if you delay too long or show any reluctance, the good mood and the offer evaporate like a drop of water on a heated griddle. Gone in a puff of violent smoke.

Ducking her head lower, she steps forward on the mattress and starts to get down.

The mattress shifts beneath her feet, realigning itself in the frame. As Ophelia reaches for his hand, though, an odd chatter of metal interrupts, breaking through the buzz in her ears that she hadn't noticed until right now.

Clink, clink, clack.

Close by. Not outside. She frowns.

Outside in the hab, maybe in the corridor, voices are raised, Ethan and Kate shouting at each other. But Ophelia can't tell what they're arguing about.

"Lark," her father snaps.

Ophelia snatches her hand back, and her shoulders hunch, her body acting instinctively to make itself a smaller target. She turns, trying to track the sound she heard. It's wrong, somehow, and she's not sure why . . .

Then she spots it.

On the floor, almost hidden under her bunk, still rocking back and forth on its rounded handle, a shiny tool. No, not just a tool. An instrument.

One of the missing scalpels from the Kellerson pack just fell out of Ophelia's bed frame.

32

Ophelia jerks in surprise, the scalpel seeming to have manifested itself out of nowhere, like an alien artifact, out of place, out of context.

Her head is fuzzy and disconnected-feeling—like in those first moments of waking up, when everything seems possible, including being chased by long-extinct grizzly bears—so it takes her a few moments to piece together what happened. While she supposes it's possible that the scalpel just "appeared," given all the impossible things currently occurring (see: her dead father very much standing in front of her), it's far more likely that it was tucked between the frame and the mattress in her bunk.

She must have jostled it loose. But . . . what is it doing here? She was looking all over for it.

Though it never occurred to Ophelia to check her own bunk. *Did I put it here?*

The thought brings a chill, but that fear feels so very far away right now.

"Lark," her father barks. "Let's go. Now."

Ignoring him, she bends down and picks up the scalpel, the cool metal in her hand more real than anything else in the moment. The sharp edge gleams in the overhead lights.

"Little Bird, you don't want that," her father says gently, the anger gone. But as always, she can't tell if that concern is genuine or just a trick to convince her to let her guard down.

Her sin is not forgiven, but to be punished properly, he needs her closer, not running or hiding.

Amazing how quickly people fall back into old habits, patterns that served them once, when they didn't know better.

She keeps her distance, just in case.

"—not leaving anyone alive behind," Ethan says. He's muffled, but clearer than before, breaking into the temporary silence.

"It's the only way!" Kate says. They must be right outside her door. "Listen, it makes perfect sense. No one will even question it. Then we can get back to our families, to the people who need us."

"We are infected—"

"You don't know what will happen. Cold sleep might clear them all out of us. Even she said that!"

"Are you hearing yourself? You aren't making any—"

"If we bring her back, it's all over. They'll bench us for good. And there will be so much attention on her, on us, we'll be—" Kate cuts herself off abruptly. "We have a chance. Right here, right now. If we say it was all her, that she went crazy, lost her shit and started killing people, then we keep our jobs, we keep doing what we're doing."

"What are we doing, Kate?" Ethan asks with an odd note in his voice.

"Come join us. Be safe, be happy. Be as one," Ophelia's father says, speaking over them, and sounding far less like himself.

Ophelia tightens her grip on the scalpel. *They* might be in her head, but they don't have control over her actions. Not yet. No way to know how long that will last, though.

"Bad metal blood," her father intones solemnly, nodding at the instrument in her hand.

A sign that the intelligence is learning. They seem to draw on powerful memories, or the memories of people for whom they have strong feelings. But outside of that, they are limited by experience. They might not have known what a scalpel was before, but they certainly do now, after Birch. In moments of alarm, they also seem to lose their ability to re-create a reasonable facsimile.

Birch. Ophelia looks at the scalpel and then flips her other arm over, finding those delicate blue veins again.

Maybe he was trying to extricate those nodules. Or maybe he was just making sure that he wasn't going to be pushed around by fucking aliens resurrecting his dead brother.

"Please, Ethan," Kate says, pleading. "I can't risk going back empty-handed." Her voice is shrill, panicked.

"You know, I never understood how Ava made it outside without triggering the alarm on the airlock," Ethan says.

The sudden shift in conversation draws Ophelia's attention again, away from the point of the blade, the paleness of the vulnerable skin.

"Little Bird," her father speaks up, taking advantage of the interruption. "You should help your friends." Those words, in his voice, set off an oil slick of uneasiness in her. Her father would never have wanted her to choose someone else over him.

These things do. They want her alive until they can get whatever they need from her, whether it's returning their progeny or the information they have gathered via the black sediment inside her. Or something else entirely.

There was a moment there, when they were operating on Liana, that all of them—Ethan, Suresh, Kate, and her—seemed to be struggling, feeling the same pain and dizziness. Some kind of malfunctioning hive mind? The Lyrians were big on community. Maybe it is their tech after all?

The ash all over the floors, in the building she and Severin explored, was that the same stuff? Pieces that had fled their hosts, like when Birch killed himself? Or maybe it was—

Ophelia shakes her head, cutting off that train of thought. Whatever this is, however it works, she's not going to be able to figure it out by guessing. Astrobiologists would probably need years of study and analysis to truly understand it. What matters now is getting everyone out of here alive and relatively intact.

"She needed help, money for her daughter," Kate says defiantly after a moment. "So I helped her. Gave her a couple of Silk Road connections. She was just supposed to bring back extra for me. That's it."

"Kate." The disappointment in Ethan's voice mixes with weariness.

Ophelia flinches. That's a mistake and it's only going to make the situation worse. With families—and with teams—judgment doesn't help. But she knows him well enough to understand that he's taking Kate's failure as his own. Trouble is, Kate won't see it that way.

"Oh, don't start with me, Commander," Kate snaps. "You think you're so superior because you follow the rules? If anything, it's all your fault. We couldn't trust you so we couldn't tell you that Ava was in trouble until it was too late. If you weren't so fucking straight-edge, you'd see that we're getting taken advantage of. My brother is in a work camp for the rest of his life because he can't buy his way out of his colonist debt. Because of people like the Brays, like her! And you're one of the fools they need, the backs they stand on. All I'm doing is evening things out for the rest of us."

"You're so important to me," Ophelia's father croons, stepping closer, his hand out, as if he would take the scalpel from her. "I don't want you to hurt yourself."

Ophelia laughs. And laughs and laughs until she's dizzy from it. "See, that's where you got it wrong. You must be pulling from our heads, maybe, I don't know, what we each identify as family? The strongest emotions that come with that?" She shakes her head. "But you must not have all of my memories, or you're missing context. Otherwise you'd know that my father wanted, very much, to hurt me."

The lock on the outside of her door scrapes faintly. Ethan.

"No! Get away from there. Don't make me do this, Ethan," Kate says sharply.

Don't make her do *what*? Ophelia can't see what's happening. Her father, even the hallucination of him, is in the way. And even if he weren't, she's too far from the door to look out the window.

Almost as soon as she thinks the question, though, the answer pops right up in her head.

That gray case with the warnings plastered on the side and the coded lock on the outside. Coded for Ethan and Kate, someone Ophelia already knows will reach for a weapon when she feels it necessary.

Kate has the gun.

"I just need you to . . . not stand in the way, that's all," Kate says. Desperation. Ophelia recognizes it.

"Kate, don't. This isn't you," Ethan protests.

And Ethan is going to get himself shot.

"Give it to me," Ophelia's father insists, stepping up to block her view of the door entirely.

Her fingers flex, once, twice, against her will. Minute movements. Only her too-tight grip keeps the scalpel from falling free.

She sucks in a breath sharply, staring down at her hand. *They* are trying to get her to open her hand, to drop the scalpel.

Ophelia backs away from her father, edging around the end of the bunk beds. She tries to reach over with her other hand, to grab hold of her fingers, to hold her own hand still. But her other hand simply hangs at her side, refusing to move.

Terror bolts through her, tearing jagged new paths. She's running out of time; she's only going to have one chance at this.

She keeps backing up until she hits the outer wall of the module, just beneath the window.

Ophelia crouches down. "My father wanted to kill me. But in his head, he was trying to keep me from exactly this," she says. He wasn't a good person, but he wasn't all bad either. Knowing that is what is saving her this time.

Using her shoulder, she heaves her unresponsive arm upward, bracing it against her knee. She flips the scalpel in her other hand so that the blade is pointing down. And then she jams it into the module wall behind her, right where the floor meets the wall in a seam. Right where Ethan said it's weakest.

Nothing happens at first, beyond a faint hiss.

Then Ophelia yanks the scalpel out, removing it effectively as a plug, and all hell breaks loose.

The enviro systems shut down with a thud that echoes through the hab—stopping circulation. The overhead lights dim, and a loud alarm sounds shrilly, followed by a mechanized voice. "Alert, breach, alert. Alert, breach, alert."

She scrambles away from the wall, the chill already taking her breath away. Or maybe that's the bad mix of air. She doesn't remember the exact percentages of the atmosphere on this planet. Just that there's not enough oxygen to be breathable. And it won't be long before it'll be the same in here.

Her father cocks his head to the side, watching her. They don't understand what's happening.

Come on, come on. Ophelia keeps her gaze focused on the door. This has to work. On that very first day, Ethan told her this would happen. That's why they had to search every single hab module, checking for leaks.

Shouts in the hallway distract her.

"What happened? What did you do?"

"Give it to me."

"Ethan, no!"

Grunts and pain sounds come from the corridor outside the bunk room, along with the fainter thud of bodies crashing into the walls.

Oh, no.

"Ethan!" Ophelia calls, coughing.

The thud of the lock retracting—the safety mechanism to

keep team members from being trapped in a breach situation, the very situation Ethan described to her—kicks in a moment later. The successive blasts of each lock firing backward, retreating into the housing mechanism, are shockingly loud. She might have described them as gunshots, except the difference is made very clear a moment later when the gun in the corridor goes off.

33

Ophelia's father remains in front of the now unlocked door. "Good," he says, beaming at her beatifically. If there were ever a moment she was truly certain that this is not solely the result of her own broken mind, it's right then. The real Field Bledsoe doled out praise like semiprecious gems. Rarely, and with the expectation that each should be treated as more valuable than it was.

She doesn't waste time trying to convince her brain that he's not actually there; instead she dashes around him to shove open the door.

Out in the corridor, Kate is bending over Ethan, the gun clutched in her bloodied hand. He lies perfectly still on the corridor floor, blood pooling beneath his right shoulder. But it appears mostly red, not yet thick with the black gunk.

Ophelia skids to a halt. Kate looks up at her and then at something next to her, her brow furrowing suddenly. Her gun hand comes up.

Automatically, Ophelia raises her hands. Or tries to. They hover around her waist, drifting and uncertain.

Sweat visibly dampens Kate's forehead. "I didn't mean to," she says. Her eyes have lost focus, with that staring-far-into-the-future look to them. Her attention jitters between Ophelia and whatever she's seeing next to Ophelia.

Ophelia can't stop herself from looking, but there's no one there.

"He did it. He grabbed it. I wasn't trying to hurt him. I wanted to hurt her," Kate cries.

"Kate. Get the medikit and PMU. Now," Ophelia says. So far, the words she hears herself saying match the ones she's trying to say.

But Kate doesn't seem to hear Ophelia, listening instead to something Ophelia can't hear. Then Kate ducks her head, cringing, lifting her hands to cover her ears. "I know, I know!"

As soon as she retreats to the central hub, Ophelia rushes toward Ethan. His eyes open as she kneels next to him, his face contorting with pain when she accidentally jostles him.

"Probably shouldn't have tried to argue with her," he says, panting.

"Probably not when she has a gun." Ophelia leans down for a better look at his wound. There's a gaping hole in the space between his shoulder and the upper part of his chest. Not his heart. That much she knows. That much any child with a grasp of basic human anatomy would get. But there're veins and arteries and important shit in that area as well.

"Projectile weapons? Really?" Ophelia mutters in frustration.

"Lower tech means less chance—"

"Of technical failure in unforeseen circumstances. Yeah, well, I hope you feel the same about lower-tech treatment, too."

"Great bedside manner, Doc," he says, coughing.

Fuck. And we're losing breathable air. Ophelia stands up and with some effort manages to shoulder the bunk room door closed. That will keep it from getting any worse, at least.

"I am not the right kind of doctor for this," she reminds Ethan as she returns to his side, trying to think.

Apply pressure. I need to apply pressure. But when she reaches for him, her hands lurch in the correct direction and then stop, hovering in midair.

Ophelia can feel them, but at a distance. It's like a malfunctioning pair of robotic arms covering her own, only she can't control them or remove them. It's terrifying, to see part of your own body as something Other.

She lets out a breath, and the one she draws in feels too thin. She needs help.

Her father was gone when she shut the door. But he is, after all, a visual disturbance, a representation intended to trigger action, Ophelia suspects.

She focuses on an empty section of corridor. "Hello? Can you help me? I want to save him. And save your . . . people in there." She doesn't think they're people so much as portions of a whole, but if they're trying to relate to get desired results, then she's going to do the same.

Ethan frowns up at her. "What are you—"

"Shhh." She focuses on the image she wants to send. These entities—whether organic or technological—clearly get some things out of her head. So, this time, Ophelia shows them. Blood pumping out of the wound, her hands pressed over it, keeping the blood and the black flecks inside. The mental version of a child's drawing.

Simplistic. But the best she can come up with. She's not sure what else to do.

The sensation that follows most resembles the ripple of chills across her skin, only it's on the inside. Something is moving inside her, along her forearms and up toward her shoulders.

Nausea rises hard in her, and she has to push down the urge to vomit. *It's in me. They're all in me.*

A sharp pain pierces her right eye, and she raises her hand instinctively to press against it, half expecting to feel the ooze of sludge down her cheek. But the pain vanishes after a second or two, and her hand is still pressed against her closed eyelid.

A hand she was able to control. Ophelia lowers it quickly and presses both hands down on Ethan's wound. The blood is slick on her palms, cooling fast, just like before. On the garden terrace floor.

"You're okay, you're okay." Ophelia recites the words, not sure who she's trying to convince.

Running footsteps echo through the central hub. Ophelia tenses up, though she has no idea what she can do in defense.

Kate emerges from the doorway a moment later, the medikit tucked in one arm, with the PMU sticking out, the gun still in the other hand.

She heard Ophelia's request. Or she heard someone telling her.

"Here." Kate drops it all near Ophelia with a clatter.

"There. See, he's going to be fine. She's going to do it." Speaking to someone else, she gestures at Ophelia with the gun, and Ophelia flinches.

But almost as soon as the fear fades, fury takes over. This part isn't entirely Kate's fault; she's not herself. But her lies, her deception, are what landed them here. This team would never have been assigned to Ophelia, and Ava would still be alive, if Kate hadn't gotten involved. People are dead because of her. And the rest are all infected, possessed, whatever the proper term is.

Ophelia's vision darkens at the edges, narrowing with building rage. Her chest tightens until it feels like a scream is coiled beneath her lungs.

"It wasn't my fault," Kate insists to whomever she's seeing. "If you had done exactly what I told you, you would have been fine!"

Ava. She's talking to Ava. Or a projection of her. Once again, these things seem to zero in on the people and situations that evoke the strongest emotions in an individual.

But based on the way Kate's face flushes with shame and anger, the invisible entities are not accepting that answer.

Neither is Ophelia.

She reaches out and grabs the PMU. Kate doesn't even seem to register the movement.

Setting it in place over Ethan's shoulder, Ophelia moves out of the way. Closer to the medikit.

"Assessing," it announces. "Blood loss. Projectile injury. Please remain still!" it lectures Ethan, as he falls into another coughing jag. His breathing slows then, his eyes slipping shut.

"Ethan, stay with me," Ophelia whispers. She slips her hand toward the medikit while Kate is distracted, splitting her attention between the PMU and whomever she's seeing in the hallway. Kate's listening to it. Them.

Right there within reach, any number of ampules. Drugs that Ophelia could load into a hypo and try to administer. She doesn't trust that Kate will give the gun up willingly, even if Ophelia could push *them* back out of her consciousness temporarily with a stimulant.

So sedative it is. Knock Kate out, take the gun away. But the gleam of the instruments in the black fabric Kellerson pack, right on top, draws Ophelia's eye. Like a delicious secret in the dark.

A few years ago, her sister Dulcie was obsessed with a QuickQ game show called *Old School Olympics*. Participants competed to churn butter, dial an actual phone, drive a car with no automation—without any previous instruction. One of those episodes involved throwing axes, apparently a normal leisure activity at one time.

Part of Ophelia wishes she'd paid more attention to that ridiculous notion. The idea of being able to strike harm from a distance sounds remarkably appealing right now.

Still, one quick slice across the tendons at the back of Kate's knee and she'd be on the floor. Easy enough to pull the gun away then.

Why stop there? Knock her down and punish her. This is her fault. They're going to die here because of her. Why shouldn't she lead the way? The image in Ophelia's head is perfectly clear. Another blade clutched in her hand, only this one sinks into Kate's suit-covered chest, once, twice, and then five times, leaving blood to well up slowly, followed by the black ooze.

The prospect offers a grim sort of satisfaction, like letting loose the leash on the monster and watching it (finally) wreak the predicted havoc. Horror is there, too. At both the idea and the gratification of her lowest impulses. But in a dimmer fashion.

Ophelia swallows hard. She would like to blame it on the entities, on the influence of its version of her father. But that's not entities in her head; that's her. The shortened temper, the rage at being defied or thwarted. She is her father's daughter in that.

But not in everything. And she gets to choose. This reminder helps ease some of the tension in her chest.

So when Ophelia slips her hand into the medikit, she bypasses the Kellerson pack. *You're making a mistake,* her father—her real father—sneers in her head. *Too weak, just like your mother.*

Ophelia doesn't love her mother's choices, either, but she knows which ones she can live with.

"Coagulation patch applied," the PMU says, and Kate jolts, swinging back toward the PMU with the gun. "Seek immediate medical attention at the nearest silver-grade medical facility."

Ophelia takes her opportunity and slams the hypo spray into Kate's calf, once, then twice. It doesn't escape Ophelia's attention that the motion is an uncomfortably close parody of stabbing Kate, just like her own imagination served up to her.

Kate stumbles back, her eyes going wide. The black flecks there are more visible in her paler irises.

"No, no," Kate says thickly. "I need to . . . I need to . . ." She sits down abruptly, looking rather shocked to find herself on the ground.

Ophelia reaches across and takes the gun gingerly from her grasp, and Kate doesn't fight her. A second later, Kate slumps over entirely, falling on her side.

"Ethan." Ophelia shakes his uninjured shoulder. "Are you still . . . you?"

His eyes flutter open. He seems dazed, but he nods. "You're still not the right kind of doctor," he says.

She's not sure it's a coincidence that Ethan and she were both the last ones to take off their suits and helmets that first day in the hab and that now they're the only two left standing, metaphorically speaking.

Ophelia rolls her eyes. "Still you."

"But I don't think . . ." He hesitates. "I don't think for much longer. I can hear them." His throat works, the sharp Adam's apple bobbing with emotion. "My sisters. They're asking me to come to them."

Shit.

After chucking the remaining sedative to the floor, Ophelia reloads the hypo with an ampule of stimulant, double-checking to make sure she hasn't screwed it up.

Then she hits herself and Ethan each with a dose.

He sucks in a breath sharply and starts coughing. "Wow, that is—"

"Better than coffee." Her laugh comes out jittery sounding, as well it should, since it feels like her heart is going to explode in her chest.

"You need to get up now, if you can." Ophelia pulls the PMU out of the way and then steps over him to his good side. She offers her trembling hand and he takes it. "You need treatment on the *Resilience*. This won't be enough."

He gives a muffled grunt as she pulls him to his feet. "What makes you think they're going to let us—"

Ophelia squeezes his hand tightly and shakes her head. They're in their heads, but she's not sure they understand what's happening at all times. Either way, better not to spell it out for them.

With care, Ophelia loops his arm around her shoulder. She's not much good as support—too short for that—but she might be able to keep him from falling face-first, should it come to that. "We're going to go find Suresh," Ophelia says aloud, hoping Ethan understands.

And either he does or he's enough out of it that it doesn't

occur to him to push back. "What did you do to Kate?" he asks, when Ophelia manages to get them turned around and facing the correct way.

"She's asleep for now. I gave her a sedative."

He frowns down at her. "But you said—"

"A gun, Ethan," Ophelia says sharply. "I was doing my best after the mission commander got himself shot. I didn't think that talk therapy was going to get us anywhere, and you definitely do not want to see my hostage negotiation skills."

"Fuck. Okay." He nods.

"I'm going to get you to Suresh," Ophelia says, avoiding the mention of Suresh being on the lander—step one of their long-overdue retreat. "Then I'll come back for her."

34

It all takes much longer than Ophelia thought, than she had hoped. Before she and Ethan can leave the hab, she has to find the right patches—the correct size and thickness—to seal the hole punched in Ethan's suit. They're out of extra suits, and the bullet tore through his on the way to flesh and blood. There are the temporary suits, of course, but getting him out of his suit and into one of those seems like a bigger risk, both in time lost and effort required on his part while he's badly injured.

"I have no idea how this is going to interact with the coagulant patch from the PMU," Ophelia warns him, as she tries to apply one without attaching it to the other.

"As long as it keeps the air in and the blood from leaking out," Ethan says, his expression strained. He needs painkillers. No, he needs surgery, at an actual medical facility, by a skilled AI. Oh, and not to be here.

By the time they get their helmets on and test the patch, the storm is intensifying. Again.

This fucking planet.

The faint pull of *them* in Ophelia's head, drowned beneath her conscious mind on the stimulant for the moment, is louder once they're outside, stumbling on the line to the lander.

Lark, we need you. Little Bird, you're going the wrong way.

Exhaustion and fear have worn her resistance to a rounded nub.

It takes effort to tune it out, to not feel it. Ethan doesn't say anything, but she suspects he's hearing or feeling something similar. Perhaps not. Perhaps he's simply concentrating on staying upright.

They're both on the line to the lander, but on opposite sides so he can grab with his uninjured side. He's in front of Ophelia so she can keep an eye on him. Her hand bumps into his on the cord occasionally as they move, vaguely reassuring.

Their journey seems to go on forever, trudging one step at a time, bending forward to make progress against the wind. Trusting that their grip on the line is leading them in the right direction when there's nothing else to gauge distance or location by.

When Ethan stops abruptly, it takes Ophelia a moment to register the cessation. She walks an extra step or two farther, her helmet colliding with the deployed landing gear, so completely does it blend in to the whiteout conditions around them.

"What took you so long?" Suresh demands, as soon as they reach him, after wending their way through the mostly empty cargo bay. Still in his suit and helmet, he's already strapped into his seat in the passenger area. "I could have regrown an entire hand in that amount of time."

"Shut up, Suresh," Ophelia says, panting, bending over at her waist to catch her breath. Gray-faced and grim, Ethan staggers past her, moving toward the ladder up to the pilot's seat.

"Wait, where's Kate?" Suresh looks around.

We should just leave her. We should just go! Ophelia's survival instinct is screaming at her. *What good does it do to risk more when we don't even know if we'll make it back as it is?*

You could be done. Just stay here.

With a sigh, Ophelia straightens up. "I'll be back." In the cargo bay of the lander, she and Ethan had passed the antigrav sled that he and Kate had used to transport Suresh.

"It's dangerous to go back by yourself," Ethan says quietly, his hand poised on a rung.

Ophelia nods. It is. But there's no one else to go with her.

And even as exhausted as she is, and as risky as the endeavor is, Ophelia already knows she can't leave Kate behind, not without trying. Not because she fears being haunted by Kate, literally or figuratively, or because she's trying to make up for her father, but . . . because that's not who Ophelia wants to be.

Damn it.

And in possibly the greatest measure of their growth as individuals and as a team—or just in an indication of how much pain he's in—Ethan doesn't bother arguing. Even though it must be killing him not to.

He inclines his head back at Ophelia, a slight nod. An acknowledgment of the less than ideal. "We'll wait."

If Ophelia's gone for too long, it won't matter. For any of them. She suspects he knows that, too.

The slog back to the hab is worse.

Because Ophelia's dragging the antigrav sled behind her and the wind keeps trying to turn it into a sail. Because she's alone. Because she doesn't know what's waiting for her and the lump of dread in her stomach expands every time she thinks about it.

Because it's taking more and more work to ignore the towers, and she's scared in a way she hasn't been since she was eleven years old.

That's when her hand on the line finally collides with the knot at the end of it and the metal ring on the airlock doorway.

"I'm here," she tells Ethan on a private channel. Or she attempts to, anyway.

His response, broken and garbled syllables intermixed with static, tells her what she already suspected. The storm is too big and they're too far apart for comms to work.

She's very much on her own.

Not with us. You're never alone.

They sound less like her father now, more like a chorus of whispers in her head. She can't tell if that's better or worse. She half expects him to show up again, to appear next to her now that she's back in closer proximity to the towers. But he doesn't. Instead of bringing a sense of relief, though, it only amps up the sensation of negative anticipation.

She lets go of the cord and feels her way around to the air-lock command panel.

It takes her two tries to enter the code for the door. When the door finally releases, with a puff of air turning white and frosted against her face, it reveals a slice of darkness within instead of the unwelcoming and clinical illumination overhead.

With a frown, she tugs the door back farther, confirming what she's seeing.

It's dark in the airlock, pitch-black. Even the emergency lighting is off. That must mean the power is down. Just like their first time in.

A shudder runs through her at the memory, at the flashbacks that it triggers.

Generator failure? Or maybe some kind of safety mechanism after she stabbed a hole in the wall earlier?

Pulling the sled behind her, Ophelia steps inside, cautiously, and her helmet light catches the inner airlock door, the entrance to the central hub. It's hanging open. Like a mouth gaping, waiting to be fed.

Fear spikes in her, jabbing down deep into tender flesh. She and Ethan did not leave the door that way.

Kate. It must be. But did she leave the hab to head to the towers? Or is she still in here?

Ophelia shuts the outer airlock door behind her.

"Kate?" she calls over the common channel. "Are you here? It's Dr. Bray." If nothing else, the mention of Ophelia's last name might get a response from Kate, and yes, maybe she is relying a little on the innate authority of both her family name and her title to keep Kate from immediately attacking.

The gun. You forgot the gun. Ophelia squeezes her eyes shut. She took it from Kate, but then she just left it on the floor of the corridor.

The comm channel crackles with static, but there's no answer.

Opening her eyes, Ophelia lets go of the sled and edges inside, across the threshold and into the central hub. Her helmet light sweeps ahead of her. Inside, everything looks much as she left it with Ethan. Only the previously piled-up bags and crates to the right of the airlock door, from back when they thought they might have the time to take things with them, have been disturbed.

Knocked over. Rummaged through. Even Kate's tool kit has been torn apart, scattering bright shiny tools across the floor, where they glint in the light from her helmet. No longer such a mystery what happened to the power.

Ophelia wonders if *they* made Kate do it. Told her to take down the generator so she and Ethan would have no place to hide.

A whisper of movement comes from her left, near the galley. Ophelia's heartbeat, already artificially accelerated, skips over itself and struggles to even out.

Kate's still here. Waiting. But searching her out strikes Ophelia as a bad idea. Better that Kate comes to her.

Ophelia makes herself straighten up. "Kate, if you're here, you need to let me know." She puts in as much of her grandmother's disapproving tone as she can manage. Ophelia certainly heard it enough in her lifetime. But also, Miranda Bray was never afraid of anything, even when she should have been. "It's disrespectful."

"Of course it's about respect for you," Kate hisses.

Got her.

But her words, distorted and strangely sibilant, drift to Ophelia from somewhere inside the darkness on the external helmet mic, not across the comm channel. Either Kate's not using the channel, or—the thought dawns belatedly on Ophelia—she's not put her helmet back on.

Suddenly Ophelia's aware of how bright her helmet light is, how the blue glow of the internal displays reflect on her face. In the darkness of the hab, she's highly visible. An easy target even for someone who hasn't had training with a gun.

"You don't deserve respect," Kate says.

Working not to make any sudden moves, Ophelia turns off her helmet light and then carefully reaches up to unfasten her helmet. The rush of air when the seal breaks is unbearably loud in the surrounding silence. And with the disconnection, the darkness around her is complete.

When she pulls the helmet over her head, the air tastes of burned metal, and the back of her throat works against the urge to cough. The air mix in here is wrong, wrong. Ophelia sets the helmet down on the floor behind her, to keep it out of her path.

"Spoiled brat, no idea how the real world works, you think your money can buy you anything, buy you *out* of anything, how many people, good people, never have that chance? Working themselves to death for you so that your family can sleep on even softer sheets at night, you are disgusting." Each word runs into the next, a hoarse monologue, dense with fury and bitterness.

Ophelia's breath catches, hard. It's Kate's voice, sort of, but not. More that rasp of unfamiliar whispers, all speaking together. But those are her father's words. Kate might well think those things about Ophelia, but that's what he used to say to her mother when they were fighting. When Ophelia was hiding in her room, taking shelter under her bunk and praying that if she kept still enough, he would forget she was there.

Are the entities sharing those memories with Kate? Or is it even more than that? There's definitely a communal aspect to what's happening. If Kate has been subsumed by *them*, is there any of her left?

"Kate, you should come out," she says, suddenly aware of

how much this resembles her nightmare, with Ophelia in her father's role. "I can help you."

Kate laughs, an eerie, raspy sound that goes on too long without a break for air.

Somewhere on my left. I think. Ophelia turns in that direction, though it doesn't help. She can't see anything. The dim light from the corridors connecting on the A side and C side is not enough.

"You can't help me, you can't even help yourself, poor little rich girl trying to make up for your existence," Kate says in that shattered voice of multitudes. "Hoping someone will love you for anything but your money."

Shame heats Ophelia's face, adding itself to the tumult, along with a roiling mix of fear and anger.

She works to keep her voice level. "Kate, we can talk about me, but I think it would be better to focus on you." Something she's said countless times in session, in response to patient deflection. But it's never felt quite so dangerous. "Can you help me understand what you're feeling?"

Silence answers. But Ophelia can feel Kate's attention, even if it's only Ophelia's imagination. Kate's waiting for . . . something.

Ophelia shivers, taking a step back automatically. It's so quiet in here without the enviro systems on. Quiet and cold. The temperature is dropping rapidly. The temptation to hide—or run—is strong.

You could just tell Ethan that she was gone. That she'd left for the towers by the time you got here. Ophelia's defensive self-preservation impulses rise up, as they always do.

But that's the problem. She's tried hiding, avoiding, too many times. It doesn't work. She keeps ending up in increasingly difficult situations, trying to make herself smaller, less objectionable to whoever is judging.

Fuck that. I'm done running. I'm done hiding.

Ophelia steps forward, toward the galley, in the direction she last heard Kate.

Ophelia's booted foot connects loudly with something metallic, and it scrapes and clatters across the patterned metal floor. Kate's tools?

Ophelia bends down automatically to pick up whatever it is, to move it out of the way, and as she does, sound and light explode directly over her head.

She reacts without thinking, freezing for a second and then hurling herself to the floor and curling up, well after it's too late.

Panting, chin scraped and bleeding by the feel of it, Ophelia lies there for a moment, still trying to process.

Not an explosion. A shot. Kate just fucking shot at her.

And if she hadn't been bent down, Kate would have killed her.

The wind whistles louder now and a glance over her shoulder shows the fist-size hole in the central hub's ceiling. Motherfucker.

"Are you still with me?" Kate asks, sounding more like herself. "If you're hurt, we should go to them. They'll take the pain away."

Ophelia wonders if that's how Kate convinced them to let her fire the gun. They could stop her, if they wanted to.

Sending her hand out, Ophelia fumbles on the floor until her fingers close around the cool metal of a handle.

She picks it up, and the reassuring heft of it pulls at the weary muscles in her arm. It only takes a quick explorative feel of the business end to recognize the tool she's found.

A wrench. Of course. Not the heavy-duty industrial power variety her father had used, but close enough. There's something poetic about saving herself with almost the same tool that he used to destroy, she supposes.

Ophelia tightens her grip on the handle and gets to her feet, keeping herself hunched down, hopefully below muzzle level.

"You should turn yourself over to them," Kate says. She's on the move by the sound of it, coming closer. "It's what you deserve."

Carefully, so carefully, Ophelia shifts a step or two to her right, praying the space is as empty as she remembers. "I'm not going to the towers. Neither are you." Then she kneels, clutching the wrench at her shoulder in a batter's position.

She's not the prey this time.

Kate hums in response. "Have you noticed they've stopped trying to pull you in? They know you want to leave. And they don't care."

Another rustle, the faint crinkle of suit material. To Ophelia's left still, maybe three meters away. It's impossible to judge in the dark, given the way sound bounces in here.

"They've been here so long by themselves." Kate pauses. "So hungry and lonely." Her voice fractures again, into multiple whispers, repeating *hungry, lonely.* "They want more experiences, more thoughts, more memories. If that means letting us go, they're fine with that—if it means spreading somewhere new."

The wrench handle grows slick in her sweaty palm. Ophelia can't tell who's speaking anymore, Kate or the entities. Is this the truth or another manipulative lie?

"But I need you to stay here. I need you to feed yourself to them. A sacrifice for the betterment of the team. My brother needs me. And you owe me. You owe all of us," Kate says. "We wouldn't be here if it weren't for the Brays. They sold the rights without telling Montrose what really happened here. And you know what?" Kate laughs again, too loud and too long to sound completely human. "They still want to have it both ways. Who do you think my Silk Road client is for this job?"

Ophelia's heart sinks. She didn't know. But . . . it makes sense in the way a missing piece falling into place usually does.

Surprising and then utterly not. Of course Kate's still actively trying to sell. She's trying to buy her brother out of his work camp. She's also the one who kept showing the team how the samples were all still in place. She could control what was taken and when, easily.

Kate's foot scrapes gently, closer still, a meter to Ophelia's left.

"You can save us all, though. Just be the brave one, offer yourself up to them. It'll make sense if anyone ever investigates. Bloody Bledsoe's kid lost it all before the towers got her." She pauses. "The rest of us can get back to our lives, save the people we care about. The people who need us. Nobody needs you."

Even knowing that Kate's trying to manipulate her, knowing that she wants Ophelia to feel shitty about herself, is no cure against it. She's right; Ophelia is not needed back at home. And sacrifice has always been the name of her game—to make up for being a Bray and a Bledsoe, to make up for being too scared to speak up against her father. People died because of her failures.

Except they weren't just her failures. She didn't choose to be a Bray or a Bledsoe. She can only choose what she does after that.

Ophelia tips her head up, hoping it will project her voice. "No!"

Kate fires, showing Ophelia her exact location in the dark, and the shot screams past her head. In the second that follows, Ophelia swings through. The wrench connects hard somewhere on Kate's leg, she can't tell where.

Kate cries out and collapses to the floor. Ophelia's on her feet and moving before she consciously thinks it through. She can't see the gun, can't tell if Kate still has it.

Kate moans, her hand scrabbling across the textured floor. Trying to sit up? Trying to shoot at Ophelia again?

So Ophelia strikes again. And again. Years of rage and frustration and impotence bubble up and flow through her, and in that moment, when metal connects with flesh and bone, she feels powerful, unstoppable.

I am free.

The second that realization hits, Ophelia goes still. The gritty, greedy sensation of power, of control drains away. This is not who she wants to be. This is not her, self-defense or not.

Her family is part of her, that's true, and running away won't change that, but they're not all of who she is.

Kate coughs and mumbles something.

Ophelia drops the wrench and stumbles back. Crouching down, and with a bit of fumbling around, she finds her helmet and gets it back in place. Almost as soon as the air starts flowing again, she feels better, clearer.

With her helmet light on, Ophelia easily finds the gun and kicks it well away. Kate regards her with glassy eyes, clutching her arm against her chest, pain etched in her expression.

"Come on," Ophelia says. "We're going home."

35

Suresh watches from his chair as Ophelia hauls Kate inside. She doesn't even bother trying to get her off the sled, where she's tied down. Ophelia turns the sled off and then secures it with cargo straps. It'll hold for now. And frankly, Ophelia doesn't want Kate to have the ability to free herself.

"Is she bleeding?" Suresh demands with a frown. "Her face is—"

"She's alive," Ophelia says breathlessly. "It was complicated."

"Great job, Bloody Bledsoe," Suresh says, clearly expecting her to be insulted and to rise to the dig.

Ophelia straightens up, after one last tug on the straps. "You have no idea."

Her body aching, she hauls herself up the ladder to the command seat, next to Ethan.

Ethan does not look good—gray, sweating, probably bleeding internally somewhere. But he's at the controls.

"Thank you," he says quietly.

"You're welcome," Ophelia says. Though in a way she feels like she should be thanking him, because now she knows. Even in the most extreme of circumstances, she can trust herself. She can choose not to be her father.

She pulls the restraint harness straps over her shoulders, her arms shaking from adrenaline and exertion.

"We're going to try this," Ethan says. "But even if we can make it through the storm, I don't know if they will let us go."

Ophelia closes her eyes. In her head it's quiet, but with a curled-up sense of anticipation.

"I think they will," she says simply. What Kate said, it held the ring of truth. Whatever they are—a technology created by the Lyrians and abandoned in their extinction, a probe from an exploratory intelligence, or some other kind of life form entirely—the chance to grow and spread is surely a priority, given their previous behavior.

The storm tosses them around, to the point that Suresh vomits and Kate is shrieking nonsense. Ophelia does what she can, doing whatever Ethan tells her to do. What buttons to push, what numbers to read aloud.

Then, all of a sudden, they're clear of it. Above the weather and heading out of the atmosphere.

The *Resilience* glows above them in a fixed orbit, a tiny white spot, growing larger by the second. She's never been more glad to see a ship in her life.

"Ophelia," Ethan says. "We can't bring this back with us. Not if it's—"

"I know," she says. "I have an idea about that. But let's just get everyone on board and patched up first."

Once they're back on the *Resilience*, everyone takes a turn through the full-size medical unit in Med-Bay—Ethan first, followed by Suresh. Ethan needs a synthetic blood transfusion. Suresh loses three fingers but manages to keep his hand.

Med-Bay has no idea what to do with Kate. Eventually it declares that she's suffering from idiopathic seizures and sedates her. That slows her mumbling and restlessness. Enough, at least, for Ethan and Ophelia to get her into a sleep tank.

While Ophelia waits for her turn—her ribs have not stopped aching since she fell under the rover near the tower—she sends two messages.

The first is to her mother. It's a carefully worded message, letting her mother—and therefore her uncle—know that Ophelia knows about the "joint venture" Pinnacle had planned and the "souvenirs" Kate was supposed to bring back. And that they would have more than enough with the returning team, but that some work would be required to safely remove them.

But if they chose to delay or not make the effort to retrieve said souvenirs, or if an "accident" happened to befall them, Ophelia would be sending another message. A time-delayed message to Jazcinda Carruthers, telling her everything.

Blackmail, in short.

What, after all, is the point of being a Bray if you can't use their tactics to your best advantage?

After Ophelia records the message for Jazcinda and sets the delay, Ethan asks her, "You think that's going to work?"

He rubs his shoulder against the remaining pain. He looks so much better now, though, his skin no longer that ashen color associated with blood loss.

Ophelia shakes her head. "I have no idea. I gave them a reason to wake us up, but I think it's entirely possible they'll leave us in cold sleep forever. If they don't just destroy the ship to begin with."

He doesn't say anything for a long moment. "We could just not go back. Fly into a star, be declared lost. Let our families claim death benefits from Montrose."

Ophelia eyes him. "Do you trust them to pay out those benefits without fighting every step of the way?"

He sighs. "No."

"Me either. And what's to stop Montrose from going back, sending another crew right after us?" Most likely they would all die, but if they didn't and they left while infected, then all of this would be for nothing. "If Pinnacle was trying to buy samples off the New Silk Road, they're going to listen. They wanted those things for a reason. We may not like what they choose to do, but at least we have a chance of stopping it this way."

At some point, some company, some team is going to leave Lyria 393-C with samples. There's no way that won't happen. Taking themselves out of the running only gives them less control. And maybe it's the part of Ophelia that is her grandmother, but if this is happening, she wants to be the one calling the shots.

Ophelia's trip through Med-Bay confirms her suspicions by diagnosing three cracked ribs and a multitude of bruises so severe that the medical unit asks her if she's been in a vehicular accident.

A car crash. Yes, this entire trip has been one.

Then it's time.

With Kate already in cold sleep, Suresh is next. Ethan, as mission commander, will be last.

"Are you ready?" he asks Ophelia when it's her turn.

She steps into the tank, naked and shivering. Even with the Med-Bay treatment, she's still bruised and strained in various places. But her self-consciousness is long gone. That moment when she fell out of the tank, slippery and scared, grasping for a towel, feels like several centuries ago. Is it odd to say that she's looking forward to it? To the quiet, to the rest. To the possibility that turning themselves into frozen corpses, however temporarily, will kill off the sentient sediment lurking in their veins, eavesdropping on their thoughts and memories.

"As I'll ever be," Ophelia says.

Ethan's hands move over her in a cool, professional manner, setting sensors and checking the line attached to her port. The tank itself will do most of the work once she's sealed inside. Ophelia gets the feeling, though, that he's doing this more to delay than to double-check.

"Everything is going to be okay." The words burble out of her before she can stop them. As if she has any business making reassurances.

He pauses, arching his eyebrows. "You sure about that, Doc?"

"Absolutely fucking not."

He laughs. "Okay, just checking."

Ethan gives the sensor on her right arm one last press, then steps back. "All right."

"You did a good job," Ophelia says to him. He did. Most of them are still alive. The Pinnacle team would have killed for their numbers. No pun intended.

He nods. "So did you."

"No bugs, no bites?" Ophelia offers. Maybe she's not quite ready for him to close the door, either.

A rare full smile flashes across his face. "No bugs, no bites," he responds, before moving the lid gently into place. Then, after two quick raps against the outside, she's alone.

Ophelia watches the light through the tiny window in the lid until it's gone. Or she is.

EPILOGUE

The dripping feels like a finger tapping against Ophelia's forehead. An index finger playing out an uneven and unknown rhythm on her skin. In her hazy state, she imagines Ethan leaning over her still, checking on a sensor on her forehead.

It's not until the drips roll down to her neck that cold seeps into her awareness. She gasps at the icy slice of water moving toward her shoulder.

Her eyes open slowly, the lids heavy at first. But she's been through this before. *Breathe, slowly. Wait. Just wait.*

She's awake. She's . . . somewhere. *Or we've been in cold sleep now for so long the tanks have run out and woken us automatically.*

Ophelia can't see anything out the window; it's fogged over, just like before.

Panic catches her anew. Did she really think that sending that message to her mother would work?

Her breath starts coming quicker, puffs of visible condensation, interrupted by the occasional chatter of her teeth.

Either way, she can't stay in here. Whether she's shoving back the lid to discover they're adrift or trapped in a secret Pinnacle lab somewhere, hiding isn't going to change that. New day, new crisis.

She can figure it out if she has to. And she needs to find Ethan and the others.

The calm center of resolve and gritty determination pooling in her chest is such a shift that it takes a moment of waiting for the paralyzing fear to catch up before she realizes that it's not coming. There is something to be said, it seems, for surviving a series of unimaginably horrible experiences. It tests your limits and changes your boundaries. What else is going to compare to confronting her father and living to tell about it?

Possibly, being possessed by the only known extraterrestrial intelligence.

Yeah. That would do it too.

She wrenches her hand up from her side, fumbling for the emergency release.

Shadows move outside the window. Ophelia goes still. Someone's out there.

Two taps against the outside of the lid. "Ethan?" Ophelia's voice sounds thick with disuse.

She strains for the emergency release. If it's Ethan, why isn't he letting her out? Is the ship damaged? Their tanks?

The fog on the window retreats, curling up around the edges, as the tank warms around her.

The shadow shifts away and another takes its place. This time, Ophelia can see enough to recognize who's staring in at her.

Her mother. Except younger than Ophelia ever remembers seeing her. Dark eyes, auburn hair cut short, with tasteful blond streaks framing her face.

Ophelia jolts backward in the tank, but there's nowhere to go. Jesus. Cold sleep didn't work; *they* are still making her see things.

Her mother's mouth moves quickly, frantically, but Ophelia can't hear anything over the rush of blood in her ears.

Which is strange. Before, Ophelia could hear everything in her head.

Her mother slows her speech down, and this time Ophelia can read her lips. *It's okay, Phe. It's okay. You're all right.*

Realization dawns slowly. This is not her mother, or even a hallucination of her—neither of them would have bothered to reassure her. Or call her by the "bastardization of a beautiful name."

This woman is Dulcie. Her younger sister, now older than she was when Ophelia last saw her, by five, maybe seven years . . . at least.

"Dulcie?" she asks in disbelief.

Dulcie grins at Ophelia, and now Ophelia's not sure how she ever saw her mother instead. "Holy shit, are you in trouble," Dulcie says. "You sent that message to Jazcinda and everything blew up. She went public with it, and the board pulled Uncle Darwin and Mom."

Ophelia shakes her head, ignoring the squeak and squelch of the bio-gel. "Dulcie, we're infected—"

"Just give us a second," Dulcie says slowly, careful to enunciate. "You're okay now, but we're not quite ready for you out here."

"Ethan? Kate? Sur—"

Dulcie nods. "It took longer than we thought," she says. "Eleven years. Cold sleep did most of the work, but it took time for the scientists or whatever to figure out how to clean the residue—"

"We're here," a new voice interjects. Ethan peers around the opposite edge of the window, holding up his hand in greeting.

Relief soars through her.

And Ophelia's sure that, in the process, Pinnacle figured out how to make money from their situation, Lyria 393-C, the tower entities, or all three, but that's fine.

She'll deal with that in her own way, as soon as she's out of here. No more running away from being a Bray. They may not like it, but she hasn't liked it from the beginning—maybe it's their turn to be uncomfortable.

"Eleven years?" Ophelia asks, taking in Dulcie anew. She would be—oh my God—almost thirty. They are nearly the same age now.

Amused exasperation fills her sister's expression. "Yes, well, I'm still younger, and I'll always be better looking."

A weak laugh escapes Ophelia, along with tears. She's missed so much.

The seal breaks on the tank with a long hissing exhalation, and the hinges squeal shrilly in protest as the lid cracks open a few centimeters.

Fresh, warm air drifts in through the small opening, and it's like the sun coming out after months of gray. Ophelia shivers.

Ethan reaches in through the gap in reassurance. She reaches across her body with her other arm, and his fingertips touch hers.

The lid is wrenched backward with a clang of metal on metal, letting light and air in fully, and Ophelia takes a deep breath. For the first time in years.

ACKNOWLEDGMENTS

Some book ideas seem to arrive almost fully formed. Others are inside out and backward, in hundreds of tiny unconnected pieces. But no matter which way a book shows up, I absolutely cannot do it alone. It takes dozens of talented people to turn an assemblage of words into the complete experience you are reading or listening to. I am incredibly grateful to everyone who made *Ghost Station* a reality.

Suzie Townsend, for always working so hard to advocate on my behalf. This is an especially tough job because I am terrible at asking for things—thank you for helping me.

Sophia Ramos, for reading everything I send, being excited with me about this idea (and all the others), answering my nervous emails, and giving such fantastic story feedback!

Pouya Shahbazian and Katherine Curtis, for the thing I can't talk about yet and all the calls and updates about said thing. Tracy Williams, for bringing *Dead Silence* to the world. Olivia Coleman, for keeping me in the loop and on track!

Kelly Lonesome, I am so grateful to be working together again. Thank you for giving me the chance to tell more of my creepy space stories!

Melissa Frain, such an unexpected joy to be able to team up with you again to tell the best version of Ophelia's story. Thank you, thank you, thank you for helping me go from what I turned in to this final version of the book, which I LOVE.

Kristin Temple, for believing in my books and me!

Timo Noack and Katie Klimowicz, okay, I know we tell

people not to judge books by the cover, but with this book, forget that. Because this cover is absolutely spectacular. I cannot express how perfect the art is for this story, Timo. The suits hanging up on the side, the blood, the cords—it's exactly as I imagined. And the design, the immediate claustrophobic effect of those letters running into the top of the hab, Katie, I just LOVE it! Thank you both for sharing your talents!

Jessica Katz, thank you for managing what must be an insane process from manuscript to final book. Also, I apologize for my comma fetish.

Valeria Castorena, Jordan Hanley, and Michael Dudding, hugely grateful for all that you do in helping me spread the word about *Ghost Station*. I really struggle with this aspect, and your expertise is truly invaluable. Giselle Gonzalez, thank you for helping me connect with readers, the horror world, and the world in general! I appreciate all that you do.

Lauren Ezzo, the best damn narrator one could ask for. You brought Claire, Kane, Nysus, Lourdes, and Voller to life. A belated thank-you for your amazing performance of *Dead Silence*.

Linnea Sinclair, for reading the opening chapters of this book so many times that I'm lucky you're still speaking to me. You always told me craft would save me. I learned that the hard way with this one. Thank you for teaching me still.

Becky Douthitt, for always being willing to read for me, even when it's scary!

Becky Douthitt, nope, this is not a duplicate. This one is for *Dead Silence*.

Susan Barnes Oldenburg, for creating a spreadsheet that set my competitive nature on fire and got me back to writing on a regular basis when I was really struggling. Also, Ben.

Matt Oldenburg, who makes sure my kitchen is lit and my smoke detectors function. Thank you for that. Also, Ben.

Read Between the Lynes, thank you to my local indie bookstore and RBTL staff for being so incredibly supportive!

Mundelein High School, especially the English department

and my colleagues in the Media Center (and former colleagues Sara Gunther and Liz Risdon). Thank you for being excited and celebrating with me!

Amy Bland and Kimberly Damitz, I so look forward to our dinners. Grateful to have both of you in my life!

Mom and Dad, Judy and Stephen Barnes, for always having my back. Thank you also for buying so many books, taking me to the library, and not freaking out when I was obsessed with the Lizzie Borden case at, like, eleven.

Greg Klemstein, we've been married for twenty-four years as I write this. Thank you for drawing me out when I've been hermiting for too long. Thank you for still making me laugh.